First published in 2010 by TheNeverPress

A CIP record of this book is available from the British Library.

Illustrated by Graham Thomas.

Cover design by Adam Sibley – www.adamsibley.co.uk

ISBN - 978-0-9567422-0-9

Acknowledgments

With grateful and loving thanks to my family for their encouragement and support. To my friends, in particular Wayne Crawford, Brett Antill, Luke Searle, Ben Alexander, Helen Plummer, Alex Taylor, Paulie Condron, Andrew Reid, Colin Morris, Ryan Wootten, Robert Goldsmith, Helena Caligari, Chris Rolfe, Kevin Hattam, Mr Peacock, Billy Corgan and, of course, the staff at The Bishop.

A special acknowledgment to my dear sister who has stood by me through it all and who has never shown anything other than great generosity and belief: One hell of a woman.

Cheers

For Donatella, of course

There are two rules that the Dream Investigator must follow:

1. Document everything.
2. Keep moving forward.

The Never Pages

Part One

1

Collar itches. Baby sitting on woman's lap staring at me. Eyes brown. Woman, probably mother, has a nosebleed. She isn't wiping away the blood. Four people are entering the waiting room. Three men, one boy. Boy around twelve. Shorts, satchel, book. Cap doesn't sit on his head properly. Three men do not seem to know each other. Dressed the same though. Dressed like me. Stiff collar. Suit. Briefcase. It is hard to write this with baby staring at me. Mother's nose still running. Three men are now staring at me while I write. Young boy is standing in middle of room looking at wall. The train is late. Days late maybe. The clock is broken. Stuck at ten-to-ten. My watch, broken. Stuck at ten-to-ten also. Missing Lucy. I am hungry. Nothing in my pockets. Gave the stale bread to the beggar outside the station. He thanked me. No teeth. Dead eyes. Only three fingers. Didn't know where he was. Didn't know when the train was coming. Saw him pacing around a few days ago. Then the clouds came. Haven't seen him since. Probably dead. Will go outside to check later.

———•◦•———

Man dead. Hat on the floor, shadow burnt on the wall. Shadow had three fingers. Dead. Probably for the best. Train still not approaching. Sand and dust extra red today. Copper red. Model-T over by the gas pump is upturned. The man who drove it long since gone. Don't know how automobile upturned. No footprints or signs of collision. Dust cloud coming in. Baby asleep on woman's lap. Blood from her nose has dried around her mouth and chin. She is staring at me as I write. Three men and young boy still in waiting room.

Dust cloud all around waiting room. Visibility zero. Man sitting next to cracked window has sand on his shoulders. He doesn't move. Sand is piling up. He is falling asleep. Head nods as lethargy takes over. Days since anybody spoke. Throat is dry. Stomach in pain. Boy has opened satchel and is playing with toy soldiers on floor. One soldier has just shot another. He is standing over the fallen soldier. Soldier is now firing into dead soldier. Dead soldier is twitching. Boy has no expression, just shaking both soldiers. One firing on the other. Woman is looking at me as I'm looking at boy. What does she want? How do I investigate her? Things I have learnt about her:

1. When the sun is at the left window, she bleeds out of her right nostril.

2. When the sun is at the right window, she bleeds out of her left nostril.

3. When the sun is overhead she bleeds out of both nostrils.

4. Her collar is high up and clasped together with a pendant. This suggests that she is grieving. It is too hot to remain like that otherwise. But she does so. Who or what is she grieving for?

5. She rotates her baby. He is on her lap, but she makes him face different ways throughout the day. She doesn't hold him close.

6. I don't think the baby is hers. The skin tone is the same, but she holds him like a book. Maybe it unnerves her?

7. Her cataract suggests that she has seen something. Witnessed something terrible or committed a terrible act.

8. When we make eye contact she clenches her jaw. She knows.

I shall continue to observe. I hope to find out more answers about her. She is intriguing. I wonder if it is the beginning of love? Doubtful.

———•••———

Young boy and his toy soldier were firing at me! He had a crazed look in his eye. The soldier was shooting me! I pretended to smile. The boy smiled back. He had no teeth and a thick, bulbous tongue. He didn't notice my fear. I was sweating profusely. That tongue! He is now asleep on the floor. Face down. I feel nauseous. I cannot go outside. Dust cloud still everywhere. I wanted to cry earlier. I am going to try and sleep. I cannot feel my legs. I want to sleep.

———•••———

I slept after counting to 1000. I remember passing the 500 mark. Then I went to sleep. I remember when I would be asleep by 250. Now it's 500. Boy is lying on his back. Man with sand on his shoulders is awake. Sand is now swept into a pile in the corner. I am disappointed to have slept through it. Who did it? Who swept up the sand? Nobody has moved. Picture of Lucy and Brekker fell out of my diary. I picked it up. Nobody seemed to notice.

It is the picture I took when she was recovering. She is still sunken-cheeked. There are copper rings around her eyes. Sitting the way she is in that picture, under the gazebo in Brekker's garden, you would think she would be in pain. Her back is straight for once. You cannot see the hump. There is no pain in her eyes. She is tired though. I should have been quicker to take the picture. Brekker shouted at me, I remember. He called me "bastard" and "time waster." I wanted the picture to be right. I ignored Lucy's pain. I ignored Brekker's annoyance. Now I have my picture and they are both dead. I am glad I took it. I would like to say this aloud, perhaps to the Nosebleed Woman, perhaps to the men, but they all stare at me, deader than Lucy and so I write it down instead. No sign of the train. Dust still outside. Feeling depressed and nauseous.

My nose has started to bleed. Woman smiled at me when she noticed. I wanted to scream. Instead the boy on the floor pointed and laughed. High pitched. A banshee. I am terrified of the boy and his bulbous tongue. I am terrified of his soldiers. I want to die. I want to die now.

I calmed down when I remembered that I am already dead. The train is coming. It must be.

WOMAN WITH CATARACT.
IT PIERCES RIGUT TUROUGU ME

2

On train now. I almost had given up hope. It came when the woman was bleeding from both nostrils. The dust cloud has dissipated. It went quicker than it came. I woke up and I saw the cloud rising, like a curtain in a play. Reminded me of the play Brekker took me to in Holstenwall - the one about the eight armed demon worshipper. The one that gave Lucy nightmares. Foolish Lucy - a woman of science and discovery but so weak to the mystery and imagination of phantasmagoria. Brekker and I tried to calm her but she fainted. We tried to revive her but the smelling salts did not work. After the play, I remember Brekker taking me to a whorehouse. I had no money. He paid for me. Lucy was sleeping. I felt shame but it did not stop me. I felt nauseous remembering that. But I couldn't help it. The curtain of dust was like the curtain at the play, my sin revealed. The woman with the baby laughed at me just as the memory faded. She knew. I'm sure she knew what I had done. She laughed loudly and her baby pointed. It is connected to her somehow. That hideous baby is bald and awful like a tumour. Like the tumours on Lucy's back that turned my stomach. Woman has a desperate laugh. It doesn't match her eyes. They seem a lot happier than her laugh. Her laugh says "save me."

———•◦•———

I left the waiting room first. I thought they would follow me. The woman, the baby, the men and the boy with his soldiers stayed behind. I stood and rested against the upturned Model-T. It's engine still warm. I don't know how that is possible. But then nothing seems possible in this dustbowl, and yet everything is, so I note everything. Just in case. These are all omens and clues. When I find you Brekker, you will be able to decipher everything. You will tell me exactly how I got here, and where Lucy is now. You will tell me the meaning of *that* dream. When I am settled in this train I will relay its details. I will note down everything I can remember around it. This will help you, Brekker. I am sure of it. I have to get to you.

Before I boarded the carriage, I counted the wheels along the train. 278 each side. I have to treat everything as a clue. Everything as noteworthy. I tried to attribute 278 to a number in my memory. The tally of days of Lucy's illness? The number of times she said she loved me? Not possible. Even so, I noted 278. It will be revealed.

The train is steam powered and the engine itself is long. 400 paces long, to be precise. I haven't seen one as large before. I am guessing it is at least 50 feet high. It made no sound when it pulled into the station and stopped on a rouble. The woman's nose stopped bleeding, the dust parted and there it was, facing the cracked window. If it had gone on further, it would have crashed straight through the waiting room. I hadn't noticed the tracks before. They are odd. Like bony spines along the dusty ground. They disappear before the horizon does. Perhaps they are not tracks, but skis? I will check.

They are tracks. I can see the train is moving on them. The sleepers are wooden, but the rails are bone. The landscape is flat. The dust clouds make it hard to gauge the horizon. There is nobody else in the carriage. Just me and the bench opposite. The corridor outside my cabin has a paisley carpet. Green swirls like smoke. Inside, the wood panelling is chipped and cracked. I smell oil. There is a large eye carved in the panel opposite me. It doesn't have a pupil. It looks like a cataract. Like the bleeding woman who seemed to know my secrets. I didn't discover anymore about her. I will re-read my notes. Maybe I have missed something about that woman. Maybe. Under the eye there is an arrow. Nothing below it.

No! The arrow below the eye is not pointing to nothing, it is pointing to the floor! I bowed my head to collect my thoughts and then I saw it. There is a symbol on the floor in between my feet. It depicts a ferris wheel with a two faces inside it. They are gleeful faces. Squinty eyes. Happy ferris wheel. I don't know what it means. I am tired. I will count to 1000.

The woman is here! I woke up just as she passed by my carriage. She was wearing a green dress. (Before it was violet, I haven't checked to note if I had mentioned the colour before) I didn't! I must mention these details when I see them! It could have been a clue and because she is now in green, I would only have known it was a clue if I had written it down. I have been lucky as I remembered her violet dress. But I cannot count on my memory so much. It is fading. This dust permeates my memory also. I think back to events before Lucy and Brekker, and even before the dance when he was bitten by the snake and already I can distinctly remember the copper-red sand on the carpet and, even though I know it wasn't there, I remember it to be so. Dust is creeping into my memory. This land is a doublethink. Must write down what I saw. Green dress. No baby. She walked passed and had no baby with her. Where had that ugly tumour gone? Thrown out the window? Left in the station? Though I would have done it, I cannot assume foul play on her part. Such judgement might cloud my investigation. I must remain impartial. To meet Brekker, track down Lucy and unravel the dream, I need a clear head. As the woman passed me, she looked into my cabin and smiled very sweetly. As she moved on, I noticed that her ears were bleeding.

3

I'm going to explore the train. Though I have not seen a soul since we boarded except her, I'm certain that we are not the only people aboard. I can hear someone coming. The woman? I will report back after.

———•••———

It was the ticket master. He only had three fingers. Dead eyes. He took my ticket, reached into his pocket and gave me some green bread. He smiled. No teeth. His uniform was dazzling. Brilliant pressed, white shirt. Mine is yellowy orange around the collar and cuffs from sweat. His navy blue waistcoat was ironed and the creases sharp. It fitted him well. I was shaking when he took my ticket, terrified of his dead eyes. I haven't eaten the bread yet. I noticed his name badge said 'Mr W_.' He didn't have a shadow. Probably left it behind at the station. There is a weevil in the bread. I am too hungry to care.

The bread was repulsive. I was sick out of the carriage window. The dust outside congealed the vomit so it became a mass of unset concrete the instant it fell out of my mouth. I felt better afterwards. I couldn't see if the extrusion plastered the side of the train. It was lost in the dust storm.

Detail to note – Mr W_ didn't take my ticket. I only thought he did because it is such a normal exchange of gestures. But I did give him something. But what? Thought it was the gazebo photograph, but it wasn't. That was in the back of the diary.

Odd as I usually keep it on the front. Could someone be reading this? Or moving my things around? Must keep diary closer. Haven't discovered what Mr W_ took from me, only that he gave me bread and I ate it. That dead eyed expression, I have seen it before. I shall write down now as I remember it and before it becomes just another sand dune in the growing desert of my mind.

Memory of Dead Eyed Expression.

The white paint on the handlebar of the tricycle was flaking. I remember picking at it with my middle finger. I am seven years old. I like the slight pain as the flakes stab under my nail. The trike is mine, although my sister will claim it was always hers. She is buried without it now, and she never mentioned it after the age of thirteen, but before that it was always her tricycle. I call it Silver Shadow. The metal handlebar is black and red from rust. It resembles a sickly bone exposed by the flaking paint. The trike is on its side upon the grass. I am sitting by it. My sister has dressed me like a doll. I don't mind. I never did. I just sit on the grass picking away at paint. I pick at everything. At scabs. Turning over rocks and pebbles to pick at the soil. I used to cut myself with glass and nails so that it would scab over and I could unpick it. I shake this habit when I meet Lucy as it repulses her. Nobody ever minded but her. At aged seven, on that morning by the trike, I have no scabs to pick and so I pick at the paint. The red dust is in the sky. It wasn't like that in 'reality', but that is how I now remember it. Red dust everywhere. I grow bored of the flaking white paint and look around. I see my sister by the pond. She looks happy and sad at the same time. Happy in her summer dress. It is white like the trike and has ivy sewn on the hems. It is her favourite dress. She is nine. I walk up to her and push her into the pond. She screams and splashes. I am laughing. Then I see a fish, it is staring up at me. Dead eyes. Expressionless eyes. Within those eyes I judge myself and my actions. The fish does not move. I do not move. My sister is gurgling and struggling. The fish swims away. I am helping my sister out of the pond. She has wild eyes, manic and livid. She chases me round the garden. She throws the trike at me. It strikes my head and I fall down onto the edge of a paving stone. When I come back around my family are all standing over me. They are all worried. My sister has a dead eyed expression. Behind her, I can now count fourteen cyclones of dust eating the horizon.

———•◦•———

Mr W_ had the same expression when he handed me the green bread. I hadn't thought once about the near-drowning of my sister since the day it happened. The concussion had wiped it from my mind. Only now do I recall it. The fish, the trike, the ivy on the dress. The eyes. Mr W_ knows something, perhaps everything. I must investigate him. I shall keep a running list of investigations.

1. The woman with the 'Tumour Baby' – where is the child? Why the nosebleeds? Why the ear-bleeds? Why the change of dress? When did she get on the train? At Holstenwall?
2. Mr W_ – how is he alive? What of the tramp? A twin? How can he make me remember what I have forgotten?
3. Who, if anyone, moved the photo of the gazebo from the front to the back of the diary?
4. The number 278.
5. The eye and ferris wheel symbols. Why in my carriage? Are they in others?

Main goals:

1. Find Brekker.
2. Decipher The Dream.
3. Find Lucy.
4. Sleep in under a 50 count.

I will now go and investigate the train. I will make a note of every carriage. I hope to find:

1. Food.
2. Travellers to talk to.
3. Some answers.

I go.

4

Carriage One.

Far end of the train. My carriage is five ahead.

Door – normal, no window. Handle – ivory, carved in the shape of a hand holding a door handle. No varnish. Just old bone. Looks brittle. Number on the carriage has fallen off. Unvarnished outline of '1' remains. Going in to investigate. If I don't come back then Lucy, the dream was true. I'm sorry. Brekker if you read this, follow the clues, and maybe you will have more success. Get to Lucy! Save her!

———•——

Back in the corridor. There was nothing to fear! How silly a thing is dread when you live through it and can look back at its illusion.

Inside the carriage there was a man sleeping on the bench. I did not wake him, but I don't think even the hounds of hell could have disturbed his slumber. The only thing loud enough to have possibly woken him was the deafening sounds of his snoring and his guts digesting food. The snoring and the gurgling were a comical orchestra. I laughed loudly without cupping my mouth. He didn't stir. He was huge. His tweed jacket had empty pockets. I didn't feel bad rifling through his possessions as I am a Dream Investigator, and it is necessary.

Pockets carried nothing but lint. Left breast pocket was filled with sand. His name was sewn into his collar. Mr H_. His belly rose and sank with laboured breathing. I got in close to his face. He had eaten meat and drank wine. The wine residue had created a clown-like smile. Glutton. He had soggy bits of meat clinging to his cheeks and beard. Filth. I prised open his eyelids. Green irises. He didn't wake. I had no fear that he might. I felt like a doctor, or a surgeon. This was work. No fear. Brekker, you would have been proud. Mr H_ had blocked ears. Wax enough to make candles. I shouted in his ear. No response. I wanted to move him off the bench and onto the floor but he was too heavy. Found his diary in his pocket. I sat opposite to read it. Nothing really to note. Had few entries. No real clues. Most entries were the same:

1. Live.
2. Breathe.
3. Don't die.

That one phrase reappeared randomly throughout. It stuck in my mind, and I know I will forget soon enough, so I write again.

1. Live.
2. Breathe.
3. Don't die.

Nonsense of course. Gibberish. He is no writer. Or at least, he has no investigation. I doubt he was even dreaming in that slumber of his. Fat-gutted Whale-Man. Why is he here? Why is he alone? I do not know yet whether I should add him to my list of investigations pending. Brekker, you once taught me three basic rules to use when casually investigating somebody's agenda. I write them down now, before they become a dune in mind.

The Brekker Rules of General Life Musings on People and Animals.

1. What is their secret? Invent if you have to. It will always be close to the truth.
2. Who were their parents and would they like what they saw if they could see what you see now?
3. If the subject were using the Brekker Rules on you what would the subject see?

Conclusions:

1. His secret is that he embezzled. I can tell this because of his chewed fingernails. Right down to the quick. He cheated people out of money and was worried that he would get caught so he took what he could and fled. Probably from Holstenwall. Yes, upon closer inspection of his 'crow's feet', you can tell he fled from

17

Holstenwall. He has the 'banker's squint' from counting money and he has ink on his fingers from forging, and there are none more bankers and embezzlers than in Holstenwall. Plus, the meat on his face is quite fresh, so he must have dined there before getting on the train.

2. His parents were slim, quiet folk who didn't have much and bent over backwards to help their son, Mr H_. He is greedy. They are not proud, but not disgusted. They are just sad. Haven't decided if they are dead yet.

3. If he were looking at me, using the Brekker Rules, he would gauge my secret to be that I am a coward and a scab-picker. He would see that my parents loved me dearly, but that it was not enough to keep them together. He wouldn't feel sorry for me. He would think that, if I were using the rules on him, I would understand his flight.

Slipped his pointless diary back into his trouser pocket. His watch has stopped at ten-to-ten. I wasn't surprised to find this out and didn't see the point in noting it, but I did out of discipline. Stamped my feet around and knocked on every panel to gauge the sounds. No loose panelling. No loose floorboards. No hidden compartments. Window was dusty. He has written on it 'Live, Breathe, Don't Die' with a chubby finger. View outside is same as from my carriage. Plains. Plateau of copper red dust and sand. No trees. It is daytime, but there is no sun.

His breathing is a lullaby. Up the gut goes. Gurgle. Down the gut goes. Gurgle. Quite hypnotic. Resting opposite him. Notice a carving on the back of the bench. It is of a carousel on fire. Round, fat people are fleeing. Symbol underneath people is rhombus with an 'X' in the middle. Looks unnerving. Don't want to look at it. Going to count to 1000. Need sleep. Gurgling gut of Whale Man is too hypnotic.

———•◦•———

Woke up and Mr H_ was on his back. Was reminded of missing the mysterious sweeping up of the sand in the waiting room. Keep missing vital actions whilst asleep. Didn't dream, no surprise. Left man on his front. Carriage two next.

5

Carriage Two.

Left Mr H_ sleeping on his front. Can't hear his breathing from the corridor. Soundproofed carriage? Doesn't seem likely as I can see through the edges of the doorframe. The light from the room seeps under the crack at the bottom of the door. Sound must only exist within its own borders. Door of carriage two is red. Paint cracking and peeling. Before I enter I am going to see what is underneath the first few layers.

———•◦•———

I picked the flakes for what seemed like hours. Order of layers: red, blue, olive, black, olive, blue, red. Didn't find any symbol or drawing. No warning or markers. No door number and no key hole. I have no idea what lies behind it. Debating entrance.

———•◦•———

Door is opening by itself! Just finished writing the above entry and as soon as I had decided to enter, the door began to open, as if my decision commanded it too. It is dark inside. Pitch dark. I am backed up against the corridor staring into the abyss. I can hear scratching emanating from within the blackness, but I am resolute and I am fearless.
Going in, for Lucy.

Back now in the corridor. Dog at feet. Mangy. Stinking. Half rotted dog. Alive. Wonderful.

Recollection of events:

Stepped into dark room. Door closed behind. I felt around the walls. Wooden as expected. Breath was held. Tried to keep as quiet as possible. Heart was beating hard. Blood felt hot. Hairs on end. Could feel sweat running down arms and legs. Mortal fear. I stayed with my back to the door as I felt around. I didn't know if there was a drop ahead. Had vision of stepping over edge of cliff and falling into the pitch dark. Bent down and felt floor. There was no drop. The room was solid. Then I heard breathing. Horrible, staggered breathing. A wheeze. A groan. It was a little sad. Then there came a scratch and a drag. Like dragging sack across ground.

I said firmly, "show yourself! I am armed with a dagger!" Groan. Wheeze. Scrape. Scratch. Heart beating too fast. Darkness too oppressive. *'Going to faint. Going to faint'*. These were my last thoughts before I fainted. Sorry Lucy, I thought of my fear and not of you.

I revived face down on the bench, bent over it, like a penitent man. Took a while to regain vision. There was a dim light in the room. Unknown source as there were neither lamp nor fitting. No window. It was just light. The sound in the room was muffled too. I thought at first it was concussion as I know the implications of it better than most, then I realised where it was coming from. The room was laid out the same as Mr H_'s carriage. Two benches opposite each other. In the centre of the cabin sat a large wooden crate. The lid nailed down. Around it there were scratch marks on the floor. Little ones showing the path someone had carved into floorboards whilst dragging crate. It had been dragged around and around. The scratch marks in floor created a huge spiral. Looked dizzying. The muffled wheezing was coming from within the crate. I inspected it for markings. Nothing. No suspect notches or whirls. The nails in the lid were hit evenly and well. None bent, none protruding. The work of a professional, like my father. Tried to prise open the lid. No chance. Then I heard a little oscillating scrape. I looked around keenly, tracking the noise. Didn't take long to locate. Where the walls were empty before, I saw now a crowbar swinging gently, as if someone had just put it back upon its holding. Took it from the wall and noticed that it hung from no hook. It was just hanging there, attached to the wall, defying gravity, swinging of its own volition. At that moment, I remembered something. I remembered drinking with Brekker in Holstenwall. Years ago when I was a student at the Academy. Drunk. The red sand is now all over the floor of that tavern and the patrons in the back of the room are now people-shaped dunes in my memory. But Brekker still stands out. The colour of the bottle stands out (green) His tie is undone and his crooked top hat is upturned on the bar, spinning around slowly.

He turns to me and says, "You see, my dear Master G_ when you take that train through TheNeverRealm things makes more sense than they do here. Things have purpose. Their own purpose. Nothing is connected because of humans. Here, the arm puts the hat on the head," he slams his hat on his head to make his point. "On the train, over there, the hat makes its own way to the head if it even wants to. You understand? It does what it wants. Don't need us to do it. We ain't the centre of things no more!"

He goes on, but his words are now drifting from my memory. Sand is coming from his mouth. He is turning into a dune. Now the memory is gone forever.

Re-reading above creates a new image in my mind, like seeing a painting for first time. I have no feeling towards it. The bar I wrote about has gone. Brekker doesn't drink there anymore. Fortunately I can still locate him in other places.

———•◦•———

I took the crowbar and prised open the lid. Nothing but soil inside. I inspected it. It was not red, but brown. Real soil. I tasted it hungrily. It was real. I took a handful and put it in my pocket. Mr H_ had done the same no doubt and I figured that this soil would soon turn to sand as it had done in his pocket. We will see. I scooped out more soil from the crate. And there he was. Curled up. Wheezing. Half rotten. Bullet hole in eye-socket. I could see his rib cage. Bones like the rails under the train. I could see his bowels. His fur half gone. Skin putrid. It was a dog. My dog. Died years ago. After my sister had gone and before I left the household. Never got a chance to say goodbye. Dog was ill. Was shot in face. Closed coffin. Buried by the pond. Never thought about him. Not once. Now here he is. I picked up the dog and put him on the ground. He stretched his legs and staggered about. He looked at me. Thankful. I have my dog back. Very happy. Good omen.

6

Carriage Three.

Dog is sitting by the door licking the black paint. Coating appears to be wet. First thought was that it was wet paint. But no, it is water. Tasted it. Salt water. Resist licking door. Tell dog to stop. Dog shakes head. Can hear bullet rattling around in dog's skull. Cannot remember dog's name.

Possible names for dog:
1. Two – after carriage number, and second life.
2. Dog – makes sense.
3. Brekker – to help me remember the man in my mind. Might help keep him from turning to sand forever. With Brekker written down so much and dog's name, could be strong enough to beat the desert's advance.
4. Lucy – see point three. Lucy is too beautiful though. If I find a cat, maybe.
5. Holstenwall – that glorious town of my youth in life.
6. Couldwell – next scheduled stop.

Decide not on 'Couldwell' as the idea of stopping there is dreadful enough. Don't need dog to remind me. Need dog to be companion. Dog has stopped licking door. Handle is dry and cold. Simple brass. Has Rhombus and 'X' on it. Easy match to symbol in Mr H_'s carriage. We are going in. Will report back. No fear now dog is next to me.

———•·•———

Carriage is completely empty. Dog asleep on the bench opposite. Its insides are fascinating. Intrigued by watching him breathe. Far less hypnotic than Mr H_'s gurgles. Far more interesting. The intestines, the liver. Can't see too much, but interesting all the same. No more symbols in the room and no hidden compartments. I used the same system of checking as I did in first carriage. Nothing on the window, no markings. There is a cyclone in the distance. Watched it for an hour and it didn't move across the horizon. Tried to use that to gauge its distance and the speed in which we were travelling. But in the hour, no other landmarks passed. No reference point.

Can't quite write down my disappointment of the emptiness of the room. Built up expectation of some discovery. Some clue. Something. Maybe the emptiness is a clue. Maybe not. Difficult to tell nowadays. Difficult to decipher my thoughts from the things around me. I wonder if I am attributing false importance to all around me. Everyone takes this train I think, so it stands to reason that it means nothing singular to one person above anyone else. Conversely it stands to reason that the train means everything to everyone. I can't ask the dog what he sees. I can't ask the dog to use the Brekker Rule Number Three. I can't ask if he is a figment of my imagination, or I of his. Perhaps we are both figments of somebody else's mind?

The people in dreams, they walk around not bothering the dream author. They must be sure to have their own lives and hopes. Must be completely oblivious to the horrible truth that they are scenery in someone else's dream. Is that what I am? A background character in someone else's dream? Am I through the looking glass? What if that person wakes up? Maybe they already have and this is the place where cast members of dreams end up? I feel alone.

I have felt alone like this only once before. In Pripyat. There, I guarded an empty town and a power plant. A reactor leak had killed most, the rest had fled. I was stationed there to guard it. Guard what? The soil and the air? I didn't know and there was nobody to ask. In the three years I sat in that wooden kiosk I saw only one other person. One day, on the horizon, after years of solitude there appeared a figure. I traced its journey as it walked towards me. From dot, to mass, to silhouette, to figure. A woman. An old woman. She walked up to the kiosk and looked me over. I went to speak but no words came out. Finally she said something in Russian, and then turned and left me. I remember almost crying as I watched her leave because I could not speak Russian. It was the first voice I had heard in three years and I couldn't understand it. For months after I investigated the meaning of her words in my mind. I explored every possible interpretation. In the end, I concluded that she had told me her secret. Her secret she had carried all that way to tell me. A secret about me.

"This dream doesn't belong to you," she uttered.

She must have she said that, because I am remembering it now. Of course, that kiosk and Pripyat itself is now a desert in my mind.

Here is an experiment - I am going to close the diary, wait five minutes, reopen it and re-read the above passage about my time in Pripyat. I will then close my eyes and objectively write down the first image or word the passage evokes. Maybe I can overcome the desert and create a new memory? Good luck. Here we go.

'Zone of Alienation'

I am overjoyed! That is the mystery of the carriage solved! The mystery of where I am! I am in the Zone of Alienation! Of course! This empty room was meant for me to feel like I did back in Pripyat after the reactor leak. I was meant to remember that old lady, her words, my interpretation, and then to succumb to the desert's erasing of my memory, only to realise it all over again. My investigation is working! I know I don't have to fight to remember, but work alongside this place, this train and everything inside it, to get to the bottom of TheNeverRealm. I wonder if I would have made this discovery had it not been for my dog, Mr H_, the lady with the Tumour Baby or the boy with the toy soldiers? Everything is here, leading me and I am unravelling it. Of course, I only know now how to read certain parts of this language. I have only unlocked one symbol in this code, but it is a breakthrough all the same. I know where I am. Right now we are travelling through the Zone of Alienation.

———•·•———

I don't know yet how everything else fits into this discovery and how in turn that discovery fits into me, and I into it. Does this affect the meaning of my dream? Will it get me closer to the truth? Closer to beloved Lucy? I do know that I badly need to see Brekker - to see him alive and well, so that he can see the joy on my face at this discovery. Locating oneself in the world, or the universe, or the mind, stops the chaos, stops the madness and helps to order. Now I know where I am, I can measure everything. Time, distance, space, everything. I am God, creator of my universe and right now I am equal to the power of this NeverRealm.

I have decided to call the dog Paisley after the swirls on the carpet in the corridor. The green matches the green of his skin. I smiled when I connected the two. And, when I called him Paisley, he barked and the bullet in his head rattled comically.

DOG FOUND IN CRATE ON TRAIN.
NAMED HIM `PARSLEY´

7

Carriage Four.

Door slid open effortlessly. On rails. Odd. No handle, just on rails. Only one bench inside, facing sliding door. Nobody sitting on it. Window above it. Maroon coloured blind drawn. Picture of a tree on blind, very fine embroidery, like the ivy on the hem of sister's dress.

Paisley looked at me, head lilting curiously. He looked into the room, then back up at me. I counted fourteen hopping little mites, fleas, or ticks on his back. Hopping around merrily. Was a quaint moment and it actually brought a smile to my face. Well, at least the thought of smiling. Can't remember if I physically did or not. Paisley stepped into the room. I followed.

———•◦•———

Examined carriage as per usual. Found only two things to note. Underneath the bench cushion (the first one I have seen on this train and I have taken it to sleep on later. May report back if it yields a good sleep filled with good omens and good dreams. Will report)

Under said cushion I found a hole in the bench-boards. Neat hole. Not smashed through. Close inspection revealed that hole was cut with saw. Possibly by left-handed man, judging by swing of blade marks. Inside was pitch. Wasn't too scared, though I did have one moment of apprehension flutter through my mind. A memory.

———•·•———

Recollection of Black Door:

I remember a black door in the side-entrance to my parent's farmhouse. I remember the knots and holes in the door. And behind it? Further black! As if black could have less, this did. I remembered the fear I had as a child, the fear of approaching that door, knowing beyond all doubt that the moment I walked past it, some devil or demon would spring forth from the bowels of its darkness and drag me down into the black-flamed inferno. I used to wait by the edge of the door, in that dashed corridor. I would count to ten, each number holding for me the weight of an entire religion and then, at ten, I would leap passed the threshold of that horrid door.

As I peered into that neatly carved hole in the bench, for a flash I remembered that door. Paisley nudged me and I reached in. The hole was deep, much deeper than the bench. I had my entire arm in and still I could not touch the bottom. I shouted into the blackness and there came no echo, but I knew that this fact held little currency here. Everything I have learned so far, and with all I have seen and all I am investigating, leads me to believe that laws of reason and physics can be bent to any objects will in TheNeverRealm. The echo was no doubt sleeping, or on strike. Whatever the reason, it didn't come.

I had sat back on the ground, facing the sliding door and had contemplated for a good hour. Brekker, in that hour, I would have written notes and jotted my thoughts, assumptions and conclusions as evidence for you but in truth, dear friend, in that hour not a single image crossed my mind.

It was in the moment when sleep was taking over that Paisley, fearless, bullet-skulled mutt of mutts, barked a heroic bark and leapt headfirst into the hole! What an animal! At first I was dumbstruck and had to quickly cycle through all the pros and cons as to whether I was dreaming. I was not, for within a minute, Paisley came leaping back out of the hole with some object wrapped in a tawdry blanket clamped between his rotting jaws.

He dropped his discovery at my feet and tried to wag his tail. Dumb creature. He could not do it. But, some mercy was shown him from whatever divinity lives within the Zone of Alienation. As he looked up to me, the one real eye shone bright and at that point a sunbeam just caught the edge of the bullet in his empty eye-socket and that too glinted. The glint of both eyes were at once upon me. It was almost convincing. I patted his head and bent to look at the package.

———•———

As I sit here now, back in my own on cushioned bench, I must describe the object as best I can in case I lose it along the way and you, good Brekker, have only this description to go by.

Object Found by Paisley in Carriage Four, just outside Couldwell. From within bench hole.

Box-Periscope.

1. Wooden casing, glued. 5" approx square, 14" approx tall.
2. Brass fastening attached to top – made for belt.
3. Painted midnight blue. Bright red piping.
4. Side of scope has painting of two eyeballs. One at the bottom, one at the top.
5. Both eyes have a brown iris. Walnut brown. Quite pleasing. Detail in veins much finer than on piping.
6. Eyeballs joined with a winding optic nerve.
7. Green ivy wrapped around optic nerve.
8. Back of scope has no marking.
9. Not finished too well, some splinters and dust caught in paint.

Have attached it to my belt ready for use. I have a plan. Tomorrow (it is night time now from what I can tell) I am going to use the periscope. I have explored all the carriages behind mine and am yet to see what is ahead. But something has come to me. Been mulling in my mind since discovery of location. The outside. What is there to see above eye level? Tomorrow, I am going to the back of train, going to climb out and I am going to try and climb onto roof of carriage and see if the periscope can see what I cannot. Brekker, I can only imagine your face at reading that audacious plan, and to think how cowardly I used to be. Of course, now I have committed to writing, I have to perform.

I don't know if I will be able to sleep from excitement. I am an adventurer! Providing I survive Couldwell and when we do finally meet, you are sure to find me a bold Dream Adventurer!

So goodnight Brekker, as ever this could be the last page I write. What a discovery I have made. A good days investigating. Paisley is sleeping by me.

Good night and maybe goodbye!

BOX PERISCOPE DISCOVERED BY PAISLEY

8

Woke up a few minutes ago to sound of scraping. Sitting up on bench, huddled in coat (cushion provided no dream). Scraping was soft. Almost a slide. A note under my door! I am staring at it. Still folded under doorframe. Peeking through the edge. Paisley is fast asleep. There is light under door and a shadow too. Someone is outside my cabin. I have swallowed my fear and am writing this as it happens. Shadow still there. Waiting for me. It is moving slightly. The note is pushed further under my door. As if the first scrape was not sufficient! How little they know how attuned I am to this place. To everything. I am a Dream Investigator. They must take me for a fool. They underestimate me, but I mustn't underestimate them. Friend and foe are easily switchable.

———•·•———

There is a place of sand in my memory. A dune that was once a somewhere, and inside that somewhere there was a friend who stabbed another over money for a drink. I remember because on that dune remains a blood-stained wallet. I look back into that desert and I cannot place dates, locations, names... but some things remain. The wind that whips through that desert is made up of the deeds of men and women. Cannot trust this shadow under doorway. It has gone. Will count to two hundred and retrieve note.

---•◦•---

It is morning, I fell asleep counting. What a fool! Though happy to sleep under a 200 count. Not by much through. Maybe under 190 but over 170. Paisley woke me up. Barking. Guttural bark. Bark had more weight than usual. He was by the door looking at note. He is more intrepid than I. And the note was not all that was there! Someone has been in this room. I know it. Things are different. A bowl of water for Paisley. I check the journal. It is here, they did not prise it from me. There is a pressed suit hanging up. Frock coat, quite fine, tapered tails and stiff collar. Shirt white. Whiter than mine. Could it be the Ticketmaster's shirt?

Smelt shirt – fresher than I can describe. A memory is triggered.

I am seventeen years old. Lucy is in the bath. We have made love for first time. I was nervous. Now I am confident. Lying in bed. She is singing. Shirt smells of freshness. Freshness reminds me of making love. Sun was warm. Grass was green. I roll over and hang my head over the edge of our bed expecting to see natural wood floorboards with perfectly flaking varnish. Perfect for picking at as I lie there. Instead I see a fine layer of sand. It is building up.

Back in the cabin, I am crying as I smell this new shirt. The memory is fading. I write as fast as I can. Lucy. Making love. She moans. Pleasant moan. She sleeps. I wake many times in night. I kiss her without realising. Gentle kisses on nape of neck. Sleeping kisses. Kisses of purest love. She has soft tanned skin. Fresh smell. Don't go. There is sand in the bed. I bury my face in the shirt more. I inhale harder. I am crying. I reach down under duvet. Sand everywhere. I break from narrative of memory as if altering it. Before, I let her sleep but now I turn her over. She has sand in her hair. Don't go, don't go just yet. Light comes in from ceiling! Hole in roof! Walls falling down! I am on a bed atop a sand dune. I kiss Lucy. Try to bring her back by kissing her. My memory cannot go, cannot leave me here! The freshness of the shirt!

I can taste sand. I open my eyes. I am alone. Lying on sand dune. A bed-shaped pile. The wind carries her song. Memory is dust.

I pull my face from the shirt. The freshness remains. But it doesn't link to anything.

Re-read the above passage twelve times. Means nothing to me. I am sitting on the bed. Paisley curled by my feet. There is more colour to him. Even an icky viscous film covering his exposed ribcage and organs. Regenerating? Most probably. "Good dog," I whisper. The sound of my voice makes his tail wag in his sleep. I smile.

Re-read passage about making love to Lucy. One memory, by the sound of it that I would dearly like to have kept. I have many more of Lucy, but I put them from my mind, lest I tempt the red devil to come and turn more of my mind into a wasteland.

I am holding the note in my hand. A dark shadow has suddenly come into the room from outside. The train is passing by something colossal! I opened the window to see. And there it is - sight of all sights:

The Exxon Valdez!

Seeing that vast hulk towering of us! The hull! The tear in her side! I cannot see the top of it, nor the beginning or end of her hull. Even the plumb line is beyond sight. It is terrifying.

This part of the wasteland must be Prince William Sound. I cannot make out any rock-bergs. The sandstorm is ever present although this monstrous tanker challenges even the sandstorm for sheer oppressiveness. A comfort inside me rises as I know that Brekker is close. His flagship, his masterpiece would not be left far from him. How he designed that leviathan ship in one evening, he never said. But he did. And here she is. Even sand hasn't taken her from memory.

I have sat back down, under the shadow of the Valdez's hull. The train is rocketing along. Moving like a cradle. Very lulling. I am opening the note. After reading, I will attach to page for safekeeping and reference. For your benefit Brekker, master engineer, keen drinker.

———•·•———

I cannot fulfil the above promise as the note turned to dust in my hand the moment I had read it. All that was scrawled upon it was a plate with some food heaped on it. Invitation to dining car. And, of course, the suit. I am meant to dress for dinner. Some person or persons demand me. Do I go? What of my plan to venture onto the roof of the carriage? If I go outside, the towering hull of Exxon Valdez will obscure my view totally. A quick answer to who was outside, and inside my room will be had by going to dinner.

I go.

———•·•———

I have put on the suit. It fits me all too well. I am unnerved by it. I know I haven't owned this suit before. Only conclusion is that I have been measured for it. Measured in my sleep by person or persons unknown who demand my presence. I have left Paisley in the cabin. He wanted to come, I said to stay and he did. Plus, the viscous film has started to smell. No film over eye socket. Bullet still inside. Can't remove it, he doesn't let me. Must remind him of my father, his master.

———•·•———

Stopped in corridor. Ahead is door to carriage. Lace curtain over window. Movement within. I will report back. I note also to remind, lest the memory is to become a dune, that once out of the shadow of Exxon Valdez, I will climb onto the roof of this damned train.

Read once more the passage about making love to Lucy. I will try to, as I approach the door to dining cart, construct a new memory, a false one. Can I plant seeds in my desert? Grow a new hope? I can only experiment.

I am at the door.

9

Night-time within the embrace of the Exxon Valdez. The woman is sleeping with her head on my lap, the bustle of her dress a maroon waterfall. Her lace collar is undone, exposing her neck. Clear sign she is comfortable. No rings on fingers. Loose ringlets in hair. Slender neck. Old and young. Difficult to pinpoint age. Cannot even pinpoint how long she has been here in TheNeverRealm. Veins across hands like mountain range. Like Urals. Scarring on elbow. Most likely an absent-minded burn. Probably day-dreaming and put arm on iron. Permanent reminder to stay alert. Mind shouldn't wander. Glad she is not bleeding out of ears or nose.

Baby asleep on bench next to me. We are close to being a family with dog on floor. Dog. Baby. Sleeping woman. Me. First family I have had since being a child. I will indulge this moment for a while. I like feeling woman on lap. Though she is not to be trusted. Notes under doorways. Shifting cataracts. Excessive nail biting and teeth clenching all add up to her being treacherous. I let her sleep and recall the evening.

———•—•———

I approached the door to dining car with apprehension, but I hid it well. Made each footstep assured. A good trick. Didn't know if those on the other side of door could sense my assuredness or not. So I played it up. Got to door. Waited. Saw movement. Crouched down with back to panel. Looked up at lace blind, hanging over pane. People on other side moving. Needed better look, but didn't want to move curtain. Got out my periscope. Peeked it under lace curtain and looked.

At least fifteen people inside going about business. Carriage cart looked plush. Waiters. Silver trays. Salmon. Caviar. Champagne. Rich clothes. Like carriage door in first carriage, there was no sound escaping under cracks. I looked harder through periscope. Saw Mr H_ gorging into an entire swan. Meat stuck to cheeks, glistening in candlelight. Grease everywhere. Saw Bleeding Woman sitting with baby, spoon-feeding him. Baby had back to door. Woman had netted hat, ruby lipstick. Net covered cataract. I felt a swathe of lust. As soon as I did, the baby spun round, its head rotating menacingly upon its spine. He pointed at door, hissed, baring sharp back teeth. Everyone in carriage stopped. Cutlery put down. Waiters slowly stood up in unison. Then they turned and looked at the door. Eyes blank. My heart froze, I cannot deny that. I knew then the following:

1. I had been right to walk assuredly. They knew things.
2. That Tumour Baby sensed my lust. Sensed my desire.
3. I had to swallow my dread and enter room.
4. Had to investigate. Come too far not to.

I stood up, packed the scope away, fixed tie and entered. As soon as I touched door handle, the shadows on other side of curtain went back to duties and sound emanated from under the frame. Typical sound of dining room. Door handle was some sort of lever to activate the lives of the souls within. I opened door and stepped inside.

Like the bench that contained my periscope, the dining carriage, from the inside was colossal. Benches, tables and trestles stretching on into the distance. Everything repeated. Everything. I felt as if I was looking into a hall of mirrors. On it went. Serving, eating, drinking, drinking, eating and serving. I was struck with a sense of weightlessness - a great vertigo at peering into this endless carriage. It was more to bear than the horizon-less wasteland outside. But I had figured out my location despite the void, and so forced myself to bear that vertigo.

I stepped into the dining carriage. Bleeding Woman stood up instantly and hurried over. Tumour Baby didn't react as before. He reacted like a babe, looking around the room, curious, free, unaware and investigating everything. Felt strange affinity towards it. Focused that feeling to see if baby would react. It did not. Felt as if, inside this carriage, I belonged. Sounds were rich and lush, odours were ripe and searing. I surfed the dunes of memory to try and locate a trinket, or a wind-song left behind to pin these new sensory revelations to. There was nothing to recall but sand so I knew that this glorious onslaught was fresh, new and altogether unreal. As Bleeding Woman swept towards me, bustle sashaying, I decided to dive into unreality with a great fervour and investigate from the inside, to do as the Romans do. I bowed, deep and long. She came up to me. My stomach turned at the sight of her evil cataract, but I did not let it rise any further. She held out a gloved arm and I kissed her hand. Her scent was lavender. A vision of the shrub by my mother's pond went off like a flashbulb in my mind and then it exploded into sand. Yet, oddly now, with her on my lap, that memory is still there. I cannot recall anything around the shrub or the garden as it is in a cyclone, but the shrub, her glove and her scent are all somehow connected. I digress.

I kissed her hand and she led me to the table. The Tumour Baby didn't regard me, even when she introduced me as Master G_. She could only have got that from her own investigation. I was on to her, but also keen to explore my new found dynamic of investigative acumen. The Tumour Baby just hit at the table with a two-pronged fork. His skin was horrid, almost translucent, his veins bright blue and his hair coarse and rank. When eventually he did regard me and offered me a hand to shake, I held my breath through repulsion and took it. Until the day I die again, I will never feel anything as cold as the touch of that baby's hand. So cold, it was almost wet.

She introduced herself as Angeline of the Theresienwiese. A meadow girl. Not rich, nor poor. Before she went any further, I asked her to describe what she thought a meadow was (feigning curiosity in her history, rather than my true interest which was in her *perception* of history). She looked at me and her 'good eye' fogged over for a few seconds. She simply said, "Flat sand."

47

10

Angeline could not recall to me her life and so instead she recalled to me a dream. The smoky cataract in her 'good eye' cleared. She smiled. I glimpsed her wooden dentures. Around me the replicated diners and waiters went through their routines.

And she said, "I have no memories to speak of, though I try to recall what went before, my childhood, my…there is nothing left. A sadness. An ocean. It started long ago, I wrote down at first what happened…then one day I forgot where I wrote it…a book I guess…left behind somewhere…on a bench maybe, or on the deck of a liner. It had inside it all my memories. All that is left now is how it happened. When thinking back to past times, the walls to rooms seemed damp (walls to which rooms? Rooms in which catacomb of my life? Never again will I remember)…but when I could recall the details, I recalled the dampness. I used to look back and see people crying…in happy times, they were crying…my memories where changing. It was so confusing. There was no difference between the realities. I was in a whirlpool. Damp walls, tears…then puddles. Wet feet. Soon, I was paddling through my memories, desperately trying to cling onto something. A keep-sake buoy or a luck-charm life raft. Anything to keep the memory alive, tangible. But no…paddling soon turned to wading and wading to swimming, as all I loved, all I hated, all I knew began to not only be swept away, but to turn into water itself! Columns cascaded down like fountains, entire cities became tidal waves and in the centre of it all, only me and my belly. I was pregnant then…and though I don't remember my life and worldly vision, I remember what was inside me - always lungs, always eyes, always liver and always a child. I felt as though I was on the edge of the sink of my mind and of my psyche and then the plug was pulled and everything whirled and swirled away. Soon I was left with an ocean in my mind. Adrift with child."

Her words rattled me, not because of their obvious significance, but with the way in which she had spoken them. Her tone was hushed. Conspiratorial. And she ground her teeth. I mistrust her deeply, but am compelled to keep her close.

"The real memories I have formed," she continued, "started many, many years ago. An abandoned harbour…of sorts. I was on a pier raised above red sand. There was no horizon. I had in my arms a baby. Already born. Look at him with his rank hair and sallow skin. He is the living drowned! I love him, yes, but here…in this place? It doesn't seem real. Seems like I do because it is ever thus. Like gravity."

Her voice hushed even further at this point. I leaned in so close that I could see the grain in her wooden teeth.

"In this place I don't know him. Is he mine? I was pregnant before, in the waking life that is now an ocean, and then suddenly, in TheNeverRealm, he was born. He could be anyone's child. He sits on my lap and I feed him, though not through breast. I cannot look at him sometimes and I will come to the reason why, but first the pier. The world had washed away, I was adrift and then, suddenly, I was on that pier surrounded by a great plateau of red sand. I stood, baby in my arms looking along the pier, into nothing but red. We walked for years and years with no food, no water, no sleep and no pain. Just walking. I counted each day, not by the sun, but by the ever moving cyclones in the horizon. Like a counter they moved back and forth across the horizon, never getting closer, always moving. Once across and back again I declared to be a day as my pendant watch had stopped."

She opened up the pendant clasp on her neck, it was a beautiful clock stopped at ten-to-ten. I carefully showed her my pocket watch also. She nodded in agreement. Her cloudy eye swirled. We seemed complicit in our knowledge of this place.

"After years of walking with the drowned baby and counting cyclones on the horizon, we reached the first sign, not of life, but of death. An oil field! Huge towering pumps, still moving up and down. But these great pumps were not made of steel, but bone. Great femurs and tibias connected by monstrous patellas. Charred, black bone drilling down into the ground. And the sound! A wailing, wailing sound of a thousand voices crying out with every up-motion of the pump. We feared that oil-field greatly. It was hell. TheUnderSide, I have no real name for it, just what I have conjured. Maybe I have named that place a million times over and maybe that name has trickled away like a stream but the vision of the giant oil-pump legs remains."

I was chilled at her words, for I know I have not been here for anything like as long as Angeline has. Not even close. Will I see such a sight as that monstrous oil field?

"And then, we were there. In that waiting room. A train was coming, and I somehow knew it. I don't remember how we got there, or how we even knew a train was approaching. We were just there. Then the bleeding came. I thought hard about the ocean, trying to recall, trying to investigate everything. I concentrated and as I did, the bleeding came; the ocean of my memory falling out of my nose. And then you appeared. You with your stiff collar. You looked new and alive. Not drowned. Not waiting. You wrote, furiously you wrote. I recognised your fierce writing as the same as my desperate clutching to the flotsam, jetsam and derelict of my life as it crashed away in that maelstrom. I tried to get your attention. I looked at you and concentrated, hoping to climb into your battle, but I just bled more. I tried to show you the baby. Tried to strike a chord within you. You just looked repulsed.

Then, we were on the train and I knew I had to meet you. I must tell you why you are here! I must tell you about this place!"

I grabbed her hand at that point and motioned for us to leave. She resisted.

"We cannot. Not yet. I will come to you later tonight and tell you. We will sleep together and I will tell you why you are here, my saviour."

We left the carriage and went our separate ways. I stayed awake, Paisley by my side. The shadow of the Valdez still there. I intently watched the crack under the door until her shadow appeared and she entered.

51

ANGELINE'S BURDEN

11

Paisley's leg is twitching. Must be dreaming. Hope it is of happier times. Playing with his master. Chewing a bone. He is a great companion. Love him dearly. Tumour Baby sleeping on floor next to him. Noticed slight puddle around him. Have smelt it. Not urine. Has brine smell. Water. Baby is motionless. Breathing slight, but raspy. Like flu. Awful veins, like jellyfish tendrils under skin.

Angeline has rolled over. Smokey eye still open. Like a pearl. Went to touch it, retreated at last second. Gently kissed her neck seven times instead. Very gentle. She didn't feel it. Sort of kiss you give a corpse in a casket. I will write tomorrow about what she tells me. Something about being a saviour. More about her dream no doubt. I must at all costs interrogate her fully. I have gained her trust. Used my new technique well. Brekker would approve. I have gained her trust, now I intend to find out my answers, and a little more about Couldwell. She has been in this transitory land for many years. She will know a lot, if not everything. I will get what I can. Upon reaching Couldwell, if I cannot get any more information, I will leave her and the squid baby behind. No need for them. Dead weight. Cannot care for her plight, or journey. I have my mission. Brekker. Lucy. Deciphering the dream. I have promised dear Brekker, to write every detail of the dream down and have not, yet.

Faint ringing has begun in ear. Pulses. Like a siren. I know that sound. We are approaching Couldwell. No signs out of window. Pitch dark. No stars. On horizon I can just make out cyclones. They do not move. Just rooted to the spot. Angeline's method of using cyclones to count days no longer usable. Stillness in air. Just the warning sign of Couldwell ringing out.

Things I hope await me in Couldwell.

1. Brekker, of course. Haven't thought about you much in last hours. Concentrating on Angeline, her ocean memory and Tumour Baby.
    a. Why does she still carry him if she doesn't truly love him?
    b. Why does she seek me out? Doesn't seem to have quest of her own.
2. Hope to find decent rest. An inn, a bed. A drink!
3. Basket and food for Paisley. Maybe bandages for his wound. Dust and wind outside may irritate him.

In truth, I hope the fear of Couldwell I have inside does not manifest. I know nothing of the town. Except that I must enter it. Paisley is by my side. Comforts me greatly.

Going to sleep now. Will not dream. But order things in head. About everything from station until now. Everything ahead. Need to think of Lucy, will focus on one memory to sacrifice. Will be turned to dust by morning. Better to think of something small. Think of important memories later. Ration them. For now. I need to think of Lucy. I will think of the way she opened the letter informing her of the extent of her injuries. Will think on the change in her expression. Not pleasant thought. Happy to have it leave forever and turn to sand, in all honesty. Going to count to 500 now, hope to be asleep by 350.

———•◦•———

My dear Master G_

I am leaving you my baby. I named him Alexander. You can name him whatever you like. You may never forgive me for striking you and I hope the gash over your eye heals. The blood stain on your shirt has formed into the shape of a sprig of ivy. Strange formation.

When you come around and read this, you will be in a rage, but I promise you, dear Master G_ that I did not read your journal, I did not! I did not! I needed to write you my goodbye and my instruction. You see I am going. Soon we will be in Couldwell amongst the Sleepwalkers and that place, from what I have heard, is no place for souls. It's a place to forget. An oubliette. But I do not have to be amongst them as I am going back the way I came. Back towards my memory. You see I have been met in a dream by a powerful truth. It was so strong and burning. The truth is that I am not here. I am there, in that deserted town far, far away. I am in a dream you see and this dream does not belong to me!

And as soon as I realised that, one single pure and bright memory returned to me. There was no water to this memory, no soggy clothes and dripping walls. A real, solid memory. Out of a void this rose grew back. I have learnt how to regain memory! I woke up from sleeping in your lap in a fever of excitement. I remembered!

I once lived in a town called Pripyat, I was old then – grey, shrivelled…but dry. Pripyat, that old workers town. I remembered there was a man, a handsome man too, who stood guard over the town. He lived in a wooden kiosk and he guarded the town long after it was deserted. I remember being old, and walking to see him. For miles and miles on broken and bootless old feet I trudged. I walked to tell him that he was dreaming...and that dream did not belong to him. It was mine! He was an interloper in my dream.

And here, now I am in his dream…your dream! I have realised now, after years of walking, holding that drowned baby, caring for Alexander Tumour, I realise that I am in your dream. And I know now how to escape it. I am leaving before Couldwell as I fear that once this locomotive stops, I will become grounded. Stuck there, like all the other Sleepwalkers. I will leap from this train now, and I will walk back. I know each step will take me back to that pier from whence I came. With each step another corner of my mind will dry out and come back to life. Reclaimed land! Even now I can recall the image of a great piece of land I once went to. Reclaimed from the sea. A hotel in the shape of a huge palm leaf. In a desert land, it encroaches into the sea. I can see it! It is my dream! Not yours, you are not in it. Alexander is not there. It is mine. You are going to the very edge of TheNeverRealm, dear fearless Master G_...but you see, you can go there, but you can also come back. And I am just as brave to attempt it. Do not hate me, for I am going alone, back through all this to find my peace. I'm sorry if this makes no sense, but what does when told verbatim the rapture of souls euphoric?

Look after Alexander. I think he is better suited to you than me because I cannot carry him back and I don't want to. He will cry and dry up. He is a water baby, and must remain a water baby. That is why I struck you! You would come after me if I hadn't...you would have tried to stop me. Or worse, you would have let me go but you would have forced me to take Alexander Slug Boy with me. He is not mine! I was pregnant in life, not a mother in the dustbowl. Who is he? You may or may not choose to find out. I dry my hands of him, forever.

Alexander, hate me if you must, but do not come after me. I will see you in my waking life when I return to it, but as my own child, not my burden as you are in this place. I am to leap. Into eternity from this train, I am to leap.

Goodbye Dear Master G_

Love,

Angeline

12

Baby safe, I'm safe! Survived the Tsar's apocalypse! Angeline gone! Gone! Turned to dust! Here's what happened. Apologies first, I am so rattled and too panicked to write coherently. Woke up to find Angeline gone. Nowhere to be found. The baby was crying. It is what woke me up. Paisley was dragging himself around in circles on the floor like lame beast. The air was thick with dread. I was covered in sweat. The wind outside was screaming at us. I have to write down what I have seen, what I went through before it turns to dust. We are approaching Couldwell and I don't know what is going to happen there. Brekker, I'm still shaking and sweating. Baby is safe now. I have to look after it. I have rested it on the bed now and he is sleeping. Paisley too is sleeping. I need to sleep. First this report.

When I woke up to the screaming I knew what had happened and when it was unfolding it was if I was not me but someone else watching. Like my body was some sort of chair and my eyes some sort of projection relaying an incident in real-time but one of which I had already seen. I cannot think of a better way to describe it.

I leapt to my feet and found my jacket neatly pressed and hanging up. There was no sign of Angeline as I have said. The baby was screaming on the floor and my diary was lying next to him. I cannot tell you the fear I had in that moment. The idea that the bitch Angeline might have read the diary or copied it or memorised it and fled to seek people to come for me was over-powering. I snatched the diary from baby and, to my shame, kicked the tumour lump to the side of the cabin like one kicks a shoe box under a bed. I regret it now as I must look after baby but then, in that moment of rage, I couldn't control myself. You understand Brekker, I'm sure. Anyway, I read her suicide note and I believed every word of it. I believed that she had not read my diary and I understood that she was in my dream just as I had once been in hers. I understood her logic but I knew that it was fool's logic. She couldn't walk back to the pier from whence she came. Nobody goes backwards, only forwards. How can somebody not understand this? It is the most underlying truth of the universe. Even in this place things go forward. I threw the diary on the floor and swung my coat on. I ran out into the corridor to find that the wind had invaded the train and the corridor was packed with sand. I panicked thinking it was a memory of a passed action turning to dust in my desert mind. Then I saw that the door at the end of the train was open and thrashing against the forces outside. I leant into the wind and trudged against it, down the carriage towards the door. The power near swept me off my feet! Paisley couldn't follow and he fell back into cabin. I pulled myself along the window ledge, my legs flailing behind me, until I reached the door. My choices were to shut it forever and seal Angeline's fate and then await mine in Couldwell or go out there into the chaos! I had no time or diary to write down the pros and cons of this decision and so went with my inquisitive heart! I went outside!

I nearly pulled my arms out of their sockets hoisting myself out onto the back of train. Wind was so fierce that I was instantly pressed against the back of train. I could see cyclones. Cyclones everywhere! Screeching all around, following the train - approaching us! Chasing us, sweeping into a formation from all sides and the sand scraped my skin and tore at my flesh.

I used all my strength to turnaround and climb up onto the roof of the carriage. I hung low to the roof for fear of being whipped into the cyclone and swept away into nothing like all the memories in my mind. I squinted and searched for any sign of Angeline and then, suddenly, there she was! Halfway down the carriage convoy standing bolt upright as if in a vacuum she stood. It was incredible to behold. She had defied the rules of this world and a flash of doubt crossed me. Maybe she was right? Maybe she had mastered it all. Maybe she was everywhere and everything? I carried myself forward, desperate to save her and to reason with her. I wanted to give her back her awful baby and then interrogate her. I was almost, so very almost in reach of her when she turned around to see me and then it happened.

Water began weeping from her sleeves, her ears and under her dress, turning into a watery sludge before my eyes! I reached out to her, my hand raw from the sandstorm. I reached out to her I said "Angeline come back, come back!" I pleaded with her and told her about love and about my feelings for her but she knew it was a lie. She said that the baby would need to stay with me and that I was to look after him. She told me to survive Couldwell and then, then she looked up at sky and said: "He is coming and he walks through walls." The mad, mad woman! And just as I reached out for her she leapt from the train! I expected her to rocket into the distance as the locomotive sped onwards but instead she just floated there, suspended in mid-air like a freeze-frame, her clothes not fluttering, the sludge not falling from her. She was simply suspended in the cyclonic air as if attached to the train by some invisible thread! Everything around me was chaos. I tried to scream in terror. I felt my larynx vibrate but no sound came out. I just got a mouthful of sand. I reached out to grab her and as I touched the heel of her boot she detonated into a plume of red sand. Angeline was no more and where she had been there sprung a new infant cyclone that spun and weaved and moved into the distance, joined by the countless others crossing the horizon like great dancers skating on a rink of packed red sand. The wind seemed to die down and calmness overcame me. Silence. An eerie inhalation and imprisonment of breath. I looked up to see a particle storm birthing in the angry sky above. Great forks of lightning all around me as though I was underneath the web of a monstrous electrical spider. The hairs on my arms stood erect and my soul shrank. I ran back along the roof, half knowing what was about to happen. I dived down into the carriage in one swing, scrambled up the corridor, into my compartment, picked up the baby in my arms and pulled Paisley close. We looked out the window and then it happened.

The Tsars returned! A blinding flash that burnt my skin but left my eyes unaffected and, at once, I was bathed in light and at one with every universal particle. I was inside the Tumour Baby, inside Paisley, inside Mr H_, inside Mr W_ and inside the panelling of the carriage and all of it inside me. I was every particle and every moment in timeless time. The flash ended and the Tsars stood! Giant mushroom clouds where the cyclones were! Huge umbrellas under the blanket sky of hell and we could see the blast wave coming towards us. I screamed so fiercely that my voice cracked into a squeal. The tidal wave of fire surged towards us and I repeated in my mind, "I miss you Lucy I miss you Lucy I miss you Lucy," and then it hit us.

I awoke from my dream some hours later and I began to write while I remembered what had happened. The train still moves, no charring and no signs of the apocalypse I imagined. I will go back to sleep now.

———•·•———

Train jolted me awake. Mr W_ opened our carriage door and said "Couldwell." I looked at the baby and said "where's Angeline?" hoping it had been a dream. W_ said, "Couldwell" and left. I picked up the baby and looked at him. Felt a pang of affection for the soggy lump. I will look after him. Paisley came to my side. Slimy viscous film over his ribcage is thicker and now with a network of nerves and veins beginning to regenerate.

Couldwell. Here we are. We walked down the corridor and alighted from the train. To either side of me I saw scores of people stepping off, unloading trunks and baggage. I wondered about each one of them. How could I have not noticed them before? Mr H_ waddled over to a large congregation of families waiting for him. Looks like local dignitary. The heat is awful. My collar itches. Paisley is panting. I covered the baby's head and took out the diary and I'm writing this now.

I can see the town ahead. I can see many buildings, mostly wooden. There is a town hall, a few stores and boardwalk-lined streets, some Model-T cars. Sign says 'Couldwell – population 278.'

I am the last person by the train. Everyone else is walking to the town. I will follow. Turned around to look back at the locomotive. It has gone. All that is left is a huge sand bank in its place. Cyclones on the horizon have resumed their metronomic movements. Someone I once knew used to count the time by the cyclones. I cannot remember who. That memory is a dune in my mind. I will read back over my writings when in my lodgings and see if I can investigate it.

I hope you are in town Brekker, I hope you are near. Need to find Lucy. Need to keep going forward. The sun is high and catastrophic. Baby is shaded and sleeping. Going into town now.

Both my nostrils have started to bleed.

Part Two

13

Much time has passed. I am dying.

Radiation sickness intense. Skin now black. Peeled away bed sheet to inspect wounds. Skin fell away like graphite powder and blew into the air. I am dying. I am not long for this middle world. I don't know where I will go. Most likely stay here. Cyclones outside are inviting. Can hear them calling.

Lucy, I have failed you. I am not going to make it. All that has happened, I could not prevent. I would have searched through the pages, but I'm too weak. My mind is a desert with only the wind calling your name. "Lucy" it sings.

The pages in this journal are not blank and pages have not been ripped out. Have I not been writing between the train and now? About Pripyat? About Paisley? Tumour baby? The kiosk? I can remember them only as words in my vocabulary. As for the events in between? Nothing. My body is ravaged. I can barely move for vomiting. I'm in my hotel room looking up at ceiling. Bedside fan does not cool me. Instead it has blown the black powder-skin from my body. Skin has flown up to ceiling. There, an impression of me hangs. Like a mirror or a shadow looking down upon me. Most of my legs are gone. Melted down to bone. Some flesh remains. Smell of cheese overwhelming. Left arm liquefied up to elbow. Flesh gone. Just radius, ulna and carpal. Hand is liquefied up to proximal phalanx.

Outside room, cyclones are motionless. Will one be for me? Buckets of vomit all around bed. Orange stained wallpaper no longer shows pretty ivy. Outline still visible. Just outline, no fill. Like me. I am an in-between outline, transitioning between lying on bed, and hanging on that ceiling. Can't turn fan off. Can't reach. Can only write. Right hand unaffected from blast and fall-out. Can barely see what I am writing. Relying on muscle memory. What can I remember? Remember the panic and the noise. Remember shouting. Crying. Remember steam. Gauges blowing. Smell of gas, of flesh. Cannot remember why I was there. Cannot remember that part. *He* will remind you.

Remember immense pressure on soul. Bleeding out of eyes, nose and ears. Remember needles in glass meters shaking. Steam hissing. Remember seeing man, maybe Sacha melting though mezzanine grating above me. Remember him just pouring though it!

Remember running to reactor. Remember Brekker shouting, then laughing. Remember being alone. Remember hand pulling me through tunnel. Then I remember waking up in hotel room.

Sun high now. Like it was before. It was no dream, though. It happened. In the distance I can see the cloud from the explosion still hang in the air. It is red. Not like the dust red. Fire red.

That's all I really can recall.

Cannot speak for townsfolk. Wouldn't know what to say. Memory gone. Eyes fading, too much strain to read over what is written. Will only write on. Sorry if I repeat. Flysheet over bed cannot stop black skin fragments drifting through. I can see my ribs. I will touch them.

——•—•—

Ribs bend like rubber. I tasted fingers. I have a metallic taste. Like ozone after a storm. How long has it been since I wrote last? I will take the strain to look back at last entry.

There is no date of entry. Just when I came to Couldwell which I now know to be Pripyat – just then and now. All that is in between is missing. Like I have leapt over time.

Need some sleep. No longer need to count to fall asleep. Happens when I close left eye. Right eye is melted through to socket. If I don't wake, then Lucy I have failed you. You may never find this journal, but miracles happen in all worlds. Maybe you finding this will be a miracle. If you find it on the bed under the flysheet, look to the ceiling, the fan will have blown my powder skin up to it. There I am. Goodnight.

——•—•—

I'm awake. Dreamt of earth. Of soil piled onto me. Then dreamt of dark water. No light. Sinking into black water tank. Was no peace, just voice inside head. Voice spoke names. Over and over. Every name of everyone I have ever met. Everyone I have spoken to. Loved. Hated. Stolen from. Could not scream. Water too thick. Thickness grew. Like tar. Thicker and thicker. I sank lower and lower. Then I could sink no more. Stuck in the purgatory of the tar abyss. Still the names repeated. Seemed an eternity until Lucy was uttered. Woke up at the hint of the first consonant. Found *him* there, at edge of my bed. Watching me. He had come back.

He sits in corner of room looking at me. Hands on lap, head tilted. He is beautiful, like I was. His face covered with scarf to block smell of my melting flesh. Paisley sits by him. Won't come near me. His ribcage is completely healed. The baby is nowhere to be seen. Where is he? Cannot see any wet patch. No clue as to his whereabouts. I asked man in chair about baby. He said, "gone." I asked about Brekker. He said, "waiting." I have told him about the dream. He will continue the journey. He must because he is me. He has sworn to continue onward. To find you, Lucy. Maybe to bring me out of nothing and reform me. Then we can all be together.

Lucy, I remember your illness. It was repulsive. But now, in my state, you seem beautiful. Now we are equal. I cast you out. Sent you away. Hid from looking at you. At the tumours. I didn't know. Nobody could have known. Now I am no longer Master G_, I am Liquid Man, I am Master Powder-Skin and I will drift into air. Into nothing. Alone. But the other man, he will continue on. He is me.

I have given him instructions for when I go to sleep for good. He knows where to leave my remains. He will then write on. He will fill in the missing days or years. He was with me for the most part. Those parts that he wasn't, I have told him about. He knows where to go. Seems a determined sort. Investigative too. I doubt he shall fail as I have done. Paisley likes him. Won't leave his side.

I wonder if...

14

Master G_ is dead.

His last words were a gurgle. Pathetic. He had a desperate look
in his drooping eye. Looked at his last entry. Didn't finish his
final sentence. Doesn't matter. Have complied with his wishes.
Have taken him here, to where I write this now. Have laid him
to rest and will continue the journal. He is me after all.

There is a lot to fill in. Where to start? End is the best. I'm
sitting against the back of the wooden kiosk. Outskirts of
Pripyat. Border of 30km Zone of Alienation. Have read back at
description of Z.O.A that Master G_ wrote on board train. To
me, the city seems different to his description. Not as much red
sand. Beneath my feet is yellow grass and concrete. Many
cracks. Deep cracks. Concrete wasteland. Hard on foot. I have
propped up his body inside kiosk. He said it was a past
employment. To sit there and keep guard of town. Don't know
why. Nobody in town. Nobody left except Sleepwalkers. All
fled after evacuation. Just useless buildings left. Whole town is
bordered by cyclones. They are lying in wait. Liquid Man said
he wanted to go back to the kiosk. He said he needed to go back
there. So I took him.

He was not alone in physical sense when he died as I was in the
room, but he was alone in reverie. Sad. Things he has said, I

believe. Places he has been, things he has done, all that he has leapt over - all for Lucy. All for nothing. His end won't be mine. I have to find her, fulfil his wish. Find Lucy, for myself.

Not much movement around. Mountains to east. Plains to south. Cyclones all around. Red flame-cloud to west. West, where we came from. Wind is gentle. Has a metallic taste. Like ozone after storm. No buds on the shrubs. Desaturated. Can see, off in distance, a great hulk. Huge. A rusty ship at best guess. Difficult to judge distance. Difficult to judge anything. Confused about many things that have gone before.

Trying to thinking back to way before. Way, way back. Very, very difficult. Difficult to remember things. Memory seems blurred. Like a veil over my mind's eye. Very foggy. Mist seems to seep under doorways, through window-panes, under chimney grates and into rooms in my memory. Mist spills out of everything. Tried earlier to remember taste of beer. Tried hard, but now I remember holding a cup of fog. Think harder now.

Now I am just holding fog in that memory. No memory of cup. Just the word 'cup' in my mind and nothing to latch it to. Very curious. Curious to see if it is contagious. Will try experiments on my memories, and the ones Liquid Man told me of. Is the fog in my memories and in his? Or just in mine? Little to worry about right now.

———•◦•———

He died mid-afternoon. I could tell because the sun was in the sky and both my nostrils were bleeding. I stayed and watched him splutter into nothing. Dog sat next to me. Taken a grand liking to me and likewise. Would like to call him different name, but will only respond to 'Paisley'. Looking over journal I notice that he has healed from his old wounds. No viscous coating. No see-through rib-cage. Only thing that hasn't healed is eye socket. Still has bullet rattling around inside. He is lying in a shaft of sunlight beside me now. Beside kiosk. He tried to eat the grass but it made him hack up. Kept trying to eat it though. I shouted at him to stop but, curiously, it wasn't my voice that came out. My voice sounded different. Loathe to write it, lest it make it true...but my voice sounded like Liquid Man's. Like Master G_. As soon as Paisley heard his master's voice, he stopped eating and lay down in the sunshine.

Wet Alexander (name I have given to Tumour Baby) is not around. I have not seen him for days. He crawled away. Left a wet trail that led to a wall in hotel room. Odd. As if crawled into wall. That was recent. I will divulge in good time what happened to him. Must report now on the dead 'me' inside the kiosk.

In town I found a shovel. Wide enough for snow, or sand. Wide enough to scoop melting body into a barrow. Scooped him up off the sheets then climbed on bed with scraping tool and scraped all the black powder off ceiling. Was a lot. Two bags full. Didn't know what to do with bags. Emptied powder into man's coat pockets. Found something. A lock of hair. Red hair. String and note tied round it. Note from someone called Angeline. Note of love. Disregarded it, put it in his pocket with rest of powder. Barrowed him out of town and through the concrete plain to kiosk. He smells awful.

Will attempt some sleep. Resting against back of kiosk. Comfort in the warmth. No need to go anywhere. No need to find Lucy just yet. There is time. There is always time.

———•••———

Couldn't sleep! Woken by approaching footsteps! I can hear them as I write this. Nothing on the horizon, nothing around me. Must be on other side of kiosk.

True! I turned and peered around edge. Dot in distance. A person approaching kiosk. Footsteps seem close, though they are a dot. Sound is carrying abnormally far. I will hide behind kiosk and see what happens. Paisley remains next to me, undisturbed. Footsteps really loud! As if walking on my ears. Will look.

No longer a dot, now a blob, formless mass…now arms and legs coming into view. A woman. Old woman. Can see her stoop, can see her bandy legs. Approaching fast from the horizon. Abnormally fast. Will hide from view now.

Footsteps are so loud. Nose is streaming blood. Ears are too. Feel like I'm vibrating apart. Boots are wet on inside. Footsteps are rattling me. She is at the kiosk now. I am unseen to her. What does she want?

———•◦•———

Morning! I don't believe it. I passed out! This is what I recall. As footsteps got louder, I covered ears. They began to bleed. Covered mouth to stop scream. Chanced a peek. Old woman, haggard and wretched. Spoke in clear cut Russian, tone and timbre of a woman three times her junior. Luckily I am fluent. She said; "This dream doesn't belong to you," and walked away. As she said those words I felt woozy. The mountains began to loom over me. The hulk in the distance began to list. Fog everywhere.

And then I woke up. Have a voice in my head. It is not my own. It sounds like the voice I used to shout at Paisley for eating contaminated grass. It sounds like voice of Liquid Man. Voice says, "You are a background character in someone else's dream. My dream."

15

Made it back to the hotel. Voice in head dissipated as I got further from wooden kiosk. Left barrow behind. Too radioactive for use now, anyway. Still has a fine coating of Liquid Man's skin inside it. Took many hours, I guess, to walk back. Difficult to gauge time. Sundial I had set up on the carousel has been shadowed at ten-to-ten for days now. Cyclones still revolve, sun still rises and sets. Shadow remains at ten-to-ten. Paisley was panting. We passed only a few puddles on the trek home. He looked up at me, metal object in eye glinting. I patted him and bent down. Let him lick the sweat off my brow. Unwise as it is high in salt. He didn't mind. Tongue was coarse as expected. But he was gentle. Good dog.

Looked around and had thoughts of Wet Alexander. Had urge to find out if he was safe. Urge passed. Thought about Lucy. Entered into the town after both nostrils had stopped bleeding simultaneously and the left one had continued on its own.

Time by blood loss = early evening.

Sleepwalkers will be out soon. More on them later. I am sat on veranda of hotel. Paisley asleep. I'm drinking sarsaparilla. From Holstenwall it says on label. Improbable. Holstenwall was obliterated 'years' ago. Subsumed by super-massive sinkhole.

Nothing left. Everybody knows that. Still, sarsaparilla tastes OK. Will finish and go to room.

———•••———

Sat on the bed (have changed rooms - old room reeks, sheets remained unchanged). Chose room closest to Liquid Man's for continuity's sake. The ivy on the wallpaper points in the opposite direction, other than that the room appears the same. Wooden floor. Each board secured. One wardrobe filled with clothes if I need a change. Kind gesture. Took inventory:

5x Starched shirts.
1x Frock coat. Black.
3x Dress trousers. Black ribbon piping.
1x Leather gloves for driving.
1x Boots.

Everything fits but boots.

Paintwork on the wardrobe is odd. Bright blue with maroon piping on edges. Each door has huge hand-painted eyeball on it. Hazel coloured irises. Optic nerve detailing spirals over the wardrobe. Ivy twisted around optic nerve. When resting on bed against plush headboard, eye-wardrobe looking directly at me. Unnerving. Too heavy to face it the other way. Will sleep on front to avoid eye contact with wardrobe.

Paisley has spent the day staring at the corner of the room. Went to investigate. Couldn't drag him away. Growled at me. Kept staring. Looked harder. Only thing to note is the slight discolouration where skirting joins wall.

Ceiling fan has curved blades. They are hypnotic in their rotation. Like helicopter. Reminds me of father's helicopter. I will test a memory.

———•—•———

I am thirteen. Father takes me up in two-seater helicopter. Cockpit is a glass bubble – model is a Bell 47. Looking out of bubble, all I can see is fog. What was outside before the mist infiltrated my mind? I can't remember. I cannot even imagine variants. Father's hands are working levers. Feet pedalling fast. Sweat on his head. Concentration in his eyes. I feel safe in that glass bubble. He pedals faster to gain altitude. I ask if I can help. He says; "who said that?" I laugh, he doesn't react. Up ahead I see the helipad. It is a small ledge jutting out of a mountainside. On the peak is a house. Outside the house, a woman is waving. Father pedals harder, faster. Says, "come on, girl, come on girl, get there, get there." I say, "you can do it father, you can do it!" Father begins to cry and look around the cockpit in a panic, he says; "get away from me demon voice, get away from me." I look back around to see who he is shouting at. There is nobody there but him and me. Outside the bubble, fog is everywhere. Father pedals faster. To the east and west of the house the fog encroaches. Woman is disappearing.

Father is screaming for the helicopter to get to the woman. I am straining my eyes to see the ledge, and my home. My mother.

She is gone. House gone. All enveloped. Just fog. It's like being inside a snow globe. Nothing to see. Father is sobbing. I tell him that it will be alright. Pedals slow down. Fog begins to creep into the cockpit. Around my feet. Seeping up. Cannot see shoes. Cannot see father. Can hear cries. Cannot see anything. Can hear cries.

———•·•———

Ceiling fan above me is supposed to remind me of above passage. Curiously I can understand the words when I read them back, but the passage means nothing. I read and re-read twelve times, fog remains but the 'memory' no longer means anything to me. However, on twelfth time of reading and tying to recreate the memory, a red light pings in the fog. On. Off. On. Off. A Beacon. A signifier of the above memory perhaps? Maybe. In times to come it will be a marker. A gravestone with the epitaph; 'In your mind, here once was a memory.' Maybe if I gain more of these lights, they will form constellations? Then galaxies? Might spell out something. Might help me find Lucy.

I am tired now. I will take off my clothes and prepare for bed. Night time will draw in. In the morning I will relay everything that has happened.

Lying in bed now, lamp is on. Bulb is red. Difficult to read. Eyes must look like wardrobe eyes. Have read everything in diary up until now. Clearly I am in love with Lucy. Upon reading the full diary, with every mention of her name I grew impassioned. In groin and in mind. Felt more than desire. Felt need to protect. She was ill and grotesque but I don't care. Tumours? I have seen worse. I watched Master G_ slowly melt, remember? I have just written a question to myself to remind myself of what I have done. Funny.

A lot of this journal makes no sense. Jottings and pointers designed to stimulate Master G_'s memory and so it is difficult for me to decipher fact from garbage. It is almost a language that I don't speak. More things will come forward. I know it. I am not as insistent as Master G_ the Liquid Man. Things will come. If you force a memory or force an action you tie yourself in knots. Friend of mine used to say that knots become tighter, the more you try to untie them. Better I leave everything to unfold in due course. Plenty of time. For now I will sleep to dream of my one true Lucy and the delivering of myself to her.

———•••———

Morning – slept well. Cannot recall dreams. Felt a comfort because of it. Feel less drained. Looked around to see Paisley still staring at the discolouration in the corner wall. Going to wash.

———•••———

Back in bed. Washed. Feel uneasy. Feel strange. Like the effect of good sleep has been erased. Unsure. Rattled. Don't want to move. Don't want to leave room.

A fine layer of sand has appeared on floor of room.

16

Paisley still staring at the discolouration. I am too scared to get off the bed. The fine layer of sand that was not there in the morning is now a fingernail deep. Paisley isn't moving. Feel like the room is sinking into a sand pit. The discolouration has grown. I can see it even from here. Liquid Man told me about his memory, about turning to sand. I have read through his journal. Read about the woman at the kiosk and what she said to him.

I have an awful sensation inside myself. I think I am inside his dream. Perhaps he is not dead at all? Perhaps it is me who is dead? His liquidation in my world could actually be him waking up in his. I must write down the circumstances that have taken him from his entrance to Couldwell (as he called it) to the explosion by the reactor. The sections of his memory that he gave to me are solid, they are not turning to fog as my own memories are. Perhaps more proof that I am not in my own world. Perhaps.

It was only yesterday that I knew everything. And now? All it has taken is a few words from an old woman, and a few grains of sand and everything has changed. Outside the window I can see the cracked concrete is barely visible. Sand is covering it. Across the courtyard, by the grocery store, the concrete fronting has been replaced with a wood veneer. Seems like the town is changing. Silently regressing. Who am I?

I must recall now what sent Liquid Man on his quest. From life, through death to the NeverRealm. To his gateway world. I must recall what he told me. How all this started.

———•·•———

She was dead. Lucy. My love. His love. She died in her sleep in the year 1815, huge tumours on her back. Last words were unheard, but they were sad. That much he was sure of. She was sleeping in Brekker's Mansion, Holstenwall, just south of Tropic of Bath. It was summer. Heat wave made her fever worse. Brekker sent word across town to Master G_. Telegram said, "Come now, she is dying. It is time." Master G_ did not rush to Lucy. Instead he finished his shift at the factory then went home. Ate. Drank. Slept. He went in morning. Lucy was holding on for him. He said he later regretted not rushing. But he didn't want to see her in that state. She was repulsive. She had to lie on her front. Tumours like Alps on her back. Oozing. Pulsating. Unknown disease but a known cause - Brekker had been experimenting on her. Testing limits of radiation crèmes. Lucy had volunteered. At least, Master G_ had suggested it to her. He had volunteered her, he told me, and Brekker had taken her in. Lucy went willingly. She knew her limp (from falling from horse and getting trampled on) made her unattractive to Master G_. Simple maths. Master G_ said he felt the way he and Brekker looked at her had made her want to take part in experiments. He said Brekker took her in and applied many crèmes to her back.

Master G_ said Brekker was obsessed with radiation technology. Obsessed with The New Future, as the papers called it. Times were changing back then, I guess. (I have only memory of this world and my life, depleting though it is)

Master G_ told me of steam-powered trains, Model-T cars, 10,000 seat dirigibles and uranium power. All of that was in Brekker's grasp. His knowledge of all worlds and dimensions was too alluring, Master G_ said. Over drinks in a bar (Master G_ could not name the bar and said something about it being a dune in his memory) Brekker laid out all of his plans for all the worlds but he needed subjects to test on. Then Lucy's accident happened. Brekker said that he could cure her using his new methods. Master G_ was happy to have her become a brave test subject. Was an honour for him. They coerced Lucy into the lab. She went and the experiments began.

At first the crèmes and tonics worked. Her skin tightened. The three moles that looked like maelstroms dissolved. She screamed in pain and Brekker held a mirror up so she could see the good effects. He thought this would stop the screaming. It didn't. Didn't stop the experiments either. After the crèmes and tonics came the balms. These turned her fingers and toes luminescent. Like Northern Lights Master G_ said. I don't know what that means. Don't know what Northern Lights are. But he said that when it happened, he and Brekker went out drinking to celebrate the breakthrough. Master G_ said that he never saw the true results of Brekker's experiments until the end days of Lucy's life. He thought the experiments were working and that Brekker was curing her. Combating her limp and its subsequent ravaging of her immune system. Brekker would not let him see Lucy. Would only feed him reports. Master G_ didn't mind, he had faith in The Master Engineer. Didn't know he was cause of illness and was blindly mixing cocktails in the dark. To Master G_, Lucy was damaged, but not beyond repair. He loved her soul but loved her looks more so. 'Weak-stomached imbecile' - that's what he called himself.

To Brekker, Lucy was canvas, palette and mixing bowl. Master G_ said they went drinking to celebrate a breakthrough in diagnosis, and that Brekker said she was nearing recovery. Master G_ professed nothing but love for Lucy. Don't know how much to believe. Could be genuine love for her. Could be guilt over what he did. Counter-argument - guilty men do not do what Master G_ has done. They do not travel to seek out their transgressions. Guilty men shy away. Guilty men stay away. This man came forth! Tracking her down, so he was. Beyond the ends of the earth! If he knew Brekker had done all this to Lucy, why did Master G_ write so lovingly about him? Could he not remember? Did he not care? Did he forgive? Why did he want to meet Brekker in TheNeverRealm? I digress...back to story.

Brekker's balms caused tumours. Tumours grew almost visibly. Lucy began to grow pale. Fevered. Experiments continued. She was force-fed Uranium Ophiochloa, an active grass compound. Stuffed down her throat. Forced to swallow. Tumours accelerated. Brekker began to sense he had gone too far and let Master G_ into lab. Master G_ saw the beast that used to be his Lucy. Recoiled in terror. He said Lucy uttered; "I am in pain, I am in pain and he won't stop." Master G_ fled the laboratory and hid in bottles of drink and factory work. Brekker had gone mad with desire to push his discoveries further. Lucy was a gateway for him. A canvas upon which to journey into his mad science and realise his dreams. The experiments continued.

Lucy died soon after Master G_ had deserted her. He told me that she had just given up and died. Alone. Brekker was in the mixology centre when she expired. Lucy died alone and dissolving. When Master G_ saw her body he truly saw the extent of his betrayal. He saw his whole life before him and all the evil he had done. Pushing his sister into the pond. Laughing at his grandmother's arthritis. Failing to rescue his love. He said he could never remember what happened to Brekker after the day Lucy died. He simply vanished.

———•••———

Must sleep now. Tiredness coming on fast. Will continue the story tomorrow. Sand on floor now mounting up around chair legs. Grocery store no longer a concrete compound. Now a wooden shack.

I feel hollow inside.

Sand in socks.

17

Discolouration on wall now two-feet tall and one-foot wide. A column. Paisley hasn't moved in two days. Tried to drag him away. He growled fiercely at me. I backed away. I am terrified and alone. Not even the dog will look at me. The baby hasn't come back either. Haven't seen anyone outside for two days. Sand in room two knuckles deep.

———•◦•———

So alone I cried in sleep. Awful to admit. Shameful. Can't remember dream. Remember now only fog and an orange light. A beacon. In my mind it is far, far from the beacon of the helicopter-dream. I had to read back to find out the origin of that beacon in the fog and smiled when I did, not because I remember it, but because the system is working. Liquid Man was good to document everything and teach me how to do so also, I am happy to continue the work.

I feel brave enough to walk out of the room. For sure, even the Evil-Eyed wardrobe does not affect me now. Though a moment ago I was deathly alone and dog had spurned me, the beacons in my mind have given me a little sense of contentment, as beacons do.

———•◦•———

Back from leaving room. Went to front desk of hotel. Old Teller wasn't there. No Sleepwalkers around either. Must keep missing them. I suspect they keep to the west of Pripyat, (wind blows from the west, thus taking poisonous dust away). Hotel is in the east so that, at least, could explain my solitude. Noticed on Old Teller's desk a newspaper. It looked fresh. Paper still white. Ink still holding onto pages. Headline read 'Oil Tanker spillage – Exxon Valdez runs aground. Engineer at fault.' Doesn't mean too much to me. I wonder if it would have to Master G_? Will look back over notes to discover any mention. All else is quiet outside. Less concrete than I remember. More sand and wood-panelled shacks. Old rusted carousel on hill now made of wood, too. Sand in shoes.

Came back after looking out of porch. Nothing out there. Nothing to see. I am alone.

Back on bed now. Read over yesterday's entry. Continue.

Brekker had vanished and Master G_ went into hiding. Locked in his room, pouring over old stenographs of the lovers, writing notes, journals and stories. He said he believed that if he wrote down every instance of their life together, he could rebuild it. Could turn the clock back. Idiot. But when he told me, I saw true belief in his eyes. Remorse? Possible. He was sorry for his actions, that much was certain. But he also loved Lucy to his core. But, as humans do, he let his eyes lead his heart. That's what he said anyway. Didn't understand it myself.

Then came 'The Dream' he said. After four days in reverie (he could not recall how or why he had remembered that length of time so vehemently when all other measurements were utterly lost to him) he fell into a deep sleep. He found himself in a vast desert at night. Not like the desert to the east of Holstenwall. This one was cold. Real. Earthly. He found himself by a fire next to a rail line. Four men sat round it. Hobos. He sat by them. A train pulled up, silently. Just appeared out of the dark and sat on the line next to them. Odd design of train. Sleek. No steam. Like a bullet. Just sat there. One man by the fire said he could commune with the dead. Master G_ asked if he could speak to Lucy. Man said he could ask one question. Master G_ asked; "now there is no pain, are you happy?" The man replied that she was not. Man said that there was no happiness on the other side. There is no memory, so there can never be happiness. There is only stillness. Emptiness. He said that Lucy was sad. In eternal sadness. Adrift. In a vacuum. Sad. Master G_ woke from that dream in sweats. How could that be? How could the afterlife be a place of mourning? And his (our) Lucy there, alone and sad!

At that, he gathered up all his notes and stenographs. He packed them into a briefcase and stood in front of a mirror. Taking his father's old folding razor in his hand, Master G_ sliced open his throat, spilling his blood into the sink. His journey was beginning. He said he had to know the truth, and if it was true, if she was in eternal sadness, he would take her and bring her back and, if he couldn't do that, then he would stay

90

with her and spend his eternity fighting off the sadness. Defending her heart from it. I was touched by his noble gesture, by his verve and commitment, (admit, for a moment I forgot about his part in her decline and death). He said the last thing he saw in the mirror, as his life blood gushed into the sink, was a reflection of Brekker. The Dark Machinist said to him; "Meet me in Couldwell, old friend, I know the way to Lucy. I am the engineer of TheNeverRealm."

Master G_ then awoke in the waiting room. Train late. Days late maybe. Boy on floor shooting toy soldier at him. Collar itching. Woman with baby on her lap. This I have assumed from reading first entry. No mention of stenographs or pictures, save one. It is possible that in transition from there to here, they got lost. Not everything survives (conjecture).

Looking back over the last entry and reading back over the journal, I do not understand why Master G_ wrote so affectionately about Brekker and why this architect of degradation so important? How did he know where Lucy was? Why didn't Master G_ note down any sense of caution or mistrust? Or further, any hatred for him? What twist had the world put upon Master G_ to make him love Brekker again?

Things to investigate:

1. Why searching out Brekker?
2. True reason for searching Lucy – through remorse? For forgiveness?

3. Who am I? Am I real, or a just a character in Master G_'s dream?
4. Why is Paisley ignoring me?
5. What is that discolouration on the wall? Since writing it has grown by nearly 6 inches.

Cyclone on the horizon has come into view. Super-massive. Wind is whipping up a dust-cloud. Coming straight for Pripyat/Couldwell. Paisley won't back away from stain on the wall. Cloud is coming in.

Speeding up! Coming in fast!

Pressure mounting.

Nose bleeding.

Here it comes.

18

Miracle! Curse! What devilry is upon me? What can this be? The words, these words, these words you are reading now are writing themselves! My mind is doing it. Storm is all around town. Walls shaking. Ground rumbling. Screech in air, blood pouring from ears. Nose. Eyes. Journal fell onto floor. I am lying on bed, looking at it. Head hung over bed. I can see the words form themselves. Book lying open on blank page atop little dune on floor. These words. My mind. I am screaming. I am screaming. I want my mother. I want my father. I want the beacons to take me home. The noise, the noise. The wardrobe, the Evil-Eyed wardrobe, its doors remain closed. Seems to not notice the bedlam. I don't want to die, I don't want to go! I don't want to be a character in someone else's dream! That is what I am, what else could I be? Must order thoughts. Must order. Maybe beat back storm. Must try!

Paisley unmoved by storm. Unmoved by chaos all around. Still he sits by wall. I scream at him, I throw my shoes at him. Hits back of his head hard. Bounced off. Didn't even yelp. Sat staring at the god awful stain. What is it? What does it mean? The noise is louder. Like feedback. And screams, and wind. Like needles in ears. Like needles in eyes. The blood pouring from me is thick. Almost black. Trying to think back to happier place. Relocate mind. Dull out the noise.

Not working. Mind is just fog. Thick fog. Swirling madly. Swirling and churning. Beacons in my mind hard to make out.

The noise in my memory is different to noise in life. Different but same. Fog noise is sighing, sad, moaning, gurgling. Like death throes of Liquid Man. Same impact. Different voice. I want to die but where will I go? Fog world? Desert World? The train station in Holstenwall? I said Liquid Man's end would not be mine and that I was going to succeed but now I will suffer failure worse than his. Total death! Total destruction! The noise! I can feel my ribcage vibrating. What does this mean?

Think man. Think.

I have rolled over onto my back. Ribcage shaking to destruction. Cannot describe pain. Can only order thoughts for you. Natural frequency! I am reaching natural frequency! The vibrations will soon turn me into dust. Vibrated apart. There is a hum in my organs, I can feel them shifting.

Can see nothing but fierce red dust outside window. Can see nothing. The ceiling has changed colour. Changed texture. It is a sandy colour.

I know what is coming next, I know what is happening. Grains of sand are falling onto my face. Scraping my skin. Grating on my eyeballs. Still I am looking.

So this is what it feels like to be a memory fading inside your mind Master G_. Though not a regular memory, but a memory aware of its part, aware of its end – a self-aware memory! I tell you, it doesn't feel good!

Nevertheless, I am still staring at the ceiling. A hole has appeared in the centre of the room like roof of a sand igloo. Grains falling down harder now and wind is whipping into room. Shout one more time for Paisley. Can see his statue-like head disappear under the sand forever. He is subsumed! Goodbye, good dog.

I am alone now but I am fierce against death. I know what is about to happen. Calmer in mind, so you know Master G_. I am in your dream. But I am also you. So listen now. Listen. Do not trust Brekker! Remember, for our Lucy. For your Lucy! He killed her. Though you were complicit in your arrogance, you were not in the vile calculations involved in her death. So I forgive you. You forgive yourself. Find her. Come back, find her and she may forgive you.

———•·•———

Bedposts are turning to sand! Crumbling slowly, and vibrating apart. It is coming. Running out of time.

Master G_ remember Brekker! He is not the man you think he is! You know this, but you have forgotten. I am telling you now. A memory aware of its demise, like you are aware of your existence. We are beating the system! Because I can send messages from your memory to you, we are beating it. Beating him. Remember Brekker and remember the experiments. Remember the dream. She is sad Master G_ - she is in the afterlife and she is sad. We will win!

Silence.

Silence.

Silence.

Storm has ceased. Calm inside ribcage. Hole in ceiling has stopped growing. Eye of the storm? Window shows clear skies. It has passed. But what now?

———•◦•———

I didn't wait long to find out. I am standing upon the dune that has surrounded the bed. Equal in height. I have no idea if journal is still recording this, for it too is lost beneath sand.

I am standing on the bed. My head is near the hole in the ceiling. The air outside is fresh. I breathe in.

Then, the walls fall away like the final moments of an hourglass. The wardrobe, the walls, the bedposts. All falls away. And I am standing.

I am in a desert. The sun above me intense. The hue of the sky equally intense. Have to shield eyes. There is a great nothingness to the west.

To the east, I can make out a white gazebo, half buried in a drift. Near that, I can make out, what appears to be a tricycle. As eyes grow accustomed to the bright landscape I am beginning to make out more trinkets, relics and monuments. I am smiling.

They are beacons. I am in Master G_'s mind. I am a beacon like the gazebo. Like everything. Like the viola to the south, like the grandfather clock to the north. I am a beacon.

Remember Master G_, rage against Brekker. If you cannot remember, follow the beacons in your desert mind to me and I will tell you. But be quick for I am sinking into this dune and soon I will be lost to your mind forever.

19

Couldwell. Here we are. We walked down the corridor and alighted from the train. To either side of me I saw scores of people stepping off, unloading trunks and baggage. I wondered about each of them. How could I have not noticed them before? Mr H_ waddled over to a large congregation of families waiting for him. Looks like local dignitary. The heat is awful. My collar itches. Paisley is panting. I covered the baby's head and took out this diary and I'm writing this now.

I can see the town ahead. Many buildings, a town hall, some wooden structures, some Model T cars. Sign says 'Couldwell – population 278.'

I am the last person by the train. Everyone else is walking into the town. Will follow. Turned around to look at the train. Was not surprised. Train has gone. All that is left is a huge, long sand bank in its place. Cyclones on the horizon have resumed their metronomic movements. Someone I know used to count the time by the cyclones. I cannot remember who. That memory is a dune in my mind. I will read back over my writings when in my lodgings and see if I can investigate it. Hope you are here Brekker or you are near. Need to find Lucy, need to investigate the dream, need to burn TheNeverPages.

The sun is high and catastrophic. Baby is shaded and sleeping. Going into town now

Both my nostrils have started to bleed.

———•◦•———

I have written that last passage twice. Copied it out verbatim. I took one step toward Couldwell and the crowds walking off into town, when a lightning-bolt shot through my psyche. That is what it felt like, Brekker. A sudden charge. Flashes of pain. Images, sounds, and smells rocketed through my mind in an instant and I staggered backwards, falling onto my knees and dropping the diary onto the sand.

As soon as I did so, the baby in my arms woke up and looked at me. Big soggy eyes. Paisley too looked up at me. I have put baby down on ground and am sitting next to it under the hot sun. Townsfolk drifting away. Last of bags and trunks being dragged away. Feel empty. Feel taut. Like muscles have been pulled. Will sacrifice a memory to better explain how I feel. Maybe that will help you shed some light on what just happened to me moments ago.

———•◦•———

I was eight and you, Brekker, were called to my parent's house. Autumn evening. Sister was by bedroom door, half in, half out, chewing blanket with worry. Mother and father were looming over me. Faces of concern. They said I had been playing in the sun, by the merry-go-round. They said my sister had sat me upon it and pushed me around and around. I had begun to feel dizzy. The light flicked between rails of merry-go-round and dazzled me. Like somebody turning light on and off in my face. Stroboscopic. Fiercely stroboscopic. The figure of my sister was moving so fast in front of me that I could only see her in left eye, then right eye – never in both. And the stroboscopic light. They said I lurched and fell backwards, convulsing. Epileptic. Awoke in bed, and you were standing over me with your medicine bags. Remember you laying out tonics, crèmes, balms, lotions and strange pots of ionic grass. Father forbade their use. Asked for simple diagnosis. You examined me. Said that I had strained my psychology. Epileptic Muscular and Neurological Tensile Exertion. Parents look baffled.

Above passage now means nothing to me. But I trust the passage before it and assume that is how I feel now. Feel that, in mind, stroboscopic events have happened. These are the images I saw in my mind's eye as that lightning bolt forked through me, for their imprint will last a little longer I feel.

1. Concrete compounds.
2. Kiosk.
3. Old woman.
4. Melted flesh and the smell of cheese.
5. A shadow on a ceiling.
6. Myself, looking at myself.
7. Pushing something in a barrow.
8. A storm.
9. Journal in the sand.
10. Poor Paisley sinking in quicksand.
11. Tumours and screams.

12. A face I cannot remember, but one I loathed. Mistrust.
13. A man in a desert. Sinking.
14. Fog. Beacons in fog.
15. A crying man in a glass-bubbled flying machine.

Brekker, my dear, it looks like I will have a lot to investigate.

Taken inventory of what I have.

1. Journal – complete as expected. Addition though – over last few pages, have noticed alterations in text. Well, scuff marks really. Faint outlines. As if I had erased something. Or that something has been faintly overlaid. Difficult to tell in the sun. Can tell that it is my own handwriting as my 'r's are distinctive. I think the pages have aged and the ink is seeping through them. Will be extra careful in noting evidence.

2. Paisley! What a companion he is. Even now his little bullet is glinting at me in that eye socket.

3. Tumour Baby – Alex, gone back to sleep. I can assume he has made my arm soggy even if the heat has dried it out. Like dolphin out on land, I assume I should keep him wet. Just in case. When in lodgings I will bathe him.

4. Periscope – tied to belt. The eyeball design strikes me now as a little more than just 'familiar'. A tuning fork goes off in my mind when I look at it. The design holds

a weighty recognition within me. Not sure if that's a good thing.

5. Note in pocket! Interesting find – says, "You will forget me, but I will not. Now I am a cyclone. Love, your Angeline" – total gibberish. No idea who Angeline is or what it means.

And that's it. All present, correct. Onward, into Couldwell. The feeling of Epileptic Muscular and Neurological Tensile Exertion has passed and has been replaced with calm expectancy.

Quick note on location. To the east and west lies a great plain. Behind me, dunes of red sand, cyclones like metronomes on horizon. North of town is a large ridge, maybe 800 feet high. Nothing larger than it around although I can see something peeking over its edge. There is something vast behind that ridge. It is glinting like a star. Reflecting in the sun. Like a beacon. Will investigate in good time.

On main street now. It is called Torpor Avenue. Couldwell is empty. The ants must be in the nest. Can see a sign for a hotel. Sign says simply 'rooms'. Going to check in. No sign of any storms on the horizon, skies are clear and blue. I am in Couldwell, Brekker, come find me. Come parlay old, dear friend.

20

On bed, in room. Check-in was routine. Sign on reception said 'under new management of Old Teller.' I stood in the doorway looking around the large reception room. Mounted animal skulls hung all around the room. Twisted horns and antlers. Bullet holes in heads. Shattered jaws. Looming down. Alarming shadows cast on the floor. I stood there for a while staring at them all when suddenly Old Teller rose up from behind the counter, as if on platform. Expressionless. A statue. Old Teller was indeed old. Possibly 200 or maybe even 500 years old. Young eyes though. Hazel, wild, alert. I greeted him. He said, "Welcome back Master G_." He spoke in an accent I couldn't place. Struck a chord but it links to nothing, not a grain of sand in my mind can offer a clue to that voice but he did know me! Or at least my name.

Unnerved me greatly. I asked how he knew my name. He said it was an irrelevant question. I pressed him to tell me. He went to speak and as he did, his jaw fell clean off his head! It hit the counter and his teeth rattled out and scattered around like marbles. His wet bulbous tongue flopped around his neck, like Paisley's does when he is thirsty. The man made no attempt retrieve jawbone. Just stood there, like statue, tongue lolling. Disgusting slurping nose. Fierce hazel eyes staring at me. That bulbous tongue; I recognised it. Then I saw two little toy soldiers on the counter. Armed with rifles. It struck a chord in my mind, I flicked back over notes. It was boy in waiting room.

Ugly, bulbous-tongued boy who shot me with soldiers! But how? Why? To what purpose? I must admit I was horrified and felt sick. Like I had been tracked by an enemy and was facing my execution. Felt as though my skull might soon be up on wall like the other animals. My skin stripped away. A bullet hole in forehead.

Decided that it was foolish fear. If it was boy, then it was just a boy. Not to be feared. I tucked journal under arm and approached. Smell of tongue rancid. Stomach held firm as I collected teeth. Fixed the rotted pegs back into jaw. Then, held up tongue and jammed jaw back into mouth. Moved it about. Could hear grinding of bone and then a 'click' as it fell into place. Like putting coin into a mechanical attraction at a penny arcade, Old Teller came to life. He said, "Welcome back Master G_ you have one letter waiting for you," and at that handed me a small brown envelope. The corners are tatty and it is severely weathered. Was about to leave when Old Teller grabbed my arm. His mouth fell open (jaw held, luckily) and a voice came from deep within as if he was a gramophone speaker. Voice said, "If you cannot remember, follow the beacons in your desert and I will tell you...but be quick, I am sinking into this dune."

It was my voice! Or at least, an approximation of my voice. Was same, but somehow different. Twisted. Pained. I yanked arm away and fled up to my room. On bed now. Haven't opened letter. Waiting.

Room is large. Bed has net over it. Bed sheet is clean. Patchwork quilt. Patches show embroideries of buildings. Not like Couldwell's architecture. These designs are industrial. Compounds, steam pipes, towers and reactors. Apartment blocks, workers, children playing. Wonder where the town is? Would quilt-maker have visited it and then constructed this quilt all from memory? Could have been made there and transported here. Have scanned each panel of quilt and found no real clues. Just a tableaux of life of a bustling town. Prosperous in layout. As a town should be. Not like Couldwell which is a ghost town. At least, it seems that way. Population 278. Though after train, have seen only one – Old Teller. Maybe they only come out at night? Under cover of night, you cannot see the nothingness which is a comfort. Only the mad and inquisitive venture into this wasteland during daylight hours. Felt pang of melancholia when looking at the quilt-town and all the life it depicts. Want company, want people. Want to go back to civilisation. But not without Lucy. Her face gives me courage. Packed away melancholic feelings. Back to room inspection.

Cupboard at the end of bed. Blank doors. Nondescript. There are clothes inside. All fit.

5x Starched shirts.
1x Frock coat. Black.
3x Dress trousers. Black ribbon piping.
1x Leather gloves for driving.

1x Boots.

Lamp works. Floorboards are clean with no loose fittings. Checked all of them. Dresser doesn't squeak, drawers empty. Interesting green paisley swirls on lining paper in drawers. Pretty. Wallpaper has hand-painted ivy detailing running around the room in concentric circles. Gives me warm feeling. Very happy with room.

Strange discolouration in the corner, though. Paisley has gone straight towards it and is now sitting, staring at it. He won't shift. Tried to move him, he growled and the bullet in his eye socket glinted evilly. I have left him to it. Alexander Tumour Baby has turned from the stain. He tried to crawl up into my jacket. Repelled by stain. Fearful of it. Put him on bed before moving closer to inspect stain.

Stain is about four-foot tall. There are two trunks at its base that join together two-foot-seven-inches up from the ground. Peculiar. Stain is dark grey and has a slight relief to it. Sticking out oddly. Tried to pick it away, could not. It was behind the paper, or at least something was behind the paper trying to push through. Very curious. Didn't smell, didn't taste. Will keep eye on the stain and detail any change in its state.

Have noticed another stain. This one is altogether more sinister. Noticed it when I lay on the bed. There is a black stain on the ceiling. Human shaped. A definite silhouette of a man. Stood up to take closer look. It is a powdery stain. Picked at it and flecks came away, lodging under my nail. Smelt ionic, tasted metallic. Like ozone. A chill ran through me when I tasted it. Felt wrong. Felt dangerous. Most unsettling.

Sat back down on bed and looking up at stain. Feel tired.

Have awoken to see that the stain has changed shape! The silhouette is now pointing! Pointing towards the window. Have looked out and saw ridge and, in the sunset, saw the glinting of the beacon-star behind it. Fills me with dread. Nevertheless, I must investigate it.

Have finally opened envelope. Picture fell out. Black and white stenograph of my Lucy! But not! She is disfigured. Horrible tumours on her back and liquid streaming down arms. Lying on her front looking at camera. Awful expression. Fear, tiredness and confused pain. Not the Lucy I know! Made me sick to think of her in that state. Under picture it had the words 'Day Four, good progress'. Will show Brekker when I meet him. He will be curious to see it.

Stain has grown 3 inches. Paisley not moved. Tumour Baby has crawled under bed.

21

In bar. Slept a bit. Woke in middle of night. Commotion outside. Town was alive! I was right, they are night owls. Town was dead during the day, but at night it is like a carnival. Lights and garlands criss-cross the main street (Torpor Avenue) and it is like being under spider's web of lights. There is music everywhere. Organs, cellos, whistles, bells and a Theremin. All of them at once. Was spectacular.

Along Torpor Avenue stood the townsfolk. Women on one side of street, men on other. Smiling. Pointing, grinning, laughing, eyes wild. I stood and watched. Strange Couldwell ritual I guess. Men all bowed at once. Then, on other side of road, women all curtsied back. Women had ball gowns on, cut off at shoulder, elasticated around upper arm. Frills and lace petticoats on show. Boots laced up to ankles. Looked like whores but had faces like Baronesses. Men all in white shirts and waistcoats. Buttoned up to neck. High collars, bow ties. Bowler hats, dusty winkle-picker boots, gun-belts. Peacemakers. Every other man had long tail-coat. All had pencil thin moustache.

I had none. Thought about drawing one on. To blend in. Decided against it. What use? That subterfuge would be undone by lack of other appropriate garb. Stood at top of Torpor Ave and watched the men bowing and women curtseying back. Then they all, in line, stepped forward into street and stood nose to nose. They kissed each other. Eyes and mouths open. Each leaning forward, lips puckered. A kiss. Then they all leant back. No emotion. Well, no emotion that matched any of mine. Each line took three steps back onto the boardwalk. Back to original position. Music continued.

The women began to laugh. There were giggles at first, then laughs, then howls, then hysterics. Suddenly a bell tolled a single solemn tone and every woman stopped laughing on a rouble. At the ring of a second bell and every man drew his gun and shot their opposite woman! Sprays of blood and brain everywhere! Like fireworks or detonations of paint. I was rooted to the spot. I could feel vomit in back of my throat. Then, the men drew on themselves, held the pistols out, turned them onto their face, pointed towards their foreheads and, as if telepathically linked (I know you scoff at the notion, but it could be possible, even more so in this world) they fired. Again, an explosion of powdered blood and brains over the shop fronts and down they fell!

Despite my repulsion, I managed to control my nausea. The music stopped and the moon dimmed. Silence.

Then a giggle…and a laugh…then hysterics! The bodies, lying on the floor, missing the backs of their heads, turned to me and smiled. Slowly they stood and all turned to me. I didn't flee. Didn't move. I was a statue.

They smiled broadly and in an instant a feeling of calm washed over me. Remembered suddenly a prayer Mother taught me. As a child, Brekker, I had awful nightmares. Nightmares of apocalypse, of death, of drowning, of atomic hurricanes. Would wake up in sweats and raw panic. Panic and fever. Mother would appear like a kindly spectre, out of the shadows with a candle and we would pray together. We said:

Sancte Michael Archangele, defende nos in praelio. Contra nequitiam et insidias diaboli esto praesidium. Imperet illi Deus, supplices deprecamur. Tuque princeps militiae caelestis, Satanam aliosque spiritus malignos, qui ad perditionem animarum pervagantur in mundo divina virtute in infernum detrude. Amen.

As I uttered those words as a child, all fear would leave and I would sleep as a baby. That memory is not a dune and I think maybe, it never will be. Though most of my mother is dust (in body and in memory) that prayer remains. Her face is blurred, but the feeling is there and I felt it when the dead smiled at me on Torpor Avenue.

I was overcome with a sudden euphoria. The blood trickling on their foreheads looked like wine, the brain matter on the floor like cake. Their lifeless bodies like pillows and duvets and I felt home again. All because of those smiles.

Then, as quickly as they had died, their life came back into them. The blood faded away, the brain matter dissolved and the music started up. The men held out an arm, the women took it, and they all danced in the street! Joyous, mad dancing. Dervishes! Under the glowing spider's web of lights they danced. Then fireworks came. Hurtling over the ridge (from the point of the glinting star) they came hurtling as if sent by catapults into the courtyard of a besieged city.

I thought they would hit us, but they detonated in the sky above, showering us all in golden sprites of light! Brekker it was as God himself had laughed. Or as you would say, it would be as if Planck himself had clapped his hands. Such was the power. I ran headlong into the ecstasy of Torpor Avenue! I was mad! Crazed! In love with these strange risen dead! I was hoisted up by a fat man I recognised as Mr H_. Hoisted right onto his shoulders and he spun me around, under the fireworks and the garlands!

The crowd all cheered my name. They cheered for me and carried me to the bar. Here I sit now, in the corner, writing this entry. The people are merry, singing dancing and laughing and joking. They have now ignored me, but I do not feel excluded, just merely taken aside by myself to document this. Of all the things I expected to find in Couldwell, this was not one of them. Going to get another drink.

I have spied a woman in the corner. She is looking at me as I write this. She looks familiar, though I cannot place her. She has the most beautiful, wondrous cataract and her dress is wrapped around her like a whirlwind. I am in love, I am sure of it! I will finish this entry, have another drink and go and talk to her!

CATARACT WOMAN IN BAR.
NEED TO KNOW HER SECRETS

22

I am hiding in an alleyway. The light is dim. Streetlamp overhead flickering. Gas must be running out. Flicker throws up alarming shadows against the wooden panels of the alley. The woman left the bar via a back entrance. I finished my drink and snuck out after her.

I was drinking, as written before, happy and left alone in the bar. I was looking at her, trying to uncover her secret. She caught me looking and threw me a voluptuous gaze with no hint of mistrust, but at the same time overwhelmed with deviance. She smiled at me, and I saw a full set of perfect white teeth. What a rarity! The brilliance! I smiled back, baring my yellow, twisted teeth. Compared to hers, mine are like the front row of a graveyard. Didn't bother her. She smiled still. She didn't come over. I didn't go to her. She just stayed there looking. Finally she glanced around the bar, and slowly made her way to a half concealed door in the corner of the room. She was about to leave, when she turned to me, winked and ushered me to follow with the flick of her neck. Then she was gone.

I looked around the bar and saw nobody looking at her, or me so I finished my drink, counted to 100 and snuck out through the same door. It did not creak, but instead slid open expelling an odd hiss of air as it did so. It was like a sigh. I stepped out into the dark alleyway. Silence. I looked both ways and could only see puddles of light from the gas lamps and, in between those lamps, awful voids of nothing. Felt as if the alleyway existed in a sort of stepping-stone of light and darkness. I would not have been surprised if, in between the gas-light portions, the darkness yielded traps of the abyss.

Plucked up courage and conviction when I made out the figure of the woman, dipping into the darkness, and back into the light. In. Out. Each time getting further away. She had a strange gait. She seemed to glide. Made no sound. I looked down at the muddy ground. I felt about. I put my eyes close to it. Inspecting. There seemed to be no footprints! I looked back up. She had stopped! She had turned! She was facing me some 25 yards down the alleyway. She was half in the light, half in the darkness. The downward shaft catching her brow, nose and cheek-bones. The upward pull of the darkness taking her eyes, her cheeks and her lips. She looked like a skeleton. Then, I swear to you Brekker, I swear to you Lucy, she slowly levitated up into the air! Up around two-foot and then she stopped. Hovering. The pinpricks of her pupils shone out, glinting like a hypnotist's and she said, "Do not be afraid, you have travelled far. Far beyond all reason. Do not hide in the shadows. He is soon to come! He walks through walls, but before he does we will all dance. We will swim in the sky and dance. Do not be afraid, this is your place of work. Your employment. Your place to be!"

She said it with such a distant, dispassionate tone that I grew cold and sickly with every word. I felt my shirt grow wet with perspiration and fever. I felt panicked. I looked at my hands because, for a moment, I could have sworn they were melting. I knew exactly what she meant, and yet, and yet I could not place it. It was like hearing a rhyme from the crib, the tone, the melody attaching to your heart, but as you have grown from babe and from cot, you cannot place the words. She then said, "Follow me, follow me," and she dropped back down slowly, turned around, and carried on gliding down the alleyway, in and out of the stepping stone lights.

I followed her slowly, maintaining a healthy distance. The fear of the voids in between the lamps replaced by the intrigue of this levitating witch. Though initially I guessed the alley to be 20-50 yards in either direction from the bar-door, I could have bet my afterlife on having walked for several hours, with no change of scenery, no hint at an end, no hope of answers. Still she glided, still I crept. The fever-sweats remained. The melting feeling remained. The understanding, and yet not, remained. I was in two places it once.

Then, without warning, she stopped floating. Without turning to address me, she said, "Beautiful traveller, interloper in your own NeverRealm, wait a while. My lover is coming to tell you something." And with that, she levitated up another four-foot and ascended upwards and away, far into the night sky.

I wanted to scream out to her, to the town, to anyone…but I didn't. And so I began to wait which is where I write this now. Who is her lover? What is he coming to tell me? I cannot see the end of the alleyway now. I have, for sure, travelled too far along it…seems that, without any passing landmarks or milestones, that perhaps, perhaps, it is not me that has been travelling but the alleyway. Stretching on, pulling itself onwards. No. Ridiculous. It's the solitude making you write fanciful hokum. You have been walking and now you are in the dark, further away than you intended. Stay calm, stay alert. Breathe. You are not melting. You are not alone. You have Lucy.

I hear something. I hear a slight wheeze. Not the friendly wheeze of Paisley (oh, how I miss him) not the sleeping, wet wheeze of Alexander Tumour Baby (who has vanished, and I have not forgotten about – will investigate when I get round to it)

Something comes, a different wheeze. I have slunk back against the wall. Tight against it. Hard to write without looking. Have to trust that hands are writing coherently. He is coming now. I see a shape, lean, tall and coming forward through the lights – shuffling, amiable. Whistling now. Approaching. He is here.

23

Dear Master G_,

My lover told you of my approach and so, when you wake, this entry into your journal will, I hope, not incur any rancour or mistrust. There is no malice or deviance on my part. I am here simply to show you a way.

My name is Nikola Tesla and I have commandeered your journal until such time as I see fit to return you to yourself, and in turn the journal to you. In short, I have commandeered you. I have run a series of tests on you, experiments to unlock your mind, to push forward the boundaries of this NeverPlace and now, I believe we are there. We are ready for the final test.

I am watching you sleep while I write this. You are strapped into the chair. I have adjusted the harness and I have inserted all the cranial needles and both eye-vices. Pre-checks are complete. There are only a few more moments before we begin and so, with grateful thanks, I write a little about how it came to pass that you are where you are.

I came to you in the alleyway. You were hiding in the dark recess of a doorway. Your heart was beating fast. You were writing blindly. Hoping for answers. Yearning for truth. I approached and smiled my kind-smile at you, and you fell under a deep sleep-spell.

You fell to the floor and I took you to the LHC Gateway (you will see what I mean by LHC Gateway in time). It was here that your mind awoke, but your body remained in stasis. For a time, you were a Sleepwalker, like those you will meet when you awake fully. This may confuse you, but really it is simple. Think of yourself as an opposite to the population of Couldwell (as you call it). When you are cold, they bake, when you are hungry they bulge. When you are (truly) awake, they will sleep. You will see shortly.

At the LHC Gateway, while under my sleep-spell I ran test after test on you. Took samples from every part of your brain. Every variation in sonic magnetism was fired into your eyes and still nothing. I read and re-read your journal, I tried to decipher everything. The train, the symbols, the dog, Alexander Tumour Baby, Lucy, Master Brekker – it meant so much, that at least was clear. But I could not understand. But I had to keep going – it was an obsession. The tests were of the mind and the body. Invasive and painful to you and for that I apologise. You must understand that I experimented on you to gain answers for myself and my own predicament. Without your donation, how could I possibly marry your journal to mine? How could I possibly understand my own dementia, my own NeverPlace?

For you see Master G_ I am like you! I too am an interloper here. I too am searching although as each day passes what it is I am searching for becomes that much fainter. It was once a vivid image; a bright and clear canvas, detailed and immaculate. Like a perfect equation. But slowly, new images and alterations began to form over it in my mind. Now it is a muddy grotesque. What was I here for? I have constructed so much, I have learned so much, but my machines do not work! Nothing works here and so I have unlearned everything. I am in a perpetual wheel. And so sculptures of memory and the machines of the mind led me to design and build this, my greatest of all inventions. The Tesla Dream Projector!

But as Couldwell (as you call it) is populated with Sleepwalkers and Skyswimmers, the machine would not operate. I tried everything, even testing it on myself, but the pain was too great to bear and hindered my results. My dream projection was simply a mirror of what I was doing. I was too focused on my physical being and so I could not release my psyche. I was at a loss. Twisted and falling into my own grotesque canvas.

Then I dreamt of you, of an interloper travelling through the NeverPlace that would illuminate the sky. Like a flash of lightning and in an instant the truth was revealed. I drew with a stick on the sand the diagrams of my motor. A thousand secrets of nature which I might have stumbled upon accidentally I would have given for that one which I had wrestled from her against all odds and at the peril of my existence. I write again, "An interloper travelling through the NeverPlace that would illuminate the sky." And you will!

Your collar is stiff and yellow. Stained from the sweat. Your chest gently rising and falling like a tide. You are relaxed, possibly serene. The dream you are having will soon be projected above you and I am overjoyed at the notion. I will see everything you are seeing, and I will understand now what it was that brought me here. I will see what it is that I am meant to do.

After the test I will take you to the ridge and leave you. When you awake, will see beyond the LHC Gateway, onto the great plain. I will not tell you what awaits you as, I would imagine, like everything here you will see it differently. I can guarantee that I will leave you on the ridge unharmed. Should you awake in pain, know that in between my leaving you and you waking, ill tidings from another hand befell you.

Before I turn the machine on and record everything you see (this will happen directly from your mind onto the page – you dream will, effectively, write itself). Before this happens, I should say that I may never see you again, but I sincerely hope you find some answers through my work. As for the answers to your predicament that I have discovered, I can give you only one truth.

You wrote that you feel as though you are in-between. That you are in two places at the once. You cannot think like that anymore for the truth is, Master G_, you are not in two places at once. You are, in fact, in the same place twice. I go now to activate the dream-projector.

Good luck NeverTraverser

With all hope and love, your friend,

Nikola Tesla

24

Frequency 10Hz, 50 microvolts…alpha rhythm. I am in pre-sleep.

I am touching both the NeverHere and the NeverAfter. My nerves are firing. The room around me is different. I do not know where I am. Am I dreaming into it, or am I dreaming out of it? I am in two places at once. There is a beam of light flowing from my eyes projecting onto the ceiling above me. It is blue, a rich azure blue waving and sighing. I reach out to touch it, my hand extends but it cannot reach it. The azure blue is above me and as calmness comes over me, the scope of the blue projection increases. It is taking over my field of vision, expanding around me, toward me and away from me. Soon the room is gone. I am suspended in blue light, warm, glowing. I feel glowing from inside and out. I am everything and nothing, I am in all space and all time. I reach out again to touch around me, I cannot. I feel as though I am in water, yet I cannot touch it. There is a closeness upon my skin, the hairs are standing up and my nerves are whispering. It feels like someone is close to every cell. The blue is a heaven and it is all around me.

I try to close my eyes but they remain open, pinned by a vice, I try to touch them, there are needles sticking out of my eyes, I do not scream as I cannot feel any pain from them, I can only feel their ends when I touch them. They are projecting the light, perhaps. Forks, lightning rods – either guiding the blue ocean light towards me, or throwing the blue ocean light out from within me. I cannot turn, or move. I cannot swim in the pre-sleep ocean, I can only hover. I liken my calmness to the baby in the womb, to the life form unaware of the dangers of the world it is about to be born into.

I am starting to feel an increase in my voltage, and a decrease in my frequency. The blue light is changing, it is becoming darker, slightly more charged, slightly more violent...I know what is happening. It has happened to every man, woman and child countless times, though perhaps I am the first to become aware of it.

I am about to dream.

As I think this, I am the point of my own observation and my waveform is collapsing. I am about to dream. A name from my past would have smiled at me for understanding the physics of the dreamer, he would have smiled...the blue ocean is growing more and more violent, on the crest of the wave flicks lightning, a net of electricity moving and breaking around me. I am a body in an electrical globe...and it is growing fiercer, but I am not afraid...I am an adventurer...here...I ...rise.

———•◦•———

Frequency 6Hz, 100 microvolt...waveform type Theta. I am in Stage One Sleep.

The angry, violent electrical waves part like a veil and I rise and rise, but the sensation is to fall and fall. My muscles spasm. I am falling fast, I cannot see the ground but I can feel synthetic wind flowing passed me, voices, songs, great speeches, utterances all – they drift past me and I have a sense that some of the aural zephyr has bled over from the world of the woken, from those that populate Couldwell, maybe even words from whoever put me in the chair and put needles in my eyes. The projection from my mind begins to grow more and more vivid and I begin to laugh an exalted and maniacal laugh. There is an old joke that rings in my ears, a name I can't remember belonging to a blurred face told me and the joke swirls round my ears as I fall. It says; "A man falls down an elevator shaft and screams, knowing death is approaching he says after a while, "this doesn't hurt…, still doesn't hurt…, still doesn't. Ouch!" Where is the ground? I am buffeting in the freefall, maybe my experimenter is jolting me, maybe it is my muscles…I see it suddenly! The ground, fast approaching, the blue veil thins and I see a vast crater, rocky with shrubs peppered upon it. Looks like concrete. I am falling. I am preparing for detonation…brace for impact.

———•••———

Frequency 13Hz, 125 microvolts…waveform type Spindle Waves…I am in Stage Two Sleep.

I do not explode on impact. I do not even impact. I stop two feet from the ground like a thrill ride, a death drop, designed to terrify, I jolt to a stop. The noise stops. Everything stops. I breathe. It is a steady breath. My heart is racing but I breathe steadily. Steady. Steady and I look at the ground. The concrete is old and there are remnants of painted lines and symbols. I see a ferris wheel with an eye in the centre. It strikes a chord. I see the grass. It is a sickly, yellowy green. It feels familiar and awful, like the memory of a crime. I am hovering over it. I inspect every blade in silence. I am projecting this, through my needle-eyes and yet it seems not from my mind at all. It doesn't seem to be my dream. I have a sudden cold fear. This is not my dream. I reach out to touch the grass. It is wet and viscous. The pigment comes away at my touch, the blade turning to graphite powder. I begin to cry and as I do, as if on a spit, I rotate around to face the sky. I want to inspect the grass and at the same time I do not. I do not want to be reminded. I am in two places at once. And then I see the sky.

———•◦•———

Frequency 4Hz, 150 microvolts amplitude…waveform type Spindle and Slow…I am in Stage Three Sleep.

The sky is no longer electrical but the waves remain, calm and serene. They pull and break, lap and coerce each other. The sky is an ocean and I am underwater looking up at it although I am not underwater. I am not wet. I am not looking down on the surface, but looking up at the underside as if I am under a giant bowl, looking through the glass. The surface is a lullaby. I look to my side and from far off, over the brow of the ridge, I can see people approaching. I call out and point to the sky. I plead for them to behold the marvel. They do not. Are they too far to hear me? I cannot tell. I cannot even tell if sound is leaving my mouth. Still they come, from all sides now. They do not walk, but drift two feet above the ground like spectres made solid. They drift and I have no fear of the apparitions. I hold a conjoined sense of place with them all. A communicable sense of shared temporality. They drift and now they are here. They look down at me with lilting necks and they smile like a mother to her newborn. Their eyes are closed. They are Sleepwalkers. One of them lies down next to me and looks up at the sky-sea. The others follow suit. I am now one man lying amongst a million. We are all lying and looking up at the surface of the sea. How deep I have fallen! How slow my waveform! How peaceful I am.

———•·•·•———

Frequency 0.5 Hz, 150 microvolts amplitude…wave type Slow and Delta Waveforms…I am in Fourth Stage Sleep.

And I am as stone. We are all as stone, like the concrete we hover above. The sky-sea ripples and then we see the recognisable figure of a woman, swimming across the sky. She is elegant, her form perfect. I do not know if she is aware of us.

Soon another comes into view, just behind and equally beautiful. I cannot look to the faces of those lying next to me, but I know they are smiling contentedly, their minds gorging on the sky-swimmers above. Three, four, now a full squadron of swimmers appear. They reach the very centre of the sky, the point where my projection needles converge at my vanishing point. A huge mass of swimmers bobbing gentle in the sprawl. There is a moment of dread followed by a moment of divine expectation and then it begins. The swimmers begin to dance in the sea-sky. They circle and weave in a choreography beyond comprehension! My mind struggles to find names for the emotions I'm experiencing. At once the Skyswimmers call forth images of mountains, of meadows, of gazebos and of couples in love. They are using the ripples created by their arms to fan out and assume the outlines of great, recognisable vistas. I see the Tropic of Bath, I see Holstenwall, that great city I once lived in, I see plains, and worlds I have once walked through…I see a face…I see a face! They have converged to make a face in the sky…the face is Lucy!

A name and a feeling gush forth from my mind. I remember! Lucy is above me in the sky. I am happy and I begin to cry, but no tears come. Instead I begin to see beyond the swimmers. I see above them a dark cloud forming. A cyclone of angry and grey cloud. The swimmers remain and Lucy looks down at me. The clouds behind her begin to break and rain falls on the swimmers. They hold the face still but some of them drift out of position changing the formation. Lucy's face changes into that of a horrible grotesque! A deformed Lucy! Riddled with boils and pain. A feeling of sickness and guilt rise in me. A nightmare. I look around to see the townsfolk have gone. I am alone in this and then the raindrops break through the swimmers and careen down towards me.

———•·•———

Frequency 30Hz, 400 microvolts amplitude…wave type Paradoxical Waves….I am in REM sleep.

My eyes are panicking. The needles are scratching the sky as my eyeballs dart around. The scratching creates a shrieking sound. My ears are bleeding the ground is rumbling. Lucy is no more, the swimmers have gone and the rain drops are falling fast. They look heavy and angry. They hit. I have a moment of relief when they touch my skin which soon gives way to pain. Intense burning pain. I can feel my skin begin to pulsate and boil. It is falling off of me, I am melting. I can see bones, I can see innards. I am melting and I cannot move. My eyeballs have gone but the needles remain, scratching around in the empty bowl-sockets.

I am standing. Reformed. I am on the crest of the ridge. All is silent. I turn to look back. I can see Couldwell. It is no longer a wooden ghost town but a sprawling city of concrete. Stern constructions of utility. Of purpose. I know the city. I once worked here. It is Pripyat. I turn back to the ridge. I am at the LHC Gateway. Below me, in the crater running the circumference at least 1000km long is a giant steel tube – an accelerator of particles – a dimension cannon. I am on the ridge looking down. In the centre, I see her! Mother Motherland is calling me! She is a giant statue 900ft high, brandishing a sword high in the air and reaching back with her other arm to call forth her people. She is powerful, alive. The tip of the sword glints red like a beacon in the fog. It glints. I look up to the sky and see two moons. Giant, bulbous moons that are joined by a thick, intertwined chain of stars.

They look like giant eyeballs joined by an optic nerve. I have seen this all before and I am overcome with fear and dread. I am leaving REM sleep now.

I am going to wake up.

Part Three

I am awake. Have been for six hours, maybe seven. The cyclones on the horizon have moved along a few degrees. I am still on the ridge looking down at the Large Hadron Collider below. Mother Motherland, that great concrete behemoth, stands ominously under the noonday sun. I am alone. It seems that even noise has left this place. All is calm and silent.

I awoke standing up. First time I can recall ever doing that. I nearly fell down the ridge when I opened my eyes as I discovered, to my terror, that I had six-inch needles sticking out of them. Thin, finely twisted and elegantly formed metal needles.

My knees were weak. They buckled underneath me as soon as I came to. The wind bit at my face. Every sense seemed heightened. I felt, and still do feel, split, in two places at once but also, I feel attuned. I feel perceptive. Doubled. Heightened.

The expanse of the LHC Gateway is terrifying. The rim of the crater maybe 1000km in circumference and, at the foot of it lays the LHC, like a cable or metal snake. An Ouroboros. I am 800ft above it. There is a large compound in the centre of the crater, a control tower with a large observation platform. It looks deserted. Even from this height, I can see that the grass has begun to break through the concrete paving. Life is finding a way.

After much building of courage, I removed the needles from my eyes. I thought of Lucy and I extracted them. Pain indescribable. I tried to do one at a time, but it almost made me vomit. Thought of Lucy and yanked them both out at once. Fluid jetted out. Almost fell down the ridge. Nausea overwhelming, then it fell away as I came back into control. Eyesight returned undamaged. I have kept the needles for further use and/or experimentation. I stripped and checked the rest of my body. Found a double-track of scars running down my torso and a series of circular abrasions, each one over a rib, parallel to each other. I can only assume tubes, pipes and cables were inserted into me. No residual pain. Wounds have healed nicely. I have been well treated for a test subject. No signs of previous infections. No mal-intent.

I have read over Nikola Tesla's notations. Need to track him down. There are so many questions now. I must order my thoughts. Need to:

1. Get back to hotel, check on Paisley, seems like an age since saw him last.
2. Find Alexander Tumour Baby! How could I have left him? Crawled away and I never bothered to look for him – must track him down. Ugly? Yes. Vital? Most definitely. Could even be the only baby in this land. Important to everything. Must find him and put my repulsion to the back of my mind.
3. Track down Tesla and interrogate him.
4. Decipher the faint words that have appeared in my diary. Noticed them a few days ago, but haven't

thought about them since. I thought they were scratching, or erased words over my entries. Now it appears that they are words emerging. They are more prevalent now. I can make out a style of penmanship. Almost like mine...similar impressions. A few words are legible....need to find paper and pen to make notes.

5. The LHC Gateway and the Compound – I need to investigate fully. Explore, document and consider. There is something about this place. I feel like I have been here before but not in this lifetime. That doesn't make much sense, but I feel it.

6. Need to communicate more with Brekker, or at least find clues to take me to him.

7. Need to get out of Couldwell. If the above threads of investigation prove fruitless, I will move on but where too? Beyond the ridge? Beyond Mother Motherland? Onto the great FurtherUnknown?

8. If following course number seven, will need to acquire transport.

First things first, need to get back to hotel, change clothes, check on Paisley, regroup and then get out to into town and look for Tesla.

———•·•———

Back in hotel – sitting on bed. Fat-Tongued Old Teller was not at the desk. Point to note – the town has reverted to its wooden basics. Not like the concrete city I envisioned in my dream. It is now Couldwell. It is a town of shacks. Like Old West from picture books my father read me as a child. Old Teller not at the desk. Torpor Avenue abandoned...though blood stains and brain matter still line the walls, left over from the ritual I witnessed. So, it did happen! It was real. Even though I noted that the blood vanished in my dream there are here, clear as day. I wonder if the Sleepwalkers in my dream were not really in my dream at that maybe I was alongside them in reality? I will chew on this.

Paisley is in the corner, staring at stain. When I patted him, he barked sweetly and his tail wagged. He did not move from the corner though. Stain has grown. It is now chest high. The stain on the ceiling has altered too. It is no longer pointing to the glint on the ridge (which I can now locate as the beacon atop of Mother Motherland's sword). The 'arms' of the graphite stain are by its side. Looks like a man in a coffin now. The wet stain of Alexander Tumour Baby still stops at the wall and, after all these days, it has not evaporated. Still a slimy, viscous wet trail.

Most curious addition to the room is now the wardrobe. It has changed although the 'make' and 'model' remain the same, it is now decorated. When entering the room and seeing it, a cold chill ran down spine, quickly followed by a strange sense of recognition like returning to a place I had once known, far beyond the small time I have spent in Couldwell.

The doors are now painted blue, with red piping and on each door is a large eyeball with hazel irises. They are staring at me. They are joined by an optic nerve, twinned with ivy. I have seen it before; the moons in my dream joined by the train of stars but, more importantly, the design is the same as that on my little periscope.

I looked back over my notes and recalled its use in the train and how it revealed the carriage. That design is with me, in the train, in Couldwell and in my dream. I will go, tomorrow, to investigate the town and I will bring the periscope with me. It could prove to be a great weapon. I feel alive, positive and ready for the next stage in my journey to Lucy. TheNeverRealm does not hold fear for me in this moment. Nikola Tesla – I am coming for you.

26

Stand a better chance tracking down Tesla at night. I have a feeling that daytime is not productive as town always seems abandoned. Night is coming in. I have washed and changed. Feels good to get into clean clothes. Shaved and trimmed hair. Feel new, ready, alive.

Paisley doesn't want to come with me. Tail wagged when I patted him, but he growled angrily when I tried to drag him away from the corner of the room. Stain still chest high. Stain on ceiling still like a man in coffin. I have packed my periscope (attached to belt).

First stop – Old Teller. I will update journal throughout the night. I intend to return at dawn. Must not get sidetracked with any spectacle. Must remain on mission. On point. Must find Tesla. I go.

———•·•———

Old Teller asleep on counter. I am in the reception sitting at end of counter. He is prostrate in front of me. Not breathing. Jaw half off, tongue lolling. The animals around the room have not changed. The skulls still remain although they have a slight purple tinge to them. Inspected the antlers of a deer, purple residue scraped off onto my pen easily. Did not corrode. Tasted it. Tasted of iron sulphide. Smeared a sample into journal for evidence/further investigation. Nothing else to report in the reception.

———•·•———

Out in the courtyard, sitting on the fountain (no water). Nothing around and no lights save for the beacon glinting over the ridge. Eerie silence. Wait, I see something, I see people.

I have climbed inside the empty fountain to observe them. They are drifting through the town, two feet off the ground. Scores of them are appearing. Among them I can see Old Teller, his tongue flapping and lolling still. They are apparitions made flesh. I read back over my dream entry, and they were there too! Almost conclusive proof that I was dreaming in reality (as I know I am not dreaming now) they were in my dream, and in reality as well. Since I removed those needles, my eyes have become sharper and I can see more clearly even in the pitch dark of night. I am not even looking as I write this, but can wager that the lines of text are straight and true. Each town member has their eyes closed: Sleepwalkers. I would try to follow them, but I cannot walk amongst them, I cannot float and so they might suspect me. I will wait until they have drifted off and then I will follow them.

Noise now! A low rumbling – a humming, from the people, bless them all they are singing, or at least, trying to. There is a low harmony that has a melancholic air about it. The song hangs in my ears as they drift away. I am not too foolish to ignore the eerie beauty of the sight and sound of the Sleepwalkers. I wait for a few moments then I will follow.

———•◦•———

The Ridge.

I followed the townsfolk, keeping a safe distance at all times. I followed them through the streets and out of the town, all the way to the ridge. It was hard to keep up in the dark despite my improved vision as the ground underfoot is treacherous. Broken and cracked rock. Concrete ready to twist an ankle. When the townsfolk reached the ridge, they descended over the brow and down into the crater towards the LHC. I stayed on the ridge to observe. Periscope does not magnify so was no real use. Had to rely on eyes.

Townsfolk drifted down, through the Ouroboros-like LHC ring and into the central compound. Then, they lined up, single file. I counted 278 townspeople. Every citizen of Couldwell accounted for. They filed into the compound.

There was silence for a few minutes. Then lights! First, along the periphery of the compound, came floodlights, then window-lights popped up. Then, at intervals of a hundred feet, came red flashing beacons running all along the top of the LHC tube, along and around the entire circumference. Quite dazzling. The compound was coming to life! Then, Sleepwalkers began to appear, rushing around the complex, moving, carrying, transporting - some in overalls, some in lab-coats, all busy and focused.

Then came a rumbling, so low at first that I could barely register it. But it grew. Little pebbles around me began hopping and rattling as it intensified. The sky grew angry and, on the far horizon to the east I could see four cyclones stop their patrol. They hovered for a few seconds then moved towards each other to unite into one magnificent cyclone! I could almost feel her power. The rumble intensified. Above me the sky grew angrier and angrier. The warning lights on the LHC tube began to flash and spin faster. Mother Motherland, in the centre of the compound, stood proud and stern, her arm extending out and pointing off towards the giant cyclone, her sword arm reaching up to the angry sky. The hue of the world changed and turned to a sickly green - a ghastly colour not of any natural saturation. Everything was charged. A warning siren began to blare. They were about to fire the Collider! A fear took me as I had no idea what would happen. The distant cyclone began to rotate in a counter-clockwise direction, the wind whipping through the plains towards me, intense it was! Then a loud fog horn like a million trumpets blared out, almost shattering my eardrums! I put my hands to my ears but the horn seemed to sound inside my head, before I heard it. Difficult to describe!

And then it stopped. We were on the point of apocalypse, and then...nothing. The clouds dispersed and the cyclone in the distance broke back into its component parts...it was a test run. It must have been. Either that or they could not figure out how to finish firing the LHC.

I stood up on the ridge and looked down, taller than anything around, eye level with Mother Motherland. I was about to descend when I saw the lights turn off and the rumbling sound powered down. The Sleepwalkers began to file out of the compound.

———•◦•———

Back in hotel room. Staring at the wardrobe door. Paisley curled up on floor by stain. Thinking over what I have witnessed. Read over what happened. Doesn't seem to be any danger of that event turning to sand in my mind. I have come up with a plan. An idea has struck me.

Tomorrow, when they go again, I will take one of them, bring them back here, use the needles to see what they see and maybe bring Tesla out.

Tomorrow, I will kidnap a Sleepwalker.

MOTHER MOTHERLAND STANDING OVER LHC GATEWAY

27

She is sleeping on the chair. I am yet to begin experiments on her. Better she has an uninterrupted sleep before the needles go in. Brekker, here is what happened. Here is what I had to go through to get a subject.

———•◦•———

After deciding on my course of action, I slept soundly and dreamt of the desert in my mind. I saw the silhouette of a man buried waist deep in a dune. The silhouette wasn't thrashing or wailing, but calmly remaining still, as if waiting for someone or something. I felt a pang of recognition, as if I was supposed to be there, or to go there and help him. Upon waking, I felt a great regret for leaving that desert dream and it has instantly become something I need to investigate further. But I put it to one side and went about my plans.

As it was early morning, I knew the townsfolk would not be around. I was right. Couldwell was deserted as usual. I spent the morning walking around, looking at places, through dusty windows, breaking into houses searching for clues and also a suitable place to become my laboratory. It wasn't until I left the borders of the town and headed eastwards that I come across something of use. By chance, as I was walking, my foot hit against something under the loose layer of sand covering the plain. Something metallic. I cleared the sand away and found a hatch. Looking around, I saw that I was alone. I opened the hatch and descended down the metal ladder (I make note that it was metal as everything else around here is made of wood). The ladder led down into a corridor which was barricaded in one direction, open in another. I cautiously walked along (firstly, I wedged the hatch door open, lest it close and entomb me forever). The corridor led to a room that seemed perfect for my needs: a circular atrium that looked like a disused laboratory. There was a bench with various instruments for dissection laid out. They were clean, and eager for use. There was a chair, similar to that of a dentist's in the centre. At first I thought I might have stumbled upon Tesla's lair and I was feverish with the notion that I had been led there, but after touching the chair and inspecting the room and it having no effect on me or my memory, I concluded that the room was not his and was probably something constructed by someone else a long time ago. Either way, I knew that the previous owner would not be coming back and that it would be perfectly suited to my needs.

I cleaned up and removed the dust and sand from the bench and the floor as best I could. I noticed a very fine purple residue on the callipers and scalpels, though. Tasted like iron sulphide. Same substance that coated the antlers in Old Teller's reception. Clearly a hangover from a past time. They are connected. Both places bearing witness to the same event. After a few hours, the room was clean and ready for use. Fortunately, when I climbed out of the hatch, the night was drawing in. Perfect timing. I had no need to return to the hotel room as all I needed was with me.

———•••———

I made my way to the ridge, descended down and entered the LHC compound. Inside was an intricate maze of corridors, walkways, vaults, silos, control rooms and laboratories. It gave the confusing impression that it was far, far greater in size and depth on the inside than it appeared to be from the outside. It was an impossible labyrinth, mined deep, deep into the ground. When standing on the central walkway and looking down into the reactor, I felt overcome with vertigo, forever it went on! I could see hundreds of service elevators lining the great uranium rods – transportation to go down into the reactor core should one need to. Everything was still. I was the only soul there. There is something altogether terrifying about being the only living soul in a space built for activity. Above the walkway the uranium rods stretched up past even the vanishing point of my eyes. Vast is not the word. I decided to make my way to the central control room, knowing I did not have much time before the Sleepwalkers arrived. I did not get lost and I seemed to know the way. I didn't double back and I didn't think twice as I weaved through the spider's web of gantries and walkways, down countless corridors and passages until I came to the control room. How could I have known about this? Again I felt as if I was in two places at once. My mind felt stretched and confused and I thought about the silhouette in the desert. I overcame my confusion and found a suitable place to hide. My plan was to wait until the operations began and then, at the height of the Test Firing, when all bedlam was breaking loose, I would leap out, incapacitate a worker and escape with them to my new hideaway. I squeezed myself into a metal cabinet and waited.

I did not have to wait long. As soon as I was ready, the control desks began to light up by themselves! The observation windows un-smoked to reveal the reactor core behind. Switches began to flick, dials turned and a humming began to rise around me. But there was not as soul to be seen! The humming grew louder and louder, yet I was alone. Where were they?

I had to think fast. I closed my eyes and focused my mind. A million images flashed before me, like a rolodex, and then one stopped. The image of the two moons, connected by the train of stars! I opened my eyes and reached for my periscope.

I opened the cabinet doors slightly and raised the periscope to my eyes. And behold! I could see them! The periscope seems to meld realities together, opening a gateway into the NeverHere and NeverThere. A Babel-glass!

INSIDE THE LHC REACTOR CORE

28

The control room was a hive of activity. Sleepwalkers bustling about, flicking switches, turning knobs, recording and cataloguing and then the hum began to rise. The Uranium Rods began to descend into the reactor core. Everyone in the room stopped and turned to the observation window to see. I was ecstatic with my discovery, with linking the images and symbols collected in my mind to make this connection. I cut short my exaltation and got back to business. I had to choose one scientist to kidnap. I had to figure out how to get them out of the room without being caught. And then a gift came my way. One of them broke from the group and drifted out of the room…and it was a woman! I recognised her immediately. From the bar. From the alleyway: Tesla's lover! I slid out of the cabinet, periscope still to my eyes, and managed to squeeze through the control room door before it closed behind the exiting woman. She was alone now in the corridor, drifting away from me. I approached from behind, ready to incapacitate her. I reached out and touched her, ready to choke the air out of her lungs….needless! As soon as my hand touched her hair, she fell to the floor unconscious! Eyes still closed, but moving rapidly in the calm internal stillness of deep REM sleep. I had no time to ponder her metaphysical state as the others might have become aware of my actions. I picked her up, hoisted her over my shoulder and made my escape.

I was unsure whether to make my escape using the periscope to guide me (to help avoid the otherwise unseen Sleepwalkers) or to flat out run for it which would be faster. I decided on the latter and trusted that my inherent and unexplained knowledge of the compound and the speed at which I could navigate at would aid me better than a cautious approach. After all, I was sure that the Sleepwalkers could not see me anyway. I sprinted along the gantries, round the passages and down the corridors all the while carrying the woman over my shoulder. I must have sent Sleepwalkers flying as on numerous occasions I could feel collisions against my body but I did not stop once to raise the periscope to my eyes to check. I was struck, while running, by the notion that perhaps my escape had gone either unnoticed or was of little consequence to the Sleepwalker Scientists as the Test Firing operation continued unhindered around me. As I ran, the ground inside the compound began shaking violently. The gantries swung wildly and it was nearly impossible to maintain balance. I fell and dropped the woman, causing a gash to her forehead and a possible fracture to the radius. I struggled to my feet and slung her over my shoulder again. The humming noise made my organs shudder and my bowels voided, still I ran. The effect within the LHC Compound was far, far worse than the effect I witnessed upon the ridge. I ran beside a long observation window that showed the uranium rods on the other side generating great plumes of smoke billowing upwards, twisting like cyclones and hissing sharply. My ears began to bleed and I slowed considerably, bowels running, ears bleeding, Tesla's lover over me. I pressed on, screaming "Lucy! Lucy! Lucy!" as it is your name, dear sweet Lucy that gives me so much strength. My vision began blurring and juddering and I was on the point of giving up when I rounded a corner and saw a long corridor with a circular hatch at the end of it! I had gotten to the exit! Lucy, your face came forth to the centre of my mind and with renewed vigour I ran at full pelt towards the exit, opened it and scrambled out into the apocalypse outside. I was in the centre of the compound in the middle of an LHC Test Fire!

I leapt down with the noise and chaos all around me, inside and out although I did not land on the ground! I stopped short of the concrete by two feet. I was hovering in the electrical storm like a Sleepwalker! I was right under the feet of Mother Motherland, seemingly safe in her great shadow. I looked towards her pointed hand and off to the south I saw, as before, the great multi-formed Cyclone. I looked back to the North, to the ridge, silhouetted against the blackest and bleakest of skies and I remembered my lair and my plan. It was then or never. I focused my thoughts and tried to urge myself along. It soon worked and I began to float towards the ridge wall, though I had barely any control of my movements. I was like a child trying to sail a boat in high winds, the inertia taking me too far left, or too far right. I began to regain control as I tightened my grip on Tesla's lover, using her force to help maintain control. I was soon drifting on a steady course through the maelstrom. Even the noise seemed to dull away slightly, such was my focus. I ascended the ridge and came down the other side just as the LHC Test Fire began to shut down. As it did, I began to feel gravity's force returning to reclaim my body. I slowly descended the two feet of air and touched down, my knees buckling slightly but I soon remembered how to compensate. I stood there, on the concrete ground on the safe side of the ridge and lay Tesla's lover down.

After a quick inspection I concluded that the gash would need treatment and her arm was indeed broken. She was still asleep, though no longer in a REM state but perhaps drifting back through stage sleep and into reality. I didn't have much time and so I slung her again and carried her to my underground laboratory.

It is here, in the chair that she now sleeps. I have attended to her wound, and set her broken radius. I have prepared the needles and set my charts. When she wakes, Brekker, I will begin my experiments on her. If I can get her to project the location of Tesla's lair, then I will be a giant step closer, if not, I will have to convince her in other ways to give up the location of the Tesla and his Dream Projector.

29

She is awake now. I have adjusted the chair so that it is upright. She is looking at me. Her eyes are cataract. Fogged up. She cranes and weaves her head around, perhaps trying to locate the sounds around her, mapping the geography through aural responses alone. Subject is quite fascinating. I clicked my fingers by her ears and she moved to look at the source of the sound, like a baby when born. She can hear.

I prised open her mouth and inspected her tongue, jaw line and teeth. She has a complete set of perfect teeth. Quite remarkable. No sign of decay or distress. Her jaw is set and sturdy with no sign of any breakage or duress. Her tongue pink, fleshy and her breath sweet.

Removed clothes, subject did not resist, perhaps feeling safe? Or unashamed? Or unaware? She has no markings on her body whatsoever. There are no similar track scars down her torso like mine. All ribs accounted for. Could not feel though her skin any signs of previous breakages. Feel somewhat guilty and sad that I maybe have caused her the only physical harm she has known by breaking her radius. Torso is lean and well-formed, breasts youthful and inviting. Hips slender and smooth, well cared for sex and long legs. In conclusion, a perfect specimen of woman and quite, quite unlike anything I have witnessed thus far in TheNeverRealm and, indeed, from what I can remember in my desert-mind, from any time in my waking life. I feel a shameful and almost overwhelming urge of lust and

I do well to suppress it, though it has been uncounted years since any form of contact that approximated pleasure. I put thoughts to back of mind, I am on a mission and need to remain focused, though I note down my stirrings to highlight to Brekker and to you Lucy, that despite this chaos I am still human.

I have prepared the needles for her eyes and she hasn't said a word, so silent that she could be asleep. I do not know what true state she is in. Here goes.

———•◦•———

It's over. She is back into her REM state. I am about to leave to meet Tesla. Experiment a resounding success.

I came in close to her eyes, as close as I could as I had to clamp her face into position. The insertion of the needles had to be accurate and I had limited apparatus. Found a bench-vice and attached it to the headrest of the chair and placed her skull into it, tightening it until I could see the pain registering on her face. She was still in her twilight phase of sleep therefore it was considerably harder to gauge any normal reaction and so I had to tighten the vice more than I would have liked. When the corners of her mouth dropped and quivered I stopped tightening. Her face was locked. I washed the needles and got in close. I held a lamp directly above her and her foggy irises focused on it intently. As I was holding the lamp, it meant I would have to insert each needle separately. I remember how painful it was to try and remove them one at a time, and was ashamed to have to subject this woman to a similar treatment.

I took off my belt and placed the leather strap in her mouth to prevent her biting off her tongue. In went the first needle. Her hands gripped the arm rest so tight that three of her fingernails prised off. The needle went in slowly through the very centre of her pupil. She began to drool and gurgle. No tears came. As soon as I felt the needle meet resistance, I stopped. I carefully cleaned up the leaking fluid around the entry wound and dried her eyeball of the specks of blood. The needle now jutted six inches out of her eye. I carefully held the lamp and took it over with my other hand as I moved around the chair to her other side, all the while careful not to move the lamp and therefore move her concentration of gaze.

The second needle went in with the same care and precision. Once in, I moved the lamp away and observed. As soon as the lamp was gone, the fog in her cataract parted like clouds after a storm or curtains in a play and they revealed the most wonderful and vibrant green irises I have ever seen. Indeed, they were so intoxicating that I leant in a little too far to see them and caught my own head on the end of a needle. It nicked me and a drop of blood ran down the needle. I was not quick enough to stop the droplet from touching her pupil and as soon as it had reached the base of the needle, it was sucked into her eyeball. Her eyes then changed to a most dazzling hue of purple and her mouth opened, letting out a great sigh. Her eyes swirled and sparked and had I not had the focus to break my gaze I would not have looked up at the ceiling! For there, projected out of her eyes was an image of the fountain in the square in perfect clarity, even in the pitch dark. And there, on the fountain, sat a man with a violin. He raised it to his chin and began to play a lament. A melancholy woe. A song for lost lovers. I was immediately struck with sadness and a sudden realisation of what I was doing and what I had done; torturing this woman to bring out Tesla. He had tortured me, but we are men of science and theory and are not privy to exception. This woman was an innocent. I almost cried as the lament continued. Then, the man stopped playing and looked up from the fountain, straight at us! For him, he would have been looking into the stars, for us looking down upon him; he was looking at us, 'breaking the fourth wall' as the saying goes. He could see me! A whisper came out of her mouth. She said; "Release my lover and come find me, come find Tesla. I am where you see me. Come find me, we have much to talk over." And at that the image began to fade, the clouds of her cataracts returned and the dream was over.

I was overwhelmed, amazed and frantic. I pulled both needles out instantly and dressed the woman, taking great care to look away and try and return some dignity to her. She is back in REM state now. I am going to carry her to the town square and I am going to meet Tesla and get some answers.

We are really getting somewhere, Brekker. Truly we are.

30

Tesla's entry.

I do not blame you, Master G_, for what you have done to find me, and I know that my lover will not blame you either for she knows that you are in desperation and in love. Fear not, she is by my side as I write this in your journal. You have passed out on the floor. We have drunk far, far too much! You were like a child, greedy for the drink! As if you had never drunk before. I sensed a great weight has lifted from you. You are curled up on the floor next to your dog. There is a curious stain on the wall, but I am sure you are aware of it. You offered us your bed before you fell down. You are snoring loudly and breathing deeply. How wonderful a sight to see a man at peace after a heavy night of relief!

I have no doubt, dear friend, that you will have no memory of the last few hours so allow me to take over your journal for the purpose of reporting but fear not, I will not reveal any moments that might be better served being buried in the desert of memory (though I will say, I have seen men set on fire, running around screaming and panicking who could be said to be better dancers than your good self!)

We met at the fountain in the dead of the night. The Sleepwalkers had returned from their shift at the LHC and my lover was distressed from not being with them, from being out of synch with her world but I, like you, am not of this world and so it is that we can move freely between the two. I think this is something you are coming to understand now. How it can be possible for us to see both planes of reality. You kept, after many drinks, thrusting your periscope at me and begging me to 'look through it and see the truth' which I did, but saw no remarkable changes like you do. But then, I see what I want to see, as you see what you want to see…or should I say, need to see. I would very much like tomorrow to sit with you and discuss the periscope and your ideas of Couldwell (as you call it).

I must admit, I truly believed that I would not see you again. After my experiments, I believed you would leave this place, or at least follow your own path. In all my calculations, I did not factor in your spirit and your drive to discover the truth that would help you on your way to your beloved Lucy. And I think, together, we stand a great chance of deciphering the LHC Gateway. Remember, I saw what you saw in the Skyswimmer's dance (thought it didn't mean as much to me as I would have liked).

After I had rested my lover upon the wall of the fountain we circled each other, you with a fierce, determined look in your eye. You were brandishing the two needles in your hands. I had no idea whether you were going to incapacitate me and use them on me, or just going to stab me with them and send to whatever place lies beyond. We circled and I began to sense that you were not seeking violence, but answers. I have told you before that you are not in two places at once, but in the same place twice.

I said this to you, those were my words and as soon as I had uttered them, a tuning fork rang behind your eyes and you realised that, standing across from you, was not an assailant but somebody similar, somebody whom you could benefit from. You lowered the needles and pointed towards my lover.

You said, tearfully, "I'm sorry. I didn't mean to hurt her. I just want the truth," and you were so sincere in your tone that I felt an instant pang of recognition. I offered you a seat next to her and you took it. I placed your hand on her head and asked you to close your eyes. You did and my lover spoke to you in her dream. She forgave you for the needles and said she would have done the same. Your tears dried and then we went to drink!

We shook hands and I took you to the bar. We drank and you relayed your journey as best as you could remember it. You showed me your diary (perhaps forgetting that I have already seen it). You showed great love for your dog Paisley and a strange mixture of love and repulsion for your missing baby, Alexander. You took me through every trial and tribulation you have experienced and you highlighted the mysterious scratches and faded writing that has overlaid some pages which, I must confess, I find utterly enthralling. Tomorrow when your hangover clears we will work together to uncover its meaning. You relayed your love for your Lucy (something so deep that the words in this diary cannot convey) and you spoke of

Brekker and of your daring aboard the train and also in the LHC compound. Brave young man! But there is much we need to do.

I have learned in these last few days that someone or something is coming. Something malevolent approaches and the LHC is truly the gateway. I hope, sleeping drunkard, that we can together get to the bottom of it and with our combined efforts either stop, or exacerbate the event (whichever is decided to be the best course of action). I am overwhelmed that you called me out, and in such a fashion, that you have unlocked so much of this place more than I have done perhaps. You are ingenious, resourceful, focused. You are a good ally and, now, I can say you are a good friend.

Sleep well NeverTraverser

Your friend,

Nikola Tesla

31

Brekker, some things men say with meaning, some things are stone, some things said in jest, some things are obsidian and this is one such thing: when we meet, for meet we shall, and you offer me a drink, as you always do, I will flatly refuse. I am never drinking again! I counted eight cyclones on the horizon, but I would double that as a thrifty estimate to the number currently tearing around inside my head. Dear Scientist, what concoction did I drink last night?

Tesla, good friend, but fiendish drink-supplier and his lover are in the shower, I am on the bed looking over at Paisley, good dog. Still staring at that stain which, seemingly, has stopped growing.

Contrarily, the graphite stain on ceiling has started to fade. However, it isn't fading as a stain would normally. It is fading from the 'feet' upwards. It is either being erased or sinking into an invisible pit. So far, feet have sunken/erased up to shins. Will keep a note of its rate of disappearance.

Read over Tesla's note and, from flashes in my memory, his report is accurate. I did circle him, I did want answers…I did cry for what I had done to the lover (I still feel immense shame). When looking back, it feels like a cloud over my mind – as if I was not doing it, but watching myself do it. How could I have been so vile to a human? Brekker, I know you would have never done such a thing and I hope my reasons and my confessions go some way to helping you forgive me. Lucy, you may never forgive me, but know I was only doing this for you!

Shower has stopped. We are all three going to explore the town. Tesla may show me his lab, may show me how he got me there. Do not know. Won't ask, won't push. Still feel like he is master and I am apprentice, still feel like he has wealth of knowledge and answers for me. I will be patient and obedient.

He seems strangely taken with the scratched and faded markings that have appeared over the pages in between leaving the train and my arrival in Couldwell…I too am taken, but not as much as he. I can see it in his eyes. It is that unmistakable gleam of a genius who has just caught the scent of a theory. I wish I could catch that. I can recognise it, but I cannot catch it for myself. How heartbreaking and worthless is the art critic who cannot themselves paint. I lament them as I too share their ability to see the looking glass, but not see through it. As if the answers are on some shelf reachable only by those who can fly. I digress.

One thing I do want to show him is the periscope again. I will take him to the ridge, we will go into the compound and we will see…unsure of lover's reaction to this as she is a Sleepwalker and out in the day, how will she cope? Old Teller seems to be able to operate although I have not seen him out of the reception. Maybe they cannot leave their places of work?

———•◦•———

Evening – Bar

Broke promise already! Tesla is at the bar getting a third round of drinks in. Much discovery and therefore, on his insistence, there is much to celebrate! I swear Brekker, if one day you two should meet, I would like to see the bar bill for all you Great Creators have thirsts not even oceans can sate. It is like you have a dam built in that place in your gut that tells you "enough!"

Before we left, Tesla laid his lover down on the bed and told me that it was too late in the day for her to walk around, she will be too tired. Come nightfall she will drift to the compound or to his laboratory. And so, we set out on our own.

We have mapped the entire town. Tesla is quite the cartographer. We explored every street, chalk marking each corner and passage. We drew up a detailed report and map in his journal (I have made a rubbing of it and placed it at the back of this journal next to Lucy's portrait) Our industry was such that I never even noticed the blood from the morning nostril move to the mid-day nostrils, and over to the evening nostril. We worked, wrote, discussed and discovered.

Come the evening, when the cyclones were approaching the end of their first passage of the horizon, Tesla led the way to the ridge. I followed eager to see what more measurements we could take. We stood upon the rim and looked down at the LHC compound. Tesla said that the LHC had been there for as long as he could remember, but it had only started firing since he had that dream about me which was part of the reason he sought me out. I admitted to him that the LHC meant the same to me as everything in TheNeverRealm – that of curious discovery. I had never dreamt of such a contraption (and still do not know what it can do, why it is here, or who could have built such a thing). Tesla said my questions mattered not. He is right, I should question forward, not backward.

As we stood on that ridge I thought instantly to you Brekker. But you were not there. When I tried to locate your face in my memory I saw instead the silhouette of the man in the desert, waiting patiently. Something about that man. I thought on him until Tesla took me by the shoulder and turned me around to look back at Couldwell in the distance. We looked at it, and surveyed our map. It seemed to be a perfect depiction of the town.

And then, as if possessed, I raised my periscope to my eye. Instead of a rundown wooden ghost town, I saw great concrete buildings and tower blocks, complexes, homes, industrial parks, playgrounds and the familiar ferris wheel! Every building was now matched by a concrete and steel variation. As if someone had taken a photograph of the future and laid it over that of the past. I could not believe my eyes. I looked to Tesla and handed him the periscope, but he saw nothing. But I saw and I know now that the place where I am is the place where I once worked. In the Zone of Alienation, where I once lived is where I am now. I am not in two places at once...I am I the same place twice. Couldwell is Pripyat.

NIKOLA TESLA,
FIERCE DRINKER

32

Tesla's Entry

Master G_ you are in the latrine. We have drunk well tonight. A celebration worthy of our discoveries. I have read over your last entry (I feel now that I am permitted to add my additions to this, most wonderful and invaluable document of the time we are in).

We have worked well today, and it fills my heart with joy to have an equal, and I mean equal, in this. For years, perhaps millennia, I have been alone in my work here. Now I have you and we are making great progress. You were right to note before that I am intrigued by the scratching in this book. I am more than intrigued and you are right doubly that I have a theory, but I will not reveal it yet as I need to incubate further, forgive me, I hide nothing from you, this is why I am telling you that I do have a theory. I will, when it is ready, when it has brewed, tell you all.

For now, the thing that has superseded all else is your quite amazing discovery with your periscope. Though I could not see any difference through it that does not mean I do not believe you, quite the opposite in fact. I believe it is meant for you and you only. You came to have that periscope in your possession by your own tenacity. It is yours, so why should it work for anyone else?

What is interesting is not exactly what you saw, but the very nature of 'seeing'.

I will explain in the morning, we'll have a few more drinks now (I have written the above as a reminder to you to tell me to tell you, should I forget through inebriation's cruel aftershock!).

You return.

———•∙•———

Master G_'s Entry

Second hangover is always more bearable. Slept in the empty fountain in the square. We are a couple of children when we drink.

We are in Tesla's laboratory now. Have not the time to relay how I got here, seems inconsequential now given Tesla's state and our discovery. Time - what does that even mean anymore? What has it ever meant? I have been shaken to my core but with the resolve I have built up, and with Tesla's indomitable lust for creation, we might, might, just be able to ride this lightning. Brekker, let me explain.

This morning Tesla was already up and measuring the cyclones in the distance using an impossible to understand equation involving the velocity of falling sand coupled with infractions of sunlight against the panes of the nearby windows. I was baffled, but his conclusion struck me.

The cyclones are nearer to the town in all directions; they are converging. As soon as he said it, I remembered how fierce the multi-form cyclone that the LHC Test Firing had created, and how far away it was. If they fire again and the cyclones are closer, what then? What then?

I put that thought to the back of my head and glanced over the notations Tesla had written down while I was attending to personal business. I reminded him to tell me what was written. He was baffled, and so I showed him his entry above. He understood. He re-iterated that the periscope was not important as an article (even though to me, its operator, it is) but in its operation. It was seeing that was important, not what we were seeing. I was too hungover to grasp and sheepishly asked him to slow down. He obliged.

It seems clear to us that the periscope is a looking glass. Or at least, as I call it, a Babel-glass. He relayed what I had written down about seeing the workers when I was in the compound, about seeing the people in the train carriage, about seeing Pripyat instead of Couldwell. He explained that he had a theory that time was not a line, but a multi-dimensional tapestry that extends upwards, outwards, inwards as well as lengthways. It was a ball, not a line. Something like that. He said that reality and time are the same (and different) they operate on the same principle. He said that the periscope had the ability to see into parallel reality and not alternative, because 'alternative' suggests that our reality is the constant and all else is to be measured by it. He said that realities are folding in on one another and soon will collide, and the periscope was able to unpick the seams of two of them and meld them together. I was confused so he ripped an empty page out my journal and held it up to me.

He said, "Imagine if every possible eventuality was laid out on this piece of paper. Beginning at this end, ending at this end…this is how you perceive time – as flat and 'a' to 'b' because it is human condition to posit one's perception at the centre of the universe…but what if we do this?" and he scrunched up the paper into a little ball. "Now", he said, point to the perceived centre of your timeline…you see? Everything is one and all."

I understood and felt cold. Then he said, "Now imagine there were infinite sheets of paper, compiled together…and then imagine if God got bored and scrunched them into a ball. What then? What then?"

I was almost sick with the concept, never mind the hangover. Tesla was giddy. He was bouncing around like a child. "Imagine the possibilities!" He proclaimed. Where I saw an end to my journey, he saw the beginning of a new one. He said the LHC was God's Machine designed to scrunch all realities into one. It was God's vice!

When it sank in, I asked (without any hint of even wanting an answer) what we were going to do.

Tesla beamed, "what do you think we would see if we ran my Dream Projector from your eyes, and through your periscope? What do you think we would see?"

I felt sick and the thought of the needles in my eyes again but it passed quickly at the thought of what I might understand! The answers it might yield.

I, Master G_ with the help of Nikola Tesla might just be able to see through all of God's papers. I might be able to glimpse into the meaning of the LHC. I might even see the path to Lucy.

I stood up, shook Tesla's hand and felt bonded with him. I felt like a true adventurer.

33

Master G_ entry

Tesla's lover stripped me and prepared me for the machine. It seems that when I operated on her it was only by sheer fluke that I was able to garner results. The equipment here is bizarre and horrific at the same time. Forks, spikes, tubes and probes all with the menacing look that says only 'insertion'. How was it that I got results just by strapping in the lover and inserting the needles?

I am behind the screen, naked. Tesla's personality switched as soon as I agreed to the experiment. Not for better, nor for worse. He just became clinical. Focused. Our friendship is aside now and I am thankful in some ways. Professional. Laudable.

He graced me with a few moments to write this before we begin. He said that he would make a small entry and then rig the journal to the machine too, so to record what I will be seeing as he did before. It should write itself. I am scared.

When it is switched on, will I feel as I did before when he projected my dream? Will I be there? Or, as this is projecting into another reality, will I be an observer? Will I be able to react? Will I be able to do anything? The main fear is that I see something that I want, or need, but will be unable to act like in a nightmare where you are meant to go through a door, but you are not able to move.

The lover has given me a two minute warning. It is soon to be time. Brekker, here goes. Lucy I do this for you. I must come to you, I must find you. I must! Where are you now when I need you? I love you. More than anything I love you.

I go...

———•—•—•———

Tesla's Entry

Subject is in the chair, positioned on his back, head in vice, eyelids pinned open. My lover has attached the pulse-verifying tubes to the tracks on his torso. All vital signs are good.

Sleep inducing algorithm tonic has been administered. Tested his synaptic reflexes. Subject has taken and is falling into a drowsy sleep. Needles are to be inserted now.

Needles inserted. No struggle, no pain, no signs or recognition. Heart rate stable.

Projector enabled. Journal about to be connected after finishing this entry.

Proud, scared and hopeful for the outcome. Though I have a theory on what I am about to witness, I will remain open minded. Anything can happen now. The periscope was easy to attach. Have rigged a small brace around his face, pinned eyelids up, instead of back. This should act as directional 'barn door' to deflect the projection through the periscope.

Retreating now to comfortable viewing position.

I am soaring. High above Pripyat, high above the cyclone's hats. High above it all I am swooping and swirling, caught in a flux, caught in an ecstasy. For once, my collar does not appear stiff, does not irritate. My arms are outstretched, fingers spread and my hands are unblemished, smoothed, softened. Everything seems in soft focus but it is not irritating, it is altogether seductive. The town below is a patch surrounded by a wasteland. The cyclones, from above, all look like plates spinning atop poles. I am above it all but I decide to descend, as even in this somnambulist state, I am of reasoned mind and I direct my focus to the ground.

I am weaving through the heads of the cyclones, flying with their flow, around and around and the patch below that is Pripyat is growing. I tilt towards the ridge and I spot the top of Mother Motherland.

Gliding now towards her, gliding up to her face. Eye to eye now with the great stone statue. I can see her pain, fear and resolution. She is complete. What love I bare to thee Mother Motherland. I reach out to touch her cheek, she is cold. As I touch her, she begins to crack and sand begins to seep from her eye socket. I flinch and fly backwards, descending away from her face as a small stream of sand runs down her stone cheek. Down I am going now towards her base, towards the compound, towards everything, I am nearly 50ft from it when a dark cloud whips all around, enveloping me completely. I cannot see, I cannot feel, I cannot taste. I lose all sense of geography. I am temporally blind.

The cloud parts and I am inside the reactor. There is panic all around but no sound. On a gantry, by a bank of terminals, a man is frantically pulling levers. Women with clipboards are running around, men in suits sink to their knees and pray. I turn to the reactor to see the uranium rods. They are not dipping, but furiously rising and falling like great, mad pistons. I am looking back now at the gantry and I can see a man crawling on the floor, crawling towards a hatch. He is near the man at the bank of terminals. There is a flash of steam. The man at the terminal screams and instantly melts through the gratings, his gushing dousing a woman on the gantry below. The crawling man gets to his feet. I reach out when I see his face. He is me. I reach out to grab him, but the black fog comes once more.

I am in my hotel room, there is a version of me on the bed. He is struggling to write in his journal. He is grotesque. Half melted. I can see black powdery skin floating from him and whirling up to the ceiling where it collects in a large black stain. It is in his image.

I am now dragging him over concrete away from Pripyat, I look down at the sack of melted me and feel nothing, again the black fog comes.

I am in a desert…I know this desert. I recognise the remnants of past memories. Tokens, affections, signifiers of a time long past, I look around in the distance, I can see the silhouette of a man, he is sinking into the sand, I want to go to him, I try to, but something grabs my ankle.

I am turning now and as I am turning, I am changing location. I am in a laboratory, there is a woman on an operating table, and she has a veil over her head. I approach her. The smell of sulphur burns my nose and eyes, there is a bright purple discharge leaking out from under the veil. I lift the sheet to see a dying figure stretched out on a gurney. It is Lucy, twisted in agony, deformed beyond hope, tortured and tormented. I know who did this. It was me…and not just me…

It was Brekker too. I look down at the travesty that was my beautiful love and she opens her eyes and looks at me, she says in a voice that isn't hers, "He is coming, and he walks through walls."

And I wake up.

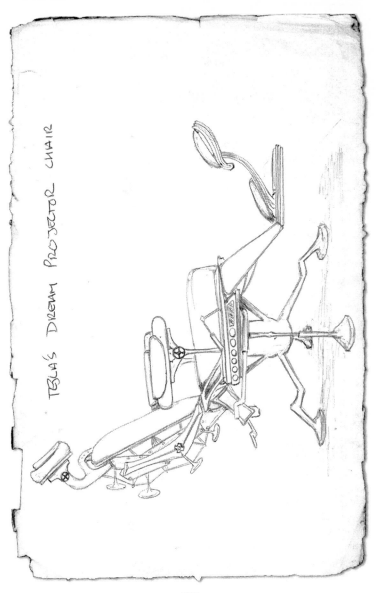

TESLA'S DREAM PROJECTOR CHAIR

34

Tesla's Entry

Silence. All is silent and empty. I am sitting on the floor of my laboratory. My lover is facing the corner of the room, hovering two feet above the ground. Brave Master G_ remains in the chair. He has been awake now for many hours, maybe days. Nobody has moved, nobody has spoken. Master G_ still has the needles in his eyes and his head in the vice.

Seems like we are all dead. Twice dead. Looking over at my lover, I find it hard to summon any feelings for her, Sleepwalker that she is, LHC operative. How can I look at her again and feel love?

Of what I have seen, I can conclude that:

1. Master G_ is most certainly in the same place twice and not only that, these two versions have crossed over at some point in four dimensional time. He is in a temporal flux.
2. It seems he will be in the bowels of an LHC disaster when it occurs sometime in the future, or past, or possible parallel present.
3. I was right and realities are indeed folding in on each other. There is a great pressure from the ground and

from the sky as the LHC pulls and presses everything together.

4. It seems Master G_'s beloved Lucy suffered greatly, a long time ago, (on the assumption that her timeline was linear and before this dimensional collapse occurred.)

5. It seems also that Master G_'s friend Brekker was instrumental in that suffering and that perhaps Master G_ was complicit in it too.

6. Master G_ seems to not know the truth about his past.

My lover is drifting out of the laboratory. This signifies that her shift at the LHC is about to start. There will be another test fire no doubt, and with it a further fold in realities. A further step closer to the abyss. She has gone. I go to see Master G_.

———•·•———

Despondent. Like a baby, vacant he was. I removed the rig, and carefully extracted the needles. He was in a state of shock. Cold. Clammy. Lips blue and puckered. I spoke to him, tried to revive him, slapped him, poured ionic tonic into his mouth. No change. Have adjusted the chair so that he can sit up. Have removed all tubes and pipes and dressed him. Have decided to leave him and go to the hotel room to collect his possessions and bring them back. He is dead weight, cannot move him or hope to carry him all the way back to the hotel. I have a theory that, if I bring his possessions here, maybe even Paisley too, lay them in front on him then a spark might ignite. Might be able to snap him back to this NeverReality.

I go.

———•◦•———

Tesla's entry (c'ont).

What a flight back to the laboratory! Have gathered Master G_'s possessions.

I arrived at the hotel in good time, the reception was empty. Old Teller gone. In reception hall where Master G_ had noticed framed animal skulls lining the walls, were now freshly slain beasts! Moose, antelope, all fresh and bleeding, their irises contracting and expanding as they still reacted to light. The past is catching up. There was a distant rumbling from beyond the ridge. The LHC was firing up. I made my way quickly up to Master G_'s room and, bursting in, I found Paisley cowering against the wall of the room on the opposite side to the stain. For the first time in days/weeks/months/years he had moved and the stain on the wall seemed more solid! It was an outline of a man! Full size with crooked top hat and cane. Standing there on the wall, like a shadow and with it there a presence. Something else was in the room. I could feel it. The hairs on my neck stood up on end. He truly is coming and he truly does walk through walls. I frantically gathered up the clothes and was about to leave when I noticed the other stain on the ceiling, the graphite stain. Now there were two people-shaped stains on the ceiling one erased up to the high chest, the other fully formed. Could it be? Could it be an echo of Master G_'s dreamscape? Could that be him? A shadow mirror into his realm? I reached up and touched the ceiling. Graphite like black residue scraped off.

The rumbling grew more intense and through the window I could see the merging of the four cyclones. I had no time to study the echo-stains on the ceiling. I picked up Paisley and the case of possessions and we fled. I did not have the courage to look back at the stain of the man on the wall, but I could feel the presence on my back. It was creeping under my skin.

Hurtled down the stairs and out into the chaos of the streets, the wind and debris whipping through the air. Paisley leapt from my arms and began to run alongside me (good dog knew he wasn't helping by staying in my arms). We fought hard against the winds and the screeching noise of the Test Fire. Reached the laboratory, opened hatch and fell in, forced it closed and all was calm.

Laid down all the possessions in front of the still comatose Master G_ and Paisley licked his cold hand, nuzzled him and curled up at his feet.

When will Master G_ recover? What is the meaning of the twin graphite stains? Are they really echoes? I have a theory. If I can get Master G_ back, I will explain and then we can get to work.

My lover is soon to return as the Test Fire is over and all is silent and calm again. All my energy is spent and I feel a great lethargy overcoming me. Everything is uncertain and, though I would love to plan for tomorrow, I simply do not know what state reality will find me in when/if I do awake.

Need to sleep too strong. Cannot overcome.

35

Master G_ Entry

I am restored. I have been in a dark tunnel, travelled through it and brought myself back from the brink. Through the periscope projector I saw too much. I saw the horrors of what has happened and what will happen. It was too much. It overtook me like the black fog and I was enveloped within my own psyche. I was awake and yet asleep and I was fully aware of lying on that chair for hours, maybe days, not bothering to remove the needles from eyes, not wanting to do anything. I was aware of Tesla writing the above note in my journal. I was aware of his lover facing the corner. I was aware of everything, and yet I was helpless to do anything. There was a great weight upon my chest, as if a slab of granite had been rested there and upon that some gargoyle sat, pinning me down. I went over the projection images in my head; the man in the desert, the melting man in the reactor core, dear Lucy's pain on her face, her tumours, the realisation that Brekker is the arch destroyer and torturer. I played it over and over in my head scanning for clues, questions and answers. Every minutia was taken apart, inspected and put back together. I cannot explain the clarity of internal focus I had but I can rationalise that it could explain my lack of physical presence. All power had been diverted internally. That is perhaps why I remained like a corpse. Tesla assumed it was shock. A rational diagnosis. But it was not shock. It was diversion of power. It was hibernation. It was work.

And now I am back.

Cannot let my unearthed feelings for Brekker come to the forefront. I cannot let the pain, guilt and anger cloud what was and what is yet to be done. If I am to escape Couldwell/Pripyat, if I am to get to Lucy then I need a calm, clinical approach now more than ever. Brekker is not here so no revenge can be exacted. Must remain detached. Am confident that Tesla, Paisley, the lover and my noting all I learn will help me to remain objective and focused on the cause.

———•◦•———

I have put Brekker to the back of my mind and I am focused on the more important plan: the desert and the silhouette of the sinking man. Can clearly recall the feeling of desire for him, to seek him out, to talk, to question. There is a divine sense of connection with him. Thinking back to a time when I felt it before. Cannot recall. Most of my memory outside of TheNeverRealm is part of the Great Desert. I need to get in there. Need to parlay with that man.

He clearly knows all. He knows the indescribable truth and, more importantly, describes the indescribable and utters the unutterable. I cannot continue toward Lucy without irrefutable evidence of how I came into this world. Of how it went down and what my true motive was. How Lucy came to be where I seek. If Brekker really is the Devil's Architect and engineer of all The Ends as I fear him to be, then I need the proof and the man in the desert can give it to me. Can double my resolve. I know it. Though reticent to call upon the teachings of Brekker now, I am willing to call upon advice he once gave me. He said one should never be sorry, one should be accurate. Get the facts, then make your tests or accusations and you will not fail. His words are prophetic as I do seek the truth. I seek it in the man in the desert.

———•••———

Tesla is fast asleep on the floor of his laboratory, snoring heavily, in a deep, deep thoughtful sleep. I will not wake him. I will make my preparations in the dark and in silence. It is better this way. I fear his questions, his ideas, his suggestions. I must act now. I must act fast. This is not the time for debate.

Paisley is curled up at my feet. Bullet resting in his eye socket – fur has begun to grow on the (previously) viscous film around his rib-cage wound. I realise now, looking at that good dog, how much I have missed him. Staring at that stain and growling at me had caused a great rift between us and I am now overwhelmed with love that he is back by my side. But also I am filled with a painful lament that where I am about to go, he cannot follow me. I may never see him again.

I may never see dear Tesla again either, that courageous and mad scientist! I do not need to document where/how I have got to where I am going. When he wakes up he will see and I trust in his abilities to concoct a way to extract me if he can…or leave me be if he can't.

———•·•———

Final preparations made. All instrumentation modifications are completed and have been checked thrice over. Clothes removed, pipes inserted and I have decided to attach the journal too. I am unsure if it will self-record this time, given the nature of the alterations I have made to the Dream Projector but I have hooked it up nevertheless. It might yet work. Everything else is ready.

I am in the chair, head in vice. It is not clamped in as there is no need to keep the needles in exact position this time given the alterations I have made to them. Not for the machine's new purpose.

I have attached the needles together, end to end, making one single, long needle and I have bent it into a horse-shoe. A croquet hoop. I will insert the half-hoop into my eyes and what is projected out of one eye will be projected into the other. I am going into my mind, into the desert of my memory to track down the man in the sand. Given the vastness of my psyche and the absoluteness of the terrain, I hold little hope of returning.

———•·•———

Needles inserted into eyes, journal attached. Tonic drunk. Falling asleep now. Journeying to the desert. Into myself.

Goodbye.

36

Collar itches. Standing on dune. Rail track to the side of me. Rails made of bone. Like spines. Waiting station a little way off. Maybe one kilometre, maybe more. Difficult to gauge true distance. Red sand dunes everywhere. Cannot see horizon. Thick fog blankets everything. Can only see desert carpet and the waiting station. Don't want to approach it. Too familiar. Been there before. Remember waiting inside it. Waiting for a train. I do not want a train this time. I am seeking the man in the sand.

Woman with baby walks past me. A memory returns. Angeline! Her face pulled out of the mire of my mind. I know she has a cataract, I know she doesn't love her baby. I know she will come to give that baby to me and she will throw herself off of the train and become a cyclone. Poor Angeline, I remember you! I watch her as she trudges toward the waiting station. I look down at the sand. I can see she has left a small dotted trail of blood, no doubt from her nose. I stand on the dune and assess the waiting station. I conclude that there is probably another version of me inside, waiting to embark on my journey. Or perhaps the same version of me. Perhaps I have looped and gone back to the start. Will not try to make contact, do not want to jeopardise my past-self's future. Will just watch Angeline disappear into the fog. Her fate is sealed.

What shatters my conception and rattles my soul most is that Angeline has the same face as Tesla's lover. How could I have not remembered that? Not realised? Is she the same person? I do not know. They just look the same, though Tesla's lover is more beautiful, with her soft skin and white teeth. My head throbs while trying to understand how, when and why...I have no option but to trust that it will be revealed.

I decide to walk away from the waiting station. There are no beacons or markers in the sand. No horizon, no visible cyclones to gauge anything. Cannot position myself. This new and abstract fog is all pervasive. I do not recognise it. It does not feel like mine. Feels like an intruder's aspect inside my mind. Lack of beacons means I have only one choice. I must pick a direction and follow. I judge the waiting station to be north, and so I turn and walk south.

———•••———

I have walked for 278 paces. Time is irrelevant now. Where my watch had frozen at ten-to-ten before, the hands now spin around in a counter-clockwise direction at varying speeds. Gives even less meaning to the concept of 'time.'

At 278 paces I stop and look back. The way station has disappeared from view...but not from memory. There is a distant howling noise, higher pitched than wind. A pained and screeching howl. Far off, far from here and in every direction. I miss Paisley.

I have no feeling now of my earthly body. I have no response to any stimulus from Tesla's laboratory. He could be running extensive tests on me. I could be on fire. I could be dead. I could be anything. I feel nothing from that version of TheNeverRealm. I am completely inside my desert mind and this realisation makes me run cold. Cold but focused. There is nothing I can do now but to continue into the void. Continue on to find the man in sand.

Further 10,234 paces now. Visibility has closed in, I could walk off a cliff's edge and not know about it until I was in freefall. Every step is a step into the unknown. I apportion a section of my mind to Tesla, the lover, Alexander Tumour Baby and of course Paisley. I wonder what they are doing? I wonder if they are concocting an extraction plan for me? I know that I cannot get myself out of here. I can only go forward. It is what has to be done. Dream Investigators must keep moving forward.

A further 1374 steps in. Foot strikes something. Small, metal – a little frame jutting out of the dune. I pull it up. It is a child's tricycle, white frame, discs covering the spokes on back wheels. I sit down on the fog-encircled dune and remember. It seems that, as I pulled the trike out of the sand, the connected memory was pulled out of the dune also.

———•◦•———

I am standing in the garden by my mother's pond. I can see myself over by the rockery. I am seven years old. I am fat, alone and melancholy. I look over to my sister. She is playing on the swing. Her white frock swaying and gleaming in the sun, the ivy embroidery catches the sun and dazzles me but it doesn't dazzle the seven-year-old me. I turn back to the rockery and begin upturning stones. I am a sad boy. I am the saddest boy in the world. I miss my mother. I try to walk over to comfort myself but I am stuck. I am in a bubble, observing myself. My sister can see that I am alone and sad. She leaves the swing and disappears into the shed. She comes back with the tricycle. It is her tricycle. She calls it Silver Shadow and she loves it. She calls to me. I turn from the rockery, look at the trike and turn back. My sister seems a little crestfallen. But she is strong. She wheels the trike over to and sits me on it. I try to remain sad, but her touch and her gesture make me smile. She wheels me around the garden. Inside my observation bubble my heart breaks. I love my sister.

I then remember a few weeks down the line. I am by the same rockery, sad once more. I am picking the paint off of the trike. I have no love for it anymore. My sister is by the pond. I know what is about to happen and out of shame I try to turn away. I cannot. Inside my bubble I watch as my seven-year-old self leaves the trike, walks over to my sister and pushes her into the pond.

———•◦•———

I drop the rusted bike back onto the dune and at once it sinks back to its original position. But the memory remains, although not perfect in clarity. I cannot taste the air, nor smell the sweet lavender scent of my mother's garden and everything around that recollection is slightly blurred and a little foggy, nevertheless, the memory remains as do the feelings it evokes –

those of heartbreak and shame. They burn brightly. I pressed on. At 439,907,097 paces I splinter my shin on a wooden frame jutting out of the sand. I pulled it out to inspect it. A memory returns.

———•◦•———

I am a young man of seventeen and I am standing naked by a door frame. I am picking at the paintwork and looking into a bedroom. The windows are open, there is a sea breeze blowing the curtains. On the bed lies Lucy, naked, strong, in command. In my bubble I am endowed with lust's great weapon; that of hindsight. I roll over in my mind all the carnal experiments I would perform on that glorious specimen. Together we traverse a galaxy of sins but the seventeen-year-old version of me instead timidly stands by the door frame, picking at the paint like a child about to be reproached. I smile as I know what is coming next. I see my seventeen-year-old self swallow, take a deep breath and walk towards the bed. Lucy, sweet, dear Lucy eases my tension and takes me in her mouth. Her knowledge, confidence and focus are light years ahead of mine. I cannot linger.

———•◦•———

I drop the frame back into the dune. The man in the sand is my mission, not this journey into nostalgia. I press on.

The fog has parted. My eyes are perceptive in this world and I can see that it has dissipated slightly. Up ahead, maybe

35,000 paces, I can see what looks like a mast, jutting up from the ground. I go to investigate.

———•◦•———

It is a mast of sorts. Metal. It juts up twenty feet into the air. At the peak I can see a five foot blade of metal hinged in its centre to the mast: a rotor. I clean the sand from the base. I have seen a gyrocopter before, but the design of this is slightly different. I do not recognise it. It is not of my world or my making. This is someone else's machine. Could I be in someone else's mind? I banish the thought and uncover more of the copter. There is a large glass bubble cockpit and inside I can see the controls and there, half buried lays a body.

I am clambering inside the cockpit, the fog has made the glass bubble damp but the sand remains dry and coarse. I am half in when I freeze. The screeching howl has stopped. It has been replaced by a slight, low rumbling. I have a volcano in my stomach at the very idea of what it could be. I climb into the bubble and inspect the body. It is my father, only not. My father had two legs, this pilot has just one, my father green eyes, this pilot's are brown…but the face is the same, the furrow in the brow, the bulbous nose and wooden teeth. I may have discovered the body of my father from a different reality. I am oddly clinical and detached when examining this body. No signs of any wounds, other than those sustained from the crash. His eyes are open. His cheeks are wet. Salty. Fresh tracks of tears. He died, alone and sad. I say a prayer for this dead father.

I move to make the sign of a cross when I knock a switch accidentally. The console comes to life. A red beacon begins to flash – a flashlight taped to the dash board. I remove it. I cross the corpse and climb back out of the cockpit.

Looking around, the fog is swirling now not in anger, just in turbulence and that rumbling noise is growing. Frequency increases, volume rising. That idea of its meaning is turning into slight conviction. I hold the beacon out in front of me and I march into the fog.

Two million paces from the way station. I freeze when I hear a voice. A voice calling my name. Its tone and timbre are more than familiar. It is my own voice! I assume it is twisted by the now virulent wind and its churning rumble. The voice calls out again. It calls out for me, calls out for the beacon. I begin to run now.

I am running and the voice is growing, as is the wind and the rumbling. The fog is turning into a vortex but the voice is getting louder, louder still, I call to say that I am coming. I call out for him to hold on.

I trip over him and fall to the floor. Rolling over I see a man, sunken up to neck in a dune, soon to go under. He looks at me and says, "I have waited so long for you…"

It is me, an exact copy of me. I am remembering my dream projected through the periscope and the image of myself dragging my other self. I am reminded of the image of myself melting. The vortex has come over us. I reach out and pull

Master G_ Version 2 out of the sand. We are facing each other. He says, "I have so much to tell you – so much!"

There is a crack of thunder and we look up to see a network of electrical beams crossing the sky in a dreadful web. It begins to descend. Master G_V2 looks scared, unsure of exactly what this is. He says, "I know this sound, but not this sight," I tell him that I know what is about to happen.

I tell him that I am trapped in this desert-oubliette and that somewhere, in another NeverRealm, a Large Hadron Collider is firing. I lie and tell him that we are going to be OK. The net falls down all around us, our ear drums shatter as the noise intensifies. We can feel our insides beginning to vibrate to liquid – natural frequency attained.

We look at each other, complicit in our knowledge, combined and united in all we know and all we feel. There is no fear behind our eyes. My collar no longer itches as it is now streaming with blood. I remember why. The collar has been an irritant as it has masked my scar. I remember that I came into this NeverRealm after slicing my throat from ear to collarbone. My life blood is falling away but I say nothing.

We step forward and embrace. I am about to whisper Lucy's name and MGV2 is about to whisper Brekker's when...

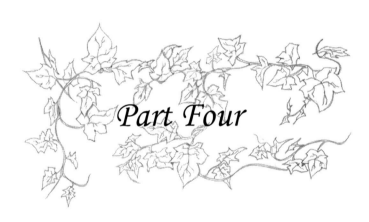

Part Four

37

Tesla's Final Entry

All is lost. Lying in a wilderness after fleeing my laboratory, fleeing Pripyat and fleeing Master G_. I am exhausted and broken, covered in soil, sand, blood and dust. Trudged a safe distance north of this Zone of Alienation. Possibly 30km safe. Behind me is a vaporous cloud of toxic gasses, burning hues of green and purple. It was more than just a Test Fire of the LHC. It seemed like a Primary Stage Fire.

You see, when I built my electrical light map, all those years ago, I could not turn it on in one go. I had power it up in stages - tripping switches in a complex sequence. I fear that yesterday's disaster was simply Stage One; a small wave forewarning of the maelstrom to come, perhaps.

The vapour will subside, I am sure of it, but I cannot bring myself to return to Pripyat just yet. What will there be left to return to anyway? What can my science prove now? What can I possibly contribute now, other than to finish this, the last entry in this journal? This is how the Time of Times came about. This is what happened after Master G_ bravely ventured into himself. Read now, whoever finds this journal, read now and understand.

———•◦•———

I was awoken by the whirring of the Dream Projector's start up charge. As I lay on my side, curled up on the floor, I knew instantly what was going on and what Master G_ was attempting. I jumped to my feet, but it was already far too late. Brave, foolish Master G_ had twisted the needles and jammed them into his own eyes. Why didn't he wait for me? Why didn't he ask my advice? I do not know. I will never know. He displayed impetuous arrogance. Youth! Foolish youth!

I could have thought of a safe way to project into his mind in order to seek the unseekable, instead what he did was to throw himself into a loop-flux; an ever-changing chain that eats itself and regenerates itself: an Ouroboros! When I saw the needle coming out of one eye and bending over and into the other I yelled at him and I tried to pull the horse-shoe needle from his eyes, but it was impossible. There was a force in retrograde acting upon it, as if being held from within his skull. I pulled with all my might. Useless.

And so, I turned my attention to the harness around his arm and tried to loosen the buckle. As soon as I attempted this, his free arm shot over his body and grabbed my wrist, as if possessed, or somehow automated! His touch was as cold as the frozen dead. He twisted my wrist and I screamed in pain. He squeezed harder and then effortlessly flung me across the lab. What strength.

I gave up trying to free him after that and instead began to study the journal as it recorded his journey. I scanned for clues, hoping to find inspiration within, in order to concoct a method to bring him out of there but there was nothing. I had no theory, I had no time. My mind was exploding and expanding in every direction at once. I could not form a single, rational chain of thought. I could not follow a single idea to conclusion. Every thought was a cosmos. My focus had scattered and it was then that I realised that my lover too had deserted me. I looked around to find her, but she had gone. Floated out of the laboratory and into Pripyat. The cold panic set in at that moment. I knew where she had gone, and I knew what was coming next.

It started with a very faint buzz in the air. I could barely register it, but Paisley was barking ferociously, scrabbling around on his side, scrabbling around in circles, trying to get away, his barks and yelps painful and tragic. I scooped him up in my arms and ran the kilometre tunnel to the exit hatch, unbolted it and threw the poor beast out. It was not an action born from hatred because I had an unshakable conviction that what was coming would destroy everything inside the laboratory and that Paisley was safer outside. He skidded and tumbled in the dirt as he landed. He got to his feet and tried to dart back inside but I closed the door just in time and I ran back to the heart of the laboratory where Master G_'s body lay.

By now the buzz had become an all-encompassing howl. The plaster-lined walls started to crack and my equipment began to spark and emit an ominous glow. The charge in the room intensified and then the instruments and tools on my work benches began to rise slowly into the air and hover, six inches above the work surface.

In the chair, Master G_ remained as calm as the dead. Even the hairs on his arms rose slowly and gently, swaying like reeds in the breeze. The plaster cracked further and chunks began breaking free and falling to the floor, the wire mesh beneath twisting and buckling. Horror took as I looked up to the ceiling. The plastered dome had already begun to splinter and crack, debris falling down and smashing into the instruments. Then larger chunks fell. I tried to dive for cover, but an apple-sized chunk struck my crown, blood gushed instantly. I fell down feeling giddy and dazed with my vision blurring in a pulsating fashion. More chunks fell and soon a hole appeared. Through my faltering vision I could see the great cyclone outside bearing right down upon us. It was so close! Like an anteater peering into a colony. Great brown swirls and green currents abounded, all twisting and howling. The electrical charges began spiking down from the monster outside and descending into the lab like charged tendrils. I looked over at Master G_ still calm and oblivious to the chaos. I laughed aloud. The LHC had fired at the worst possible moment, when Master G_ was under. In a world where time means nothing, it had chosen a very apt moment to strike. I laughed at the obvious predictability of chaos. My laugh grew manic as more chunks, electrified now, fell from the ceiling. My papers and documents ignited. A life's work, an eternity of questions, reduced to ash before my eyes. The laughter was twisted and delirious then, as quickly as the mania came, it passed and I regained composure. A moment of clarity hit me. This journal! It could not turn to ash! It could not ignite. I rallied and dove upon Master G_ - shielding his battered and bruised nakedness from the LHC's wrath. Debris smashed into my back as I tried to unhook the journal with one hand and, with the other arm, shielded Master G_'s face. With a scream and a final yank, I pulled the journal free and fell backwards onto the floor just as a fork of green serpentine-like electrical current descended through the hole in the ceiling. It moved in a controlled way, awfully, almost supernaturally slowly. It weaved down to the chair and lingered above Master G_'s head for a few seconds as if contemplating the corpse-like NeverAdventurer. Then it gently licked downwards, touching his lips in a curious, almost desirous way.

There was a sudden burst of purple light and with it came a tremendous blast wave that threw me back against the broken wall, leaving my eyes stinging and burning. The flash burnt itself out and in an instant the storm had ceased. The instruments, twisted and deformed, fell back onto the benches. The cyclone dissipated and the rumble and howling died down. I stood up and looked at the chair.

My eyes focused just in time to see the last recognisable shape of a human, Master G_, on the chair, blackened and stinking of sulphur.

I motioned to touch his body, but as I did, the pulped mass melted through the chair, leaving a black graphite-like powder stain over the chair. The horse-shoe needle, buckled and half-melted, rested on the seat.

Master G_ is now a puddle on the floor. Physically, he is no more. I cannot speak about what realm his mind occupies. Stage One Firing of the LHC is complete…Stage Two to come. I was clutching this journal when I left my laboratory for the last time.

38

Tesla Entry

Cannot leave the journal like that. I have overcome my despondency. Slept heavily for a long time, maybe days. Shirt cuffs are frayed and my jacket is threadbare possibly from the LHC Stage One firing, possibly from time spent in slumber far, far from Pripyat.

I did not dream. I wanted to. I wanted to go back to that dream I had many years ago, that glorious dream prophesising the arrival of one who would come and illuminate the sky. I wanted to see him again and talk to him even if in a dreamscape. I knew it was an impossibility, but even men of science dream of the impossible sometimes, even of the supernatural. Even men of science dream.

But I did not dream. For however long I spent on that dust covered concrete plain, all I saw was blackness. No sound, no weight, no depth, just calm nothing. Of all I have seen, I assume that the nothingness was as close to heaven as can be. Hell is stimulus, heaven is nothing.

———•·•———

When I awoke, Paisley was sitting on my chest, panting and looking down at me. He had followed me here, good dog. Had waited patiently outside the lab, amongst the chaos. He must have held firm in the heart of disaster. Good dog. He was sitting on my chest, head tilted and his bullet-eye glinting.

It was in that moment upon waking and seeing his face that I regained my resolve. Paisley remains chipper and so shall I. It isn't over! It was only a Stage One Firing after all. I ran through theories in my head and classified the stages as numbering between five and eleven. At the most, there will be ten more Stage Fires and then the Final Firing. What the Final Firing brings, I do not know but I must investigate it. For Master G_, for his Lucy, for my work, for my legacy, I must investigate it.

Stood up, took inventory of assets. Not many. My mind, Master G_'s dog, Master G_'s odd little Dimensional Periscope (no real use to me so far) the journal and that was it. Flicked through the book and a photo of Lucy fell to the floor. I can see why Master G_ loved her. I too feel love for her, but it is a love for her because of what she inspired in him, not what she generates in my heart. I would have very much enjoyed an evening in the company of my two friends. Put the photo back in the journal. It seems this journal is mine now. For my eyes only. I have nobody to pass this too. It is mine now only to document.

Noticed that corners of my vision have a slight purple discolouration. It's like wearing tinted spectacles that I can't take off. Edges of my peripheral vision are just slightly blurred. I can conclude that it was caused by the LHC (what else could it be?) Notice also a fine purple residue on my skin. Tastes metallic. It is a similar residue that coated the bones in Old

Teller's reception. Clearly, the residue came from the staging of the LHC and, as I have not been through such a severe event before, I must conclude that it has happened long ago (or a long time in the future) or in another reality. This residue is clear proof of the folding and melding of realities. All things are beginning to become one. This sparks my curiosity greatly.

I have cleaned off the residue down one half of my body. I will make note of any change in condition that the coated side has. I could never bring myself to perform this test on Paisley despite his adequacy for being a test subject. No, cannot test on him. He is an innocent. Test on myself instead. Put my clothes back on (which, to note, bore no residue. The purple coating appeared all over my skin and not just my face and other exposed areas. Conclusion? The residue came from within. But how? And why? Come on Tesla, question forwards, not backwards!)

Packed everything away now. Feeling confident. Heading through the Zone of Alienation and back into town. Will continue to update.

———•◦•———

Tesla Update.

Standing on a ridge. Taking a moment to collect thoughts.

Ahead I can see Pripyat and, past that the taller ridge, behind which stands the LHC Gateway. I can see the mighty, imposing figure of Mother Motherland calling me and despite the chaos of the test fires, and the Stage One Fire, Mother Motherland seems unaffected. The LHC Gateway always seems to withstand all. Construction not the same as anything have seen. Not the same as my laboratory which, I can see, just to the east, lays ruined.

The town itself seems different. It has somehow expanded in all directions. Not just in surface area – buildings are bigger, taller and seemingly newer too. Hard to be more concise as the distance blurs my vision somewhat. The purple tint around my eyes hinders me slightly, also.

Have noticed to the west, some distance off, a small wooden structure. Taking a detour to investigate.

Wooden object is a kiosk, similar to an old style toll booth. Bizarre location - middle of nowhere. Looked back through journal and found a mention of it. Master G_ recollected that he used to work here, in this kiosk. In life he used to guard the empty city of Pripyat. A past employment.

To note – found a similar mention later on in the journal. The etchings and scratching that cover a portion of the journal (which was a source of great interest and curiosity to both me and the departed Master G_) have become more legible. I can make out certain words here and there. 'Graphite', 'gurgling', 'kiosk' 'old woman'. Wonder if that is a reference to the old woman who came to Master G_ when he worked here? She said to him, "This is not your dream."

This new etching seems to reflect it. The folding in of realities includes the pages in this journal it seems. Perhaps Stage Two LHC Fire will fold even more? Maybe make more words legible. Maybe. Perhaps all will be revealed before the final Tenth Stage is released.

Walked around the kiosk and found two, altogether familiar, graphite stains. One inside the booth covering the seat of the chair and one on the outside, smeared against the back of the kiosk. The second one resembles a man sat against it. They are like shadows, imprinted or burnt. Both shadows bear the same shape, just in different poses.

The same person in the same place twice - Master G_.

39

Tesla's Entry.

Slept by the kiosk after surviving a cold night. There was a bitter frost on me when I woke. First I have seen since I can remember. Frost in a desert? Paid attention to the icicles that had formed upon the guttering around the kiosk. They shimmered in the sun. Very beautiful. Have decided to stay here in case the woman in dream (Master G_'s dream) returns.

———•·•———

Woman did not come back. I held out little hope for this to occur, but thought it prudent to exhaust the possibility anyway. Paisley shivered and moaned through the night, his leg twitching. He was having a fever dream. What do dogs dream of? Getting chased by automobiles? Dinosaur bones?

Have inspected the kiosk once more. Found only one new change. The graphite imprint of the man lying against the back has dissipated. Not entirely vanished as a shimmering outline remains. What is new however, are footprints leading from the kiosk and off towards the town. Graphite footprints. As if the shadow got up and walked away…pure fantasy of course, shadows can't walk.

What is not fantasy, however, is the possibility of recording and playback. A memory has returned.

———•·•———

Nitrate Experiment - recollection.

Notes on this were destroyed during Stage One Firing so must recall purely from my muddy and blurred memory. Like my purple vision, many memories upon my canvas have melded together. I will focus and try to pull the correct method from the amalgamations of memories.

Nitrate Experiment – carried out in early June, 1828, Dalmatia.

Reputable socialite reported to me of her haunted house. She came to me desperate. Priests did nothing but exorcisms and endless masses. Still she heard ghostly voices emanating from her parlour. I inspected the residence. The house was near the municipal railway and predominantly constructed of strong, varnished wooden beams. Woman held many parties. Riotous laughing, cheering and singing. During the quiet times, she reported of distant singing and voices in dead of night floating from the parlour.

Took extensive samples from the house. From the wooden beams and varnishes. From the plaster mix of the walls and even from the cosmetics she applied to her face daily. My methodology remains vague in my memory, however the outcome remains.

The nitrate solvent varnish use to coat the beams, coupled with electrified rail-lines created a static field. Whenever a train rumbled over, it made the film of nitrate coating the beams vibrate. The resonances of the voices and singing within the parlour when this happened were at a pitch high enough to be captured onto the film! Later, in times of quiet, whenever a train rolled passed the parlour would vibrate at a low frequency and nitrate film rumbled, releasing the captured sounds which amplified off walls. Put simply, the parlour was a giant voice recorder. She was hearing playback of parties. Woman changed varnish, solving the problem and she paid handsomely.

———•·•———

Now, perhaps instead of a shadow walking away, the footprints and silhouettes are echoes? Perhaps they are playback from events past and future (future on this plane, past on another) as realities are folding in and the LHC is discharging this residue, this stain. It is entirely possible that this world is a giant recorder and amplifier? Recording and echoing events, realities. Entirely possible.

———•·•———

Followed the steps, they soon fade away into nothing. Like wavelengths, they stretch and dissipate until nothing (at least nothing recordable by my meagre tools).

I have an idea.

———•◦•———

I was right! And a major breakthrough! Master G_'s periscope works for me! At least in a small way. I put it to my eyes and looked at the kiosk and saw a man resting against it. It was Master G! He was neither alive, nor dead but instead a representation of his form; a still image that was presented in multi-dimensions. I could walk around him, viewing him from all viewpoints and even put my hand through him.

I have heard of an innovator in Greenland who has pioneered work into the field of 'solid-still' projection. The pretence is that several similar, yet conflicting images are thrown at different parts of the eye simultaneously. Then, when they are compiled together and rendered fully, they combine into a solid form representation. He called the science 'holographonics.' This must be an example of it.

I looked inside the kiosk and, in place of the previous graphite stain, I saw a horrifically disfigured Master G_. He was in a frozen state of liquefaction. Similar to the fate the real Master G_ had suffered in my laboratory only this Master G_ seems to be in the middle stages of decay. Seems to be slowly melting. Whereas my Master G_ resembled a bucket of water being emptied, this poor variation seemed more like a candle melting away in sombre melancholy. His left hand has melted away to a skeleton, even his fingers are calcified nubbins. His whole face is drooping. Totally grotesque.

Feel both alleviated and sad to discover that across all dimensions, one's fate remains the same. Circumstances and details may alter, but it seems that, essentially, all deaths are the same.

I cannot take samples as the periscope does not seem to make things real, it only shows what is real. I have scanned the environment with the periscope to my eyes and nothing else seems to have changed. I holstered the contraption and looked with my naked eyes.

The sun was beating down so I put my hand up to blot the glare and I noticed the unmistakable outline of my skeleton through the layers of my skin on my hand only the light seems to penetrate deeper through the skin than before. I can make out little details. Nerve clusters, veins and musculature. I rolled my sleeve up and held that up too. Similar reaction, but a lot less pronounced due to thickness of my arm. This is the side of my body that is covered in the purple residue. I am probably disappearing. Well, one half of me anyway. If it gets too debilitating, I will focus on a remedy as it is my belief that there is no chemical known to man that cannot be countered. Until then, I will leave it be and note the progression.

Discoveries are coming fast it seems. I must speed up my pursuits. Although glad to have made detour to kiosk and made crucial breakthroughs, I do hope that there are not many more like that around here as I need to get into town and have a look around at ground level.

214

Must find my lover! What state will I find her in?

I hope to fi….

———•·•———

Second Stage LHC Firing just occurred! Though I am at safe distance from the Gateway, this Stage Firing was different to the first. There came no rumbling and no howl, no wind or electrical nets. Instead, from where I stood upon the ridge, I saw only a curious pulse. A bubble came up from the ground and formed over the town. It was a huge orb of shimmering light which refracted into an oil-stained pattern. Within the bubble, the town seemed to swell into an awaiting belch. I winced at the sight of the swelling town, waiting in trepidation for it to reach a critical point and detonate. Within the bubble, the town held at its zenith for a few seconds, seemed to contract slightly, and then the outer bubble burst! The pulse filtered out into the wasteland in a rumbling, iridescent wave. As it approached me, I raised the periscope to track the effects of the blast. There were none and the blast wave fell away harmlessly. A moment of bitter disappointment washed over of me and, to some extent, still lingers within. I do not know whether that was truly Second Stage Firing. I must assume so. I must assume that 'time' is running out (at least on my timeline).

I go now with haste back into Pripyat.

40

The town is horrific! It is a nightmare vision I am aghast at the monstrosity that has been forced upon me. Pripyat has been irrevocably disfigured. It is not partially melted like Master G_ in the kiosk and not levelled like my laboratory, but it is in the most painful stage of transmogrification possible. The reality of Couldwell, as Master G_ saw it, has morphed with the reality of Pripyat. Then is there, when is now, there is here.

Every building that was once wooden is now fused to some twisted steel and concrete structure. But neither is fully integrated. Neither one is complicit in their amalgamation. It is as if each structure is being forced together against its will and so is still pulling away. It is as if the buildings themselves are reeling in horror at what is being forced upon them. When tectonic plates collide, land masses crash together forming vast mountain ranges and it seems therefore that when two realities fold in on one another, the constructed landscape does the same.

I should have guessed this when I discovered the dual fates of Master G_. If it seems that death in all realities is the same, save for inconsequential details, it follows that the same be true for buildings and monuments (have not seen glorious Mother Motherland yet and I feel ill at thought of the grotesque that will await me there).

However, the transition of one town's reality into the other is not yet complete. Each iteration of building in this universe has one foot still in its other. The fold is not sealed. I am standing in the middle of open-city surgery and it feels as if I am the only whole object around. Must investigate.

Luckily, I have the detailed map of the town Master G_ and I chartered a while back. Will make similar studies to find what is new and what is not. After Pripyat, I will go to the ridge and view the LHC. I will brave the sight of the new Mother Motherland.

I have not yet contemplated what might have happened to the population of this place, given what state the architecture is in.

———•◦•———

Street markings seem to be congruous with before. While some corner-markers were difficult to locate, some were easily found which made it easy enough to gauge the overall geography of this mutant town. I have made map on the reverse side of our old map. This way, when I hold it up to the light, I can see a detailed map of all three states – Pripyat, Couldwell and the mutant town in between.

Found a newspaper on the floor. The headline read, 'Exxon Valdez, pride of Engineer Brekker's fleet sets sail!' doesn't mean much to me but I made a rubbing of the front page in the journal. Ink came straight off and left the original page blank. I used the blank paper to make copy of new map.

To note – I have started to bleed out of my left ear. Nothing alarming, just a trickle. Paisley noticed it first. I had bent down to mark the west corner of the fountain by Torpor Avenue when the good dog barked and licked my ear. I laughed until I saw the blood on his tongue. I will keep track of this leak.

The purple residue is still causing half of my body to disappear, although now it seems at a somewhat slower rate. Though I do not need to hold hand to sun to notice nerve clusters and I can make them out under normal light, the rate of degradation is in no way congruous with the rate of disappearance of but a few hours ago. Curious. I have also not lost any feelings, dexterity or tactile feedback from the disappearing half of my body. It could well be a purely aesthetical dysfunction of either my body or my eyes.

I am writing this now leaning against the fountain, Paisley by my side. I'm hungry. Imagine Paisley is too. Haven't seen him eat. Ever. Or drink. No water here. No rain. He doesn't complain. Energy of fifty. Good dog.

I'm looking at him as he inspects his shadow. He is tilting his head curiously to one side and then tilting it the other side in surprise when he sees his shadow copy him. Back and forth he tilts his head. Like a metronome. Sweet mutt.

Took another look at the picture of Lucy. She is beautiful. Looked around the town for signs of life. None. Scared for what my lover will look like, if she is even alive.

Wonder now about the mysterious Alexander Tumour Baby. Though I have never seen him, I have heard Master G_ talk about him and the curious mixture of love and revulsion at the constantly soggy baby. Wherever he is, I am pretty sure he is not here. Possibly crawled away at the right time perhaps.

The fountain makes me sad. This is where I met you, dear friend Master G_. You were fierce with the needles. I imagine you to have had the same look about you when you recklessly threw yourself into your desert mind. Determination for the truth, at all costs. I miss you.

I am alone and sad.

———•◦•———

I was flicking back through the journal as I rested against the fountain. Scanning over entries, clues and discoveries. Noticed an oddity. Where before I could make out specific etchings, scrawled over Master G_'s writing, I can now read them as clear as day, and they occupy their own space! They are no longer faintly scribbled over Master G_'s original notations. All subsequent entries have shifted down to accommodate them. It seems that as the realities collide and merge, this journal is shifting too. Making space, making order. What kind of journal am I in charge of? Clearly it is more than a book, that much has always been obvious…but now this? Can it self-edit? If it can move text, copy entries from alternate realities and paste it all into one single form chronology then what can else can it do? Can I trust what I read over? I rely on it for information from Master G_s travels, for answers from his discoveries and also to remind myself of what I have learned (as my memory is slowly blurring and turning into a muddy canvas like a chalkboard never once cleaned after a million physics lessons).

Can this journal self-edit? How is it moving entries? I have studied it through the periscope and there is no change. It is impervious. How is it doing this?

I cannot contemplate the alternative, but I must.

If this journal is turning into some sort of NeverDiary, and it is not doing it of its own accord, then who is doing this?

This entry will no doubt delete itself.

41

Tesla Entry.

Previous entry did not delete. Not yet anyway.

On ridge now. Mutant town behind me. LHC gateway compound below. The Ouroboros-like Hadron ring that circles the crater floor has changed. It is no longer made of gleaming steel. It seems to have dulled somewhat, perhaps aged slightly. It does not reflect light and therefore, it must be said, does not capture the imagination anymore. It just looks like a functional necessity now.

But Mother Motherland, miracle of miracles, remains untouched! She is still powerful, still inspiring and her sword remains held aloft with the red beacon flashing atop its point. Dear God, how I am in love with Mother Motherland now, seeing her here like this, stern and brave. To be certain, I viewed her through the periscope – no change either! Truly she is an anchor for all realities and how that fills my heart!

I am about to descend the ridge and inspect the LHC pipeline's one thousand kilometre circumference. I will inspect a portion and then tomorrow inspect another and soon gather an aggregate idea of its entirety. I may even try and find a hatch that lets me inside. No idea when Stage Three Firing will occur, that's a chance I will have to take.

Paisley is under instructions to remain here on the ridge. He will obey because he is a good dog. As soon as I commanded it, he sat down and became as still as a statue, only his eyeball moved, alertly scanning the horizon. Good guard dog indeed. I descend.

Difficult descent. The terrain has become like a mountain range tilted upon its axis. It dips and spikes in an angry fashion. It is extremely hard not to fall, or twist an ankle. The jagged rocks have melted and fused together, pulled by the LHC's powers. They are treacherous rocks. I scraped my hands, back and face on my way down. Ascension will be near impossible.

New discovery: gravity within the crater has altered slightly. Upon descending, I dislodged a rock and it slowly fell, bending towards the LHC pipeline as if it were magnetized by it. The rock landed two-foot from the base (which in fact is a hundred-foot from the wall). Therefore, there seems to be a ninety-eight foot gravitational drift. To test, I dislodged another rock and dropped it.

I counted the time of descent. I estimated myself to be two-hundred foot from the crater's floor. The rock should have taken approximately five seconds to hit the ground. It took eight. Terminal velocity has stretched.

———•·•———

Climbed down and inspected a full two kilometre section of the LHC pipeline. From ground level, the pipe appears even more monstrous. It is far taller and far wider than I imagined. I can see that the steel is, indeed, distressed. It is covered with grease marks, oil stains and its structural integrity has been compromised. Its outer layer is buckled, notched and stricken. The LHC Firings have clearly taken their toll. I wonder how much more can this pipeline take? What if, during a Stage Firing, it accidentally breaches? What then?

I closely inspected the outer-casing and found a thin purple residue coating it. Of course, it was the same residue that I have on the left side of my body although the skin of the pipeline seems to be impervious to this residue's talent for erasure. I used my sleeve to wipe away a portion of the grime coating the pipeline. I saw insignias and symbols photo-etched into the pipe - tiny murals like a great tapestry all over it. Engravings of ferris wheels on fire, of gyro-copters and dirigibles falling from the sky. Men with the faces of pigs dancing on clouds of fire. The intricate delicacy of the work was staggering. I cannot comprehend the time it must have taken to coat the entire LHC pipeline in this vast, sprawling pictogram. Who did it? From the section I uncovered, I did not find either end or beginning of the engraving which suggests that it does, indeed, cover the entire thousand kilometre circumference of the pipe. The scale of the work makes me nauseous. And of course, it is battered, scarred and mistreated. This art work has gone unnoticed. This labour uncared for. It makes me nauseous for the scale, and sad for the artist.

———•·•———

Now standing on top of the LHC pipeline. I managed to scramble up the ridge-face, high enough to see the top of the pipe. I pocketed the journal and leapt from the ridge wall onto the top of the pipe. It was a great distance to leap, considering the size and curvature of the pipe. The apex standing a good hundred-foot from the ridge wall, thus making the radius of the pipe one-hundred foot and its diameter two-hundred foot. It was an impossible leap but I remembered the gravitational shift I had witnessed in my falling rock experiment and trusted in my maths. I was sure the gravitational dilation would carry me safely over the distance and onto the top of the pipe. I was not wrong. I sailed over the distance easily and landed like a ballerina.

The roof of the pipe has a flat, grated walkway presumably used for servicing. I can see a hatch ahead.

———•◦•———

Inside LHC Pipeline. From the hatchway I found a ladder attached to the interior wall. It was difficult to descend that inverted parabolic ladder and the periscope nearly fell of its latch. Managed to climb down, though.

On the ground there is a walkway wide enough to drive vehicles down which, I assume, is necessary for maintenance. I cannot see any carts or carriages and no workers either. Abandoned. The middle of the pipe houses the Collider Tube which is an inner pipeline in which particles are hurled at catastrophic speeds until they slam into each other. This is how realities are brought together. Not by folding, but by smashing. The Collider Tube is transparent and inside I can see floating globules of liquid. Wonderful globes of green, violet and purple. There is no gravity within and the balls gently collide, merge and break apart. The Collider Tube's shell is cool to the touch, but nevertheless charged. I feel connected to it when I place my hand upon its sleek glass casing.

———•◦•———

Curious to note - when I placed my right hand on Collider tube, nothing happened however, when I placed left hand (the hand coated in residue) upon it, the globules of liquid inside the Collider Tube were pulled towards me. They were instantly attracted to the residue on my disappearing arm. They fell flat against the inside of the tube and merged together to form a perfect sculpture of my hand. I was mesmerised. Before long, from farther down the Collider Tube floated more globules of colour, all attracted by my touch. They merged into each other and I saw a perfect copy of myself form within the tube. It started at my hand and then my arm grew back and, as more globules arrived, my shoulders and torso formed. Globules from the floor rose up to form my legs and they joined my torso. Lastly, my head rose up. It looked at me – myriad of colours changing through the spectrum as it seemed to decipher who or what I was. I smiled at it and it smiled back. The colours then all assumed the same identity, that of a blood red hue. A burgundy head stared at me and smiled. I tilted my head, he tilted back. I was reminded of dear Paisley and his confusion and curiosity at his own shadow. I reached out and touched with my other hand. As soon as my 'clean' hand touched the Collider Tube, the liquid copy of me broke off our 'connection' and 'he' stepped back into the centre of his world. Slowly, he fell away breaking apart into his original component globules. They floated away, back to the turbulent chaos of zero gravity.

I am speechless. I cannot move. I am overwhelmed with beauty. Even as I write this I can sense the onset of rumbling. Stage Three Firing is about to commence and I am in the heart of the beast! I cannot move and I care not to. I am too awed and excited. Stage Firing intensifying.

This will be a ride!

42

I am weightless and I am drifting through the infinite. I am the stars, I am the cosmos, I am light, I am the way. I am millennia. I am thought. I am all things. I am all particles. I am all time. I am observation at all points.

I am writing in a journal, I am seeing, I am calculation, I am a singularity, I am returning from the void, I am accelerating, I am gravity, I am falling through space, I am leaving the stars, I am leaving the cosmos, I am leaving light. I am something. I am at one linear time. I am focused. I am carbon. I am at my own point of observation. I am Tesla again. I am dreaming. I am feeling warm, I am feeling pushed and pulled.

I am waking up.

Systems check.

Musculature – active.

Nervous system – responsive.

Heart – beating.

Lungs – breathing.

Open eyes.

Eyes open.

Focus eyes.

Eyes focused.

Purple tint clouding vision. Peripheral vision feathered 14%

Sit up.

Tesla Entry.

Against all odds, against all hope, I am back! I survived the
Third Stage Firing and from within the Collider itself no less. I
am sitting still against the wall of the pipeline, staring at the
Collider Tube. Everything remains the same. I feel as if I have
merely slept.

Diary entries have shifted again. I can make out passages
written my Master G_ Version 2. I shall now divine them as
MGV1 and MGV2.

The skin on the left hand side of my body is transparent
down through the musculature and I can see the network of
veins and nerves. I can even see the blood vessels floating
around inside my veins.

They collide and repel, pushed and pulled around the tubes giving me life. I can see them all. Zero gravity inside my veins.

The Third Stage Firing occurred and I was indeed sent into space. I was at one with everything and nothing. Stage Three, from inside the LHC, seemed to fold reality outwards. Perhaps like opening a book and sending the trapped dust particles into the air, then slamming the book shut again. I was outward, and inwards. Like breathing in, taking air into lungs and then expelling it.

I'm lucky to have survived that! MGV1 was not so lucky and, as proved by the periscope that shows different realities, he was not so lucky twice. Cannot put myself in the position to test my luck a second time. Getting out of the LHC pipeline and heading for the hotel complex. Back to the room.

———•••———

Brow of ridge.

Clearly the reality of Pripyat took another assertive step into the reality of Couldwell. Less wood, more concrete. I cannot help but think of my lover. Will I see her? Will I find her awake? Going confidently to the hotel.

———•••———

The town is filled with signs of life but bereft of any physical evidence, save for shadows. There are strange shadows moving around, silhouetted against the ground and the walls. I hid behind a barrel on Torpor Avenue and looked out at the silent, empty town. The footprints in the ground, the tyre tracks and the wheel ruts from carriages all appeared before me. And so, I tracked a pair of footprints in the dust-covered concrete floor as they walked passed me. I saw along a concrete wall, the shadows of people coming and going, dragging trunks and boxes, pulling carts and all laughing jovially. I was like a moving projected image. A zoetrope.

I put the periscope to my eyes. No change save one. With the periscope to my eyes, there came the sounds of the city. I could just about hear the sounds of life - of laughter, of horns, of street callers and children playing. All the sounds of town life.

Either I am newly dead, brought into a confused existence by which my mind refuses to see the living, or it is the other way round. I can conclude that, as Pripyat has been brought from one existence into this one, so too have its inhabitants. I am not dead. I am not a ghost. I am real. I think I am witnessing souls walking through a doorway. It seems that folding reality brings everything else with it. Are they aware of it? Are they conscious of the intrusion? Have they been folded from one moment into the next and continuing onwards as if nothing had happened, or have they been folded into a specific timescape and doomed to repeat actions and gestures that they have done before?

How do I explain better?

Equation... X+time/Y=time continuous where / represents Fold?

Did the townsfolk in reality X experience time as A, B, C /[FOLD INTO REALITY Y] D, E, F, and G....completely unaware of any such interference in their position in time and space, oblivious to being ripped from one place to another?

Or:

Does the timeline of the Townsfolk run as in this equation?

Reality X + Time < A, B, C> /[FOLD INTO Y] = A2, B2, C2,

The second solution seems to run with supporting evidence of the holograms of Master G_, and the footprints leading from the kiosk. This might also help explain the loss of memory. As we shift from X into Y and begin to run time as A2, B2, C2 so our memories unwind, re-order, and rebuild to create a singular line. Therefore, as we reorder our psyches, we witness echoes and shadows from other variations of ourselves.

Highly possible.

For now though, it is clear that the townsfolk are indeed in this NeverRealm but also in their previous time/space/reality.

I can assume that the next Stage Firing will bring them either fully into this world, or one step closer. If I survive the next stage, will I see full bodies walking around (and will I be able to interact with them?) or will I see skeletons? Or nervous systems wandering around? How far into this world will they step? And of the Sleepwalkers? What of them?

My theory goes that the construction of the LHC brought with it the ghosts or their souls. Like pioneers, they came first, and now, everything is ready to bring their physical forms through. Possible, though I cannot be sure. It would be foolish to conclude that the realities folding inwards consist of merely two…how many facets of the psyche are there? How many cells in the body? Each one is its own entity.

The numbers are great indeed. I go now to the hotel.

43

Outside the hotel now. Journey back was chaotic . Made great care to hug walls, dart down alleyways etc. Was almost impossible. I was shunted and pushed by all the 'ghosts' of Pripyat. They clearly have some physical presence here. After the first few knocks, I decided to experiment. I traced some footsteps and, from the gait and the size of the footprint, I judged them to be of a grown man (and one not carrying anything). I spent an hour looking for a suitable subject as I did not want to experiment on a child, or a woman, or someone elderly. I found a suitable mark coming out of a cold, grey official building. I almost lost the trail, as I was fascinated by the handprint the ghost made on the glass pane of the revolving door. I made note of the direction the steps were going then quickly darted into the door-well to study the hand-print. It was as expected. The clammy sweat evaporating quickly, but it wasn't just the physical implications of this ghost's touch that interested me but the faint purple tinge it carried with it. Before I could take a sample, the print evaporated. I stepped out of the carousel door and caught up with the footprints.

I followed them for a few paces and then, when in the time was right, I shoved. I felt contact, I felt resistance and I felt my muscles having to push against thin air and then the footsteps stopped and were replaced by the clear markings of a body falling onto the floor.

Most interesting.

My next experiment utilized the same method, but this time with the periscope to my eye and as I pushed, I could hear the gasp of shock from my test subject, the thud as they landed, and the cry of pain as they had obviously twisted something. I stood and listened for it was the response I was eager to hear. I was hoping for either, "Who did that?" or, "Why did you do that?" What I got instead was, "Stop pushing me, you're always pushing me, if you don't, you're a dead man!"

I was shocked! I could not bring myself to answer, or apologise or to move on and try out my experiment out again. A mixture of embarrassment, fear and shame rose up. Once more in this realm I am presented with more questions than answers! I fled Torpor Avenue and now, here I am, outside the hotel. The exterior is both grand and imposing, more so than any other building in Pripyat. It seems as if the hotel has fully arrived here. I cannot make out any vestiges of the old, wooden shack that was once stood here.

I go in…

———•◦•———

The hotel is the same but changed. Or perhaps it is the same, and I have changed around it? That's absurd. Cod metaphysical musings. MGV1 would raise an eyebrow, but wrote it as it came to me. The thought skipped over my reason, like a word skipped by a hiccup. I am standing in the corridor outside the room that MGV1 (and MGV2) stayed in. Have not entered yet. Collate this first.

The lobby matched the grandeur of its exterior - plush carpet, drapes and mahogany decked reception. Periscope revealed the sounds of footsteps – high heels, bus-boys, hand luggage on wheels. A functioning hotel.

Noticed that there are no longer skulls of dead animals lining the walls. Instead there hang portraits. Stern, strong faces. Kings, Tsars, Princes, Queens, Engineers, Physicists etc. Recognised some. All looming down upon me, casting their judgement. None of them have my intellect, nor have they ventured where I have ventured and sought what I have sought. Felt revulsion for these 'leaders'.

Walked over to the reception. Could see the key to my room hanging on the wall. Dilemma presented itself. Should I brazenly take the key? What if I disturbed the harmony of the reality in which this hotel was full of bodies? What if, while going about their daily business, they suddenly saw a floating key. What then? What then?

The chair behind the desk wheeled itself backwards and sprung up an inch, as if someone had stood up, then the saloon style hatch-door raised and lowered. Someone had left the reception. I took my chance, leant over the desk, seized the key and fled.

Before leaving the reception, caught glance at newspaper folded on the counter. Headline read, "Crown Engineer unveils designs for revolutionary oil fields," beneath it, etching showed giant oil-drills. The pumps resembled like huge femurs. Giant legs thrusting into the ground. Bizarre.

———•◦•———

Left to find my room. I write this now, in the corridor, facing the door.

I am going in now. After I have looked around, I will take stock of this journal/possible NeverDiary as more entries have moved to make room for suspected MGV2 entries. Paisley, as ever, is here, although…Paisley is not here. Suddenly struck by his presence and how I had not factored it into my calculations. I did not notice him getting jostled about while in town.

Just looked at him through the periscope. He is indeed not here . Through the scope, although everything else remained the same, Paisley did not. Whatever realities have melded together, this dog is not a part of either. Poor mutt. Will hold him with me for as long as possible. Every Stage Firing that brings forth realities and seals them together could, and theoretically should, push Paisley further and further out.

The room is same but different. Bed is now an iron frame, thin mattress. Walls are plastered, unpainted and poorly sealed. The stain on the wall is vivid and foreboding. A clear outline of a figure filled in with dark, black light.

Ceiling is dark grey. Can see outline of stain. No longer of two people side by side. Now resembles two people embracing. It is a lighter shade than the rest of the ceiling. It is a negative space. It carries with it an overwhelming sense of understanding and melancholia.

I feel a presence. I focus. No, I feel not one single presence, but the presence of two. I am writing this now with the diary at my side. The same method MGV1 adopted while I was approaching him in the alleyway for the first time. It is by my side. I am not looking at these words, but focusing on the room instead.

I can feel a presence in the room.

And I can feel a presence in the corridor.

My sense of existence of splitting into pieces.

44

Tesla Entry.

I, Nikola Tesla, am not afraid of the chaos. The sky is green and glowing. There is a blanket of black smoke spreading out from behind the ridge. I am standing by the fountain and people are fleeing in all directions. Absolute panic. A great catastrophe has come about. Brave firefighters, soldiers, scientists, even fathers are running towards the ridge. Running towards the LHC and the scene of the disaster. I can hear people screaming and crying, but worse, I can feel their panic. I see a child of six or seven trip over and fall to the floor by the base of the fountain. I can see a crowd of panicked folk charging towards him. I reach down to help him up but he does not see me. He wails and cries on the floor. I reach out to grab his collar but my hand goes through him. I go to jump down onto the floor, but instead I float. I am a ghost. A Sleepwalker. All I can do is observe. I scream out to the crowd to stop panicking, but nothing happens. They trample the boy. Heavy boots, sharp heels and walking sticks pulverise him. Nobody stops to help him up. I can see his skull reduce to pulp. I can see his organs burst out of his tiny ribcage.

I can see looters, I can see the panicked men, gathering their families. I can see people on fire. There is a line of men carrying stretchers from the site of the LHC, the stretchers are leaving a trail of liquid. They are ferrying melted workers from within the reactor.

I am floating now, without control, following the trail of melted flesh. People pass through me as they flee. People cry, people burn and people laugh hysterically. I am floating down Torpor Avenue and I can see a line of twenty women standing still along the boardwalk. Their skin purple and their faces drooping like candles aflame. On the other side of the avenue I see a firing squad comprised of lovers, brothers, husbands and sons. They too are drooping and ailing. They raise their weapons. As I float down the avenue, I see them fire and the bullets glide through me and onwards to their targets. The women are no more. I leave Torpor Avenue just as the firing squad turns their weapons upon themselves.

The black cloud belches rain. Large globules of black graphite sludge come crashing down. When the droplets hit, they leave a thick residue that runs like tar down the faces of the doomed.

As I float, I pass a great window and see my reflection. I am here but not. Just a representation in shimmering green. I am a hologram, projecting into this event. It exists and I do not. I conclude as I approach the ridge that I am a witness to an event that has already taken place. This is not an amalgamation of melded realities but a pocket of history. Of one time. Of one place. I am this disaster's point of observation.

As soon as I make this conclusion I leap forward into the LHC control room. Inside, there is no real panic. There is only the laboured, drawn out moans of the dying. Inside is worse than in the town. The mania is more pained, more real. People do not move as fast, or as wildly because they cannot, they are dragging themselves mostly. Arms, legs, torsos fused to the walls and floor, to tables and chairs.

I see another hologram approach me. This is MGV1 and he has my Evelyn over his shoulder. He cannot see me. We are two interlopers, each in their own realities, observing the same true event in another reality. We occupy the same space and time, though only I seem to be aware of the existence. I know that MGV1 will soon meet me in my reality. He will soon catch up with me. He will soon experiment on Evelyn and soon we will drink and become great friends and, of course, soon he will send himself into his mind and seal his fate forever and his reality will merge with mine and overtake it. He falls down, dropping my Evelyn, she cuts her head open and breaks her radius. I can see the fracture but I do not feel anger. I know he will look after her. I drift on past him, through corridors of melting workers and frantic terminal workers, through the reactor core and up towards a gantry that leads to an observation room. I can see on the door of the room there has been painted a familiar sign - that of two eyeballs joined by an ivy-twined optic nerve.

I float through the reactor core and to the control room where I see a man lying on a desk. He has a crooked top hat lying on his chest and his legs are crossed. There is a vacant look in his eyes and he seems oblivious to all around him. Catatonic shock.

He says, "Nikola Tesla, in whatever reality you are watching this in, you will soon be with me. This is only the beginning. This will happen again and again until I am right. I will see you on the other side." And he closes his eyes, and melts away to a black graphite stain on the desk.

Bright light. Wake.

———•—•———

Stage Four Firing complete. I am back in the corridor, looking through the doorway to my room. I hardly noticed the beginning of the Stage Firing, so terrified and transfixed was I. A shudder and then a pulse of energy swept through me and the corridor. The pulse seemed to begin from within me, from inside my stomach and it spread outwards. Then a green hue began to invade my vision, the purple tint falling back and the green hue intensifying until it was all-encompassing. Then a flash of brilliant light, and then back. Back to the corridor. I cannot tell how long I was in that vision of the disaster, it seems to be only the briefest of moments on this side.

I am frozen.

I am numb.

As soon as my eyes adjusted to the light, Paisley yelped and fled. I called after him. No answer. Could not turn to chase.

Could not move. I am staring into the room and I am utterly terrified. Within the room, there is no longer a stain on the wall. That growing stain that Paisley has been staring at has gone! All that remains are footsteps starting from the wall, walking up it, across the ceiling, and out of the doorway. The steps are black stains, like graphite powder.

But they are wet. Dripping wet.

Whoever they belong to, they can play with gravity. Whoever they are, they have come and they have walked through a wall to get here.

I can feel a presence in the corridor.

45

Angeline Entry.

Nikola, my lover you sleep so soundly. You snore so loudly! You are exhausted and drunk. I have given you drink and I have given you food. I have given you speech, sight, sound, and I have given you my body.

When I saw you standing in the doorway to our secret room, looking up at the ceiling my heart became all things at all times. You had a look of horror on your face and you seemed to be looking up at nothing. As soon as I saw you, my heart was yours once again. A distant, awful dream I have been in of late. Since you left, I have done nothing. I have not eaten nor slept. I cannot say I have even walked. I feel as though I have drifted through my days.

You have come back to me! You were there, writing in your journal without looking, mouth open, eyes wide in horror. I called your name. I could not be calm, I shouted out "Darling Nikola, my love, my heart, you have come back." You said nothing. You did not acknowledge me at all. Then I thought that perhaps I was dreaming, perhaps I had finally fallen to darkness. I walked over and touched you on the shoulder. You snapped awake and turned to…well half turned! I was stunned by a magical trick of the light that manipulated my amorous eyes, for you appeared to be half here and half not! As if half way in a room. The left hand side of your body seemed to have disappeared. I rubbed my eyes, you had returned. And your eyes saw mine and you said, in a voice I had not heard before, you said, "You're awake."

And yes, my dear Nikola, your wonderful and alive Angeline is awake. We embraced and as we kissed, I felt as if I was once a closed book that had once more been opened.

We fell into our secret room (despite your protestations. Oh, how you do like to play) and we made love over and over again. It was calamitous in the most amazing way. And after you collapsed down breathing hard, muttering under your breath (and who exactly is MGV1? Sounds like another of your scripture headings or perhaps it is code for another woman?) You mumbled and murmured and, as lovers do, I left to find you food and drink.

When I returned, I found you kneeling by the wall in the corner measuring an empty space on the wall. You have been strange before, but this was so strange that I laughed loudly and your eyes looked wild. I had to have you again. I fed you and poured drink down your throat and, as ever, you tried to get back to your work. After all this time apart, you tried to deny your Angeline her wants and rights! Foolish scientist! And so now you sleep, comatose and my world is back to normal. It no longer feels like I am caught in a typhoon or a thunderstorm. I no longer feel like I'm stuck on some ghastly train to nowhere. I feel reborn. When you wake up, I will wash and dress you and then, of course, we will go straight to the power plant.

———•◦•———

Tesla Entry.

Woman is in the shower. I am frayed around the edges. Angeline she calls herself. Angeline was never her name. I knew her as Evelyn. Though she is the same in looks, and in tastes, she is not my lover in spirit. This version is a beast, vibrant and volcanic. My Evelyn is serene and graceful. When she said her name (Angeline) it struck a chord. As soon as she went to the shower, I grabbed the journal and read back. Master G_'s accomplice on the train, the nanny of Alexander Tumour Baby. She is Angeline the Cyclone. Her ramblings above echo the events surrounding the Other Angeline's fate. Her feelings of being trapped on a train, of being in a storm are all concurrent. But this answer throws up one, terrible question. Whose dream is this? Where has the Evelyn of my reality gone?

Though I thought this NeverRealm belonged to many, it is clear that the LHC Firing are folding in all realities concerned with Master G_.

Evelyn has now become Angeline, and Other Angeline has now become Evelyn with a melded mind. The fate of the Other now just a feeling in the heart of the New Angeline.

I will keep this journal close to myself now and go with this New Angeline. I will go along, and see where it takes me. Paisley will accompany me, though I cannot tell if she can even see him. I have not looked at her through the periscope yet, but the thought occurs that she would not appear.

The residue on my left hand side has faded now. My fullness has returned. Rubbed off during Angeline's attacks? Or maybe I have stepped into a new reality. Stepped into Pripyat of old. The room has become more concrete than wood. The footsteps over the ceiling remain. They fill me with utter dread.

To note also – the pages of this NeverDiary have re-ordered even further. I can read now a sad passage over the fate of Master G_ in his earthly-bound days. The experiments on dear Lucy, Brekker's insanity and malice, Lucy's pain…and Master G_'s suicide. Every moment that passes and with every new entry that reveals itself, I feel more convinced that, like MGV2, I am inside Master G_'s dream.

Will my fate be like that of MGV2? Now that MGV1 is locked inside his desert mind, how does this world continue? Characters in a dream do not live on after their puppeteer has woken up.

The sky is still pulsing supernaturally green.

Angeline returns.

46

Tesla Entry.

Night. Moonlight intense. All pervading, like a sheen over the clear sky. No clouds, no cyclones on the horizon ergo no time. The stars innumerable, the planets, galaxies, nebulas are all visible, all clear as crystal (to note – purple tinted vision receding – edge feather now at around 3%).

I do not recognise any of the constellations. Spent a good deal of time lying on my back on the little fountain wall looking up at them all. Found a few moments of solace. Mind fell to rest. No questions, no answers, just a sense of calm, silence and peace. Sensation almost alien to me. Before I had time to really enjoy those moments, my mind started questioning. I started trying to understand these almost forgotten feelings. Mind started up again. For a moment, the briefest of moments, I was at peace. Like a body seconds from an expected death. It was glorious.

Sitting up now.

Town is asleep like before and, as ever, I am the only soul moving around. Always seems to be some sort of quantum state in which I find myself as 'other' compared to my environment. As I told Master G_, where they go hungry, I bloat, where they laugh, I cry, when they sleep, I walk.

Angeline is sleeping. After an exhausting day; she has finally taken to her bed, though I am sure that she did it out of convention, rather than necessity. She seemed not tired, but as a child commanded to go to bed. She was talking, as she incessantly does, then an expression crossed her face. No…not an expression. It was the lack of expression that crossed her face. It was wiped from her in an instant like a blackboard full of a day's equations and notations being cleaned away in one great motion. She stood in front of me, blank and distant then she said in a voice without inflection, "I am tired. I sleep now," and she lay on the bed, stiff as the dead, fully clothed. She crossed her arms, corpse like, and fell 'asleep' instantly. I was shocked at her sudden change of state. I lay stiff too, pretending to sleep. I counted to a thousand in my head before moving as I needed to make sure she was asleep. I waved my hand in front of her eyes. There was no reaction. I listened to her heartbeat – slow, low frequency; second stage sleep and progressing further.

I crept out of the room and left the hotel.

(To note – reception dead, neither a soul nor sound)

I am by the fountain. Since the Stage Four Firing, not only have the population turned from ghosts to full flesh, it seems they have bought with them the remaining buildings from Pripyat of then to here.

I can see a complex of tower blocks to the east of the central business district. They are high-rise, cheap living, and practical. Impressive scale and functionality. A pleasant mix of design. I can see green areas for the children to play in. I can see roads and verges. Planning has gone in to provide a good level of comfort to the wives and homeowners. And yet the functionality of the vast concrete blocks bears clear reminder that they are machines for living. Best estimate, there is accommodation for around 60,000 families. Monstrous workforce. Sheer scale and concentration of people brought he for a single (awful) purpose is quite chilling. I can see behind the east tower something even more chilling – a wheel. A giant wheel.

I scanned back through Master G_'s notes. Yes, it is here! The symbol he discovered in his train carriage was of a great ferris wheel, and under it fire and children running and screaming. A great eye in the middle and I too saw a similar affectation of that huge wheel on the side of the outer casing to the giant LHC pipeline that runs against the crater floor. Great wheel, fire, panic. Of course, I have borne witness to this panic first hand through my holographic state earlier.

Do not need further proof that a catastrophe has befallen this time before and maybe countless times before that. I have not checked further the extent of the engravings but it is a near certainty that the burning wheel will repeat itself and more than likely in different iterations denoting the variance of its temporal occurrence.

West of the residential tower block reveals more of the town. It is expanding out, further out than before. I postulate that one could walk from here all the way to the ridge without leaving the city limits. Before, Couldwell stopped a good quarter-cyclone's trudge from the ridge.

Have noticed also that the concrete appears to be newer. There is less weed growth breaking through and less cracking and discolouration. Layer of sand is negligible. Would be impossible to track the townsfolk by footprints alone now.

There is a clock tower too (ten-to-ten), a town hall and various official looking buildings just north of Torpor Avenue which is no longer a wooden clad boardwalk, but a grand avenue wide enough to drive carriages eight-abreast down. At the fountain end there is a great archway. At the arches zenith, a great cast-iron head. Perhaps twenty foot from chin to brow. Wide eyed, stiff moustache, greased hair. Stern. Powerful. Focused. Do not recognise the face.

Packing diary away now. I feel I am ready to return to the scene of the tragedy. I think it is a necessity that I return now to my laboratory and survey the damage, sift through the rubble and see what I can find. There may be clues. Of course, it may not be there at all. I half expect some great tower block or municipal structure to have folded onto it. Or perhaps the laboratory itself has folded and transmogrified into something else? Could be conclusive proof that I, Nikola Tesla, were here at some other point in time and have been folded here (to follow that theory, I could very well find another version of me running around this place as MGV1 himself did).

I go now to find my laboratory in the name of science.

I also go now to the grave of Master G_ in the name of friendship.

KEY

ZONES

    A. HOSPITAL COMPLEX
    B. MUNICIPAL PARK WITH FERRIS WHEEL
    C. UPPER CLASS RESIDENCES WITH PRIVATE, GATED PARK
    D. OFFICES
    E. TOWN HALL AND OFFICES
    F. CENTRAL BUSINESS DISTRICT
    G. WORKFORCE HALLS OF RESIDENCE
    H. OFFICES

POINTS OF INTEREST

    X1. HOTEL
    X2. TOWN SQUARE AT FOOT OF TORPOR AVENUE
    X3. FOUNTAIN. WHERE I MET TESLA
    X4. BAR
    X5. DARK ALLEY WHERE TESLA 'KIDNAPPED' ME

↑ TO THE LHC GATEWAY

↓ TO THE TRAIN STATION

↖ TO TESLA'S LABORATORY

- - - - - - COULDWELL BOUNDARY

:::::::::::: CONCENTRATION OF COULDWELL BUILDINGS

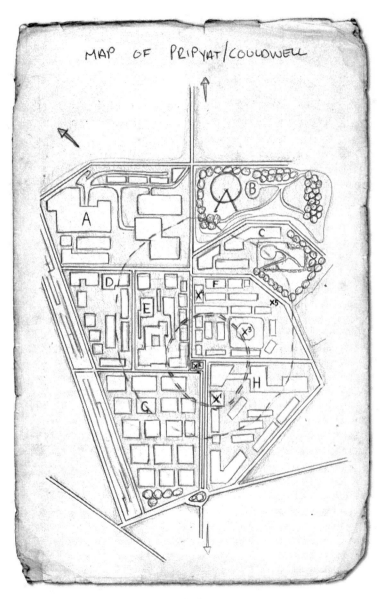

MAP OF PRIPYAT/COULOWELL

47

Hiding high. Can feel presence. Have felt it since hotel. Something/someone/persons unknown watching/studying me. Led them a merry dance.

Could not let them see where I was going or let them on to my mission. Could not let them follow me to my laboratory. Led them around the houses, so to speak. Luckily my morph-map of Pripyat and Couldwell is firmly ingrained in my head (and, should that fail, in my pocket) so I was able to wind and weave through the town.

Proved also useful to take note of any changes/similarities now that Couldwell is seemingly no more. Noticed that the alleyway in which Evelyn (before she was Old Angeline) lured Master G_ for our first fateful encounter has changed. Instead of the narrow near endless alleyway there is a simple street, wide and well lit and lined with townhouses (more up market than the towers blocks of the workers. Clearly I had weaved through the area of residence for the management).

After possibly two hours of walking in circles and doubling back, I found a small concrete compound used for housing metal oil drums. I hid there and looked out. Nothing. Could see, hear and feel nothing. Did not want to give up my position so I waited longer still. After another two hours, crouched by the barrels that gave off a smell that almost tasted metallic, I decided to creep out.

Had not gone far before that uneasy feeling returned. While I had one phonological neural loop processing my upcoming endeavour my other neural loop (my subconscious) started firing faster, sending messages through to my conscious. Primal messages. Messages alerting me to imminent, unseen danger. Something was coming for me. That dread soon became conviction and I ran.

I bolted through the deserted streets, focused to not run randomly and so no doubt ending at a dead end, or trapping myself. I ran purposefully and near silently until I came to a building with an exterior drainpipe. Caught my breath. Waited. The dread was there, but my sub-conscious assured me that, while present, the danger was not clear. I scaled up the building and found a decent vantage point with almost a three-sixty degree field of vision. I scribble this now from that high point.

So far nothing. The view is decent. Can see over most of the town (though not the tower blocks) can see the ridge and the tip of Mother Motherland's great sword, the red beacon blinking in the clear light. Under the celestial blanket, the tip of her sword itself could be a star.

Looked harder at Mother Motherland and I can see something in her outstretched hand. Something in the palm of it. Cannot make it out (Periscope offers no clarification). Something large (to be seen from this distance, and by my eyes, I imagine it to be 25ft high in itself). The object shimmers slightly. It is so faint that I have to stare and focus to be sure that there is actually something in her hand. Looks like an Orb. Curious.

Dread has returned. Looking down now. Can see something. Moonlight is throwing a long shadow from down a narrow street two blocks to the north. Whatever is throwing the shadow is approaching my building and soon it will come into square.

———•◦•———

It was Paisley! Good dog! What a mutt! Tesla Crown Prince of Cowards slunk behind the wall of his high-hide and looked out with dread at the growing shadow looming and ghastly. Into the light it was growing and lurching...and out from the narrow alley stalked Paisley leading with his nose to the ground and his tail in the air, haunches up. Sweetest creature. He caught my scent and froze, as if an enemy whose eyesight was based on movement had spotted him. Frozen for a few seconds. He sniffed the air.

I could not resist. I thought not about waking the townsfolk and I shouted "Paisley, Paisley! I'm here, I'm up here!" I waved both arms for joy. I could have whispered and my voice would have carried, such was the stillness of the air but I shouted and it was like a crack of thunder through the plains. Paisley's ears shot up and he looked at me. Tail wagging furiously, he fell to his side and began scrabbling around in circle as if trying to catch his tail whilst lying on his side.

I scrambled down the pipe and ran to him. He jumped on me and began licking my face. We rolled around on the hard concrete and laughed. I playfully pushed him and hit him, he bit and nuzzled back.

Instantly a section of my memory returned, as if a portion of my blurred canvas had been pulled into focus. I remembered a time when my older brother still loved me.

———•·•———

I am nine and playing with my toy zeppelins and he is reading a picture book on soldiering. He looks at me over the brim of his comic. I do not register his glance physically, but I do sub-consciously. I am warm. He yells "bundle!" and leaps on me, punching me and ruffling my hair up. I am struggling and trying to resist, all the while laughing madly. He gives me a dead leg, I laugh off the pain. He straddles me, pinning my shoulders down with his knees. He rips open the top two buttons of my school shirt and holds up his two index fingers.

"Nikola Tesla!" he cries "today's lesson is how to be a typewriter!" I smile-scream to stop, but it is too late. He thunders his index fingers into my breast-plate repeatedly shouting out the letters of his name as he does so "S.T.I.V.Y.A. SPACE [DOUBLE HIT] SPACE T.E.S.L.A SPACE SPACE W.O.Z. SPACE E.R.E EXCLAMATION MARK [OPEN PALM TO THE FOREHEAD]"

I am in agony, breastplate burning red. I contemplate correcting him on his spelling but decide against it. My brother laughs. I laugh. He ruffs my hair and climbs off.

———•◦•———

The memory of my brother and the time when he still loved me hits me like my own LHC Stage Firing in my heart. Paisley keeps me grounded. The calmness and serenity I felt under the celestial opera, and the reunion with Paisley and what he gives me has answered a question that I have not yet asked. A question I, perhaps, should have asked from the beginning; who am I?

I am Nikola Tesla, and I am human.

I have posited myself in the Multiverse and, by doing so, in this instance, I have ordered everything. It is chained to me, from me, behind and in front. I have a timeline. And that means I matter. That means I am alive. I am ready to go to the grave of Master G_.

Ready to see my friend again.

48

Sitting on what used to be roof of laboratory. Dome caved in. I can sit on its edge and look down into laboratory. It looks like an archaeological dig. Paisley is sitting by my side peering down into the ruins.

I was surprised and a little relieved to find that the laboratory has remained unaffected by the Stage Firings (save for the destruction). It has not folded in or out of this reality. Indeed to note, the reality of Pripyat has not overtaken the reality of my laboratory. Lab now sits in a clearing surrounding by high-rise buildings of low quality most presumably designed for the lower grade workers. The concrete paving leading up to the lab ends abruptly. I have noticed that a few compounds that encroach the edges of my building show signs of distress and disrepair at their bleeding edges. It seems as if they cannot fold into the space my laboratory occupies, but they want to, or they are trying to. Coupled with the lack of Stage Firing incurred degradation I am lead to believe that the laboratory exists in the Couldwell reality, not the Pripyat one. Or at least, it exists in its own reality altogether and the space it occupies does not affect Coulwell's landscape, but it does Pripyat's. It seems like my building has a force that can withstand the LHC. Of course, structurally it is decimated, but it still remains and it has not morphed into some sort of twisted hybrid. It has strength to resist the pressure induced by the multi-worlds collapse. Interesting. It is an anchor - a place that spears through many realities and, as such, is unchangeable. Similar to Mother Motherland who seems to remain the one constant in all worlds.

Going into the lab to inspect the damage and investigate.

Sitting in the Dream Projector chair. Have investigated. Strange findings. Melancholic discoveries. The laboratory remains effectively untouched since I fled those days ago. Since the LHC broke through and vaporised brave Master G_. My journals and maps are now ashes and dust spread over everything. A lifetime (maybe many lifetimes) of ideas, dreams, confessions and discoveries are reduced to a fine membrane, a gentle dusting that covers everything I have known.

My instruments and apparatus are ruined beyond repair. They lie where they fell, twisted and half melted by the power of the LHC. They are hideous. Like a demon's instruments of torture. Curiously, they are all heavier. Picked up some forceps, some scalpels and some thumb-braces and they are much heavier than muscle memory recalls. It seems that the melting has re-ordered their composition at a molecular level. There is alchemy here. Titanium alloy has now become some sort of obsidian (at least comparable in density, the colour however is more like dulled mercury).

The chair I am sitting on has changed also. It is now a foul construction melded into the floor as if it has grown from it. This new Obsidian2 does not yield clean lines, as steel does. Its natural state is undulating and there are wire-like reliefs that run over the arm rests like a network of veins. There are no rivets or bolts anymore. The Obsidian2 here has replaced them with small balls and sockets with a porous impression on the surface. Like bone. It is a ghastly aberration.

Paisley does not like the chair. Does not like the laboratory. His fur visibly rose as he entered. Part fear, part electro-magnetic echo charge. He stayed by the door. The most curious and ominous discovery here lies at the final resting place of Master G_. Instead of a pool of melted flesh there now lie two small pits of sand. Real sand unaffected by the OBs2. Unaffected by anything. Almost as if someone has come in, and shovelled two piles of sand on the floor and left.

Tasted sand. No hint of iodine. This sand does not appear to be from anywhere around here. Old fashioned sand. Fine, red and pure. I pushed my finger into the pile, attempting to take a sample – hand almost disappeared! I did not feel the touch of the laboratory floor as expected and my hand went past the knuckle, passed the wrist and half way up my arm. I felt a force pulling in retrograde upon it. I yanked my hand clear and staggered back. The surface of the sandpit did not move and did not fall into the cavern I had created, did not sink away. It remained calm as the Dead Sea.

I paced around, and then decided to makes these notations though the chair repulsed me, I felt drawn to it. To sit where my friend had sat in his final moments. I thought maybe it might reveal something. It did not.

To note – I could not find any evidence of the Dream Projector Needle that master G_ had fashioned into the fateful horseshoe. Gone.

I can feel a presence.

Not Paisley this time – another presence.

Paisley is not here. I just looked round, hoping to see my loyal friend at the doorway. Gone. Where is he? The presence is strong now. While one phonological loop is writing this, my other phonological loop is screaming at me. It is saying; "There is someone here, there is someone here. You are in danger. Get out.

Ge…

———•◦•———

Tesla Entry.

Taken prisoner. Journal taken from me. If I get the journal back, I will paste in this notation. Head throbbing. Cannot see anything. Pitch black. The walls of my prison are cold and smooth and there is a curvature to them. Twenty paces from wall to wall. Room circular. I am inside a globe. A globe with no windows. No light. Writing this on the map, though I cannot see what I write. Hope is legible.

Struck over head with rock. Assailant came out of the dark like a ghost. Couldn't see face. Like a nightmare. Phonological loops synched up and screamed to me to leave and I turned to see the ghoul and it struck me with a rock. Darkness took me. And then I awoke.

Inventory.

Periscope – taken.
Journal – taken.
Paisley – not with me.
Map – here.
Pencil – here.
Shoes – wearing.
Suit – wearing.

Events of the day unfolded thusly, as I have not yet noted the moments between Angeline showering in the morning and my notations of Pripyat at night.

How it was:

New Angeline returned from shower and took me into town. I had to keep calm and cool. The town was now thriving with life. No more Sleepwalkers, no more ghosts. Convoys of supply trucks, Model-T's, horse and carriages bustled about. The population exceeded the 278 that MGV1 thought used to dwell here. The population was in the thousands.

As New Angeline pulled me through the town, talking incessantly and loudly, she waved at the citizens who waved back and tipped their hats to me. As all this went on, I felt cold and ill because I knew, and I still know, that these people are the same people I saw during my Stage Four Firing recall. The same population I witnessed being destroyed. We walked giddily down Torpor Avenue and I saw wives, sisters and girlfriends all walking arm in arm with husbands, brothers and boyfriends.

I saw a young boy, maybe seven, playing by the fountain. He was trying to catch a little ball on a string attached to a cup. I recognized his face. He was the boy who was trampled under the panic. I reached out to him, he thought I was waving and he waved back. I almost cried.

There are all dead, and yet alive! They have all died horribly in another time and now they are here again, to go through it once more and they are unaware! They have been recalled into existence. They have been folded into reality and time is melding together. I have a thought: what if, during the Stage Four Firing, I did not witness the past destruction of Pripyat but a future destruction? Before, I concluded that I was in one reality, and everything was catching up to me.

I think now that maybe I am the one catching up to the reality. The wound on my head throbs. I have difficulty ordering thoughts.

These things are clear.

1. The LHC is folding reality – bringing in past, future and alternate events and melding them into one.
2. I am aware of all around me.
3. It is of no use trying to figure out how bad the storm is when you are in its eye; it is only of use to survive it.
4. The LHC, when it reaches its Final Stage Firing will clearly be cataclysmic. I have witnessed as a hologram one version that has/could happen. MGV1 and 2 have also.
5. I must try and prevent it.
6. If I cannot prevent it, I must survive it.
7. I must save as many as I can.

I would assume that I am close. The man in the crooked top hat, lying on that desk in the middle of that meltdown knew I was there and so must know that I am here. He must know that I can prevent it. That man is the architect of all of this. Obviously, he is Brekker but what has he to do with me? Apart from my intellect, why Nikola Tesla?

In life, I had never met Master G_, Lucy or Brekker. I remember only this place, my laboratory, my failed work, my distress and my Evelyn. I remember living next to the LHC that never fired and just lay dormant. I remember Mother Motherland abandoned, sad, and lonely.

And then that dream concerning the one who would illuminate the sky - Master G_, that most unassuming of men. Where I held genius in my hands, he had nothing but questions and a goal. I sought him out for my own answers and I became drawn into his world and onto his path. My questions were answered in him. I am not here for any other reason than to exist in his realm. I was folded into his reality the moment I had that dream.

And then the Stage Firings started and Mother Motherland became glorious, noble and powerful once more. Everything was pulled apart and reformed and we bounced and hurtled through dreamscapes, realities, time and space aware but out of control. We were fearless and reckless and, in all truth, we have been truly alive in TheNeverRealm.

But now that he has gone, the possibility of the end of all things still remains. His dream is over and all the actors in that great play are left behind in the theatre.

The end of all things is coming so now it is me who is aware of it all and who must prevent catastrophe. I must escape this oubliette and prevent the apocalypse. If only for saving that boy by the fountain.

Tesla Entry.

I am in the air! Suspended in a glass globe! After writing the above entry, I sat upon the cold floor to gather my thoughts.

Thoughts of escape, thoughts of rescuing the town and of ascending. Then, as I felt a great lethargy begin to rise inside of me, the walls of my black prison began to grow less opaque. My vision began to penetrate slowly though the walls and the murky shapes behind them soon formed a horizon. I could see the ridge of the LHC in the distance. I could see the compound below me. I was looking out to the west. Soon in the distance, the Tsar cyclones became visible, moving along their horizon like clockwork.

My black globe-prison became a glass bubble. I looked out and around and as I turned to look behind me, I saw her and I knew exactly where I was.

I am standing in the palm of Mother Motherland's outstretched left hand. When I was hiding from Paisley, atop of the building, I glimpsed an odd shape in her hand - a shimmering trick of the light. It was this glass ball I was looking at. And now I am inside it.

Mother Motherland's fierce, glorious face is gigantic. It looms over me, calling beyond me, calling to the Tsars on the horizon. The beacon on the tip of her sword flashes brightly and the sky so clear and the celestial blanket so vibrant that I can almost reach out and touch it.

How I got here, I do not know. How I will leave? I cannot begin to calculate. Although, the most probable theory is that this glass ball is intrinsic to the next Stage Firing. I have survived all of them so far (even from within the LHC itself) and so I can survive this. I have to, for Paisley, for that boy by the fountain. For Master G_ and Lucy, for the Evelyn I loved, her soul stolen from me, and the imposter Angeline poured into the shell of her body.

I must survive. Running out of space on the map to note these things down. Glory of Mother Motherland overwhelms me.

I can see people on the ridge. The townsfolk have all come out. They are standing on the crater's rim, covering its entire circumference. What will happen? I cannot tell if they are looking at me, or looking out at something else.

Above me, the celestial blanket is merging. A wash of green, azure and purple merge. The most beautiful light-shower is unfolding about me.

It is the Aurora Borealis! I know this. I can almost taste it. The magnesium in the atmosphere is thinning. There is a solar wind coming. The colours are waves, the symphony! The opera of light! I am lying on my back in my perfect observatory and my hairs are standing on end. I feel a charge. I feel electricity flowing through me as this orchestra of light builds its crescendo all around me.

I am one in light, one in stillness, one in peace.

Three in one, one in three.

Part Five

49

To my darling Tesla,

Find here what happened to you in the majesty and tragedy of your most memorable hour.

I stood upon the crater's rim looking up at the glass ball in Mother Motherland's outstretched hand and I was in awe of the spectacle. The Aurora Borealis fell down from the skies, and gathered around the dome, hues of violet and green, washing over Mother Motherland like the flailing veil of a dancer. Everybody was there. The whole population of this great city. We stood around the rim of the crater and held hands and felt at once unity, hope, fear and energy. Our minds seemed to synchronise as one great feeling of power swept over us. The lights were hypnotic and seductive and I felt alive and did not spare a single thought for you, poor Nikola Tesla the literal lightning rod.

You stood in the centre of your glass prison as the waves of the Borealis swam around you. You were illuminated so much so that your great silhouette was projected high up into the sky. We could not see your face, but I imagined your expression to be calm and rested unlike any expression I have seen upon you before. I imagined the fierce look of concentration you used to carry to have been washed away. I imagined the crazed glint of discovery you bore to have been dulled back. Simply tranquil. As if sinking into a dream.

Slowly, inside the globe, you began to levitate. Gently you lifted up until you were in the centre of the orb, arms outstretched, legs spread also. You tilted your head back. Then, great tentacles of electrical light began weaving from your body, from the very epicentre of the dome. They began to lick the edges of the ball, charging everything. I could feel the hairs on the back of my neck stand up. I looked briefly at my hands and saw small blue sprigs of current leapt from my fingers and into those of the man whose hand I was holding and on from him to the woman next...and on and on. I could see the tiny blue thread of electrical life weave its way from person to person, connecting us and enlightening all.

Mother Motherland's great sword began to glow a molten colour and her eyes became aflame! What a sight! What power you, Nikola Tesla were generating! What triumph Brekker was creating and the town was galvanised.

The glowing beams inside the glass ball continued to lick the walls in a free, chaotic motion. You remained still though, hovering in the centre of what seemed like the universe.

I was about to scream out my admiration and my love for you. I was about to offer up every inch of my soul for you, man of light. I inhaled to do so, and took in a lungful of hot, metallic tasting air. I began to shudder. We all did. A thunderous hum began to emanate from the base of Mother Motherland, ascending in pitch and timbre.

Then, a blinding flash and all was silent. My eyes took seemingly years to recover. After the all encompassing light of the Borealis, the glow of the Tesla Dome, and then the burst of light from Mother Motherland all sense of time and space were washed from us so I cannot accurately gauge how long it took to come back to my senses.

———•◦•———

Sight came first. Focus returned, everything remained the same and the statue stood, the LHC still ran the circumference of the crater floor and the reactor complex in the centre remained. The glass ball in the palm of her hand shimmered in the light.

What had gone, however, was colour. Saturation came slowly back, as if reluctant to do so. Even as I write this, it seems that the sky lacks a certain vibrancy. I looked around at the townsfolk, they looked at me and at each other. An all-pervasive sense of melancholia hung palpably in the still, metallic air.

As silence reigned, we began to believe that our sense of sound had abandoned us forever. I know now that it was not a mass deafening but a shared melancholy that quelled within us all any desire to utter a sound.

I looked up at the ball, hoping to see your heroic figure standing there, arms raised in triumph, enticing us to cheer and toss our bonnets and hats into the air. You were not standing there. For a moment I thought you had vanished. I looked harder and I made you out. My heart almost broke. You were there, sitting against the glass dome, hugging your knees and gently rocking, like a terrified child or an aged man lost to dementia.

Slowly, the townsfolk drifted back into the town. I could not do likewise. I felt that leaving you, my lover, in that moment to be the ultimate betrayal. But I could not get to you. I could not fly up to your glass dome and I could not climb up the robes of Mother Motherland. I could do nothing and so I stood and watched you rock back and forth until eventually, under the celestial blanket, you laid down and fell asleep.

I walked back into the city, never once looking up, instead gazing down at the pristine concrete below. Muscle memory must have guided me back to our hotel, for I did not look up once to see the street signs.

My memory of that walk is nothing but the image of my feet trudging and the ocean of sadness I felt adrift in. There seems nothing more painful than to be in a glorious city but feel nothing but the ache of solitude.

My darling Tesla, I will find you again. I will see you alive, hold you tight, make love to you, taste you and listen to you spin your theories all night long. I will do this.

As a token of devotion, I have written this letter with the aim to paste it in your journal so you may one day know of what happened to you. It was, as you were, everything. It was glorious, awesome, tragic and empty all at once. I carry the faintest hope that this thought might somehow find its way into your heart and behind your eyes to once again ignite that crazed spark you once carried.

Your lover, for always.

    Angeline

50

Angeline Entry.

Nikola is no more. His body remains, but his mind has gone, wrenched from him and channelled into Brekker's Large Hadron Collider. I feel that I am complicit in his destruction. I feel that we all are – every worker, every scientist and every lover.

We stood on that ridge and watched as Brekker took from him all that matters. We watched and we did nothing. I see Nikola every day now, and I feel nothing but wrenching guilt and pity for that broken man.

It seems the Stage Firing that involved the Borealis and the glass dome has taken his mind. It was an awesome and glorious lobotomy. Brekker now uses Nikola's intellectual might to power the LHC and the reactors are working at two thousand percent increase. His plan to fold all realities into one is nearing completion.

We all work hard, we are energised and enthused and yet, I see Nikola and pity him. Brekker has him working a menial job in the reactor. I see him every day pulling the same two levers up and down, up and down, up and down for twelve hours at a time. His eyes are blank, fogged over – he is lost. His head lilts to the side. In the morning, he drools out of the right side of his mouth, in the evening, the left side. At midday he drools from both corners. Slowly side to side his head rocks as he pulls his levers. He is the saddest metronome I have ever seen.

However, I have a job to do, and I perform my responsibilities professionally and in a way in which to make Brekker proud but it is increasingly hard to walk past Nikola on the gantry where his terminal is. I pick up my pace and look to the floor as passing him is one of the worst moments I have ever encountered and I have to go through it over and over (the gantry leads from my observation deck and into the reactor proper). I have read over Nikola's entries in his journal and he notes that death is the same throughout the Multiverse and that only the details change. Walking past him and feeling the guilt time after time proves his theory. I am in a perpetual cycle of shame. And he is there, a constant yet oblivious reminder of our crime.

After his shift, he is released into the town. He drags his feet and walks like a Sleepwalker. Nobody pays any attention to him. It's as if they cannot see him. Nobody talks of his gift to us, of his past genius, or of what we have taken from him. If they avoided him, or looked away, I could cope. I could understand that. But they utterly ignore him which is worse. He doesn't exist. He has no position in the Multiverse anymore. I cannot bring myself to even guess what sort of internal landscape he is wandering through. I just pray that it is no worse than the one he physically occupies.

As my shift in the reactor observatory ends, I slip away and catch up with Nikola. I take him to our hotel. Bathe him. Feed him. I try to sleep with him and hold him tight. He is cold and stiff. In the morning, I always seek to love him. He cannot become aroused as his circulation is as lost as the gaze in his dead, shark eyes. I still love him, I still yearn for him, I still lust for him…but he is beyond useless now. Every morning, I shower him and dress him and then I clean myself. In those minutes of solitude in the shower I weep and curse and pour anguish over myself, raging against what we have done to him. I feel better afterwards. I leave my pain in the shower and this sense of duty to care for him returns. Every day, after this ritual, I step out of the shower to find Nikola gone. Every day I look out of the window to see him trudging off towards the LHC gateway, his gait sloped and his path winding as if he is a walking drunk. Back to his terminal. As if somehow connected. Somehow calling him. He has been given a name tag for his white overall. He is known as 'Sacha,' a nondescript entity amongst the workers of Pripyat, but I know he is Nikola Tesla, I know what he has done. I know how his mind was taken. I remember his greatness.

I am writing this now in the remains of his laboratory. The moonlight is shining through the hole in the roof. Everything here is destroyed. Twisted, melted and not how I remember it, though I now recall the times spent here without a clear definition of time and space as if I had been dreaming, or indeed only half awake. But still, I do remember that I used to help my lover work here.

There are two piles of sand next to the operation-chair. They seem curiously real compared to the buckled and bent furniture and fittings that still remain. There has been no trail of sand leading to, or from the piles. They look like they have just sprung up. As if they have grown through the concrete floor, like puddles signifying a leaking pipe under-floor.

Curious.

I have decided to leave the journal here along with the map and periscope. This laboratory is the grave of Nikola's intellect, so I feel that his tools should rest here too. I no longer have my love, I have his shell but I will continue to care for him. But I leave the last parts of him here, to rest.

To rest.

I placed the periscope on one pile of sand and slowly and solemnly, it sunk into it, like a coffin being lowered into its final resting place. After I have finished this entry, I will consign this journal to the depths of the sand-grave.

Once Brekker has fired the LHC and all the realities in the Multiverse are one, I shall leave. Once my duty has been seen through to completion, I intend to walk out into the desert, alone. I will walk forward and never look back.

A solitary death awaits me. I deserve to die alone and sad, somewhere in uncharted and indifferent territory.

51

Master G_ entry.

We were almost gone, buried up to the head. Swallowed by the dune. Pulled in by the slipstream of dissolving memories we were holding hands as we sank slowly down. Our heads were tilted back, facing the azure sky, the sun bright and the air crisp. Grains of sand began to creep into our vision, their harsh forms grating against our corneas. We were falling into an hour glass. Into our mouths, ears, nostrils, sand trickled.

Breathing became painful – dyspnea - the pressure of the dune crushing against our chests. Malfunctioning respiratory system. Then apnoea. Lungs still. No air. No movement. Like holding your breath. The sand had an iodine taste. Our eyes began to water as they tried to wash away the grains of sand. Only served to create a muddy sludge that pooled around the corners of our eye sockets.

Deep within the belly of the dune, I felt something grip my arm tightly like a vice. It moved down until it found my wrist, then my hand. It wove into my grip and a voice came into my head. It was my own voice. The other version of me was holding my hand and talking to me. I could not turn my head to look into his eyes, I could only hold my hand and talk in my faltering mind.

We told each other not to worry, not to fear and together we began to count, hoping to fall asleep before the pain of suffocation overwhelmed us. We longed for a peaceful end, we longed to forget our failings, and we longed for sleep.

We never reached our end. I was about to close my eyes and resign myself to the NeverLasting when a figure filled my vision and blotted out the sun. The figure stood over us and looked down at our disappearing faces. The figure sighed. An involuntary pang of recognition flared up in my mind. I knew that sigh! And as soon as that recognition fired, several more detonated, my memory alive like a fireworks display. The shoulders, the neck, the gentle slender arms, I knew them. The figure bent down towards us, the face being revealed at last.

It was Lucy! She was perfect. No scarring, no sores. No pain, no tears. As she was. And she smiled at us.

This time, the water in my eyes was not produced to combat the sand infiltration; it was produced to echo my shame and sorrow. I had forgotten her, I had failed to find her. I had given up on my Lucy and resigned myself to the slow suffocation in the desert of my memory. I tried to speak with my eyes, to say that I was sorry and to tell her that I loved her. She must have understood because she smiled that luminous smile, shook her head, kissed her finger, and then wiped the sludge from our eyes. She leaned into my face and spoke, the words bypassing my now defunct ears, and blossoming straight inside my mind.

She said, "We are not over yet, you still have fight in you, come my darling, there is work to be done, there is journey to be made. You are not falling away from me yet."

I became resolute, I became energised. I felt fierce and volcanic. I felt my other self tighten his grip on my hand. Lucy stood up and took a step back, the sunlight now dappling her face. She began to sing a love song, one of her favourites, the one whose name I could not recall, but whose lyrics spoke of her believing in me as I believed in her. With each passing phrase, softly sung by my love, I could feel air returning to my lungs, I could feel my blood beginning to circulate. I could feel sand falling out of my nose and mouth. I could feel the dune receding. Soon, my face was free and I gasped in air and knew that never again will I taste air so pure and vital. Those breaths taken in those moments, under the sun and carrying Lucy's song may well have been the only real breaths I have ever taken in my NeverLife, and in my real life and also in every life across every reality. I was breathing.

I moved my head and looked over at the other me; I looked back at myself, the same energy, the same conviction behind my eyes.

Then, our necks and shoulders were free and we could feel our hearts beating again, hard and powerful in our chests. Lucy finished her song and began it again. The sun still danced across her face. Her white cotton dressed swaying in a gentle breeze.

Next came our chests and arms, then our waists and finally our legs. We were back, standing on the surface of my memory. The three of us. Myself, myself and Lucy. The final grains of sand fell out of my ears, my hair, my sleeves and my trouser legs, each grain seemingly weighing a universe, each one freeing me all that much more.

Lucy finished her song and began to walk away. I called out to her. I asked her to stay. She looked back, shook her head and walked off into my desert memory.

I called out to her. I said, "Tell me something!" And just before she disappeared from view, her voice appeared in my head once more.

She replied, "He seeks the answer to his question. He seeks and seeks. You will give him his answer and he will rest and rest." My other self called out, asking her how we would get back to the world. She said; "To go back to the world, look to the sun, climb up to it, and pull it from the sky. The sun is a window!"

The voice fell away and the speck on the horizon vanished. Once again we were alone in the desert, but this time we were elated. We were inspired. I looked over to the other version of myself. I smiled at myself, I smiled back and then we both turned and looked up at the sun.

52

We did indeed look towards the sun, we did indeed climb up to it and we did indeed pull it from the sky. The sun really is a window. We climbed through the sun, leaving the desert behind and we pulled ourselves back into TheNeverRealm.

We were standing on the dune, Lucy's song fading away in our minds. We looked up towards the sun and reached out to it. But instead of the air, we felt resistance, like pressing on an invisible ceiling or wall. Only, it was not solid, it was pliable like a film above us. We teased, prodded and investigated it. The film, when prodded, distorted the light, bending the shape of the sun into an oval. Its touch was warm, sleek and dry.

We were abruptly interrupted in our pawing of the sky-ceiling by a ripple and a shudder emanating from the centre of the sun, and spreading outwards like a stone thrown into a pond. As the ripples dispersed, the colour of the sun dulled, the saturation falling away slightly revealing a black spot in the centre. We sat back on the sand to study it. The black spot grew until it was the size of a fist, then the black spot lost its absence. An image appeared like a hole cut through a sheet of paper to reveal a landscape behind it. We could see, in the spot, a vista behind, we could make out a sky of a different hue, we could make out the partially collapsed roof of a building, we were on the floor, looking up at the ceiling, and past it. I knew instantly what it was. I was looking up at the ceiling of Tesla's laboratory.

I was about to stand up when, without reason, an oblong object fell through the hole and landed in the sand next to us. It was my periscope. I picked it up and looked through it. The sky that we knew, the sky in my desert fell away, and the full vision of the laboratory was revealed to me. I saw, from my vantage point below the floor, the cracked walls, the melted desks and twisted chair, the hole in the ceiling, the sky above and I saw a woman walking away.

We knew immediately what had to be done. The second version of me began talking in my mind and we formed a plan. In seconds I had holstered my periscope, and climbed onto his shoulders. My face was so close to the hole in the sun that I could taste the air on the other side. I could almost hear the cold dripping of the broken water pipes in the laboratory. I reached up and grabbed the edges of the sun-hole and pulled it open. The resistance to my efforts was immense, but I overcame them, pulling and tearing at this window back to TheNeverRealm.

The second version of me held my feet and with an almighty heave he pushed me up. I was half in the laboratory, half in my desert-mind with a pile of sand around my waist. The suction from the desert world below was dragging me back down. I was struggling against the pull and below me the other version of myself was pushing my legs up with all his might. I could feel the sand falling into my pockets, I could feel it in my sleeves grating against my skin. I scrabbled around to find something to hold onto. I found a good purchase on the cylindrical chair leg. Gripping it tightly, I was able to pull myself fully into the laboratory. I lay on my back, panting hard. I coughed, hacking and spluttering up the muddy sludge from my throat.

After coughing up the mass, I lay on my front and stuck my arm into the sand-hole, shouting at myself to leap up and grab hold. He did and, our strength working double, I curled my arm, shouting loudly in exertion. The other me grabbed the edge of the hole and pulled himself up, the sand pouring into him as it had done to me.

With one final pull, I got him out of the desert and fully into the laboratory. Like I did, he heaved up a vomitus mass of sand and mud. I slapped his back hard and helped scoop the remaining sludge from his mouth and throat. We were about to embrace and laugh at our accomplishment when a look of panic overcame him and without a word, he dived back onto the floor and into the second sand pile, falling halfway back in, head first! I dived down and grabbed his legs before he sank back for good. I yanked him back, the force against me even greater. I fell backwards, smashing my coccyx. I screamed in pain, but kept a hold of him. I kicked against the floor, trying to pull myself (and myself) backwards. Slowly I began to get a purchase, and slowly I dragged him back from the pit.

As soon as his head was free, I rolled him over. His eyes were closed and he was not breathing. I punched his chest plate repeatedly until he was revived. Again he vomited. I screamed at him to explain his actions.

He pulled his arm free of the sandpit just as the portal closed for good and in his hand he was holding this journal. My journal. The NeverDiary. It had been sinking into the pit, seemingly thrown into it as if it were garbage!

We sat on the floor in the laboratory and laughed. Exhausted, elated. Alive. Beyond all reason and hope, we had traversed time, space and even death.

———•◦•———

I am writing about our return to TheNeverRealm while the other version of me inspects the laboratory. He has sand in his hair and he leaves a trail of sand from his trouser legs wherever he walks.

We are back and we have work to do.

53

TheNeverRealm is now an alien place. When I left it, Couldwell was still here. Now it seems Pripyat has arrived fully. I have read over Tesla's entries. Amazed at his discoveries. Amazed at how he carried on investigating, even in the face of all this chaos. Touched by his dedication and kind words regarding me. Heartbroken at reading Angeline's entries and learning how Tesla's end came about.

After some time investigating the ruined laboratory, MGV2 (have adopted Tesla's name for him) and I headed into the city. The map left in the diary by Angeline helped greatly. Tesla was canny to integrate the maps of Couldwell and Pripyat and we found our way through the town with ease. Even tracing some faded markers on walls and corners where we had originally began to map the town.

Good discovery: we exist.

We were corporeal to the other townsfolk. Though they bustled about and though fixated on getting from 'A' to 'B', they avoided us like we were really there, a part of their lives and environment. One man even tipped his hat to us as he rushed about, offering us a greeting in a language we don't speak.

We were giddy at the long forgotten feeling of existence (at least, existence in comparison to other living entities). Of course, we could all be ghosts, or projections. However, the acceptance of each other's temporal occupancy in a shared environment proves that we are a part of this collection of souls and in that, we can divine an existence. Our excitement caused us to bump into many people, caused us to walk into poles, snag our ankles on steps and rails. Townsfolk paid no real mind to our shambolic nature. Must have assumed we were drunk.

After a while of stumbling around, soaking in our new-found existence, our shared consciousness began to throb. We both began to endure a monumental headache. A sensory overload. Our minds perhaps not capable of dealing with all the folds of reality in one place so soon after our rebirth.

We sought refuge. Our staggering and stumbling soon turned from giddy disbelief to tortured anguish. We had to leave! We had to get away. We stooped low, our arms around each other, shielding our eyes from the sun and the sights of the town and we focused on the concrete and made our way through the town.

Eventually, after many blind turns, we stumbled upon a dried out and deserted concrete canal. The pain in our heads fell away and we slid down the dry wall, onto the canal bed. I write this now, sitting against the wall.

The canal extends at least five kilometres in either direction and we can see tributaries branching off the main tract that we occupy. We are relieved to be on our own again. We assume that, in 'time' our minds will become adjusted to the 'living conditions' of actually existing in this thriving town. For now, we need rest.

I have noticed that sand is leaking from my trouser legs also. MGV2 has a gentle trickle. Now I do too. Curious. We will sleep for a bit.

———•◦•———

Woken at sundown by sound of whimpering. We both woke from our black, dreamless state at the same time. A gentle, sad whimpering. Seems to be emanating from south of the concrete canal.

We are going to investigate.

———•◦•———

The whimpering is now louder. Louder and disturbing. Something is in pain. We have taken a few turns to get here and the sun has set. The section of the canal we are in is dirtier and more dilapidated. It seems that the further away from Pripyat we venture, the greater the disrepair. The concrete is cracked, discoloured and damp in places. There is even moss and reeds breaking through the floor. The whimpering is coming from up ahead. We go now.

———•◦•———

Found the source of the noise. There is something trapped behind this storm drain. We found a metal grate over a culvert, sealed with rust. Behind it, the sad tones of the crying beast.

Our collective strength is not able to budge the grate. We cannot see what animal is making the noise, we just both feel that we need to get to it. MGV2 says he can see something. A glint in the darkness.

———•·•———

It's him! It's Paisley! The glint was the bullet in his eye-socket, shining in the moonlight, wet from his tears, poor creature! Stuck in the vent. How did he get here? I do not know. I would assume after Tesla was destroyed in the plasma globe, Paisley was alone and with nobody to see him in the world and nobody to care for him he fled to this dark and awful place. Poor thing. We cannot get to him. The grate is sealed beyond hope. He is moaning and crying. He has dragged himself forward, and we can feel his fur, he is nuzzling MGV2.

Discovery:

We have gotten him out of there and by the most unexpected means imaginable. We have discovered that, while we exist, we are not flesh. We are something else.

While MGV2 was stroking Paisley, and as their cries grew and their sorrow compounded, I noticed his hand begin to disappear into Paisley's fur. Sand began to trickle through has scraggy neck and collect on the floor. Soon, MGV2's arm began to fall away. He began to scream. I was shocked. Dumbfounded. He began to pour through the grate and within seconds he was no more, simply a great pile of sand with Paisley standing in the middle of it! I rattled the grate and screamed in terror and pain.

Before I could think to do anything, the sand began to shift and stir. Paisley leapt backwards as a shape and form began to push and pull from the pile. I fell backwards, aghast as Master G_ Version Two reformed himself in his entirety before our eyes! Every detail was correct, every molecule in its right place, even his clothes had reformed. He looked at himself in disbelief and then smiled.

I scrambled forward to the grate, fixed my eyes upon my two compatriots in the culvert, took a deep breath and extended my arms through. The feeling was sublime. I was in control of every single atom and I had total omnipotence over my being. I poured myself through the grate and reformed on the other side. It was almost effortless, like jumping out of a tree – once you overcome the initial trial, you can do it time and again. We hugged Paisley and, from the inside, we managed to kick the grate free, releasing us. We climbed out into the starry night. I picked up the journal and the periscope (which I was unable to convert to sand) and all three of us walked back to the sleeping town.

54

Paisley is sitting on the hatch of the LHC pipeline. Though he came with us, he cannot go any further. He must stay guard and though it pains us all to leave each other yet another time, it must be done. MGV2 and I are going into the LHC.

———————•—•—•———————

Inside the LHC Pipeline. Read over Tesla's entry about surviving the Stage Firing from within here. Quite incredible to have done so and to have gone through space and become entwined with fabric of Multiverse in such a way is astounding. We have now to find a way to get from inside the pipeline to inside the reactor complex that sits in the centre of this great ring. Must find a service tunnel.

———————•—•—•———————

The service tunnel runs for the radius of the pipeline ring, right to the centre of the compound. Flickering red lights line the hexagonal corridor. Wires overhead like veins. Cannot see the end of the tunnel.

———————•—•—•———————

Seemed to be walking down hexagonal service tunnel for centuries. On and on it went, the repetition of the blinking red lights almost tipping us into dementia. We held fast. Made it to a hatch. The other side of it lays the reactor core!

———•◦•———

We are in the reactor core and it is a hive of activity. We must be tens of leagues beneath the surface of Pripyat now and above us an impossible maze of walkways and gantries that cross over the expanse of the open reactor. We opened the hatch from the service tunnel and we were greeted by a descending ladder that led down into a murky abyss. The only sign of depth were the blinking lights every kilometre or so (blinking blue this time. The beacons did little to dilute our sense of unease at our approaching descent. Down we went).

———•◦•———

We are now at the base of the reactor core, tucked into a dark corner. Perhaps nobody has ever been so far down here (since its construction anyway). Great columns of glass stretch up, way out of sight. The column glass must be a yard think and inside, balls of liquid float in abstract gravity, colliding, morphing and breaking apart. Sometimes they form recognisable shapes – a dog, a Model-T, a church, a man, a trombone. Sometimes they even form vistas, dioramas that look like they have been moulded from jelly. They form and hold their position for a few seconds before falling apart. The scenes are uniformly of devastation; mushroom clouds over cities, great tankers capsizing in oceans, tsunamis engulfing whole islands. Everything is chaos inside these tubes.

Above, across the myriad gantries rush workers. Some in overalls, some in radiation suits and others in white coats. The sense of industry is palpable, but is overshadowed by the sense of dread and of expected disaster. In my mind MGV2 tells me of the dream of mine (the dream in which he lived, and the dream in which I melted inside this very reactor core) He tells me of what is to come and he tells me that we must prevent it, or if we can't, we must save as many as we can. He echoes Tesla's last coherent thoughts. I agree, though the images he shows me in our conjoined mind of that existence horrify me. This was my death in that reality, and most probably my death in this reality. All death is the same, it is only the details that change.

———•·•———

We have taken rest at the base of the core as we are overawed at the sight above us and agree that notation is important as we (and others) have carried on this NeverDiary over dimensions, through time and across landscapes of life, death and the great FurtherUnknown. We need to take stock of all around us, all we witness and experience. We need to take time to 'smell the flowers' as my mother used to say (my final image of her, half frozen in winter, on that crooked rocking chair does not turn to sand like other memories…instead, falls now to snow). Time to smell the flowers indeed, perhaps more than ever MGV2 and I need to do this, we are on the edge of the precipice. This is our inhalation before we plunge. This is us.

———•◦•———

After we left the dry-canal with Paisley, we ventured back to the hotel. We expected to find Angeline and Tesla there (after reading her entries) but it was morning and so we assumed that they would be working. So far, we have not seen either of them here. Tesla works on the walkway leading to the observation platform which is a hundred leagues overhead. We will make our way there. We will explore floor by floor.

MGV2 is now running his hands over the glass walls of the reactor columns. The globules inside are attracted to his touch and they form a replica of him, mimicking his movements, just as I do in life. It is quite calming to watch this little mirror-dance. Everything is a copy. Everything is a silhouette. Everything is everything else. Our minds reflected a conjoined stillness as I wrote that last statement. We agreed.

———•◦•———

He has suggested that it is time to go. We'll advance through the internal network of the vast complex, room by room, floor by floor, back up to the very top of the reactor core. Bold spies we are!

———•◦•———

We have advanced up to level 278 and so far we have encountered workers who have, to a man, ignored us. No shouts of "Halt!" No questions at all. We were simply passed by.

Everyone is programmed to do their duty it seems; gloomy machines of industry. Mechanical flesh beings. We passed through endless rooms of desks and terminals, wires everywhere, pipes, steam vents, bulbs, switches, everything is connected in some way to something else. It seems that not one rivet is wasted in this construction. We have no hope of understanding how anything works, instead we are focusing on finding that one mistake, that one agent of chaos that must, inevitably be floating around here somewhere. There will be a document, there will be a lose wire, or a hidden room that has been overlooked.

We seek a 'time' or a 'place' where Brekker will abound when this final, catastrophic Stage Firing occurs. We need to know the secret.

55

We have climbed into a ventilation duct above the observation gantry. We can see Tesla. Poor, broken man, pulling on his levers in a slow repetition. If there is one terminal, one process in the LHC reality reactor that is menial and meaningless, it is Tesla's terminal. Our hearts break for him.

We have chosen to hide in order to observe. We can see all the way down to our starting point, back to the floor of the reactor where MGV2 interacted with the reactor-tube. It is a tiny dot. The gantries criss-crossing, the electrical beams that dart across the space create a maelstrom below us. It is even more impressive to be above it than to be below. The noise is wondrous and almost symphonic. Before, we had ear-bleeding reverb and gut churning bass rumblings and now we have a gentle hum with a higher toned sparkle that complements it gracefully. Hard to believe that such a machine of destruction can also create something so wondrous.

Our vent is at a cross-passage, the grate below views the walkway, turning left, the grate on that passage looks down onto the observation booth. It lies empty at the moment, save for a strange grotesque bronze bust, maybe waist high. The arms are sharp, rectangular and without hands. The head is long and pointed. Could be a hat, could be a visor, could be an interpretation of a horse's skull, such is its shape. Can't tell when looking down upon it. The shoulders are large and smooth, almost like it is wearing plate armour. The bronze finish of the statue is buffed, cold and menacing. Cannot see what it rests on, looks like a set of three thin, long legs, with four joints a piece. Like a ghastly easel. The room is filled with dread. The shadow the bust casts is not of its true form: shadow across the wall looks like a human wearing a top hat. Do not want to go into room. MGV2 does not want to either.

But go we must.

———•·•———

Cannot open grate to fall into room. Going to try and pour our way instead. The incident with Paisley and the culvert could not have been a one-off. We can turn to sand. We know it. We can feel it. We can reform too so we can move through grates and keyholes. Though the room fills us with dread, we are compelled to investigate the odd room. It has no obvious place in this complex. No rhyme or reason.

Leaving journal in vent, will pour in as sand, investigate, leave, double back to where we climbed into vent originally and pick up journal. From here we will continue to observe the gantry and mourn our working-corpse friend Nikola Tesla.

———•·•———

Returned.

Back in vent at cross passage. Journal still here. Periscope still here. Infiltration into room success. We poured through and reformed. Like human hourglasses.

Made discoveries and found a document.

The room we entered was thirty-five foot cubed. In the centre stood the bronze bust. It was indeed standing upon a hideous tripod/easel construction. The entire piece stood eight-foot tall and the spindle-legs were filed to points at the end. They seemed both sturdy and fragile at the same time.

Its face was not of a horse's and was not a visor. It was a sleek, long helmet. Ribcage looked like the front grill on Model-T. The shape of the torso and the width of the shoulders suggested the statue to be male, however where the stomach should have been were not the contours of a strong set of abdominal muscles, but instead the feminine shaped contours of a foetus. A progeny!

I got in close and I inspected it. No warmth. No humanity, not even in its progeny. The one thing that overwhelmed us completely was its sense of menace. Purposeful menace. I looked over the foul machine and MGV2 went about inspecting the walls, running his fingers over the seams and counting bricks. He found nothing to note.

We were about to leave, when there came a sudden, cold gust of air through the room, accompanied by a sigh that carried the weight of pain and history that only mortal souls can bear.

No mere draughty sighs like we humans do. MGV2 and I froze in dread. There was something else living in the room. The statue? If I had my periscope I would have looked, but I could not bring it in through the keyhole. Was it the statue's shadow cast upon the wall that sighed? Twisted and non-representative of the statue's form? Most possible.

We turned to look at the statue, and that is when we saw it: a piece of paper. A torn, stained and sorry looking document, folded over and over, poking out betwixt the statue and the stand. How had I not seen it before? We could not stand to be in that room any longer and so we took the paper, slid it under the door and then together we poured ourselves through the keyhole and out onto the concourse.

When we reformed we looked over at Tesla again and called his name. A whisper at first, then a shout. No workers seemed to care about us and Angeline was also not around. Tesla did not respond, just moved his two levers up and down.

We did not dally any longer and so we moved quickly down the gantry that ran alongside the office wall and into a utility laboratory where we climbed back into the vent overhead. Here we are now, back in the vent with the journal. We do not want to look back through that grate into the room with that statue. MGV2 is watching Tesla. I can hear MGV2's tears dripping onto the cold metal vent. In our conjoined sadness, each strike of sorrow on steel is like a cannon firing.

———•◦•———

Angeline just came! While MGV2 was crying, she walked past Tesla and as she past him, she let her hand gently brush against the hem of his suit jacket. Nobody but us saw the gesture. That tiny gesture. That hope of a connection. We could not see her face, but we didn't need to; the subtle contact said it all. Tesla did not react. She walked off and he carried on with his levers.

I have attached the document found on the statue below.

What happened to me in MGV2's dream has happened before in another reality. In another time. In 1986. In this town, but not this location. Before it was folded into this realm, it suffered a fate that, it seems, it is doomed to repeat again.

The note is attached.

56

Brekker's Journal.

1986, Pripyat, Chernobyl.

Catastrophic failure. Cannot comprehend my disappointment. I am a vacuum. Nothing left in my mind. Cannot describe anger at the workers. They have failed me. Failed the universe. Many dead. Many more will follow. Over the years and across dimensions this will be felt, the reach of this disaster is immeasurable. I predict now that there is a hole underneath the reactor that splinters through all realities: a whirlpool of space-time.

Chain of events as follows:

1:00am: Organised test-firing of reactor's safety features. Power reduced down to 3200MW. A single turbine should be enough to power coolant pumps in event of emergency power collapse. Simple test.

1:06am: Turbine Nicolai is powered down. Routinely executed. Notations precise. Systems checked. Stable.

3:47am: Thermal power reaches 1600 MW.

2:00pm: We disconnect the core cooling system as scheduled. Intention now is to continue power reduction. Stivya informs me of power shortage on grid. I order Reactor 4 'Lucia' to be held in perpetual usage. Stivya disagrees. Attempts to override test-firing. Attempts to undermine experiment's integrity. I have Stivya removed from observation deck. Reactor 'Lucia' continues to operate. Experiment is not halted.

11:10pm: We intended to reduce power. I note the names of all workers who cast doubtful eyes at my conviction. I can hear the murmurs of dissent in their minds. I feel their doubts. It is that combined negative energy that pushes the power reduction much further than anticipated. Bottomed out well below expected baseline and now I know that we are heading for cataclysm.

01:00am: I can smell the build-up of Xenon. The others cannot. Their senses are not as attuned as mine. The build-up has been caused by running the reactor at a low power. We have raised it to 200MW but it has done little. I compensated for the Xenon build up by pulling out the control rods. An operator detects the Xenon build up. He screams for an emergency shutdown. I force us to press on, we have come too far and we continue with our preparations for the next test stage.

1:23am: Turbine Nicolai is gradually denied steam flow signalling the commencement of the next test stage. The water flow through the core is reduced, thusly boiling increases. Reactor Lucia signals that power is rising. Rising too far. I push for an increase even farther. I am wrestled to the floor by three operators. I gnash and flail and threaten murder. They are too blind and too foolish. I know what they are about to do, and I know what effect it will have.

1:23:40am: The foolish mutineers attempt an emergency shutdown. We are beyond that now. They do not see it. They thrust the control rods back into Lucia. The effect is opposite to that intended.

1:23:43am: Just three seconds after their emergency shutdown attempt Lucia goes Prompt Critical. Exponential increase in fission events. We have entered the catastrophe in just three seconds of irreversible stupidity.

1:24am: From the observation platform, I witness the gargantuan steam explosion, the upthrust rattles my soul. The operators on the outside gantry are vaporised in nano-seconds. Those not hit by the steam, are hit by the sonic blast. They have barely enough time to react as they resonate into pieces.

Inside our room we fall backwards, part shock, part awe, part despair. Only I retain focus. Operators scramble for the door. I yell to stop. I yell to wait.

1:24:53am: A chemical explosion follows the steam. A wonderful column of light and gas rockets up past the observation window and blasts the roof of Lucia, breaking into the night! The sound is like static, or feedback. It is electrical, powerful, almost inconceivable. The lights that swirl the chemical fire are vibrant reds, yellows, purples and greens. We are transfixed. It is like the Aurora Borealis.

1:24:54am: The chain reaction we have started fires a chain reaction in my mind. The Aurora Borealis. I have been struck with a monumental idea. I laugh. The operators are screaming.

1:36am: Internal firefighters beat back the flames. Many perish in chaotic backdrafts that swell and belch at their choosing, in three dimensional space, in mid-air, under the floor, on ground level. The fire is almost impossible to contain. Firefighters are courageous. They do not flee.

1:45am: Lucia stops firing chemical gasses into the night sky. The light show is over but the chaos continues. I release my operators from the room and I order them under Lucia and into her crawlspace to investigate and take readings. Cowards turn white, but go. None expected to return and none do. All melted and fused to the underside of Lucia's core. I am reminded of a previous failed experiment – that of the USS Eldridge. Must find more suitable operators.

05:1am: Firefighters from Pripyat along with townsfolk battle back flames successfully. None wear protective clothing, almost a generation of men wiped out. Young boys and underfed teenagers sent back into crawl spaces around Lucia and reactor core to tighten or loosen fittings. To quell flames and plug leaks. They succeed at huge coast to population and morale of Pripyat (speculation). Many children dragged out of tubes and pipes. Crushed, deformed, melting.

06:00am: Against my wishes, Reactor Three 'Gregor' is shut down to prevent further catastrophe. Calm and control are returning to the scene. I begin to retread the events. Begin to piece this together.

———•◦•———

6th May, 1986

21:00: Reactor 'Lucia' is sealed to avoid further spill and atmospheric contamination. I offer humanitarian gesture and I order five thousand tons of boron carbide, limestone, lead, sand and clay to be dumped into the devastated Lucia. Dirigibles fly over and men dump the sand bags into the reactor hole in teams. Others walk the mix in by hand or by barrow. Operation is immense. From my observation room, they look like industrious ants. The possibility of a further chain reaction is minimal, though underneath Lucia there still churns white hot toxins. I can feel that reality across the Multiverse is under strain. It is twisting. The sarcophagus over Lucia will hold, but the downward damage is irreparable. I must use this to my advantage. This catastrophe, like the others are combining to form ideas. This could be the merely the beginning: a preliminary sketch for my masterpiece.

57

Brekker's Journal.

The clean-up operation is fully underway. I have supported their ideas and suggestions. I have even volunteered to help (it was actually invaluable to witness the devastation from ground level).

We have effectively evacuated the city. The relief convoys came in the night. Schools, nurseries, offices are all abandoned. I have walked around the city and saw in the school, books lying open and lessons half written upon the chalkboard. In offices, telephones left off the hook. The ferris-wheel stands empty, the carts at the top swaying in the breeze. I can see charring on them. The yellow paint burnt off from the blast.

An office of operations has been set up at the hotel. The entrance is still buffed and shiny, but the portraits in the reception hall have changed. Atmospheric distortion has warped the oils and sealants causing their faces to desaturate. Cold grey skin, their eyes drooping. The paint has run and coagulated in places causing the subjects to look like they are covered in boils and mutations – they are both fascinating and hideous. They strike a chord in my memory, but it is a chord to a song whose melody is only half recalled. I am fascinated by the paintings. I make excuses to inspect the offices so I can stand in the foyer and study these pained and mutated faces.

The evacuation of Pripyat extends in a thirty kilometre radius and nothing living (after workers have left) will exist within the plant. I have been informed by Stivya that all that is needed to watch the city is a single guard. The unfortunate will sit in a kiosk at the edge of the Zone of Alienation and watch. We have positioned the kiosk east of the town as the wind blows predominantly westwards. He should be relatively safe, save from boredom. I should like to meet him when he arrives and explain to him the magnitude of what happened here but I'm doubtful he would grasp it. Doubtful anyone can grasp the importance of this disaster. I expect I will never meet him anyway as I intend to leave soon. I will post notifications of his duties for him. Stivya will no doubt remain here to brief him.

The biggest challenge, in terms of engineering, is containment. Though Lucia has been filled with limestone and boron carbide, we still need to seal her completely. We need to build a secondary sarcophagus around her. This is highly dangerous work and, as many died in the disaster; it is difficult now to send workers to work! They demand improved conditions, safety goggles, lead lined tractors. I have acquiesced to their requests. They have panelled the tractors with sheet lead and they have constructed rudimentary goggles. However, due to the potency of the air around the disaster site, workers can only operate effectively for a matter of minutes. Any longer and they risk lethal exposure thus diminishing the workforce. They work in shifts of three minutes. They drive in, run out of their tractors, shovel some debris into barrows and run back to safety.

Any sheet led that has not been panelled to the vehicles is panelled to the men. Each one charged with the construction of his or her uniform and they beat and shape the lead into helmets, chest plates, back armour and greaves. I have seen some men who refuse to do so, and others who cannot find lead (or who have had their own stolen) none of them last longer than a day on the site.

They are hosed, soaped, wire-wool scrubbed hourly and then sent back into work. I have arranged additional cigarettes and vodka to be rationed to the workers.

Lucia's roof is the most dangerous duty. The men there have to clear the toxic graphite and radioactive dust and rubble. It is almost an alien landscape: silent, cold and grey. The men run up the stairs and onto the roof. The maximum 'shift' allowed is 45 seconds of work. Enough for two shovels worth. The operation is minutely slow. The men are brave. In thanks, and in order to entice more volunteers to perform this task, each man who completes five shifts receives a certificate of duty, signed by myself.

The reports of illness are rife, as expected. There is no real way to tell who will survive or who will die. Some men who were weak in life, survive many shifts on the roof of Lucia, many soldiers die the moment they set foot inside the Zone of Alienation. Many still come, though. They believe in the site, they believe in its purpose and they believe in Brekker.

Today I saw a boy of only seven working dutifully. I have seen him once before, a long time before this. I remember walking into the town and seeing him playing by the fountain. He held a cup and attached to it by string was a ball. He was attempting to catch the ball in the cup. I remember feeling pity and anger at that boy. Anger for his playing when there was a world around him to discover, and pity for his obvious lack of intellect.

Today I saw him working. He took off his little lead helmet and gave it to a worker without one and then he went about trying to shovel with a little spade and pail. The worker went to the roof. The boy's duty was ineffective, but his gesture of comradeship was astounding.

It is acts like these that spur me onward. It is acts like these that galvanise my belief in my work. I am leaving Pripyat tomorrow to find a new site to build upon. I have, in my mind, a grand scheme, perhaps the grandest of all. I will walk out east, into the winds – east into the desert.

I have heard there lays a great crater, perfect for my specifications. I have heard also that nearby there is a little town in which I can live and work.

The town is named Couldwell. That is where I go.

If I have my way, I will eventually bring Pripyat with me.

58

Master G_ entry.

The above pasting details much. Answers a lot of questions. By that I mean, it orders much into a congruent timeline. It positions everything in a chain, albeit a chain with links that intercept each other at various points over various realities. Seems to be that Brekker's need and desire is to order. That is the engine that drives him. One could suggest that by doing so, by ordering everything, one orders all the Multiverse around oneself. One has a position. A finite place amongst all things. When one has position, then one is the baseline to which all variants are measured. One is the point of observation for the Multiverse. One is God.

MGV2 and I are calm in our understanding, but also resolute. No more proof is needed (Though MGV2 had known all along) that the man I sought out for answers and help is unconditionally the man who deals in chaos. I am a fool to have believed in him in life, and carried through that belief into TheNeverRealm. My love for him was so strong that I carried it over to here, and when all else was turning to sand what seems like millennia ago, I kept him more alive than anything. More alive than Lucy herself.

MGV2, Paisley and I have occupied Tesla's old laboratory. The hotel is a place for Angeline/Evelyn and the brain-dead Tesla. Seems fitting that this place is where we should operate.

To note – the two piles of sand that we climbed out of (and nearly lost the NeverDiary back into) have vanished. Instead there are two black, obsidian-hard plaques.

Paisley is with us. After our escape we found him sitting on the LHC pipeline, calm as the dead…until he saw us. He barked a bark that said "Hello!", but also nearly chastised us for not being quicker and for making him worry. I do not like leaving him on the sidelines. MGV2 and I believe that a fight is coming and we believe it is time to put the mutt in harm's way. The dog is a good dog and he will not fail if we task him with something. His tail wagged like a gyrocopter when we told him this.

We left the reactor via the roof. After exploration of the lower levels, and the room with the evil statue and dreadful presence, we ascended level by level. We occasionally turned to sand to gain entry into areas through keyholes, grates, vents and under doors. We have become so used to it now that we do not have to conjoin our minds, we simply approach a door, dissolve through it as we desire and then reform. It is as effortless as walking through an open door when made of flesh.

We found files, documents and maps and we pieced together other experiments. The USS Eldridge that he spoke off for example. There he attempted to move an object, a battleship, through realties and back again. The aim was to distribute and recall with the goal of attaining identical molecular reformation. He failed. His mistake was to equate all things on a single plane. Steel, iron, flesh and bone have different patterns, different agendas. His calculations were too simplistic. He learned from this and moved onwards to more 'successful' experiments (at the expense of many lives).

We found his designs for the Exxon Valdez, her hull integrity critically flawed. We found the transcripts of the distress calls – notations all over. Criticisms of emergency procedures – blame cast everywhere.

We found a diagnosis for an illness made out to him. We did not recognize the name of the disease. We found designs, concept through to final, for that horrific sculpture in that room. We have taken one (a final rendering of the bust and exposed progeny) it is pasted in here, thought I am loath to look at it. There was also a portfolio on Lucy. I could not bear to paste it in. I fear the need to do so is redundant as I may never forget what the document outlined; the torture, the balms, the ionic powders and tonics he forced her to drink. The mutations, the pains, the screams and the acts he visited upon her would have made the Devil himself scream in horror.

We learned from that document a valuable outcome: all his experiments across time and space before were concerned with the effect on all reality. However, The Lucy Experiments were concerned only with her and with *her* limits, with *her* boundaries and thresholds.

His conclusion perplexed us. He stated that he learned nothing from her. Throughout all his catastrophes he has orchestrated the results had all fired him off in another

315

direction. They had all given birth to some new theory. Except for the Lucy Experiments and because of that, he concluded that somewhere in that series of tests lays the secret to it all. He stated that every experiment after was designed to recreate that procedure so that he could re-enact the process and explore his great question.

We do not know what his great question is; he does not write it down. But Lucy knows it, and has charged me with delivering the answer. Neither of us knows the question or the answer nor even how it will come about. We hope that its deliverance will also deliver us from this place and onwards to Lucy. We believe it will. We believe in Lucy. I believe in her, as she believes in me.

While reading over Brekker's demented notes, MGV2 and I both shared a pang of sadness for this madman who has struggled and traversed time, space, death and reality in his insane quest for answers, his failures twisting and burning in him and the lives he has squandered, the dead bodies at his feet and the blood on his hands! Even with what he did to Lucy, and even given what I feel towards him for that we have to believe that he feels each of his crimes. We have to believe that he is not lost to the cold and that he is human, somewhere inside that twisted oubliette of a soul. He must feel the weight of all his crimes and hear the screams of his victims in some capacity!

If he does not and if inside he is truly as blank as The Void then we are not dealing with a human at all. We are dealing with a God. And that makes us fear.

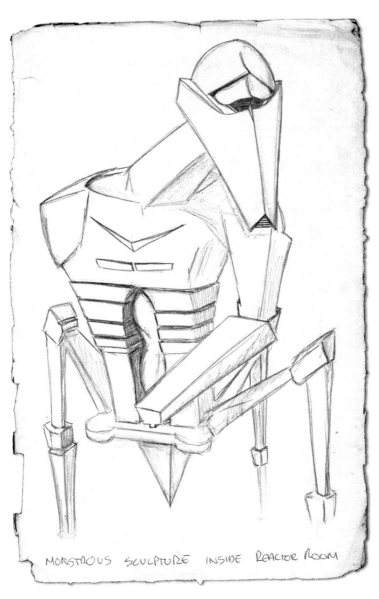

MONSTROUS SCULPTURE INSIDE REACTOR ROOM

59

There is a noise outside. Footsteps. Paisley has sprung up and is staring at the hole in the laboratory ceiling. Something is coming.

——•·•——

It was Angeline! We saw her shadow spill over the hole in the roof. It was twisting and contorting as it passed over the ruins of the laboratory. As her footsteps approached the edge of the roof, her shadow retracted into the more recognizable human shape and, just before she appeared, the shadow snapped back into her unique form.

We looked up at her, she looked down at us. Paisley barked at her pleasantly but she did not respond.

She simply whispered, "I have come to help." She climbed down from the roof into the lab and we sat together. Angeline recounted her shame and guilt in the participation of Tesla's destruction and the love she still bears for him. She was honest and sincere and the angst she carried was genuine. We sat upon the cold floor, MGV2 with his hand in Angeline's and my hands on Paisley's back, stroking him.

We told her that she was not to blame, that Brekker was the architect. She began to cry, mournfully at first before broking into fits of confessional sobs.

She said, "It was me! I betrayed him. I didn't want to, but I felt compelled. It felt natural. I was asleep, yet awake, in control and somehow not. It was dark, dark outside, night-time, but also dark inside my eyes. My vision was tunnelled and blurred. I walked from our bed all the way here, though I do not remember taking any steps. It was like in a dream where one flies. I drifted to this laboratory and I felt like a shadow. A ghost. I entered and saw my love standing, facing away from me and without pause for breath or thought I struck him with a rock. A clean gash opened on his head and he fell to the floor. I did it! I hit him. I betrayed him and I took him to Brekker, and delivered him as if he was weightless. We placed him inside the glass dome and stole his mind and now I am awakened with the knowledge that my nightmare was real and I have done this terrible act. I want to die. I want to leave."

Her sobs grew in intensity and her words became inaudible. MGV2 hugged her tightly while wiping away her tears with my handkerchief. Paisley nuzzled her. At his touch, Angeline flinched in surprise. She couldn't see him! I handed her my periscope and pointed her in the direction of the mutt. She looked down and saw him. Her tears were vanquished and she smiled broadly. She reached out and touched him. "I can feel him," she said, "he's really there...good boy, good boy." Angeline calmed herself, relieved at having confessed.

We showed her the notes we found in the laboratory and the diagnosis of Brekker's mystery illness and his repeated experiments. She was silent. When we are done she looked us over.

MGV2 spoke to me in my mind. He queried whether we should have relayed our findings and whether we should trust Angeline. He reminded me of the Old Angeline on the train, of her warning of the man who walks through walls and of her fateful transformation into the cyclone. While we looked at her, we colluded in our minds. Secret parlay. We fell on the side of trust as we have not trusted too much to anything, even reality and so maybe now it is time now to trust to this woman. So we do.

Whether she was privy to our talk, I cannot say, but as soon as we had spoken these words to each other, she seemed to react. A light behind her eyes flared up slightly. She stood up, dusted herself down and declared that we go. A lightning bolt of conviction flashed through us all and we knew what needed to be done. We all stood up and shook hands.

And so we go. We go to the LHC compound to terminate the experiment and evacuate the city before it is too late. We are prepared. Paisley and I are to evacuate the workers first. We will falsely trip the alarm and cause manageable panic. We will rupture steam vents and set off controlled explosions that lead the workers out to safety. Through the smoke and darkness, Paisley will lead the people out. When they are a safe distance, he will return back to the laboratory.

Angeline will infiltrate the observation room and destroy the reactor uplink before all realities reach Prompt Critical. Once that is done, she will disable the service tunnel to the LHC pipeline. She says she is able to do this and we believe her. We have to as we do not know how anything inside works. Once she has stopped the experiment, she will escape with the others through the panic. Once outside the compound, she will break away from the crowd and make her way back here.

MGV2 is to get Tesla out of the complex and back to the laboratory. It is understood that the man is lost and that he will not react to any situation. He will not move from his terminal and his levers. Not of his own accord anyway. MGV2 will either drag him away, or incapacitate and carry him out. They will meet back here also.

My charge is, once the compound is clear, find Brekker and extract him. Perhaps we can force him to reconstruct Tesla's psyche? Perhaps I can get him to show me a way into the FurtherUnknown and to Lucy perhaps? This is best case scenario. Worst case scenario: if we fail to stop the final firing of the LHC and all realities are folded into one, then we cannot foresee a path in which anything will matter. We cannot imagine what a folded Multiverse will appear to be, so we cannot predict our reactions.

In short two things must happen now

1. We must not fail.
2. Brekker must be captured alive.

GLORIOUS MOTHER MOTHERLAND CALLS US TO ACTION, AND SO WE ANSWER!

60

The cyclones have crossed the horizons and back again. Twelve times, in fact and we have not yet caught up with Brekker and Angeline. Twelve 'days' pursuit on foot, over red sand and under an ashen sky. No food, no water.

Paisley has led the way, the courageous animal. He runs, nose to ground after that woman and that monstrosity. I call to him to stop, I cannot keep up but he does not heed my words. The sand mixes with me and every few steps I become merged with the dunes. I cannot keep up! The sole of my shoe sticks, then it turns red like the sand, then my legs begin to fall apart and I begin to feel the dune overcoming me and I struggle free and continue onwards. It is like running through quicksand but where you yourself are intermittently becoming that very same quicksand. The chase is impossible, yet Paisley's determination and lack of consideration toward my physical condition drives me on. A saviour he is.

I am writing this now, twelve cyclones since the time we stormed the LHC compound. Has it really been twelve days? We are resting on a dune that is has a bedrock of iron. Like much in this desert it seems the sand only covers a percentage. Some of it has rock underneath, metal and even coral. In other places the sand is deeper than my sadness.

We rest now because we have to. I need to document all that has transpired. I have not touched this journal since it began. TheNeverPages were forgotten while we battled. Then the chase came and it is only now that we have time to recount. Paisley lies on the peak of the dune, his head over the brow so he can see into the distance. On the horizon I can see a tiny pinprick of light. I know what it is: Brekker and Angeline have also made camp.

Storming the LHC Compound – Chain of events:

And so, we left the laboratory determined and energized. It was a calm night, the town was asleep and the stars alight. We moved silently through the ghost city, fully aware of the chaos that was to ensue. As we walked we took time to appreciate the architecture, the archway, the statues, the pillars and, when we got to Mother Motherland, we sat on the ridge, held hands (and paw) and looked upon her glorious face. It is quite something to be alive in a place when all else is absent. It is quite something even more to be alive in a place when only you know that everything around you is only moments from cataclysm. We had a calm sea inside us. I saw it in Angeline's eyes and I felt it in Paisley's slow, controlled breathing. I knew it in my mind because MGV2 was quietly humming the melody to Lucy's song (the song she sang in the sunlight as we climbed out from the dune).

We tested the gravity field of the ridge on the LHC side by throwing a rock and timing the descent and tracking the direction of its parabolic trajectory. Its fall was slow and it angled sharply towards the LHC pipeline, like a coin to a magnet. The rock struck the pipe, clung to it for a second and then fell to the ground. It seemed that the entire crater was a sort of 'bath' for irregular gravity.

We all turned and looked back at the town, bathed in moonlight, silent and asleep. Pripyat. We all blew her a kiss, turned and as one we leapt from the ridge down, down, down into the crater.

The freefall was exceptional. While there was no wind resistance in the traditional sense we did feel an upwards pressure upon us, like pole-to-pole magnetism. We fell slowly and for a few seconds poor Paisley scrabbled around trying to figure out what was happening. MGV2 reached out and stroked his belly and his leg kicked sweetly. We performed complex and conceived gestures in that timeless freefall and even the bullet in Paisley's eye worked its way free. He was on his back, falling down, and the bullet gently floated up, free of the socket and hung a few inches from his face.

The joy and novelty of our obscure descent threatened to overcome us. However, as we approached the LHC pipeline, we started to speed up slightly and we began to feel the pull towards the outer casing. Linking arms and legs, we repositioned ourselves ready to land feet first. It was approaching fast and we were about to strike when we halted suddenly.

Suspended above the pipe, we combined potential energies, converted them to kinetic and managed to right ourselves gently onto the pipeline. Paisley's bullet as if divinely connected to him, floated down and found its home in his eye socket once more.

We wasted no time in contemplating our bizarre free-fall. To business. Angeline rushed over to a service hatch, swung it open and climbed in. MGV2 followed. I picked up Paisley and followed lastly.

Inside the pipeline, Paisley took the lead, sprinting in the same manner as he has done during these last twelve days pursuit. We followed and just about kept up. MGV2 and I pooled our adrenaline and our energy but Angeline? She was something else. She overtook us, overtook Paisley and we could not see her feet touch the ground. She literally flew down the pipeline.

We got to the service tunnel and entered. I was about to close the hatch behind when Angeline instructed I leave it open. I did. Again we sprinted down until he came to the drop to the reactor floor. Paisley's eye could not perceive the drop ahead and so he bolted straight over the edge! At seeing the dog careening over, MGV2 dived forward and grabbed his hind leg just in time. However, he slid forward, carried by the momentum of the falling mutt. At the last second his free hand grabbed a rail and he brought them both to rest. Angeline glided over them and hovered above us all in the atrium of darkness. Paisley swung below, MGV2 holding him, me standing in the entrance to the service tunnel. Angeline, hovering, looked at us with a blank, clouded expression. She gazed at us and smiled. "I go," she said. "I go to him! Master of Engineer, the God

Machinist commands me!" and she rocketed upwards into the black.

We felt sick. Betrayed. I pulled MGV2 and Paisley up and back into the service tunnel. We took stock. Our conclusion? Press on. I climbed down the ladder to the reactor floor. MGV2 followed with the still shaking dog slung over his shoulder. It was clear that we would have to fight our way up the hundreds of leagues from the reactor floor to Tesla, to the observation decks and to Brekker himself.

When we climbed into the reactor floor we looked up and saw it. Sight of sights! Above was the Multiverse! The Final Fold was in its initial stages. Everything had a glow. Everything was warm. Everything was charged. Paisley's hair on end like steel. The grains of sand that made up the outer layers of our 'skin' seemed to separate and hover around us. We were breaking apart and yet held together. It seemed the magnetic field in every atom had expanded! We looked up into the Multiverse and we bore witness to many, many levels of light, stacked on top of each other, like sheets of paper, each showing a new or alternative view of what we were seeing.

It was like looking at a picture of a cat, but in the lens, you can also see a faint picture of a leopard, a lion, a jaguar, a tiger etc - each individual, each real if you focused on it, yet all merged if you focused on the whole. Imagine that, but extrapolated to an image of everything around you! We saw the reactor columns going up to the ceiling (these seemed constant) but around everything else, well on the gantries we saw many people burning, and yet many people cheering, all melded over each other. A deck of holograms. Disorientating is not enough to describe it.

Tesla. We had to get to Tesla and, of course, we had to get to Brekker. But the climb! The climb through this pandemonium of realities? It was too awful to contemplate, but had to be done. To Tesla we went.

61

Master G_ entry – in pursuit of Brekker and Angeline:

Campfire on horizon has not extinguished. They await us. We are advancing upon them. Fell asleep on the rocky dune. Lethargy finally overcoming us. Cursed myself for sleeping and losing time and distance when I awoke. Peeked over the brow of dune and was amazed to see fire still there. We continued our pursuit. We have covered good ground and there is no change in the fires position. They must be waiting for us. Waiting for what? To parlay? To kill us? Only one way to find out.

Resting now. Noticed that the pursuit is easier today. I have not been wading through the sand and have not fallen apart or melted into any dune. I have remained solid and focused throughout the day. Decided on a test. I tried to fall away into sand and reform myself. It worked but only after considerable concentration. The pain in my mind was almost unbearable, but I held my focus for long enough and I managed to disintegrate. Reformation was equally hard and I almost did not make it. I will not attempt full dispersal again, only localised - a hand or a leg. Now that I am resting, I will recount further the events that took place thirteen days ago.

————•◦•————

Storming the LHC Compound – Chain of events (con't):

We went to Tesla. We ran through the labyrinth of corridors and passages that led up towards the observation deck. It was a fever dream. The collision of realities was nauseating and as we ran through each one, we felt pulled apart, punched, kicked and crushed by the chaotic gravity. The abnormality of the fold ravaged us as we passed through many, many iterations of the same journey. By the time we got only halfway up, we no longer knew which reality we occupied fully and had the divisive and confusing feeling of being posited over a myriad of spaces at the same time. We vomited constantly as our run fell to a walk then to a stagger until eventually a crawl.

We were about to halt for good, overcome with the impossibility of our physical location and the subsequent strain on our psychology and we lay upon the grated walkway in the centre of the Multiverse. All around us electricity spiked off the walls and the noise, the noise originated in our very souls before hitting our ears, our atoms faltering, our blood boiling, our skin liquefying – we were done for! And then, at the end of all things, I felt a tug on my collar and a pull followed by a growl. It was Paisley! He was dragging me on along the corridor, his one eye bright and his bullet eye gleaming with electricity as it flailed around the bullet in his socket like a plasma dome.

I held out my arm and grabbed hold of MGV2's wrist and Paisley dragged us both, seemingly unaffected by the impossibilities that wracked MGV2 and I. Of course, he was invisible to all but us and he does not exist in any of the realities of this one Multiverse. At least, he didn't in that moment as the realities he existed in were yet to be brought forth into Brekker's mad cauldron. So he remained alive.

He pulled us along to the end of the gantry when an almighty thunderclap came. We looked up and saw the force blast the entire roof of the reactor out into the sky. Corridors and walkways above us shattered and melted with the force but no debris fell onto us as it was all instantly turned to ash. The sky was angry and the Borealis was all around, the washes of green and purple ripping across the sky. There was a spider's web of electricity above linking the celestial blanket and it seemed to be descending upon us.

The explosion of the reactor roof seemed like the lid of a pressure cooker had blown. We settled atomically as air returned to our lungs and our circulation regulated. Slowly, we got too our feet.

MGV2 and I barged our way through the connecting door at the end of the gantry and made our way further up the compound towards the observation room.

———•◦•———

To note – while I write this, a development has come about. Looking out now at the campfire, I can see that it hasn't moved. The change is in the landscape. A dust cloud has descended on the horizon, dimming the firelight. I can see within the cloudy hazy shapes. Giant forms moving up and down slowly like seesaws. Gargantuan! I have to strain hard to see them. When I think I can understand their structure, they vanish again behind the dust clouds.

————•◦•————

Storming the LHC Compound – Chain of events (c'ont):

We reached the observation deck in stronger character, our confidence growing with each level ascended.

We reached the final level and saw the T-junction ahead. It was where we split up. MGV2 had to get to Tesla and I had to get to Brekker. It was clear now that Angeline had betrayed us totally and the Final Stage Firing was in full swing. We had no chance of saving the workers, or the town – at least, not as priority. Was Angeline in control of her actions? Probably not. Still accountable? Most definitely.

We split up as we had work to do. Hopeful of success. Fearful that we would not reunite.

MGV2 ran off one way, I the other and soon I came to an empty observation room. The far wall was one giant window that looked out over the reactor core. It was a perfect view of the chaos around. I stood for a few seconds, amazed at the scale of the operation – the gantries criss-crossing, the monumental Uranium rods and the great glass columns standing firm against the Final Firings onslaught. I snapped out of my wonderment and went was about to leave when another thunderclap rocked the complex and I was thrown across the room, smashing into a terminal. I staggered to my feet and fought against subsiding gravity. I felt as if the whole room was on a listing ship on the brink of capsizing. I fought forward to the window and I grabbed onto a rail just as the gravity in the room shifted 180 degrees. Paisley shot to the ceiling and would have impaled himself on a twisted upturned desk leg had I not grabbed his tail at the last second. As I held on and the gravity shifted once more and I saw through the observation window a giant shard of concrete and steel come crashing in through the reactor roof. It fell between the great glass columns and pierced the floor. It was her sword! Mother Motherland had lost her broadsword and it had come crashing down upon us! The impact obliterated many gantries, shattering the windows of reality as it anchored many eventualities into one single conjoined fate. Many people across the Multiverse expired when Mother Motherland laid down her arms.

A hairline crack appeared in the corner of the observation window and, as the gravity began to shift again, I could see the furniture begin to bend toward the glass. A single blow to it would prove catastrophic – we didn't have to wait long at all. The gravity shifted in one swoop and both Paisley and I were flung against the glass. We smashed through it and were blasted into the reactor core. I tried to hold Paisley close to me, expecting to take any impact on my back but as soon as we were clear of the observation room and out into the reactor room our gravity suddenly re-aligned top to bottom and we shot upwards along with the shards of the window and the debris from the sword as if we were in a vacuum, sucked out into the Borealis!

The floor of the reactor grew small as we were being pulled up alongside the blade of Mother Motherland's sword. I could see the blazing night sky through the hole of the roof. We were headed for destruction but we were saved by the sword's hilt. I crashed, back first, into the underside of the swords cross-guard and stuck to it, pressed against the great concrete quillons looking down at the chaos below. I held Paisley tight to my chest, praying the gravity would not shift again and send us crashing back down to the floor.

Directly below I could see a walkway, perhaps 200 feet lower than us that had so far sustained no damage. I could not understand how that could be, given the wanton destruction all around. Through the smoke and shimmering light, at one end of the gantry below I saw a worker next to a terminal, still working away, totally oblivious to the chaos. I knew instantly that it was Tesla, that poor creature.

It was then that my vision changed. The view of the walkway, the reactor floor and the sword fell away and there was a moment of blackness and panic which passed as, while my body remained pinned to the crossguard of the broadsword, my eyes told me differently.

My new vision showed me that I was walking along on a gantry, the gravity constant and real. Up ahead I could see a closed door. I opened it and stepped out on the walkway in the reactor room. Directly ahead of me, at the far end of the gantry stood Tesla, monotonously operating his terminal.

While my body was pinned to the underside of Mother Motherland's sword hilt, my eyes were projecting the vision of Master G_ Version Two.

62

Master G_ entry – in pursuit:

I am in an oilfield. The giant seesaws are oil pumps made of
bone – like giant legs plunging into the earth – I have walked
towards the campfire and I am getting close to them, I can tell.
They are not moving and I am certain now that they are waiting
for me. In the morning Paisley and I walked from the dune and
into the red dust cloud that masked the giant leg-drills. The
wind was severe and I had to wrap my coat around me, holding
it close and leaning into the sand-blizzard. Paisley this time
struggled to keep up as the loose sand collected around his
paws, the grains battering his face, filling his eye socket and
weighing down the side of his skull. The wind became so
intense that the grains of sand were pulling my skin off also –
grains flaking away – I was in full control, and yet I could feel
myself turning to sand against my will. Strange paradox. The
sand-skin fell away but only so far as to reveal bone! For a
while I was literally a walking skeleton! Real bone – cancellous
and cortical composition – why did that not turn to sand? Why
only partial dematerialization? I am becoming human once
more – rebuilding again. I regret losing my ability to turn to
sand as it has proven useful. Saved my 'life'.

Writing this now as the wind has died down. We are in the
centre of the ghastly oilfield. Read over old notes, seems Old
Angeline from the train has walked through here before. Before

I met her at the train station, before she turned into a cyclone. I wrote before that I would fear coming across the place she described. That now, I know, is not true – I do not fear this place. I seem indifferent to its biomechanics. Perhaps I have seen too much. Numb to TheNeverRealm. Perhaps I am too focused on my meeting with Brekker and New Angeline that all else is secondary?

The Bone Drills have large, calcified rock bases, like coral, supporting the giant femurs – they are large enough to provide habitable cracks and holes. Good crawl spaces in which to find shelter. I have crawled, feet first into a crevice a metre above the ground on the south facing drill. The wind is calm and I have a view of the pinprick campfire on the horizon. Less than a day's pursuit. Paisley remains outside, sitting and watching the campfire. He is breathing steadily. I have little room to move and can barely write. It is like being loaded into a cannon, the campfire being my bullseye. At least I am safe from the elements.

───•◦•───

Storming of the LHC Compound – (c'ont):

My body was pinned to the sword's crossguard due to the inverted gravity that the Final Stage Firing had incurred but I could see through MGV2's eyes. However, his vision had not entirely replaced mine but was more of an overlay with reduced opacity.

He (I will write it as 'he' and not 'I') was on the walkway and the gravity was 'normal' – the gantry seemed to be impervious to disorder around. Ahead he could see Tesla still at his station, operating his levers with that same metronomic sadness. He screamed at the automaton – screamed his name, screamed for him to move – it was only when he said, "It's Master G_," that anything registered. Tesla began to slow his levers down. His head twitched a little. MGV2 began to advance along the gantry.

It was then that gravity pinning me to the sword began to slip – I felt as if being gently lowered on a rope – a rope whose tensile strength was weakening. I held Paisley tightly to my chest as we began to lower towards the floor and all around me, a whirlwind of debris and electrical charges cackled.

MGV2 was almost on him when Tesla stopped his terminal operation completely. As soon as he brought the two levers to rest, the gantry was rocked by a crippling sideways force! It buckled awfully in the middle, as if it had suddenly materialized into this chaos. The buckle forced the gantry to rip its holding from the reactor wall at MGV2's end. The centre of this now 'V' shaped walkway smashed into the side of one of the reactor columns causing the globules within to charge like boiling water. Tesla's side of the walkway was barely holding on to its stanchion as MGV2, on his freed end, swung wildly and repeatedly crashed into the reactor tube. He was shouting for Tesla to get safe, to get away, but the scientist just stood there.

I was screaming too – screaming at MGV2 to get clear, screaming to Tesla to wake-up. Paisley was barking also and we could both feel the 'chord' of gravity connecting us to the underside of the sword slipping, soon to send us plummeting down the hundreds of feet to the ground.

MGV2 looked up at me and I looked down at him. In my mixed vision I saw myself, and then he said to me, "Go now, go save yourself," and he pointed up to the hole in the roof.

It was then that MGV2's vision faded away and my true eyesight returned. I managed to rotate myself in that faltering gravitational field so that I was now facing the hole in the roof and the ocean-like Borealis in the sky. The crossguard of the sword was only a few feet above me. Paisley barked at me and nodded towards it. We understood each other. I pressed him off of my chest, held him up and with a monumental heave I threw him up. He scrabbled in the air, his legs kicking and scraping through the resistance and he made it! He managed to grab onto the edge of the quillon, his hind legs, digging in and he scrambled onto it and looked down at me. I unclipped my belt and swung it up to him. It took just one attempt for the animal to catch it in his mouth.

Paisley braced for the strain and I began to climb. I was almost there when the 'chord' of gravity finally gave way and it shifted to its natural state. My legs swung down violently and Paisley scrabbled forward, falling half over the edge of the crossguard. He dug his back legs in, gripping harder so hard that three of his teeth shattered and still he kept his grip! He began to backup, and I climbed faster. I was in reach when the poor dog's jaw dislocated and snapped open, sending the belt flying out of his mouth! I swung my arm up and just managed to grip the concrete quillon in time. I scrambled up and crawled towards poor Paisley. He was lying on his side in great pain, his legs kicking and scraping against the hilt. I bent down and looked at the damage. It was a clean dislocation. I held his head firm and fixed him with a stern gaze. I nodded three times and on the third, I snapped his jaw back into his socket. A look of relief washed over the dogs face and he got to his feet.

We were now standing on the hilt of Mother Motherland's sword, the tip of which was impaled into the reactor floor almost out of sight below us. As we looked over the edge, we saw the folding realties continue and the complex begin to twist and distress under the great weight. I looked up and saw that the pommel of the great sword was resting against the edge of the roof. It was our escape route. With Paisley slung over my shoulder, I climbed the handle with relative ease and within minutes we were standing on the outside of the reactor at the highest point possible and the very tip of reality. The Borealis was all around, the colours penetrating us, flowing through our veins, through our bones. We were glowing!

The downward curve of what remained of the dome roof was easily traversed with many foot and handholds available to us on our descent. Paisley went down head first and I followed feet first. Though we had escaped the chaos inside the reactor, we were not done - we were not out of the fire or the fight! We had to reforge our strategy. The new plan was to find a way back inside the complex. We had saved ourselves from the sword, but we still had not seen to Brekker! We had not even seen any sign of him or the treacherous Angeline. It was at this point that I was still sure that we had a chance. I still held spirit. It was then in that flash of warm hope that MGV2's vision overcame mine once again.

It was then that all hope fell away.

63

I held fast my grip against the dome and pressed against the vibrating concrete. Eyes closed, almost frozen and still MGV2's vision projected straight into my mind. He was stranded on the gantry, swinging wildly and crashing into the Reactor columns. On the other section, Tesla remained statue-like by his terminal. MGV2 was calling out to him, but now his voice carried panic. He was clearly fearful for his safety for the first time and my stomach turned with guilt at the realisation of my abandonment.

MGV2 was braced against the handrails, the section of the gantry bending and twisting towards the floor and as it swung back against the reactor column it lodged against it for a few moments. MGV2 slid downwards, hitting the column with the full force impacting upon his back. His jacket, shirt and first few layers of skin were instantly flayed off. He screamed in agony as he began to melt against the heat of the column. His section of walkway was now in decline whilst up ahead, Tesla's section still held onto the wall on the other side of the reactor room. MGV2 looked up, his eyes wild, the pain numbing his senses and above him, we (for my eyes were still his) saw a fracture running up the concrete blade of Mother Motherland's sword, splintering and cracking upwards like a stubborn river carving its way through a mountain. We knew instantly that once the crack reached the great crossguard the stress fracture would be fatal and the entire hilt would come crashing down and, given its position, would smash straight through the walkway sending MGV2 to his death and leaving Tesla stuck on his side. The fracture continued to climb and so MGV2 gripped onto the handrails and clenched his jaw, slowly pulling himself forward. His flesh began to peel away from the reactor tube exposing his musculature and his spine. He pulled harder, gripped tighter and eventually the glue that used to be his skin and flesh gave way. The fracture reached the hilt. The whole crossguard, handle and pommel dislodged, wavering precariously on the blade, coolly teetering like God's finger choosing which path of destruction to plump for. MGV2 looked over at Tesla who did not look back. A moment of clarity swept through our conjoined consciousness: an idea.

MGV2 pulled himself to his feet and began to run up the inclined walkway. He was halfway up and gaining speed when the great hilt chose to topple towards the gantry. It broke free, careening down and bringing with it a meteor shower of concrete debris. MGV2 and the hilt were destined to collide, the shadow of the falling hilt casting itself over him and with a groan it stuck the gantry. MGV2 dived into the air as his section shattered into a falling heap of twisted metal. He was in mid-air, diving straight towards the hilt and, on the other side, Tesla's section of walkway when the hilt leaned over, the gravity below pulling it so. The collision had all but shattered the hilt and it broke apart as it toppled away from Tesla and towards the diving MGV2 and the ground below. MGV2, twisting in the air in an impossible dive, turned himself into sand just as the hilt fell upon him. Magnificently, he was able to command all his grains to fly through the cracks and out the other side of the falling hilt as it tumbled down, thundering into the reactor column in its descent. Still as sand now, MGV2 with his vision projected into my mind by willpower alone, brought all his grains together to form a long spear and towards Tesla they headed.

The MGV2 Sand-Spear poured into Tesla's ear, filling him like an hourglass and suddenly the broken scientist was active and possessed by the sand and spirit of my other self. My vision was his, my mind now a shared third. Tesla, though comatose in appearance, still had an active mind and as our minds melded, Tesla's voice came into the back of our thoughts. He kept repeating, "What is happening? Why am I here? Where is Evelyn?" But his confusion didn't last long. With our minds fully integrated a fire was ignited under his feet and he began to run with the speed of three, off the gantry and into the observation room. Through corridors, leaping over desks, ducking under fallen masonry, he ran. And that is not all! As he passed through field upon field of realities, he pulled with him survivors! As if he had some magnetism, they were wrenched from their panic and from their distressed world, and they followed him all the way towards a ground level service entrance. He must have taken with him at least fifty workers, technicians and scientists.

Outside on the reactor dome, the well of hope sprung once more inside me. I scrambled down until I found myself on the roof of a lower building. Paisley was waiting for me, barking and running around in circles, trying to hurry me along. With our overlaid vision, I tracked Tesla's escape route from the roof. Paisley and I began to run at full pelt over exposed pipes, exhaust vents and leaping great extractor fans. Below us, inside the complex, Tesla ran with his group of survivors. We were almost there!

I could see the edge of the complex approaching fast and I prayed that the gravity would still be attracted to the LHC pipeline. Paisley and I leapt into the air and sailed unnaturally far, perhaps kilometres as the gravity of the LHC pipeline pulled us towards it. And, as before, we gently landed upon the top of the pipe. We turned to see if the others had exited. We looked down at the hatch below the roof we had leapt from. I concentrated my vision on Tesla's. He could see the hatch ahead! He was almost there!

It was in that moment that I looked to see the heart breaking sight of Mother Motherland, her great sword-arm broken and her other arm drooping like a candle over flame. She was melting into the Reactor Dome. The great statue was falling.

Her melting, outstretched arm gave way and fell into the reactor core. There was a flash of pink light and an eruption of liquid! The reactor columns had finally shattered. In my mind I heard manic screams. I looked inside to Tesla's vision. They were at the hatch, but the corridor was pulsing and breaking apart. The complex itself was melting. The survivors were screaming as electricity and fire began to rise from the depths of the tunnel. Tesla, under the control of MGV2 grabbed hold of the hatch, his hands fusing irretrievably from it and he yanked it open, pinning himself twixt hatch and wall. He shouted to the survivors to run out but they barely needed speaking to. They piled through the hatchway onto the ashen ground of the crater and fled in all directions. I screamed in anguish and scratched at my head, trying to pull the horrific image from my mind and from my reality.

The LHC complex was liquefying, with Mother Motherland melting into it as if sinking into a pit of purple lava. The corridor collapsed slowly, almost organically and Tesla dissolved first into the wall and hatch then, like the statue above us all, he joined the great lake. The image in my mind faded out and a part of my soul followed. He was gone. They were both gone. No longer, no more.

Distraught and almost numb I sat on the pipeline as it too began to sink into the rising lake. The survivors of the Final Stage Firing did not become survivors of the lake. I sat and wept as each became as one with the liquid. Some waded forward, desperate to live, some embraced others and stood still, some even fell on their backs and floated along, consigned to their doom until they were no more.

Tesla and MGV2 had saved not one: they had died in vain.

If it weren't for Paisley I would have joined them also. Not wanting to die, the animal had been barking at me since the final destruction of the complex. He did not sit next to me. He did not give up. Despite losing teeth and dislocating his jaw, he still found it in himself to bite my arm hard enough to snap me out of my despondency. It worked.

Had I sat a minute longer, I would have dissolved with the last of the pipeline. I grabbed my great dog and slung him over my shoulders and around the back of my neck, like a hunter carrying a dead stag. He gripped me tight enough to maintain purchase and I leapt off the pipeline, grabbed hold of the hard ridge wall and began to climb.

My pain and sadness were put to the back of my mind as the climb was hard. The heat from the rising lake below was intense and made my grip sweaty and loose but still we climbed and, eventually, we reached the safety of the crater's ridge.

As we climbed over it, we were greeted by an orange glow in the distance. But this glow did not carry the intensity and wonder of the Borealis. This glow was fierce and dreadful. We knew what it signified.

Ahead of us, Pripyat burned.

64

We had failed utterly. We stood on the ridge looking at the burning city while below us churned a lake that was once the epicentre of the Multiverse. Countless lives from countless realities now drifted through that primordial soup: None of whom needed to be there, all of whom failed by me.

MGV2. Nikola Tesla - How I failed you both.

Paisley and I walked slowly through a no-man's land of cold grey earth towards the town. The Borealis had been replaced by dulled stars in an indifferent sky. We didn't know why we were walking towards the fire. To Angeline? To Brekker? Where they even there? We didn't know. We didn't even know if the Final Firing had even been successful. Maybe it had and this was intended? We knew nothing other than bitter failure. We had no real control over our legs. They just began to trudge by themselves.

The ground had changed too. The concrete was cracked and charred but also loose, like walking on unset paving. Through the cracks we could see a bedding of sand indicating that the desert below was pulling the ground apart. In time, as the sands shift enough, the whole site will be disbanded. Maybe subsumed. Maybe spread so far apart as to be a puzzle only solvable when viewed from the cosmos.

The town of Pripyat burned as if it was the town of Couldwell. By that I mean it burned as if made of old, dry wood and not concrete and steel. By the time we got there, the fires were in their final stages. Everything was blackened and everything was silent, save for the crackling of the flames. No wind, little heat. A cold pyre for the town.

We were able to walk through it quite easily as the outlying streets were deserted of debris and bodies. We walked slowly, sadly, all the while looking around for signs of life. None came until we reached the top end of Torpor Avenue where we finally discovered the bodies. Not fallen, not crumpled and not piled over each other like rats looking to escape. No - every person was like a statue, arms by their sides, upright. Gently burning. They were lined along the pavement of the avenue facing each other like chess pieces.

We walked down the middle of Torpor Avenue holding back the tears and the vomit as the smell of burning flesh invaded us further than a sensation should be allowed to - right into the pit of our stomachs so that we could almost taste it, to the back of mind so that we could almost feel it, to the corners of our eyes so that wherever we looked we could see the black, charred skin and the grey, cooked flesh beneath. They stood and burned.

Further we walked, past the hotel and out to the other side of the town, back to where the train had left me, seemingly years before.

We stood on the sand bank with all that was left of Pripyat behind us. Ahead lay the nothingness of the red desert. We both sat down and just looked out. It was only then that the tiredness hit me. Eyes heavy. Body broken and battered. Psychologically torn to shreds. I felt as I did when I was sinking into my desert mind with MGV2. Only this time he was not there, and I felt that Lucy would not come to pull me through. I was so tired. I tried to sleep but I could not. Not for the repetitive question in my head: what happened to Angeline and Brekker? Over and over it went, in turn generating other questions. Did they survive? Where are they? There was no peace to be had.

Paisley was curled up next to me, his head facing the remains of Pripyat, while I looked in the opposite direction, out at the desert. He whimpered slightly and sat up. I looked down to see his head lilting to the side in that inquisitive manner of his. I turned around to see what had caught his attention.

I stood up to behold. It started first as a movement of the sand under the concrete slabs then. Then, sand gently spilled up and over the paving, carpeting Pripyat. Wind picked up all around the edge of the town two hundred feet from me and moving in a circular motion, like a huge wheel. As the motion intensified more loose sand whipped it into a large ring, almost enveloping the smouldering remains of the city. I dug my feet in to stay on top of the dune. The ring of sand began to rotate faster and faster, and then began to contract in ever decreasing circles, all the while growing upwards into the sky – a cyclone forming before our eyes!

I tracked its epicentre as it seemed that the sand was being drawn from under all of Pripyat and being pulled towards the site of the LHC Compound. It grew and creaked until finally it was fully formed and monstrous in size - taller even than Mother Motherland had once been. Towering over everything, it swirled and howled. I looked into its heart and saw forms, reliefs and impressions emerge. I saw huge faces form for a moment and then break apart, distinct in their separate features and terrifying in their size. One wailing and sad the other angry and tyrannical. Angeline and Brekker rose from the desert around us.

The tornado held its position and the faces swirled, as if surveying their work, and then it slowly made its way into the distance, crushing the buildings in its path and pulling those behind it to the ground. Into the distance they weaved.

That was my quarry and my charge. They were who I sought. Brekker had a question for me, and Lucy had answer to give him. I patted Paisley and he nuzzled my hand. The journal went in my pocket and towards that great tornado the two of us gave chase.

Part Six

65

And so, after twelve days arduous trekking we find ourselves here, burrowed into the base of the oil-pump, safe from the elements and facing our enemy.

Our pursuit, as noted, was hard and determined and only once did we almost give up. It was on the day, perhaps the tenth or eleventh when we lost sight of it all. We had spent half the day climbing up a particularly treacherous dune made entirely of loose sand and many times we had almost reached the top before sliding down and almost burying ourselves. Our endurance pushed to the very limit. Not ashamed to say that a few times I screamed in anger. Cried in frustration. Paisley did not. Every time he found himself half buried he would dig his way out again, growl at the peak and trudge forward. As ever, I followed him and after a full day we finally made the top, exhausted.

We lay there on that dune breathing hard and elated to have conquered the beast. It was only after a few moments respite that we noticed the tornado to have gone. Though we lost sight of it, we could not give up, not after the trial of the dune and we spent the next day heading towards the tornado's last position, praying that we were not straying too far, or that it had not vanished forever. It was in the night that the pinprick of fire appeared. It seems that Brekker and Angeline can turn themselves to sand and reform at will like I am able to. Upon spotting the fire, we realised that we had held true to our course and we were not too far from them. This lifted our spirits, and we proceeded. It was after half a day's trek that the mirage of this oilfield appeared and we entered into it still with that campfire on the horizon. That campfire was our beacon – still is our beacon – and they wait for us. I am confident it will still be there in the morning. Going to sleep now. Little point walking out through this storm. Could lose sight and lose way.

Sleep now.

—————•◦•—————

I dreamt! A real dream! It was set in a realm that I have not been to and have not even seen in a daguerreotype. I was in a large bedroom, modest but spacious, perhaps in a mountain lodge. It was high up and through the window I could see the lush and verdant tops of mountains and below the room I could see lakes of crystal waters. The room I was in had a large open bay window and the breeze blew the white lace curtains seductively I was standing with my back to a wall, an unmade bed to my side. I was happy, excited and my heart beat pleasantly fast. Everything felt right. I could hear faint singing from another room. The air was so fresh. I felt no pain or unease but only a desire to look out of the bay window and to stand with the wind upon my face and gaze at the mountains and the lakes below. I stepped forward…but I could not move. I tried again. Failure. I was stuck to the wall. I tried and struggled and slowly all serenity washed away leaving only anxiety. I tried to move forward, but I felt pulled backwards, into the wall itself! The colour of the brick filtered into my vision as the brilliant sky and white linen in the room turned to terracotta. The singing faded and soon all was the colour of red sand.

I woke up, not with a start, but with the dogged tiredness of a factory worker consigned to work eternal. Paisley was up already. The sky was cloudy and we could not tell what time of day it was. There was a bitter wind. My lips chapped and cold, my throat dry.

We can still see the pinprick fire in the distance. We go to it now and we believe our enemy to be within a day's march. I hope that between the edge of the oilfield and their encampment lie no obstacles as, if they do, we could find ourselves trapped in this bitter desert without shelter. We go onward. That dream is still with me, bittersweet it is. With that in mind, we go.

———•◦•———

At a ridge – we are upon them!

The walk here was uneventful, the wind came and went, sometimes bitter, sometimes warm. The cyclones kept their usual route across the horizon and back again. The oil pumps disappeared just as they had come – like mirages, shimmering into nothing as we pressed onwards.

We are standing upon a ridge, similar to the LHC crater, but much smaller and much shallower. On the other side we can see their fire and we can even make out the shapes of Angeline and

Brekker sitting beside it. Cannot make out the detail of their faces. They are just silhouettes by a fire. Behind them there lies a great plateau, surreal in its flatness, like a plate of sheet steel. Red like the desert around and stretching on in all directions for an eternity. On the horizon behind them we see no cyclones. Perhaps we are at the very edge of TheNeverRealm.

This could possibly be the final entry in this journal, though many times I, MGV2 and Tesla (writing their names still pains my heart) many times we have written "this may be the last," many times it nearly was. But we have never been so close to the end and to Brekker. I know I may now never see Lucy and never get to wherever she may be. All that remains for us to do is make this last passage towards them, hold parlay and then when he asks his question give him his answer.

66

I am sat on a pier watching Angeline and Brekker walk back the way we have come. Back into TheNeverRealm. Paisley sat next to me. We have parlayed. We have exchanged questions and answers so now, they go. Behind me, at the end of the pier (the edge of TheNeverRealm) lies the FurtherUnknown: The steel flat plateau that I am soon to sail across.

I am overcome with what has passed me, what I am watching walk away into the desert and of what awaits me now. Relief, fear, hope and trepidation – they are the realities that are folding into each other within my soul.

Before we begin our last voyage. Here is how the end of it all came about.

———•◦•———

My last entry detailed the crater that divided us from them. We climbed down in good time. It not as treacherous as the LHC crater and was easily traversed. We walked happily through the bed and as we did I felt a sudden twinge and then a jolt inside my limbs. I felt hardened as a solidifying presence came over me. It was a long forgotten feeling of substantial weight. I thought back to the effort it took to turn to sand during the pursuit and I thought about the pain and trouble of reformation. Looking up to the forthcoming ridge and the quarry thereupon, I thought about turning to sand one last time. It was a risk to attempt it, nevertheless, I was fearless and I concentrated every atom to channel one thought: "turn to sand, reform." I concentrated but I could not fully fall apart. Only a few layers of skin disintegrated and no more. I am so very nearly human again. So nearly.

I reformed the few layers and we continued to the shallow crater's rim. I climbed, what I thought, would be my final climb with Paisley slung over my shoulders. We reached the top and I dusted myself off and looked over to see, not ten-foot away, sitting around a small fire the treacherous New Angeline and what I assumed to be Brekker. Angeline sat on her knees, hands together, her head bowed. Brekker…well at first I did not know what to believe.

Next to Angeline stood the awful bust under which I had discovered Brekker's journal entries. The cold, bronze angular frame, the long face, the thin limbed tripod it stood upon and that foul metallic progeny in its belly. It now stood before me. And it was animated!

"Welcome Master G_," it said with a processed voice that was at once Brekker's, but at the same time not. It had a lower register, a hum that was held in whatever voice box was inside that throat before appearing in the air. With its arms, lacking of hands, it gestured to sit by the fire. I stood in shock.

"Please," it said, "you and your animal are tired." He then looked down to Paisley, "Hello dear boy, it has been many centuries."

Paisley slunk behind me, cowering in fear. Brekker's tripod-legs folded into each other and his bronze body slunk down to be by the fire side. Angeline did not raise her head to greet me.

Mesmerized by this abomination before me I sat down and, sensing my calm, Paisley sat next to me. The poor mutt was trembling.

"Please excuse my present form," Brekker began softly, "some lifetimes I am encased within it, some lifetimes I am not...most lifetimes I am neither. It is needless to ponder the vessel. It always falls apart."

The reflection of the flames licked over the bronze finish of his 'skin'. His coolness and his control rattled me greatly. I debated whether to refer to him as 'him' or 'it'. I keenly searched for that elusive spark of life within the recessed pits where his eyes should have been

I could not speak. I was numb. All the questions. All the pain. Revenge, fear and anger burned through me. I was at tau zero travelling through my cosmos of inquisition and I managed to splutter only one question. After I had come so far, been through so much all I could mumble were the words; "what happens next?" Shameful question. I cowardly blurted out an apology directed more to myself and to the fire, rather than to the dark machine in front of me. That metallic voice resonated in the air. It said, "I have missed you dear friend."

It was then that my courage returned. Maybe his response was designed to illicit anger? I cared not and I screamed and dove forward to tackle him. He did not move, but struck out his arm, crashing it into my sternum and knocking the wind right out of me. I fell backwards gasping. Paisley roared and leapt forward and he met a similar fate and was sent sprawling down next to me.

With the sound of a clockwork watch being wound, the Brekker Machine stood up. He looked out towards the great plateau ahead. He looked up at the starless sky, and back to where we had come from. Somewhere back there lays the toppled ruins of Pripyat.

"I cannot count the ways in which we have died," he said, "the ways in which I have constructed, deconstructed and reconstructed all things. I have searched through all realities as if they were scriptures baring secrets. Passed through time, space and death. I have occupied all things, studied and unravelled dimensions like old tapestries and yet the answer defies me."

He bent down and ran his truncated arms through the sand with the intention of letting it sift through his fingers like an hourglass. The grains did not stick to his sleek veneer - his gesture meaningless.

He stood up once more, again with that clockwork ticking. Nearly eight feet tall. I scanned him for signs of life. Nothing. Not even that gleaming progeny in his abdomen looked alive. There was not life, there was not death, nor heaven or hell, beginning or end…for what business do any of those childish impositions have in the unfathomable expanse of the Multiverse? I suddenly felt confident.

He looked over to me and, in an authoritative key, he generated a statement. A statement that intoned a question, as we both knew it prescribed a specific response. One he had been waiting for.

"Tell me something."

"Firstly," I countered, "tell me what happens next". It seemed now that the second time round, my question felt not so shameful. I could see that answering his question was all I needed to do to progress. A simple answer. No grand fight, no final confrontation. Just a question and an answer.

I suddenly eschewed all sense of revenge and anger. I felt no need to place myself at odds with him, or anyone. MGV2, Tesla and many others had died, but many others had died before and will again. Brekker's journey no longer mattered to me. What mattered was what lay ahead and I felt compelled to seek ascension. I remembered the two rules of Dream Investigation and so I repeated my question, imbuing it with an emotionless resonance that seemed to match his.

"What happens next?"

He mechanically lifted his head to both sides.

"You will leave us," he said. "You will sail into the FurtherUnknown which lies behind me and beyond TheNeverRealm. You will keep going onward. Maybe to your end, maybe to your NeverEnd. I do not know. I only know that you will leave."

His words carried finality and relief overcame me. A great feeling, perhaps the greatest of feelings. I was going over the great plateau. He must have recognized the understanding and acceptance in my eyes, as he nodded at me in compliance.

"What have you to ask me?" I said, preparing to deliver my answer, stand up and leave immediately after it was given as there would be then nothing more to say or do but to simply go.

The flames licked over his sleek face, imbuing the dark recesses around his 'eyes' with an approximation of humanity.

"I understand everything," he said, quietly, "I can control realities and I can control the full psyche." At his words, the firelight lit up Angeline's face to show her eyes clouded over and her expression blank, like she used to be: A Sleepwalker.

"I have done and undone everything all to search for my one answer. It concerns Lucy. I have never understood anything, nor felt anything in all my incarnations as I did when working with her. I was fervent. Inspired. And a great subject she was. Brave." He stopped there and looked at me, eager to illicit a reaction and gauge my internal landscape. I gave nothing away. Lucy's answer was to be greater than any puny actions of retribution I could administer. I was sure of it. Of her.

"When she expired," he continued, "I was lost. Plagued by visions and teased by dreams and theory that dangled and pulled away from me before I could grasp them. We had made the final discovery, Lucy and I, but I was not there to witness it. It was in her moment of transition from one world to the next that she created The Unified Theory of Everything. But I was in another room, mixing tonics and balms! After she expired, I tore through realities trying to rediscover the fire that we had birthed – trying to recreate it. As I broke worlds and souls apart I got further towards it. My designs got more complex and more wondrous, edging ever closer. I spun around in that wheel of trial and error until in a mechanical dream I heard a sentence floating through a field of black. The words 'Master G_ knows' came to me and it was then that I was shown the course that would lead me to build the LHC complex, Mother Motherland, the bringing together of all time and place to find my ultimate answer. My question is thusly: Master G_ what were dear Lucy's last words upon her earth?"

I was incredulous. That was it? This machine had turned the Multiverse upside down and crushed it in upon itself a million times over and again to find the answer to such a little question? For a moment I was blank. How could I answer? I was not present when Lucy died…I did not know her last words and, as I realised that, I felt the same desirous need to turn the Multiverse upside down to find it. In that moment I would have gone to the lengths Brekker had gone to in order to find out. I closed my eyes, searching for her last words. I had to know the answer!

It was in my blankest of moments that I saw her. There, in a meadow by a crystal clear lake she sat against a mulberry tree. Her white cotton dress dazzling in the sunshine, her eyes flecked with light of the Borealis. She looked at me and smiled and with that smile carried her final words, drifting towards me like dandelion snow on an autumn breeze. I opened my eyes and flashed a brilliant glare at the Brekker Machine. My Lucy, dear Lucy, in her final moments of unspeakable pain had uttered a Couplet from her most beloved poet. So I told him what her last words had been:

> 'Always will God Machinist be lost,
> Twisted and mad inside Great Ouroboros'

As her words carried over the campfire the flames flickered and a zephyr blew the words into the sleek veneer of Brekker's armour and they entered his mind. He froze. His bronze turned to a sickly grey as he comprehended his ultimate answer. His head jolted slightly then slumped loosely. Like the victim of a hanging, his head lolled. A second gentle zephyr came through the air and at the gust's gentle touch the engineer fell backwards onto the sand with a great thud. We sat there for a moment, unsure how to act.

We sat in silence for a few moments until a sickly wheeze came from his torso. We leaned slightly towards him and heard an awful scratching from within his abdomen. The progeny! The bulbous lump in his abdomen was moving! We could see hands pushing and pulling from inside, the bronze seemingly now having the viscosity of skin. Fingers broke through! They pulled the abdomen open from the inside and from within the carcass of Brekker came a wet, ugly baby. Angeline picked it up and held it to her chest. She carried no look of love. The nauseating baby rotated its head towards me and smiled a revolting smile: Brekker Tumour Baby /Alexander Tumour Baby.

67

And so here we are, watching Angeline and Brekker walk back into TheNeverRealm. After the Tumour Baby birthed itself, we all stood up, our meeting at an end. Angeline looked at me, almost awake, almost asleep and with one of her eyes holding recognition for me and for what we had been through. There was definite pain there and I hoped that it was pain for Tesla and not for herself. I could not be sure. Her other eye had clouded over into the awful cataract I used to fear, then had forgotten and now recalled.

I offered my hand to shake, but she did not take it. She simply turned and walked down the pier into the red desert. I wonder whether she will meet me again. Whether a version of me will be there at that train station, or maybe she will meet me again in another life, or another reality? All fates are the same; it is just the details that differ. So we will meet again.

———•◦•———

I am now at the pier's end.

Beyond me is just an expanse of flat red sand. Curiously, there is a small rowboat pitched to the side of the pier. It does not bob or move when I push on it.

I put my hand on the flat surface below the pier – I lay down on the decking and ran my hand over the red sand and my fingers sank in...but into nothingness! There was no sand beneath the top layer. I could just feel a cold nothingness. I fear that if I were to leap off the pier, I would fall straight through the façade and fall into the void! A terrifying concept: frozen in space. No gravity, no force, no sensation of falling or rising. Just stuck.

Before we embark on our journey into the FurtherUnknown I will take a moment to look back over TheNeverRealm that I have travelled through. Inversely to my physique reforming, the desert in my memory is falling away and I am beginning to remember things now. My fears, my spirit. I remember Tesla's wry smile; I remember his giddy explanations of his theories and his capacity for drink. Tesla, my love, I am so sorry for what became of you. But what do I know of other people's death? Maybe you are alive in another reality driving others crazy with your wild schemes. There is no logical evidence to support this conjecture, but I am choosing to support it nonetheless.

I can also think back to my life before TheNeverRealm. Back into my flesh life. I can remember staring into that mirror in the bathroom. Looking blankly at myself before slicing my open my throat. I can remember my shirt growing heavy with the blood.

I came this way for Lucy whom I hope to meet one day– but I do not think it possible. Though, like with the unsubstantiated belief that Tesla is not dead, but in fact happy somewhere else – I am choosing also to believe that I will, in this reality, see Lucy again.

On the horizon behind me the cyclones are still moving in their regular fashion just as they have always done and just as they always will do.

———•·•·•———

We are now in the boat. I must admit that there was a moment of fear just before I climbed in. Would it hold us or would we crash straight through? As soon as I got on it, it suddenly began to act like a boat, pitching and yawing and it gave me great comfort to be welcomed by recognisable natural physics given the insanity at the LHC compound and our various, twisted escapades. I steadied the boat and beckoned Paisley in. Poor thing flat out refused. Paisley doesn't like boats...so I left him!

It was a cruel joke, I admit. I rowed out away from the pier without saying goodbye. He sat there, his ears flat against his head, whimpering. I rowed out as far as I could bear to see him like that and then I beamed a smile at him and rowed back shouting, "Come on boy! Come on, let's go!"

His ears shot up, his tail wagged and he began running around in circles on the pier until I was within reach before leaping out across the lake and landing in the boat with such force that we nearly capsized. I hugged him tightly and he nuzzled and licked my face. We were happy and to sea we rowed and so here we are!

The surface of the plateau acts like water and we bob and weave as we move along with no discernible current taking us anywhere. Oddly, there is no wake or waves - no pattern or evidence of my oars. Everything is deathly still and yet we drift.

———•—•—•———

I have rowed for days now (maybe weeks or years – there are no cyclones on the horizon anymore). I have put my oars in their rowlocks and taken time to drift on the invisible current and write. We are not hungry, nor thirsty and we cannot see land in any direction. Only us and our little boat.

I have never written about my father. I have not mentioned his likes or dislikes or what he stood for or his journey. I have never theorised what might have happened after I slit my throat and left them for TheNeverRealm. How did he feel and how did he grieve? If he even did grieve. I never once thought about it, such is the eternal selfishness of the child. I cannot talk about my father in descriptive terms that are unique to him, only in terms of how I perceived him. The truth is, I do not know how to. I should like to have spent more time with him. Listened to him more. Asked more about him.

I do not know why I write this. Something about the solitude of this lake compels me to. This gentle melancholia that I am drifting on makes me ponder.

I would like to say that I am at total peace and fulfilling my destiny of continuation but, as I am human, there is a niggling thought remaining. It is like a scratch in my mouth or a hair in my throat. There is always one duty left to perform. One face you need to see and whose name you need to speak again. Lucy.

371

68

We have run aground! After perhaps millennium upon this lake we have run aground. But we cannot see what we have hit. There must be some invisible mass. Luckily whatever it is we have stuck has not scuttled our boat. I was lying on my back, dreaming of my childhood and all that it meant (as I have done of late these last years at sea) when we hit something. Paisley almost fell overboard as we pitched to the side, the hull of the boat creaking under the strain.

I prodded and poked at the invisible mass with my oar and there was most definitely something there. We have tried to sail around it, but it is impossible, so vast it is!

After many years of rowing and drifting, work and dream I have taken this NeverDiary out to document this. We are beached against it and I feel compelled to write. I have not documented the revelations and bittersweet recollection of my memory in the years between the pier and now. In all honesty, and as unbelievable as it sounds, I did not occur to me do so! As my memory returned, it seemed my duty as a Dream Investigator had been forgotten. This journal that has documented everything lay forgotten on the bottom of my boat for however long we have sailed for and only now that we have struck something, as if awoken from stasis, I resume my duty. We struck this strange 'NothingBarrier' and I suddenly remembered the journal. So here we are.

———•·•———

I have an idea – my periscope.

It is a mountain! Through the scope I can see a mountain, taller than anything I have ever encountered. Taller than anything I have read about, imagined or dreamt off. It stretches up past the clouds and into…who knows? To note – through the scope, I scanned all around me and nothing changes. It is just a flat plateau of never-ending red sand and this mountain. I put the scope to Paisley's eye and tilted his head up…I could tell he was shocked. He held his breath upon seeing the great mountain.

I have a duty that I now remember. A duty that I have been brought here to carry out. As Brekker has said, as Lucy has said and as life itself has said - the duty is to carry on.

I have used my jacket as a papoose which Paisley now sits in.

We are to climb!

When I reach a ledge to rest, I will write what I have learned and what I have felt. We climb!

———•·•———

Summit.

I am a God of no use. I am above the entire NeverRealm and I can see forever and not just *across* this realm, but through it! After lifetimes of climbing, I am on the summit of the FinalMountain and I can see with crystal clarity the plateau. I can see the lake at Pripyat and I can see a holographic projection of Couldwell above it and other towns as well!

I can see hundreds and thousands of settlements and a circulatory system of roads, railways and electrical lights all layered over each other, and below too. I can see down forever. I can see every variation of every thought and every possible reality. I am God.

But I have no use for I am bound to continue and yet a great impossibility now faces me. At the summit of the mountain is a flat brick wall. No idea of its thickness. Could be inches, could be leagues. It stretches upwards into, presumably, the very roof of the Multiverse. It stretches across in both directions to who knows where.

Looking down at the all the worlds below and seeing all the eventualities fills me with a coldness. I have no attachment, despite my understanding all of it. I hold out my hand, and the perspective of my hand over the vista seems to cover vast countries, blotting out their existence. And yet it means nothing.

I can observe everything, and yet I cannot act on anything. I cannot change anything. I cannot affect anything from this height and so, from my ineffectual state of observation I have truly no use and that, truly, makes me God.

And so there is only one thing left to do: Perform the impossible. I am to walk through this wall. Like all humans, I am 0.01% substance and so if I concentrate every atom and, if I move slowly enough, I will merge with this wall and be able to pass through it to the other side. It is not whimsy. Not fantasy. It is science. Theoretical science yes, but science all the same. It can be done and it will be done because it must be done. My conscious state will guide me. My love for Lucy will guide me. It will guide every molecule as it always has done.

I have to do this, but I also know what that means. I will have to leave everything I have behind. To continue I must leave my clothes and my scope and this diary. If I am to pass through this wall, if I am to be reborn on the other side I must be naked. And…I will have to leave Paisley.

I think he understood. He was looking out at TheNeverRealms below when I bent down and kissed him. He nuzzled me and whimpered. I think he knew that he would remain here alone, surveying everything. If anyone where to find this mountain and climb it, they would be met by a pile of clothes, a little journal and a canine deity.

We sat together and hugged each other. I stroked and kissed him and his tail waggled slightly. He nudged me. His nudge said, "go find her, go find your peace."

———•◦•———

I have taken off my clothes and they lie neatly folded next to Paisley. I have unravelled my papoose-jacket and draped it over his back. He cried a little when he smelt my identity in its fabric. But he understood. I am standing next to him now, naked and sad. Once I have finished this entry, I will leave the book by him.

TheNeverRealm - I am taking stock of all I have done. I am realising that my insignificance in the sense of temporal occupancy does not mean that my actions are insignificant.

Nothing is insignificant. Everything matters.

I miss my friends.

This is the last of TheNeverPages.

MY LUCY

Lucy's journal.

Stripes was acting very strangely this morning. He did not want to go and run in the meadow. He did not want to swim in the lake. He didn't even go to his bowl for his breakfast.

When I woke, I found that silly dog staring at the bedroom wall. He was very close to it and growled when I tried to pull him away so I left him there.

Particularly beautiful weather today – the mountains are lush and verdant. The wind is gentle. It makes the white curtains billow peacefully. Took my coffee on the balcony and looked out at the mountainside and the lakes below. So perfect.

Went about day – made bread, wrote, practiced piano (can play Rachmaninov's Concerto Number 4 through to end now…took four hours though).

Carried on with a strange feeling all day though. An expectant feeling. Felt like something was supposed to be happening, or was about to happen. It felt good – like that feeling you have when you meet someone for the first time and await their love letter.

Came upstairs to bed and to write in my EverPages and Stripes was still sitting by the wall. His tail was wagging happily and his tongue was lolling. His eye was really glinting (his pretty eyepatch I embroidered also seemed to glow a bit).

But the wall – the wall was different! I have noticed a stain on it. A large dark, life-sized stain like a shadow. Not my shadow – not anybody's. It does not dissipate when I run my hands over it...but it feels warm. It feels good. It feels like it is linked to my sense of joyful expectancy. Don't know how to explain but I think someone is walking through the wall!

Things need names and so I have named the Shadow-Stain 'Gavrilo'. Yes, it will be called Master Gavrilo. Ridiculous I know...but it just....feels right.

Feels like I am in love.

Appendices

Brekker's Journal

Joints stiff. Bones ache. Laid in bed for thirteen minutes thinking on nightmare. Couldn't move and so reflected. Searing nightmare, complete in its terror. Unknown enemies, unseen threats. Dread.

Was in metropolis – abandoned. Unknown architecture, unknown city, unknown location. Did not recognise the vapour trails in the sky – seemed thin, like threads. Some flying machines that I did not know. I shouted 'hello' to the city but no answer came. Just me. I remember that my knees felt as they did in my youth, or at least as they did just a few years ago. I could walk without a cane, but my gait was slow. Cumbersome. As if ground was treacle. Ankles wading through unknown slurry. Had an overwhelming compulsion to advance down the wide, concrete street. There was a place I had to get to, a door perhaps that I had to open but everything around me conspired to prevent this simple action. I thought to empty my pockets and find the key to whichever door it was I had a dire need to open and step through. Hand felt heavy in pocket, seam snagging on wrist so that I could not pull hand out. Took great effort. Pulled hand out and spilled contents on floor, just as sun crested a nearby building. Shaft of light straight into my eyes, near blinding me – could not see contents of pocket on the floor. Bent down to feel around, but could not grasp objects. Had no tactile feedback in fingertips. Could not grasp. Bent down, put knee on ground and felt a panic rise. Like something was close, something watching or approaching. Gripped wrist with other hand and held it steady, like a surgeon holding knife-hand for more precision. Picked up key and held it tight. Stood upright and opened hand. No key in my palm, but a button. Still the dread was on me, but I did not vex over the transformation of object. Seemed to me that it held the same purpose as the key. Tried to move forward, but feet were heavier. The approaching person or object was so near to me. Behind me, but I could not turn. Neck frozen stiff but not through fear – seemed like a sudden reversal of my joints abilities of just a few moments before – as if it was a cruel glimpse of what was to come when my affliction becomes all-consuming and I am completely immobile. That was when the fear came over me. I felt cold and dizzy, back of my neck icy. Tried to lift hands, tried to move on but I was a statue. Looked to feet, saw boots had merged with floor – like concrete. Edges of vision began to grow dark, sickness now overwhelming me – could not move, everything – even jaw, locked in painful position – not clamped shut, not wide enough to make any discernible sound. Felt great pressure on my body, felt great weight pressing against rib cage and shoulders. Like being in a vice. It was as my vision began to close for good when I said, in my mind and with a sudden strange, disconnected voice, as if narrating or observing the events. I said, "You are dreaming, you cannot die in a dream so do something," and then I pushed. I clamped my eyes shut (in my darkened dream state) and concentrated all my effort in waking up. The terror was so great that all I could do was pull myself out of that nightmare. I said over and over – "this is a dream, this is a dream, you can't die in your own dream."

And then, as if suddenly a law of science had been explained fully to a child and their fog of confusion parts to enlightened understanding, I saw myself looking at a large block of concrete, freestanding and forming around some unknown character in the middle of the street. Literally, they were being subsumed by a wall. Cocooned within it. With a sad groan, the vertical crack closed and all that was visible of the fellow inside that sarcophagus was a strange, dull shape. A shadow.

I woke up at that point, safe from the terror but still with a start. The dread remained because, as my eyes shot open and I thought I was safe, I could not move my arms or legs. It took a few moments to calm and recall that it had been a dream and that I was back in my mansion, in my bed and my stiff joints being nothing more than the slow advancement of my condition. I lay for thirteen minutes contemplating the meaning of the nightmare and becoming somewhat fascinated with my inner self's ability to control the madness of the dream-world. To recognise that it is strange and not real and to objectively pull myself out of the dream. I wonder if others can pull themselves out of dreams?

Didn't bother to wake Agatha with my thoughts and contemplations. She was snoring next to me and she wouldn't understand nor care to either. I waited in bed until she had awoken and dressed. Then she came to my aid. As per the ritual I dictated to her, she applied some ionic balms of my own concoction with some lavender and tinctures into a bowl and washed my joints. Soon, I was able to sit up in bed and then, after she had washed my back, shoulders and elbows, I was able to grab hold of the hoist and lift myself out of bed and upright. It is strange how my bones work these days. By lunchtime, I am a man of nearly half my age. I can walk freely in the garden and I can even ride my horse through the mansion grounds. But come the evening, my bones begin to seize up. The joints in my body freezing. Daily I become like a statue come midnight. Carefully Agatha lays me down at night, like a board. It is this reflection of my reality within my dreamscape that causes such dread I believe. For if I am like I am in reality as I am in dreams, why the fear? Why the panic of the seizing joints? I can only conclude that its meaning is more than the physical, perhaps metaphysical. Perhaps it allies with my fears for my work – my fear of stasis of the body. With my theories circling in my mind like cyclones, I can sense that they are soon to coalesce into my grand masterpiece. But there are too many stages, to many tests and theories of theories to explore before I can begin to assemble everything and I fear that my body will not be able to keep up. What if I am consigned to my bed, looking up at the ceiling knowing what to do, but unable to perform? I cannot dictate my actions to Agatha. She has not the patience let alone the intelligence to understand what it is I am doing. She can tend to my joints, but that is the extent of her use. She is a daily distraction to what I have to do and having her in the house irritates me beyond belief. But how can I send my wife away? I would be consigned to the bed far sooner if I did.

And so, the course of action seems quite straightforward. To unify everything – to realise my brilliance and to venture into what I dream of venturing into I need to cure myself so that I can be free of Agatha and can focus on the next stage of work.

But to test on myself is dangerous – techniques are highly experimental, highly complicated and are only in the exploratory stage. Ideally, I need test subjects to begin with. Experiment on animals until I know the parameters of my methods and have mastered the boundaries. Then, perhaps, it will be time to apply my science to my bones. Fix my joints.

So, to work.

Brekker's Journal

Agatha inconsolable. Tried to comfort her. Even attempted apology. Didn't work. She has locked herself in her bower. Been there for six hours. I can already feel my arms and legs seizing up as the evening draws in and so I should try and take myself to bed before I cannot even pull myself up the stairs, or winch myself into bed.

In bed now – legs paralysed, journal held by makeshift arm. Lying on back, pencil in mouth. My dexterity with this pencil is improving by the day. Can see that this is relatively legible.

Experiment partial failure, partial success. The benefits are that I now know how I should be mixing my compounds and just how far a living creature can withstand the injections I concocted. I overshot by a distance. Tomorrow, I will halve the measures, but double the dosage of countermeasures and hopefully this will provide me with a baseline upon which I can now measure everything else. The failure is that one of Agatha's dogs, the Afghan hound named Matty currently lies in on my workbench, half of it melted to the floor. Have not cleaned up the remains – I want to wait until the morning to see if there is any reaction to the oxygen in the room overnight.

Took the dog while Agatha was cleaning bed-sheets. I was at full mobility and so offered to take dogs for a walk. Selected Matty as he is, relatively, the same age as me. Took all five dogs into the grounds and let the four off the lead. Walked Matty around to workshop while offering of treats from pockets. He was happy, tail wagging. Easily bent down to feed him. Approached door and I smothered him with chloroform handkerchief. Animal passed out and I carried him into the workshop and strapped him down. Shaved a large patch of skin around his side, exposing his ribs. Drew outline around each and prepared a variation of my experimental ionic balm and tonic for each rib, increasing in strength by 10% each time. Fed rubber tube down animal's throat and funnelled down a cocktail of phosphorescent luminance and water. Presumed harmless. Injected solution into the marrow of the bone using prepared needles – planned to use on myself so have already built needles thin, yet strong enough to easily penetrate bone. Turned on black lights – specially treated gas lamps with tinted glass from those exceptional glassblowers in Holstenwall.

Immediately through the animal's skin, I could see the glow of his stomach, intestines and bladder as the luminous liquid made its way slowly through the animal's digestive tract. Put on gloves and began to prod and inspect each rib. For thirty-eight seconds nothing seemed to happen. Then, like a slap in the face, a pungent odour of mouldy cheese hit me. I stepped back from the animal and held my nose as the smell grew stronger and the air in the study seemed to grow hotter and heavier. I backed away and saw the animal begin to kick slightly. The effects of the injections stronger even than the effects of the chloroform – the animal was in pain, clearly. His eyelids were half open and his black eyes were rolled over.

The smell stung my eyes, but I became resolute and brave. I stepped up to the beast and bent down to my canvas. I barely touched the first rib when, like a deflated balloon, his entire side sank. Seemed like when Agatha and one of the maids open out a bed-sheet to fold again, or when she flings out a rug to lay down as a picnic blanket. The whole ribcage collapsed with a hiss, ebbs of smoke rising. The animal stopped kicking and his jaw hung open, his tongue hanging out. The animal began to drip slowly onto the concrete floor like a guttering candle. The beast kicked no more.

I stepped back to take notes and observe as the skin around the ribcage began to shrink-wrap so tightly that the bones sliced through like knives through butter. Prodded the bones – though they pierced the skin easily, against something of more substance, they flexed like warmed rubber, bending to the touch and losing all elasticity. Documented all I needed to and left beast to return to the mansion for lunch.

Agatha, following her nose, found Matty at three O'clock. Her screams and wails almost burst my eardrums. Tried to explain the invaluable lesson the animal had given me in its death. Asked if she would rather it be me? She fled to her bower and has stayed there ever since. Can hear her sobbing through the walls. If she sleeps in that room, I will go to her in the morning before I see the remains of Matty and before I select a new test subject.

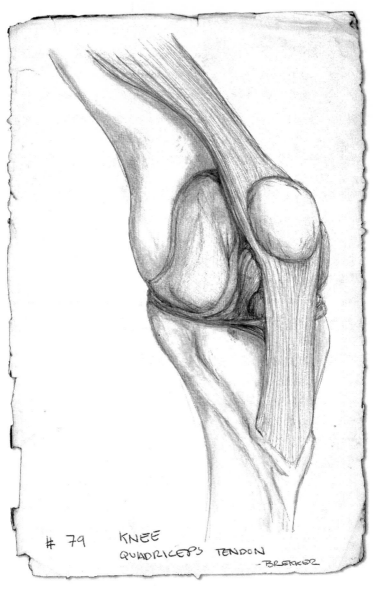

79   KNEE
       QUADRICEPS TENDON
                    BREKKER

Dear Vasili,

I hope this letter finds you and Kamila well. No doubt it will. I am sure you are giddy with excitement, trepidation and maybe even a smattering of fear (the good, butterflies kind). Firstly, thank you both so much for your invitation to your upcoming nuptials, how very exciting for you both. I am happy. Happy for you both. I see that you have chosen the Abbey at Holstenwall just as we did when we were married all those years ago. Doesn't it seem like a lifetime has passed? It is a beautiful location and should be used for such things – it is a good choice. Did you take Kamila to see it, or did she already have the place picked out? Does she even know that we were married there? I'm sure all girls dream of a Holstenwall wedding. Tell me - Will you be married at dawn as we were, or will you take your 'eternal' vows at dusk?

I must admit, to my shame, that receiving your invitation vexed me somewhat. Not out of personal sadness, please believe that I am so very happy for you both. No, because the letter arrived the morning I had hoped to find the letter from Commissar Sukhoi concerning Gavrilo's placement in military academy. I know it is so important for you, for our son to follow in your footsteps. To be strong, to learn discipline and to perhaps march to war and glory as you had once done. I know what you are thinking. I know I was never so keen on the idea when he was a boy and I know you used to get so angry at me and my ideas for our son. Oh, the arguments we had concerning his welfare! They seem so funny now, but do you recall how we raged? The man of discipline against the silly woman with dreams filled with air like a balloon! How we argued, but it goes to show much we love our son, doesn't it?

Remember how I would stay up all night talking to him, making up stories, having adventures with him. We would build worlds and traverse strange lands until he was too tired to continue. He was a boy then and I so dearly wanted him to explore his imagination. Perhaps find a talent and become an academic...or even an artist! I have told you many times, over the years of my own sadness and anguish over my own school days. Having my secretarial lessons in the art classrooms. How the children who could afford a creative education were allowed to paint and sculpt and how, children that came from poorer districts learnt only typing and clerical tasks. Being stuck in that room, surrounded by all those easels and paint boxes. Well, you know how it made me as a child. I so didn't want that for our boy. But, boys grow up and he is a young man now and you were right. Such dreams and ideas are foolish to pursue. And so, I was expecting the letter of acceptance from the Commissar. It didn't arrive, and so back to my original point – it made me vexed somewhat.

But still, the wedding – how exciting. I am sure that Kamila will look so beautiful in her dress. You have caught a great butterfly in your net. Youthful, strong, beautiful. I hope that she will be able to bear you more children as the years of your perfect marriage continue. I am sure she will stay forever young (my tip for her – rub olive oil into the corners of your eyes before bed. It stops the advance of age and the crow's-feet! Ha-

ha, not that she needs it now. Girls of 19 think women of 21 are ancient. Lord knows what she will think if you told her a beauty tip that came from the shrivelled lips of a 50 year old woman!)

I should go soon – I shall wait by the door in case the Commissar forgot to deliver the letter and comes back. Yes, I still have this habit – some things never change. Some things do, well, a lot does…but some things remain.

I do hope that you and Kamila will permit me to continue to write and keep you abreast of the Gavrilo situation as it transpires. The boy is so sad and sullen sometimes that if this course of his future does not pan out as we have planned…well, I don't know what I will do. Of course, when you are married and on your honeymoon planning a new family with young Kamila, I will not continue to keep you abreast, unless you specifically ask. Newlyweds need their privacy! But, like I say, if you request after that time that I continue to write, then I will. Until then I will keep doing so. Lord, I pray that he gets into the academy. I cannot bear to think.

Look at me, going on and on. I must go now!

Goodbye my dear Vasili,
With love and kind regards

Elizabeth.

PS – I am not sure if I should accept the invitation to the wedding, wonderful and generous as it was. I cannot help but think it was not Kamila's idea and that it was your doing, out of the kind charity of your heart, big and deep as it is. Pray, in confidence, what should I do? I cannot deny that I will feel a twinge of nostalgia seeing you so fine in your dress suit once more at the altar, but that is my sadness to bear. I can handle my own heart! I would dearly like to come and wish you well and say my goodbyes, but I am concerned about Kamila. If she does truly want me there, or indeed is ambivalent to it, then I will attend. If you have bent her ear and championed my cause to be allowed a seat at her wedding then you must tell me. I could die of shame if I went and was met with begrudging smiles from the bride - not when it is her special day and she should be beaming! I remember my day so I speak from experience. So please, in confidence, write me and let me know.

Brekker's Journal

Agatha now sleeping at her sisters. Tested on all her dogs and have made great advances. Each expired but have been able to minimise effects of my tonics greatly and even been able to localise some of the destruction. The major breakthrough, however, is that I have managed to also construct a device that can apply the ionic balms to my own joints as Agatha used to. I anticipated the woman would leave me, and so whilst also pushing forward the boundaries of my understanding, I spent time constructing a bathing device. It is simple really, but not easy to construct given my dexterity. All is controlled by a series of hanging ropes that a suspended above my bed, by the pillow. I can lie on the bed, bite on the end of a specific rope and receive a wet sponge over my knees. The action is like that of a church bell ringer, but using jaw instead of hands. Ruins bed-sheets as the tonic is not particularly controlled as it douses my ankles and knees and I spend a good while, when I am mobile, cleaning the bed. To note – maids have also left, apparently horrified at my experiments on Agatha's dogs.

Though it was sad to see her take the carriage to her sister's house, I can honestly say that I feel a new lease of life returned to me. I am no longer bound to her in a healthcare sense and, I would imagine, in a marital sense. I am free to work on a cure for my condition (or at least, a method that will abate the symptoms and grant me more hours of mobility throughout the day). I shall miss the carnal benefits of having Agatha around – even though her physical form does not stir me in the way it used to, she was at least willing to perform her martial duties and receive me as and when. But it matters not, I have never been one to let those pleasures overtake my work but when the need comes, I will be somewhat regretful that she will not be around to oblige. But, if I can grant myself just two hours extra mobility a day, it will be enough to do my work and take a carriage into Holstenwall and visit one of the bordellos that line Window Street.

More distressing than the departure of Agatha and the maids is that this morning, I received the curriculum from the Holstenwall Academy. I had no idea that the term starts so soon. Of course, I have informed them of my condition and even over-exaggerated the severity of it in order that I might not be required to give too many classes. However, I need the money – if I do not work for them, I will not be able to afford the upkeep of the mansion and the laboratory. A necessary evil and one that has made me vow to work harder and with more fervour so that I may have an hour before and after my lessons with which to conduct my experiments, (can also acquire raw materials from the academy).

But how I dread the start of the academic year. The children with their ideas and theories, their desire to make a name for themselves with questions, questions, endless questions. Why can they not simply accept what it is that I tell them? Or at least question forwards, and not ask me to clarify or repeat. Question forwards, always. Still, go I must.

Interesting to note, the documents of the curriculum and the outline of what's to come arrived with an addendum. Due to my condition, and also my esteem – the academy do not want to lose me and want to keep me in the classroom and lecture halls until my dying breath it seems – they have assigned me a technician to assist. Their précis is included. I must admit that at first, I was incensed with the notion – I felt nauseous with the idea that I would have to teach the children and no doubt have to explain my methodology also to whoever this assistant is. But then, upon cold reflection over a glass of port, I recognised the benefits. A mind to mould can be useful – this is assuming they have a basic grasp of the sciences, theology and don't scrunch their face up at the mention of Dream Investigation – if they have just an ounce of that, then perhaps they can help me in my experiments outside of class. They may even be eager to explore and question forward – this could provide results more quickly and push boundaries with greater force. It could be worth pursuing. Of course, that is counting on a lot of assumptions. Have very clear memories of Mr Reeder of five years ago (assigned when I had a three-term bout of near crippling pneumonia) He had not even the slightest grasp of the basics and hindered everything. But then, at the time, I was not (thankfully) pursuing what I am pursuing now. Had I been, Mr Reeder would be cast adrift in a rowboat with no destination. No, the element in this equation that provides a glimmer of hope is that this assistant to be is young. Mr Reeder was 43, and his précis was adequate (if one were hiring a teacher and not looking for an adventurer). He was past his prime, which is why he taught, his mind stagnant and happy to re-tread old theories and parrot back passages from textbooks. No, this new assistant is young. Not even twenty. According to the notes, she has studied and written theses on astral projection, radiation therapy, uses of uranium in powering flight and a spiritual dissertation on the places between here and the afterlife. Though the theories are ill-founded, trite and inconclusive they do at least show promise. I shall write back to the academy and request formally an interview with the applicant so I can better gauge their abilities and see just how far they are willing to go.

Applicant's name is Lucy.

Brekker's Journal

Writing this in bed. Papers of divorce came this morning. Delivered first mail. The bell rang, but I had not the mobility to open the front door. Mail posted and I found it later that morning. Read over the declarations from Agatha and feel unsurprised that she would seek to leave me. She is weak of will and of stomach. She possesses not once iota of courage to see the task through to the finish – least of all our marriage. I should have married intelligence, not beauty. Hard though it is to even recall how she looked all those years ago. I have signed the letters will send them back. Her conditions were that I can keep the mansion, my laboratory and machines herein. All she requires is a modest settlement so that she can afford balloon passage over the Long Sea to the new lands. Presumably so that she can start again. Unsurprised as I am to receive letter, I was rather taken back by the fact that she is not pursuing an angry vendetta against me and seeking to take the house and the contents. She just wants to leave – to get as far away from her mad husband as possible, I would assume. That is fine; I will acquiesce to her wishes. I shall pay the sum and then some more on top of that to show that I am not mad or angry but simply wish to continue my work undisturbed.

The mansion will be cold as I wander around it alone, but if I can cure or abate the problems with my joints, the awkwardness of existence will not be too great. Indeed, it could vastly improve – my mansion becoming an extension of my laboratory. More space to think, work and dream. The divorce is good all round. It shall be granted.

After I read over Agatha's letter, I returned to my work. Today was spent predominantly mapping out the great vessels and containers that I shall need to build. I have located on my map a suitable site for my grand final design. I can see that it will take years to get the site operational, so I must begin now. The vessels I am designing, nobody has ever seen the like. The engines themselves are greater in size and power than many think possible. I know that if I presented the blueprints for the Valdez now to the scholars at the Academy, their eyes would bulge trying to comprehend her scale and then they would resort to mocking laughter and incredulity, to cover up their own intellectual failings. They would call me a mad fantasist because they lack, to a man, the vision I possess (though, I am sure they are happy in their existence and would gladly keep what they have – limited understanding in return for free joints and limbs, whereas I am blessed/cursed with near infinite vision yet mobility limited to just a few useful hours a day) Still – the drawing up of plans is easier for me in these days than experimenting. Indeed, such is the dexterity of my tongue and jaw that I can happily either sit in my wheeled chair at my desk or even lie in my bed and accurately draw out my schematics.

As for the Valdez, the plan is complete and it took me just one afternoon. I need, tomorrow, to bind it in a leather portfolio along with all the other instructions and documentation to ferry it far away from here, far from Holstenwall and the Tropic of Bath across the channel to the great shipyards at the Greenwich

Sound. My contact there, Mr Knudsen, will oversee construction of the great ship. We have held good correspondence over the last eighteen months and the commissioning process has been as smooth and trouble-free as the conception of the ship herself. It appeared in a dream, floating over a flat, red sea and as I stood upon the water in my dream I saw her sail past. But I did not see her as a completed ship. No, I saw her fully rendered and formed schematic. As if her skin was see-through. I saw every beam, every rivet, every joint and joist of that magnificent ship. And so I awoke and felt twice blessed. Once, for receiving the inspiration for the great ship Valdez, and the other for the manner in which inspiration came to me. Not just as the skeletal ship – but my Muse came to me and told me to investigate the skeleton of everything. To look through the skin, to look at the joints of all the world's bones so to speak. To peel back layers, to pick away scabs and see what lies beneath.

It can be truly said that the birth of the Valdez was the start of my intellectual journey to pull apart the veils of reality and look beyond. I need to understand my own innate structure, and the structure of everything. It is an obsession that started with a dream, manifest in diseases in my bones (which has sped up my investigations) and will conclude with me stepping through the veil of reality and into the beyond – whatever may lie beyond this world. And it all started with a dream. That vision of the skeletal ship.

And so, the designs were finally drawn up today after eighteen month's negotiations with Knudsen. I knew I could pull the design together in one afternoon as the image of the ship resides in my mind so vehemently – as if it were branded to the inside of my eyelids, I see her whenever I close my eyes. But I have spent this last eighteen months investigating more important parts of my journey – namely my diseases and making steps to prolong my time. Like building a great ship, first you must build the shipyard, you must gather smaller ships to ferry materials, you need to build supply lines, and you need to build everything around the final product. And so, as my final product will be a gateway into the great beyond, I am still at the initial building stages. But I hold little fear that I will die before it is completed. I have initiated many stages in this long journey and I am approaching a moment in this timeline where all these projects will reach Prompt Critical – and the completion of all these primary stages will fall like dominoes in quick succession and propel me rapidly towards starting construction of my Great God Machine.

So the Valdez is designed, it will be ferried to Greenwich Sound and construction will begin. That leads me now to have more time to concentrate on abating the symptoms in my own joints. This is the next phase. I have not long until term starts at the academy and I will lose some time for myself if I am not more mobile by then, That is my deadline, that is my goal.

The assistant Lucy arrives for her interview tomorrow and I shall pay the academy's questions on curriculum mere lip service and instead probe her on her own theories and ideas. I hope to find an inquisitive, young mind that is easily moulded and pushed forward. I need a fellow investigator.

There are no dogs left in the house to experiment on and time is running out. If Lucy proves to be up to the task, we shall soon reach a stage where we will be able to test my potions upon my own body. We shall see.

I shall sleep now and cycle over the day's events, consigning everything to memory and ordering all. Poor Agatha, if you had been only half intelligent, you would see where I was going and you could have come with me. Now, you shall spend the rest of your days in ignorance. But that is your choice and I can no longer apportion any more thought to you.

And so, in short, good bye to the image of you Agatha.

You were, for the most part, an adequate wife.

To sleep.

422 TEMPOROMANDIBULAR JOINT

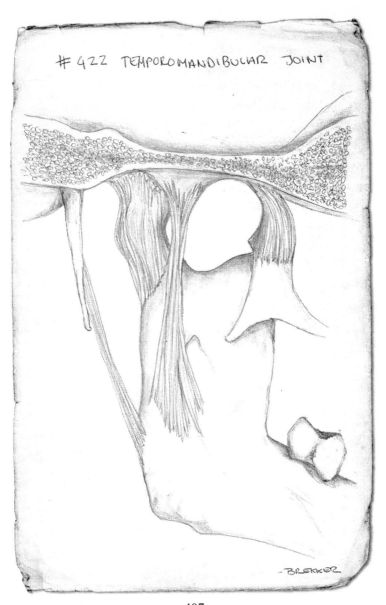

Brekker's Journal

Hope ignited, timeline compressed. Happy. Very happy.

What a wonderful young woman my new assistant turned out to be.

She arrived at one o'clock this afternoon and she stayed until 8 in the evening. I am extremely happy to have her in my service and to push forward now with more vigour and aggression.

She arrived by carriage and my joints were active enough to answer the door and immediately I was struck by her beauty. She has fair, creamy skin with just the hint of blood to her cheeks. She has flowing golden hair and a hue to her irises that looks so azure blue, they could be Austrian lakes in spring. I was taken aback by her beauty. I cleared my throat and showed her into the house, leading her through the great atrium and in to the conservatory so that she could sit in better light and that I could conduct the interview. As she walked, I watched her and knew instantly that she was right for the position. As she walked, her eyes barely rested. They darted around the house, gauging everything – taking in every detail, documenting everything. She said nothing, she just walked and looked.

We sat and I poured some juniper tea for us both. The official interview lasted just twenty minutes. She spoke efficiently and eloquently about her laboratory and classroom experience. She has studied for three years in the field, as she called it, plucked from her class by an old lecturer who noted her innate talent (she blushed at this point, perhaps embarrassed to be talking of her own gifts. Though this would irritate me in other peers, in Lucy, I find this modesty to be quite charming). We spoke freely of the curriculum and she told me that she is willing to work late and arrive early so that the laboratory is always clear or set up for when I arrive. I asked why she thought that was important and she said that ordered preparation equalled happiness. I smiled and agreed, though I would not have put it quite so contritely. Still, she is young.

I probed her regarding other areas of study and she spoke of poetry and of art, claiming to feel genuinely torn between her love for those areas of study and her love for science. I asked, if she were to choose, which way she would bend. After a few moments intense thought, she replied that instead of choosing, she would try to reconcile all she knew in order to marry the two fields together. I spoke of unification and marriage; she said they were not the same thing. We laughed and I broke protocol and told her of Agatha and the impending divorce. This was a tactic to test her manners and sense of propriety. I rationalised that if she blushed, or tried to change the subject then perhaps she might not have the fortitude to probe and investigate alongside me. There may be no place for manners and propriety along the paths I am forging. She did not falter, instead asking me about the marriage and my history. I spoke at length, freely and cannot deny that I told her things that I had not spoken aloud, perhaps ever – thoughts of regret, of anger and remorse. How beguiling a woman that can disarm a man such as me in that manner.

We finished our tea and I could feel that my knees were beginning to seize a little. Lucy sensed my unease and suggested a brief walk around the grounds to loosen the limbs a little. I tentatively agreed and we stepped out of the conservatory and walked over to the gazebo by the small lake some fifty-yards away. It was warm, the sun full and overhead.

We walked and talked and by the time we reached the gazebo, I knew that she had been given to me. A divine gift. We sat down and I looked at her profile, as she pulled her hair back over face and tied it up. I asked her about love. She said she loved God, her family and work. I asked her about suitors. She said they did not interest her.

The young woman wants to study and be free. Cannot deny that I fell in love with her instantly, but I am nearly three times her age. Besides, if we are to work together, our feelings must remain on work, on the end goal. That is the most unshakable of all things.

We sat under the gazebo for an hour in near silence, just looking out at the grounds. It was a captivating time and I did not feel anxious to return to my laboratory. Instead I looked at the grounds, the grass and the trees and in her presence I let my mind wander – I began to imagine and daydream. Of all the theories I have, of all the places I wish to go, or all the things I wish to see.

Sometimes, I have learnt, instead of doing, it is good to take the time to dream and wonder. To marvel in the miracle of simply dreaming of a destination, rather than tearing the world apart figuring out how to get there. It was a revelatory feeling and Lucy gave that to me, under the gazebo.

The hour passed and my knees started to seize again. I stood up, painfully and Lucy hooked her arm in mine and led me back to the house. I told her of my pain and my limited hours of mobility and with a smile and a pat of her hand upon mine she said: "We shall have to do something about that."

A divine gift to me is Lucy.

Dear Vasili,

How is Kamila, how are the preparations coming along? You have not replied to my last letter – Lord, I pray that it did not get lost in the mail! Perhaps it is still in transit? A recap – I asked about the wedding and kindly asked whether my invitation was borne from genuine love or was out of charity. If you could please provide an answer to that question, I can go out and buy a hat and a dress. You remember how I used to drive you mad about my hat boxes and dress boxes that littered the house! Well, at least now I am free to keep the hatters and tailors in the Tropic of Bath happy! Remember how young Gavrilo as a boy used to take the boxes and make great fortresses out of them? I can see now his chubby little self, hiding inside a dress box and pretending it was a coffin! Even as a youngster he was alive, but sad! Silly, silly boy! So sweet! But, before I get to Gavrilo and how he is now – you must tell me one thing. How is Holstenwall? Oh the dear, dear Holstenwall – how I miss that city so much! The twisted spires, the crooked streets and houses that seemed to topple over each other. When I was a young girl living in the meadows of Theresienwiese, I heard tale of Holstenwall and that it was not for all people. Some of the farmers and bakers in my hamlet said that they went there once and nearly ran home screaming the moment they saw it! But not me – not you! Remember how crazy we used to become when the sign for the annual Fayre was erected at the start of every Reaping Season? Do they still have the Fayre? Do the attractions that come still amaze and dazzle? I am too old now, of course, to dance in the streets and whirl and twirl like I used to… but I am sure Kamila cannot wait. Does she love the Fayre too? Is she a girl born for Holstenwall? I know that when we left that town to head back into the country to raise our baby, we thought we were done with the town and I believed it too. But as soon as you told me you had met Kamila and were moving back there, I must admit that I was jealous…but now, I can say, at least one of us made it back to that town. Dear Holstenwall – please, tell me all about it so that when I do receive your reply it will fill my day with light.

Well, the time has come for the…well… the sad part of this letter. I hate to disrupt any of your wedding preparations with my news and bring a rain cloud over your playing field. But, it seems that Gavrilo did not get into military academy. The letter from Commissar Sukhoi came two days after I last wrote to you. I knew it was bad news. The letter arrived in a black bordered envelope, as if someone died. It reminded me of the letter I received when you were at war and how sick I felt when I saw it. Then I fearfully opened it to find that they had the wrong address. The relief was great and I think I have never loved you as much as I did then knowing that you had died and come back! Nobody dies and comes back… but you did in that moment. Divine clerical error. But no, the sad news here is that our son's future has died. At least, that pathway we had prepared for him. I sat Gavrilo down at dinner and told him. He was filling his face with broth and he didn't seem to mind. Can you believe it? I had tears in my eyes as I told him. He shrugged

413

his shoulders and said he was glad! Glad! I asked him what that meant and all he said was "now I can go to school." I think he means to attend a different academy. A centre of higher education.

Please do not scream.

Please do not tear this letter up.

But I think our son is coming around to the idea of being a scholar.

You must be furious and if you please tell me what course of punishment I should deliver onto him, I will follow your word to the letter. I will beat him, confiscate his notebooks. Anything you ask if it appeases you. But that is the truth of the matter. I do hope that you will not be angry at me. I have a feeling that you may suspect that I had a hand in this – that I might have filled out his application for him, or at least falsified some information or omitted some vital detail in his lineage on your part and in your absence. My dear Vasili, to do that? To besmirch your good name – never! I think perhaps the interviewer was not impressed with Gavrilo's demeanour. I sat quietly in the interview and observed (I was not permitted to talk as I was the mother. You could have intervened, but you were not at the interview. Did you get my invitation?) Gavrilo sat, quiet and stony faced. He answered in monosyllabic tones. The interviewer ticked his boxes. Thinking back now, as we took the cart back to the farmhouse, I noted a wry smile across his lips. I attributed it to the pleasant sunset but now, with hindsight, I think he sabotaged the interview. Isn't that a terrible thing to think of our son? I don't know if it is the truth, but I am just thinking/writing aloud to try and understand what went wrong and to think of ways to calm you down. I know how angry and frustrated at the world you can be and you are so far away from him and me to punish. Well, tell me what to do and I will do it.

And so you don't forget - if you could reply with you guidance and also an answer to my original question regarding my invitation to your wedding.

Thank you, my dear.

With my love,

Elizabeth.

PS – I found your father's old folding razor this morning, while clearing away some of your old possessions into the attic. I know how much you were attached to it. Would you like me to send it to you?

Brekker's Journal

It has now been three weeks with Lucy in the mansion. What a change she has brought. She arrives early in the morning and has not once hinted at any discomfort in applying lotions and balms to my joints in the morning so that I might be afforded a few hours additional labour. Indeed, the effect of Lucy upon my work ethic has been insurmountable. She cleans the laboratory, she sets things the way I like them and mixes my potions with a skill and rhythm that is a marvel. However, it is not just in her assistance with the everyday tasks of setting the laboratory. It's in the way she approaches the idea, the way she sees things, the way she probes theories. Never afraid to ask questions when she doesn't understand, and never afraid to question my rationale when I have perhaps leapt too far. We have made great progress.

My joints seem to be healing or at least abating and I have now three additional hours of mobility a day. It is in the last two hours, just as the summer lights begins to wane that Lucy and I retire to the hearth and share some brandy. We talk. Of course, not of personal issues (I have little care for her private life, as long as it never interferes with our work – and unspoken pact that I know she would never break) No we talk of work, we discuss our findings of the day and we postulate and hypothesise on what is to come. We cover physics, chemistry and spirituality with a breathless verve. Soon, as the sun sets and the fire by the hearth is lit, the conversation turns to what is my favourite subject. Not what lies ahead, but what lies between.

The space in the afterlife between the here and there. At first when I theorised of the place in between, I could see Lucy's brow furrow and so I explained it thusly. The sitting room is adjoined to the dining room by a doorway. To pass, you step through the door – obviously – but the passage across the threshold is not instantaneous – you pass through, there are moments when one foot is in the sitting room and one in the living room. There are moments when you are in neither, perhaps fully in the door way. To me, it stands to reason that when we pass over to heaven or hell, we too step through a doorway, we cross a threshold and it is not instantaneous. She understood, her eyes firing with a galaxy of questions and ideas. Pure creation, pure inspiration.

"But how long? How are those moments measured?" she asked.

I could not answer – how does one measure time when one is dead? When alive, all we do is measure time, all we do is pursue, deny or try to rail against it. In death, when there is no flesh, no ageing or decrepitude, how does one measure time...could stepping through to heaven take an eternity? A never-ending journey...or could it indeed be instantaneous because we can still recall even in the exact moment of death, the passage of time. Is the 21 grams that leave the body at the moment of death the soul, or is it time? Many questions puzzle us, very little understood but that is why we are here, is it not? Why we have turned our world over and over, raped her natural beauty and resources to understand our eternal questions – why are we here, what are we doing, why are we doing it? We must go forward and understand our place and position.

Lucy and I must question forward, we must pursue at all costs what this means.

I told her that I have spent many years working towards this pursuit and have put much in place (the shipyards, the public engineering commissions I took to fund it) all this to take me closer to diving head-first into this abyss of uncertainty. But I tell her that it is only now, now that she has come into my life that I feel ready to accelerate. She is been sent to me. Divine providence has given me Lucy and so I must leap across the divide – I must cross that threshold from the room of theories, to the workshop of practice. Lucy will help me, Lucy will inspire me.

Today, by the fireside, I tell her that I love her – but that the love is not sexual but platonic. I tell her that whatever happens, wherever we go, we will go together and that I will never let her down, never let her go. She smiled when I blurted this out and I think, by the orange firelight, that I saw her blush. She coyly pulled a golden lock behind her ear and looked at me. She did not say anything, but instead smiled and nodded with conviction. And I know that she was by my side. She was with me and that was that.

She doesn't sleep in the mansion, though I have suggested it so that she could perhaps aid me earlier in the morning, rather than travelling from Holstenwall to my mansion, but she prefers her little quarters in the Academy. And so, after the brandy by the hearth, she ups and leaves. How typical of inspiration – it warms your heart, tonics your tongue and then when you are about to fall into glorious discovery, it ups and leaves. Still, I shall not complain of her daily abandonment – not when she makes sure the laboratory is squared away and ready for the morning. Not when she aids me in dressing into my night robes (as my joints have seized by this point) and lowering me into bed. I wonder if one day she will kiss me goodnight as a mother to a child? I wonder. She turns out the lamps and tells me that she will go to get rest and that I should too.

"Tomorrow is a bigger day," she says every evening before leaving me.

And so, I am writing this in my bed thinking on the glorious inspiration young Lucy gives me. I think of the power she generates in me. I think of the energy and what that could do if it were somehow harnessed. Somehow.

I hope to dream of energy, or crossing over, or power and strength. Immortality through creativity, for what else is there for humans, locked as they are in these decrepit vessels of flesh and bone.

So to sleep, perchance to dream as the saying goes.

Dear Vasili

Why do you not reply? It has been many weeks and the wedding is right around the corner? I would like to know if I should attend. I have bought a lovely veiled hat and dress, just in case. I look younger, even if it is vain of me to say so. Not as young as Kamila, not as firm or invigorating – most of my body and my mind has migrated south, as they say. But I would like to know, I must know – for my peace of mind. Just one week to go. Shall I attend?

Gavrilo…well, were to begin? I have not seen him properly for days. He has locked himself in his room, pouring over books and notes and Lord knows what else. I ask him about which academy of higher education he is applying too. He doesn't answer. He has a little job though. He works in a factory on the nearby town of Sollen. I don't like the job, I must say – from our house I can see the billows of black smoke rising from the chimneys. They look like a collection of great, black cyclones on the horizon. When he comes home, he is covered in a residue – this thin covering of black graphite powder. Plays hell with my carpets! But he likes it, he enjoys the work. But I know that it is not for him. I know it is not for him. The more I think about his studies and what could be achieved, the more I believe it is right for him. This will make you angry, but you are not here anymore and so it is difficult to leverage two opinions and to dictate what he should do with his life. I have taken it upon myself to lean him towards a path of study and creation – it I could just get him out of that damned factory. This will enrage you, I am sure.

Anyway, I am sure Kamila is out of her young mind with giddy excitement for the wedding!

Please reply immediately with any thoughts you have on our son. Any at all. And of course, an answer to my original question regarding my attendance at the wedding.

Kind regards,

Elizabeth.

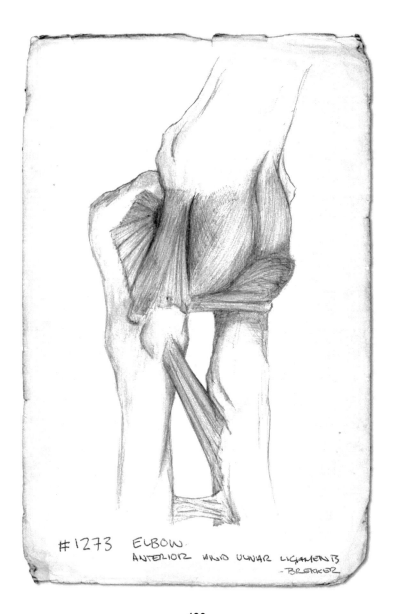

#1273 ELBOW.
ANTERIOR AND ULNAR LIGAMENTS
- BREKKER

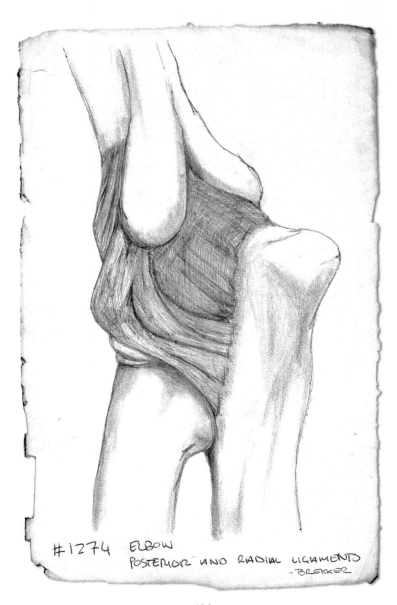

#1274   ELBOW
POSTERIOR AND RADIAL LIGAMENTS
-BREKKER

Brekker's Journal

Rage almost overwhelming, propensity to violence near prompt
critical. Lying in bed, fists locked, writing with pencil in jaw.
Everything nearly lost, but I feel should be recoverable. This
thought helps me from screaming and tearing apart everything I
know to exact revenge on Agatha.

She came unexpectedly to the mansion, perhaps to deliver
some letters – more likely to snoop. She came to the bedroom
and found Lucy applying balms to my knees. Of course, the
stupid woman could not understand and could not see Lucy's
clinical behaviour. No, she wailed and thrashed and cursed at
dear Lucy. Calling her all manner of disgusting names. I
screamed at Agatha to cease, I tried to leap out of bed – the
desire to throttle that bitch powering my every thought, but my
bones locked and I fell out of the bed, landing on the floor.
Lucy, shocked at the intrusion rushed around the bed to help
me, but Agatha that mad woman, pushed Lucy to the floor and
hauled me up onto the bed. I scratched and clawed at Agatha,
but she easily batted away my protestations and ignored my
hateful words as I spat them into her face. Lucy, poor Lucy
rushed from the room – no doubt fearful for her life! I called
after her to return but she did not. She fled the house. At the
sound of the door slamming, Agatha turned to me and smiled.
Victorious.

Lucy will return, Lucy must return – our work is too
critical, my ideas too important and I need her. I explained this
to Agatha, tried to explain the platonic nature of our

relationship, that she is aiding in my recovery and that we are preparing for the new term at the Academy. I dared to try and explain our extracurricular experiments into traversing the threshold but it fell on deaf ears. Mobility returned and with begrudgingly accepted help from Agatha, I managed to get out of bed and get dressed.

Upon standing up, calmness came over me. The hatred for the woman remained but the violence had gone. And so I asked what she was doing in the house and she said she had only come to collect some of her journals and her viola. Agatha went about her business and then I showed her to the door. I thought that it would be the very last I would ever see of that bitch.

———•·•———

Lying in bed, rage like lava. Agatha lies next to me. We made love tenderly, with no hatred or malice and that, now, in the cold analysis of our actions disgusts me. I am rage.

What betrayal of Lucy, to succumb to my lust and desire – to fall back into nostalgia instead of moving forwards. I hold out hope that Lucy will return and we can continue. Term starts soon and we should use the time in between to do as much as we can concern our traversing of the threshold. If she comes back, we can. Now I cannot move, I cannot throw Agatha out of our bed. I cannot even move her naked thigh that is draped over my waist. Though the idea of her and I conjoined repulses me, it seems my body cannot resist. How I hate that woman.

Dear Brekker,

Firstly, let me apologise to you for fleeing your mansion and our place of work yesterday. I was startled at first, then fearful and then angry and as I try to remain as good and calm as I can be, when my anger flares up I act irrationally and so I apologise to you, my mentor, my friend for abandoning you in that state. I do hope you can find it in your heart to forgive me for that.

I fear that you won't forgive me for what I am about to say. I must resign from my duties as your home assistant for the time being. Though you must understand how deeply I believe in your work and the discoveries we have made together, I just think that I need some space after the incident with your wife. I am not sure I want to be in that environment and though you may promise it will never happen again, I do not think such a place conducive to a healthy state of mind. Of course, I shall (if you will have me) assist you in your lectures and classes during term and if you ever need to talk or tell me things – please let us do so over coffee or brandy in one of the taverns on campus. Some place of common ground.

I may, in time, feel safe and relaxed enough to return to your mansion and continue our work but for the time being I cannot return.

I realise that this letter may well stir up great anger inside you and you may never wish to see me again, let alone have me assist you in class and that is something I have thought deeply about. But I must be resolute on this and if the cost is your eternal hatred, then that is a great sadness that I will have to carry with me for the rest of my life.

Please let me take this opportunity to express my great thanks for the opportunity you have given me and the insights and ideas you have shown and offered. You have been truly inspirational to me and I hold you dearly in my heart and always will.

I hope, truly, that we can remain friends and that you will indeed take me for a drink in the coming days and update me on your progress.

I have enclosed an ingredient list and recipe for your applications and balms that, if your wife is to remain in your house, should follow so that you can continue to have your hours of mobility.

So goodbye, for now - I truly hope not for ever.

Your assistant, your friend.

Lucy

Dear Lucy,

I understand and accept your resignation. You may continue to assist me in class and in lectures. Our friendship is guaranteed and perhaps after my first class we will go for that brandy.

As for our personal experiments and theories, I am afraid your resignation will preclude you from being privy to any discovery and theory.

Thank you for understanding and I will see you in class next week.

Kind regards,

Brekker.

Brekker's Journal

Through anger, perhaps. Rage, despair, frustration – all of these, I went forward. Agatha left the house and I received Lucy's letter of resignation the following day. I was courteous and civil and there was no lie when I told her that our friendship would remain but it is clear that I cannot trust her professionally. To look over the edge and dive in. She has shown a weakness of character that disappoints me and so, somehow I will need to find an assistant and furthermore a worker who is bound to me, who will never fail and will obey at all costs.

And so, with the anger inside me I took myself to the laboratory and decided, against rationale and reason, to experiment upon myself in an effort to expel my disease once and for all. Lucy and I had been working on a variation of the experiments I carried out on Agatha' dogs which had ended inconclusively. We had mixed our balms and balanced our compounds and with construction of a small distillery, we created a potion to be drunk, rather than injected. The idea was to test the subject on a rat but now that I am alone and pushing forward, I intend to take the potion myself and report back on my discovery. Our prediction is that by the next morning, I should find at least a 23% increase in mobility and if our wildest hopes come true (now my sole hope) I should be able to work from the moment of waking until the moment my eyes close in the night – a full day. The possibility of returning me to my former physical self is almost too much to consider. I have to stop myself smiling at the thought of it as that giddy 'what if' is not productive. I need my rational wits about me.

And so, with hopeful thoughts of the future put to one side and thoughts of Lucy and her inspiration and light dispelled from my heart I have taken myself to the laboratory below the house. I am stripped naked and currently sitting in my thinking chair. The potion is mixed and sits in a carafe upon the workbench beside me. The lamps are dimmed, the potion glows green – bright luminescence. There is no sound. There is nothing but the green glow beside my face. I write this without looking, my eyes locked on the carafe. What fortunes will it bring? Maybe death…and if so, how then will I be able to document the journey? How then will I be able note down what I see, what I feel and most importantly, how time is perceived to the soul when passing through the doorway of this world into the next? How will it occur?

I have no immediate option other than to just drink the potion and see. And so I do. This may well be the last of this journal, it may be the beginning.

I drink.

———•◦•———

All is blackness, all is still. I do not know if I am asleep or dead. I flex my fingers – my knuckles do not ache, my joints work. I reach beneath myself, expecting to find the touch of leather from my thinking chair. I feel nothing. I am prostrate, but there is nothing beneath to support me. I am in a void. I reach for my eyelids and find that my eyes are open, despite the absolute pitch all around me. I try to scream. No sound comes out. I can feel in my chest, my heart thumping harder than I can recall it ever doing. I feel intense pain in my left arm, I feel light, distorted, stretched. My heart rate increases, the pain now crippling my shoulder. I try to grab my shoulder, I try to clamp my hand over it but I seem to pass through myself. My hand falls through my shoulder and out of my back, the inertia of the force turning me over as if on a spit. The pain is replaced by fear. I am dead. I am dead. I paw and grab at myself but my hands pass through my body. I am a non-corporeal entity in the void. The pain fades, the fear dies down and I accept this. As soon as I say this in my mind, calmness washes over me and I close my eyes. As I do, the edges glow orange and little orbs float in that never-space between eye and inside of eyelid. The light dances for me and I can feel the muscles in my face moving. I am smiling at the dance though I do not open my eyes. I do not need to open them to see anymore. The golden orbs stop dancing and they begin to merge. At first I think them are merging to form an all-pervading hue of gold, but soon I realise that the mergence is providing shapes and images. I see the orbs peak and trough like waveforms presenting me a perfect silhouette of the skyline of Holstenwall, even with the shimmering reflection in the Charles River that bisects that great city. I see Holstenwall and feel warm. But no sooner has the image appeared and been recognised then the shapes change again, presenting a differing version of the city. I can still see some of the buildings, the unmistakable great church and academy, the clock tower ... but new structures now abound . Tall oblong buildings, great architecture of function and utility. A future Holstenwall? The shapes change once more and together the orbs merge into one, great oblong, shimmering in the blackness of my vision. I do not know what the image represents but soon, the oblong pulls and twists and forms the figurine of a beautiful woman whose face I cannot make out. The woman stands tall, mightily so. She is powerful, she is strong. She is brandishing a great sword high above her head and her other arm reaches out behind her – as if beckoning forth a great army, calling back to the ranks behind, calling to arms all to follow. The great woman rotates and her face comes fully into view.

She is my mother.

And I wake up.

———•••———

I have returned from my dark dream. A near death experience, perhaps. It was terrifying and revelatory. It was everything. Where was the other Holstenwall? What significance to the warrior woman who bore the face of my departed mother whom I have not thought about once since the day she left us when I was a boy. What of her?

Though these quandaries perplex me, two things are immediately apparent and maybe even more revelatory.

1. The potion appears to have worked. I have full mobility in all my joints.
2. While I was under in my dark dream/sleep-spell I continued to document, I continued to write. My mind controlling my fingers. Total free association writing.

And so, how far now can I travel into the dark dream to decipher the locations and the statue…how far into the void can I travel and still document? How far into this dark dream can I investigate?

How far I have leapt. How much farther I still have to travel.

Dear Mother,

Holstenwall, Holstenwall, Holstenwall! Well, what can I say
apart from 'you were right'? When I was a boy…well, a
younger boy, remember how you told me stories at bed time?
You would never read from storybooks but instead invent whole
new worlds of mystery and imagination for us to venture
through – great deserts and jungles. I think, upon arrival in
Holstenwall not two hours ago, that all that wonder, splendour
and verve you managed to conjure from your mind must have
sprung from the well named Holstenwall. This city is alive and
is already more than I could have hoped for. Even more than
you prepared me for. Your love for the town and the times you
and father spent here must have been mightily powerful. Indeed,
I can already dare to say that I hope I never leave this place.
Foolish, I know – it's just the first day!

I have installed myself in a rocking chair by an open fire
inside a little wine bar on Villiers Mews which is a few side
streets from the main square. Everywhere I look there seems to
be young men and women ferrying trunks and luggage around
the city. The start of a new academic year and the city is
buzzing with fervour, and trepidation. All these young minds in
the same place, at the same time each eager and unsure. It is a
potent mix, mother, for sure. I arrived in good time, the train
pulling into Holstenwall Main just before nine o'clock. It came
to a halt on a rouble, jolting everyone near out of their seats. On
my journey from hearth to here, I travelled with my face
pressed against the window. The morning fog obscured our

farmhouse and the Heavy Hills and as it did so, my melancholia also faded, soon to be replaced by the dark, black tunnels as the train went under the Heavy Hills. In those few minutes, in near darkness except for the carriage lamp and the rickety-rick, clackety-clack of the train I felt a cold sense of abandonment – leaving home, leaving you behind in that house of memories alone. For a moment, for a moment, I saw the face of Bella in the window and I sighed loudly at the vision. I think of my sister a lot in these months, especially as I have just surpassed her age and to leave you in the house, near her but not? I admit, beloved mother, that I felt great shame in the abandonment. However, call it youth, call it selfishness...but as soon as the train passed through the Heavy Hills and burst out into the bright morning light, my sadness too passed and was replaced with wide-eyed awe. Indeed, everybody in the carriage collectively returned from the darkness and introspection and there was outpouring of giddy talk in the carriage. We could see ahead and all around us, the city of Holstenwall.

We pulled into H. Main and I alighted. A kindly student named Sacha helped me with my trunk and we loaded his bags on top of it, together carrying our belongings across the platform and into the city proper. He was a decent fellow, wide of smile. He wore a hat that I read was called a 'bowler' and quite unlike any style I have seen before in our little village. I wanted to enquire about it, but for some reason a shyness came over me and I thought he might consider me blunt, or rude. We spoke of the city, pointing out things we saw that took us – Bakers Row for example was exactly how you described it and, you will be happy to know, hasn't changed since you used to trundle through it. Fifty bakeries, twenty-five either side of the narrow street and the line of young girls outside with little trays bearing a selection of bite-sized samples. The Row was immensely busy and we had taken four strides down it, before we decided to double back and find an alternative route. Alas, it was too late – like fish caught in some great stream, we were pushed and shoved down Baker's Row. I didn't even have a chance to reach out and grab some slice of cake or tart as we went. In a few days, when the calamity of arrivals has died down, I will go back to that row and see for myself what it was that you and father saw when you were here. If you write back immediately with an order, I can use some of my roubles to buy you a specific cake and have it boxed and sent to you. That way, you might feel a little taste of Holstenwall in our farmhouse! Write back if you think this is a good idea.

Well, as I say, I am in a little wine bar on Villiers Mews – after we made it through Baker's Row, I suggested to Sacha that we find some place for a bite and a drink, some place away from the hustle. He agreed and we walked on with our luggage until we came to the great town square and what a sight that was. The great church with its automaton clock – we arrived at ten-to-ten and waited amongst the crowd, staring up at the clock face, waiting for the hour to strike. It seemed as if the whole city had stopped. Well, at least the people within that grand square. The cafés that lined it – all the waiters stopped and turned, the diners in their furs and hats held their tiny coffee cups half to their lips and turned. We all turned, staring at the clock face, waiting. A city of statues. Then, it chimed! Loud, powerful strikes that rattled my insides! Beside the clock face there were two little doors, high up on the tower. On the first strike, the doors open and little puppets on rails stepped out of their homes. The crowd smiled as one puppet, an old man stopped and crookedly waved his walking stick at the people below. Then, from the other door came Old Tick Tock, the Grim Reaper himself! The puppet, in his little black cloak and cowl, moved on his rail around the clock face towards the Old Man and, upon the final strike of the clock, swung down with his scythe and sliced across the Old Man's throat. The crowd laughed and clapped as the Old Man's head fell back and a charge of red streamers were detonated from his neck. The red strips of paper fluttered through the air and fell down on the outstretched hands of the people in the square. The pantomime above us ended. The Old Man, head lolling and the 'blood' dangling from the slash across his neck retreated back to his home by the clock face. Old Tick Tock then turned and bowed to the audience below. Then, as one, all the residents of Holstenwall shouted up to the clock.

> "Until the next hour, hark and heed to me,
> Don't come for us, Old Tickety-Tock,
> We'll all be good as can be!"

And everybody turned to their neighbour and shook their hands with friendly abandon and broad smiles everywhere. It was a bizarre ritual and though I shook hands and smiled like everyone else, the sight of the red streamers in the sky and the lolling of the head was quite affecting. The crowd dispersed and then went about their business. The waiters attended to the diners and the new students in town carried on ferrying their trunks and luggage. Sacha and I walked on, down the side streets until we found this café.

So I entered first and then, as I turned to Sacha I found him standing in the street staring off down the way. I held the door for him and awaited his crossing of the threshold so that he might help me take my trunk to the bar in order to buy some bread and a little wine. But he stood there, staring off into the crowds. And then, before I could hurry him he absently picked up his things from the top of the trunk and walked off as if in a trance. I peered around the door to see, but already he had disappeared, subsumed into the masses. I suspect I will bump into Sacha sometime over the next coming days. Perhaps at registration and induction – there are plenty of programs for the new students and academics to engage in. Classes and showcases for courses to view, even a ball at some mansion somewhere. Yes, no doubt I will see my friend again.

So here I am, sitting alone in the wine bar in Villiers Mews having a little drink and some wine. I have my feet up on the trunk and the fire is warming me. I have been left relatively undisturbed as I write my letter to you, mother. The bar is busy and talk is happy and loud – not shouting, just loud. You could stay here and not complain of the noise.

After the wine and bread, I will try and flag down a carriage to take and my trunk to my residence and check in with the Dean. When I am settled, I will write again to tell you about the room and how I found it. Then, in the evening I shall put on my greatcoat and my thick scarf and go exploring this great city of Holstenwall.

What a choice I have made to come and I thank you, beloved mother, for your encouragement. I never wanted to go to the Military Academy as father had done and I know that you knew this. So thank you for helping me take this, my very first step on the road to becoming a scholar and an artist. What wonders will Holstenwall present to me? What wonders will I create and present to the world?

I feel born for the second time, and like the first, you dear mother have pushed me along.

Write me soon.

I am not sad.

With all my love,

Gavrilo

Dearest Mother,

Well, it has started! I have moved into my accommodation – the Dean of the hall is a kind man, but he is huge. I don't think I have ever seen a man quite as large as he. He walks sideways into the room and he is always eating, or if he is not seen to be eating, you can tell that he has recently just finished. First time I met him, I was a little lost in the halls and a young lady escorted me to his office. I was shown in and the huge man smiled at me. I could see remnants of greasy meat clinging to his ginger beard. He was trying to dry his hands with a filthy napkin but the grease was just shifting around. He shook my hand and left an awful residue upon them and his huge grip overlapped my shirt and stained my cuff. It was a rather stomach-churning encounter, however I am not the type to judge a man on his eating habits or table manners and verily this proved to be just. He is a kind man who did not admonish me for intruding into his office or his day. He took me to the window of his office (which overlooked a great courtyard to the academic residences) and he pointed out the various halls and libraries, even giving me a brief potted history of the grotesques and gargoyles that adorned the high walls and rooftops of the great academy. A nice, man indeed. After our little meeting, he instructed the young lady in the reception to show me to my dormitory. He bade me good day and returned to his plate. His name was Harrington and I hope, throughout my time at the academy that we may indeed become friends.

The young lady did not reveal to me her name and barely spoke in the ten minutes we were together, walking the long halls of the dormitories. She walked with her hands clasped and her head bowed. I enquired of a few things as she led me around – her name, for one, then a few cursory questions regarding the many portraits that lined the walls. No doubt former deans, scholars and great thinkers of a bygone age. She did not answer.

Well, she showed me to my room – number 278 should, when you write, desire your letter to reach my room rather than the central mailroom. Letters delivered there are handed out at breakfast, so I am told.

Room 278 is, I assume, much like everybody else's. It is a modest room, with wooden panelling and a single bed. The wardrobe is large and dominates the room. Inside, more than enough space for my clothes twice over. Underneath the little window sits a writing bureau where I intend to spend my every moment outside of lessons at the desk, reading and studying. Also, I hope to be able pick at ideas that I have been gestating in my mind and my heart for a while – maybe try some poetry. I will pick at the surface and see what is underneath. You never know what I might uncover. Also, to note, that I shall not be too distracted at my little desk – there is no view from my window! By that I mean, barely six inches from the pane of glass stands a great brick wall! If I sit at my desk and stare ahead, all I see is the wall and a strange reflection of me. It is most curious, seeing the dull reflection of my own face staring back at me – it looks as though I am walking through a wall! Most comical. Nevertheless, I am curious to see what will come out if I write at my desk and stare only into myself – the only distraction around being my own reflection. No doubt it will ensure that my studies will take effect!

Well, my beloved mother – tomorrow I am expected in the great hall where all the new year students will gather and listen to the lecture by the great dean and we will be assigned our classes. I see on the pamphlet provided that there will be classes in anatomy as well as modern physics, spiritual sciences and engineering.

I am truly here, mother – amongst the young, the eager and the willing. What discoveries will come? Whatever may lie ahead for me, whatever destiny – be assured, I will traverse the worlds and I will adventure through it all side by side with you, like the stories you read to me, now I feel it is my turn to relay the magic of imagination and discovery to you.

I must turn in now, I must try and sleep. What dreams will come when I close my eyes and will they seem dull in comparison to the majesty of Holstenwall? I can only find out.

Your loving son and academic adventurer.

Gavrilo

#641   BACK OF HAND
ANTERIOR

-BREKKER

Brekker's Journal

Awoke this morning in pain. Knees and elbows locked. Minimal movement in wrist. Lay in bed panicking. Thought before that I had cured disease. Seems to have abated only. Strange how symptoms returned so suddenly. Went to bed late last night, worked long hours. Retired through mental fatigue, rather than physical. No sign of stress in joints and tendons.

Had dark dream concerning myself and the unnamed, abandoned concrete metropolis that abounds my dreamscape. Where before I have found myself alone in that vast city, this time dread of being watched returned. First time in many weeks my time in the city has been filled with trepidation and fear. Stalked through city, trying to be brave. Trying to beat back the anxiety and stalk the other inhabitant. Was taken on journey through streets and back alleys. Buildings tightly packed together, steel pipes and tubes criss-crossing the alleyways, great steam fans. Difficult to pass through. Felt like adventurer through dense jungle, hacking and pulling away at steel vines as I ventured into the darkness of the city. Eventually, came out onto a town square. In the centre, a stone fountain. No water. Old. Concrete in the ground cracked, grass pushing through. Walked over to fountain and sat down. Looked around town square, large apartment buildings bordering square save for the east entrance. A large avenue, above which a great stone arch upon which, at its centre, there hung a strange stone bust. Not a human's face, not an animal's. A strange, sleek representation of an animal at best guess. Looked like horses head. Long, thin snout – straight edged, square ended. No eyes, just a dark visor. Looked upon the bust for a few moments and felt no dread. Felt no fear. Instead, a disconcerting recognition welled deep within. A familiarity. I turned my attention from the bust on the arch and looked down the wide avenue beneath. And there I saw my stalker. Half way down the avenue, perhaps 200 yards away, stood an abomination. A creature not of flesh and blood, at least not on the outside. In the sunlight, I could see beams glint of the surface of the creature. Reflected light. A sheen. Creature was either made of metal, or was wearing some sort of armour. At eight feet in height, the 'thing' stood upon three spider-like legs. Thin, long and tapering to fine points that dug into the ground. The 'thing' did not move. Did not approach. The bulk of the torso seemed almost human like – triangular from waist to broad shoulder. Two arms that appeared to have no hands. Head seemed, in silhouette to be humanlike. Staring at me.

For some reason, upon seeing this interloper into my dream and my city, I did not objectively step out myself and say "this is a dream." I did not attempt to pull myself out of the dream. Instead, I sat on the fountain feeling that deep familiarity with the location and even that interloper. Slowly, I raised my hand and waved.

And then, a processed, automated approximation of my own voice sounded in my mind. Directly inside my head. Wavelength not carried, but generated within.

Voice said:

"This is you. Come to us. Step over the threshold. Walk through the wall. Come."

———•◦•———

I awoke to seized joints. After thirteen minutes my joints suddenly returned to normality. Not ease of tension or pain. As suddenly as symptoms came, they vanished. Was reminded of automaton fortune-tellers on penny arcade who remain motionless until a young child places a rouble into their coin slot and they spring into ordered life. Am I being operated like that? Am I not in control?

Preposterous.

And so, I set to work. Took detour from usual plan. Mixed my balms with boiled gelatine and let them cool and set. Rolled up trousers and sleeves, applied glowing jelly to knees, elbows and wrists. Turned off all but the black lights and waited for the application to activate.

After thirteen-minutes, skin began to feel warm. Pleasing, warmth. Like injection of iodine. Held out hands over a nearby black light. My concoction had been mixed perfectly. I could see through my skin. I could see all the bones in my hand. I could see the cartilage. The tendons. The same for elbows and knees.

To my distress, I could see that my dorsal radial-ulna and radial-carpal ligaments across the back of my hands have degraded significantly. Can see the frayed, snapped and slitting threads.

In my knees, the same applies for fibular-lateral ligament and the annular ligaments in my elbows.

Have noted the amount of degradation. Will repeat experiment in day or two whilst continuing apace with my work. If degradation worsens, I shall have to seek a new remedy.

First thoughts on possible solution is to construct a series of braces for my joints. An automated suit of armour, so to speak, within which to operate. I have a list of possible designers to contact should situation worsen.

For now, to work.

My beautiful, beautiful boy,

My son, my child, my bold adventurer! Thank you so much for your letters – you cannot know how happy they make me. To imagine you there, in Holstenwall – young, fervent and eager for life! I wish dearly that I could have been there, when the train came out from under the Heavy Hills, to see your face change at the sight of the city. Of course, I know that these experiences are better left to be experienced alone. The last thing you want is your haggard old mother hanging around, slowing you down!

Have you managed to go exploring in the city? If you're feeling brave, you should venture into the Latin Quarter (my advice, leave half your roubles at home or you will spend more than you can afford!) The Latin Quarter is awash with taverns and dance halls – in our youth, your father and I spent many a night there, drinking and dancing. And though, as your mother I should warn you off the perils of such activities when there is serious study to be had, I would not begrudge you a few nights there. It does the soul good to release itself from the strictures of routine. And also, while you have a day or two to acclimatise to the city before school starts, why not explore a little? As for Baker's Row, if you do manage to go there – please, enter from the east entrance, walk down ten stores and stop. On the right hand side of the road, you should (I pray) see a tiny little bakery without sign (all the others are quite garish in comparison with their signage). This little bakery is modest and small. Go in and get yourself a cranberry and orange Kugelhopf. The finest in all the city! I do hope that little shop is still there. Maybe, if you have a coin left, you could box me up a slice or two and send them home so that I could take one, final journey back to Holstenwall and to my youth?

Ah my boy, how happy you make me. It is quiet in the house, too quiet sometimes. Especially at night. I walk from room to room when it all gets to me, leaning in the doorway of Bella's room and then to yours. It is a little sad to know that you were in that room just a few days ago. I haven't touched the room – I will preserve it just the way it is...at least until the smell from your socks on the floor becomes too much!

Have you heard anything from your father? I have not heard a thing. I have written to him about your move to Holstenwall and about the upcoming wedding, but so far nothing in reply. I am not sure if I should go. Will you?

Well my beautiful boy, the moon is high and my eyes are heavy. The candles are soon to bed, and so must I.

Please write again soon!

Your adoring mother,

Lilly

Dear father,

I do hope you and your fiancée are well and are excited about your wedding. I am sure you are. As you know, I have just stepped onto a path of academia at Holstenwall and, unfortunately, one of my lecture days falls upon your nuptials and as such, regrettably, I shall be unable to attend.

As a man of duty, I am sure you will understand my decision. Work comes before play, always. But please do not think that I wish you anything less than happiness.

Kind regards,

Your son, Gavrilo

Brekker's Journal

I am standing on the threshold of a great hangar. The sun sets behind me. A vast expanse of concrete all around. A few buildings in the distance. I look into the dark hanger. I can see the semi-circle of daylight at the other end. A great mass lies within. I can see the outline. Looks like a great, sleeping whale. I step inside.

The building contains a great jigsaw puzzle, laid out before me. A huge, steel machine broken into pieces and laid out like a daguerreotype of an explosion. I walk around the great mass. It is sad, broken, dead. A flying machine reassembled after a catastrophic accident. I have never seen a machine so grand, so sleek – even in its broken form. The fuselage resembles a bullet. Four great engines buried inside the wings, one of which has been recovered in its near entirety. The second wing, sheared off at the outer engine cowl. Along the fuselage, a row of square windows. Like dead, black shark eyes staring back at me. A machine for passengers. I step around the wings and up to the fuselage. I can see her name inscribed onto the steel - 'Comet G-ALPY.'

I feel a great sadness rise inside at the sight of her, once grand, now decimated. Through a breach in the fuselage, I can see the broken and twisted seats. There are no bodies inside. Removed, buried. Given a resting place, while she lies here for all to see. No dignity for her.

I walk around the fuselage and regard the shark-eye windows and I know explicitly what happened. Her design was flawed. She suffered great fatigue. She wanted to fly, to ferry people, to work…but her structure was weak. Her structure unsuitable but she was pushed onwards, passed her boundaries. Her failure was not of her own making, but of her designers and those that applied needless pressure onto her. The windows were designed to be square, purely for the elegance of design. To attract loving gazes from other designers – gross pride and hubris caused her to become weak. Corners of windows square and sharp thus concentrating stress and increasing fatigue during pressurised flight. Propagating crack appears in corner, plastic zone increases, fatigue grows, crack increases – catastrophic burst of fuselage.

I step back from the sad machine. She was beautiful, almost perfect. She wanted to fly, but her design was insubstantial.

I sigh, but the sound that comes from my mouth is distorted. Mechanical. Mine and, yet, not.

The sun sets, its last beams cresting the frame of the hanger and flooding the inside with orange light. My silhouette is cast upon the steel hull of the Comet. I have assumed the shape of the interloper. I stand upon three, thin legs. My torso broad, strong, my face now a sleek muzzle. The sun does not penetrate my visor. Does not blind me.

I am a Brekker Machine.

———••••———

Have awoken from deep dream after administration of my sleep inducing tonic. Self-recorded the above while under. This was no traditional dream. I know that now. This was not a subconscious exercise in ironing out physiological anxieties. This was real. I was there. I was the Brekker Machine. Must now test ligament degradation.

———•••———

All ligaments appear to have degraded slightly since last experiment. I have not long before I am totally immobile. I must rescue my body to preserve my mind. If Lucy had been brave enough to overcome her petty fear and return to the laboratory, we could have built what I needed together. As it stands, I have not enough time to do it myself. I must employ somebody to dedicate their time solely to lengthening mine.

I have sketched my design and have sent it to someone I know who can flesh out the concept and produce an adequate brace for my joints so that I may work on.

Must keep moving forward.

Jacob Epstein will help me.

Unsent letter to Vasili Koromov.

My dearest love, my heart, my heaven, my hell.

This morning you are getting married to that child! You never replied to my letters, not once. Do you hate me so much? You have turned away from me to be with her and that was a dagger in my heart, but I can understand that…but the lack of correspondence? Not one letter. Do you hate me so much when you know I love you? Still. I have always loved you and I always will. Won't you please tell me what I did wrong? I can change; I will go to surgeons to make myself youthful again. They have made advances on ageing creams – I have read about it, radiation therapies to make you forever young. They are experimental and expensive but I will do it for you, I will sell everything if it meant you would desire me again, that you would come home. I will take you inside me whenever you command, I will do whatever you desire because I love you and I need you. You can bring Kamila with you, we can all three be together if that would make you happy. Please come home, please come back to me. Don't you remember how you used to love me; how you said once that you would cross space and time to be with me, to do anything? Do you remember that you went to war to protect me and you lived through that hell to return? You told me it was my face that kept you alive when all around you was folding into mad chaos. You said that, you said you would walk through walls for me. You fucking liar! You fucking liar, how dare you say that to me and then turn away to her. Please, can't you see that I love you, please, please come home. Come back to me, my only love and bring Kamila if you need to.

Just come back so that you can be reminded of how you loved me once and how you still love me.

Just come home.

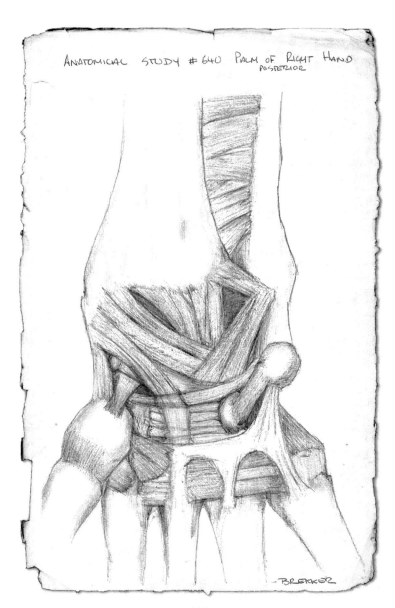

ANATOMICAL STUDY #640 PALM OF RIGHT HAND
POSTERIOR

BREKKER

My darling boy,

Thank you for the Krugelhopf. It was delicious. In return, please accept this small food parcel. I have been clearing out the house and found some tins that you might like. You must keep your strength up! Please excuse the brevity of my little note my love, I am a little under the weather. A chill came over the Heavy Hills a few days ago and I was out in the garden, tending to the lavender bushes and I had not my shawl. So now I have a cold. I will be alright though, you know me. Please don't worry…although if you want to send more cake, then I am sure my recovery will be hastened.

I have been clearing a few things away lately. Making more space around the house. Have taken my easels out of the side entrance of the house and I intend to finally use them. All those years hidden behind that crooked black door in the side of the house, rotting away. All that potential shall now be realised…just as soon as I shake this cold! Apart from the spiders, guess what else I found in that dingy little coal shed? I found that painting of the Tsarina Angeline that terrified you as a boy! Poor sweet child! I must admit, I can understand why. The degradation of paint around her eye gives her a sinister look – an evil cataract indeed. Lord knows what possessed us to keep that hanging above the mantel.

Attribute the melancholia to my cold, but when I held that portrait and remembered all the times you saw it and shied away, or had nightmares about her and came into our bedroom in the middle of the night. Well, I got a little overcome. How silly of me!

Anyway, my darling boy, please eat the food I have enclosed and be good. Study hard.

Don't have dark dreams about Tsarina Angeline, and don't be sad.

Write me soon, my beautiful boy.

Your loving mother,

Lilly

Dear Vasili and Kamila.

Congratulations on your wedding. I am sorry our son and I could not attend. There must have been a terrible tragedy at the post office as the invitation did not arrive until the day of the wedding! Can you believe the service? I am so sorry; I would have loved to have attended and seen the happy couple. Our son too.

Anyway, you are on your honeymoon as I write this. The Prince William Sound? Marvellous - I remember our honeymoon there. Beautiful scenery.

Have a marvellous time and we both wish you a wonderful and happy life together.

Best wishes,

Elizabeth
Gavrilo pp.

Dear Brekker,

Please regard this note as acceptance of your commission. Your preliminary sketches are more than adequate and your advance payment generous. Be advised that I shall meet the deadline you have specified and the brace should be with you before the end of the year.

As soon as the maquette is made, I shall send you a pictogram of it. Any design feedback at that stage would be greatly received.

Kind regards,

J. Epstein

Dearest Mother,

How are you? Your infrequent correspondence troubles me somewhat. Are you alright? Does the emptiness of the family home press upon you? I dearly hope not. I think of you always, sometimes at night when I am alone in my quarters, I think of you alone in yours and I must admit that my seemingly inherent sadness comes to the forefront of my mind. Maybe you are in your rocking chair with your needlework, or rolling out your pastry with that faraway look upon your face. How I remember that look. When I was a boy and in the kitchen, oftentimes banished from father's workshop for getting under his feet or spilling paint I would sit by the warm oven, next to our dog and look at you as you rolled out the pastry and you seemed so sad. So lost to your thoughts and your nostalgia. Now, having moved to Holstenwall, I can understand fully that desire to retreat in your mind back to this place. But now that I am here, your only living child, and you are all the way over there, away from me and Holstenwall – I wonder how you cope with it. Of course, the hope in my heart and the little light I carry tries to convince me that your rare letters are simply because you are too busy – perhaps lost in happy activity. Painting the spare room? Tending to your garden and pruning the lavender bushes? Maybe you have even mustered the energy to attend to the rockery by the pond that you always spoke of seeing to, but never did. Maybe that is why.

I cannot deny that the loneliness I feel often, away from home, is projected back to you and how I feel you must be.

Please, do not be sad for what I am about to say but I feel I
cannot lie to you. I find the studies to be so hard here – it is not
what I thought at all. The other students, they are true scholars
and they take to study and to learning as if it were coats of their
own making. Of course, I try hard in every lesson. I put my
hand up to answer every question and I spend many hours a day
in the libraries catching up on the lessons, revising and trying to
pick at the subjects and get to the flesh! This, of course, leaves
little time for socialising and I am sad to say that, in truth, I
have not made any friends here. I sit alone in the dining halls
and have my broth, the other students tucking in and laughing
and joking. Nobody approaches me, nobody wants to know me.

But I try not to let it bother me too much because I am here
to understand, to learn and to become a scholar and an artist, to
make you proud of me. This keeps me focused and from being
too sad. But it gets lonely, sometimes. I feel like I am in two
places at once – knowing that exams are round the corner, I
know that I need to work twice as hard in lessons and in the
libraries, but the more I do that, the other half of me yearns for
release. I think that is only natural, though, isn't it? Contact,
friendship, comrades! I never went to the Latin Quarter like you
advised. I never took the chance.

Ah, listen to me mother – my old, sad self coming out
again! I thought that stupid side of me had gone for good. We
both did. The saddest boy in the world you used to call me
when I was a boy. I remember. When Bella used to do all she
could to make me happy. Letting me play with her toys…even
dressing me as her dolls so she could practice her make-up

techniques. I think she thought that playing would make me a happier boy (though she could have at least one played with my toys and not just hers!)

"Eat your cabbage and don't be sad," you used to say to me at dinner as I pushed my food around the plate. I remember that, and I say it daily. It's like the sound of the train over rails in my head – "eat your cabbages, don't be sad, eat your cabbage, don't be sad."

Mother, I am sorry for my sudden deluge of melancholia – this place and time of my life, coupled with my thoughts of you and longing to hear that you are happy and not feeling so alone just compounds sometimes! But fear not, I will be fine – I must succeed and keep moving forward! Destiny awaits – there are canvasses to paint, books to read, poetry to write!

So now, I go back to the books!

Please, please, write to me soon.

And don't forget to eat your cabbage and don't be sad!

With love,

Gavrilo

PS – If you hear from father and he enquires as to how I am doing, please say that I am doing well, studying hard and doing my duty in a manner of which would make him proud.

PPS – Burn that damned painting of the evil Tsarina Angeline! Get rid of her, once and for all.

Dearest Mother,

Well would you believe it, no sooner have I sent a letter loaded with sadness and the Gavrilo of old, but along comes a most wonderful surprise? The Holstenwall Fayre is coming... but not only that, but this year they are going to create a Fayre bigger than any before it. The posters went up around the town this morning. Scientists, artists, explorers – exhibits of every kind, from all the corners of the globe will be here. Can you imagine my excitement? They are going to create a great crystal pavilion in which to house everything – I have seen the plans and it seems you could fit the entire world inside the palace. It is going to be quite, quite something. As academics of Holstenwall, we receive one complimentary ticket but I beg and plead with you mother, sell the remainder of my possessions so that you can afford a ticket. Come back, come back, and come back to Holstenwall! We'll go the Fayre and see the exhibits of old (yes, even the Somnambulists will be here, how quaint!) and we'll see the new exhibits (I overheard a whisper in the library that even Nikola Tesla will be here – but I cannot let that idea fester in my mind or I will never able to concentrate on my studies...I shall chalk that up as just fevered hysteria!)

The academy has put up notices suspending some classes so that we all might have more time to explore the wonders. Like you used to shout as you chased me around the garden and through the house when I was a little boy, making me giddy with happiness and out of breath from laughing – "The Fayre, the Fayre, the Fayre is coming. Coming, coming, coming to

Holstenwall! And the price of a ticket, the price for joys…a bite of a belly from a fat little boy!"

Come to the Fayre.

With love,

Gavrilo

My beautiful boy,

Tell the bakers on Baker's Row to fire up the stoves, tell the painters by the Charles Bridge to ready their easels and prepare for portraiture. Ring the bells in the square and buy a drink for every drunk in the Latin Quarter, for I have a ticket and I am coming to you, coming back home to Holstenwall.

I am coming to the Fayre!

With the love in my heart,

Lilly

Brekker's Journal

Have just been informed that 'the great' Nikola Tesla will be in attendance at the Fayre. Guest of honour. Must corner him and test his intellect. If he is indeed as miraculous as the notices want me to believe then he will see my genius and will be bewildered by my theories. He will then assist me.

Must go to Tesla and test him.

Must show Tesla that I am the way.

Beloved Mother,

It with a heavy heart and great sadness that I write this letter. Detest me if you will, but I must forewarn you of what might occur when you come to Holstenwall.

Though I was over the moon to receive your letter informing me that you had purchased your ticket, I received a graphein that very evening from father informing me that he and Kamila are also attending on that same day. He said he shall attend the Fayre with Kamila and stay with me. He also said that as a present and thanks for my hospitality, he has taken it upon himself to pay for my following year of study in the academy.

How could I refuse and so, to my shame, I must accept this offer. It is for the greater good, I am sure you understand.

So please, do still come but I wanted to forewarn you that if you do, they will be here too.

Please don't be sad, please don't be angry. Come and let us try and enjoy the Fayre?

Your loving son,

Gavrilo

Unsent letter from Gavrilo, to his mother

Dearest Mother,

Please forgive my lack of correspondence over the last few days. It's been a strange time indeed. I should say that while father and Kamila did indeed come to the Fayre, I did not see them once. I found an envelope in my room with money stuffed in it. The note said "for study" and nothing else. I found it this morning when I came back to my room after a few days away. Turns out you could have come to the Fayre on that day after all. If only that cold of yours had cleared up, if only you had the strength to come. Anyway, on with my little recollection of my last few days. Quiet an adventure.

I write this now at the great Fayre in beloved Holstenwall. It has been going for a week now and this is my second visit and I am with a friend! But first, let me tell you of our meeting just a few days ago – of all the attractions and wonders on offer (including the somnambulists!) I can barely believe who I ran into here. At the moment, I am sitting in a makeshift tavern while my friend gets some drinks.

They have constructed a great wooden structure within the crystal palace to house the diners and drinkers – this particular one reminds me of that great beer hall father used to fondly describe at that great drinking carnival in Prussia. Rows of tables and benches in the centre of the room, and women in traditional Holstenwall garb ferry huge glasses of beer to the patrons. When I first entered, I was awestruck and I went up to the bar to order my drink…but it seems you cannot do it there. Suddenly, I felt an arm link with mine and a giddy maid swept me away from the bar and sat me down in the middle of a group of drinkers I did not know. I was a little apprehensive as I am not the greatest at making company and so I took my glass with both hands and stooped low over the table. But I had little to worry about. After a few seconds, the middle-aged man next to me nudged my elbow and introduced himself. A fine fellow he was indeed – Mr Grayley his name was and he had travelled with his family all the way from Barston to be here for the opening night. He told me how much he had paid (not out of pride or to brag, but to demonstrate just how extraordinary this Fayre is and how much ordinary people are prepared to put aside or sell off to attend). My Grayley introduced me to his wife, a quiet and respectful woman who never took off her lace gloves and ate her pork knuckle and sauerkraut like a bird. Mr Grayley had a young daughter, of about eleven who was cherubic in her wonder and even managed to drink a whole glass of beer! Miraculous. She was a wide-eyed sort and could barely keep her gaze from the ceiling (eighty foot high and patterned with intricate wooden beams, entwined with golden garlands). Mr Grayley also introduced me to his mother. I was kind and polite, but she was a twisted old bat – shrivelled and shrunken, like her face was recoiling inside her own skin. And she had the most terrifying cataract. Everywhere she looked, that eye seemed to be always on me, as if she knew me, as if I had perpetrated some great crime and she knew about it. The living embodiment of the Tsarina Angeline come from beyond the grave to haunt me! The deep, primal fear I had of that strange painting was reflected back to me in that old hag's eye. But, like I say, I did not let my fears or revulsion show. I shook her hand and wished her a pleasant stay in Holstenwall. I conversed thereafter mainly with Mr Grayley and we talked over the various wonders we had seen. To that point, coincidentally, we had only been in the annex which housed antiquities and artefacts left over from the Superstitious Age. We laughed at the quaint appeal of the somnambulists, dressed in their black body stockings and the way their 'masters' presented them – each upright in an open coffin, sleeping away while their masters stood upon upturned potato crates, bellowing to the crowd about how and when they discovered their sleeping treasure. We laughed at the tradition of it all – that they all had to be in coffins, that they all had to be in black body stockings. Superstition is rather sweet, really. That is not to say that the other artefacts were of equal sweetness and juvenility. The army of clay soldiers, all two thousand standing in regiments, each statue seven-foot tall. It was quite something to be walking amongst their ranks, feeling the texture of the clay. Getting so close, to the age, to the history – thinking of the people that made these giants and how they believed then that they would protect them, and how these soldiers stand now, while those they were to protect are long since dust. It was most melancholy and easily my favourite artefact. My Grayley agreed, though he did not feel as I felt. The soldiers were his favourite because of their identical nature – identical insomuch as they were all designed from the same mould and how time had carved its own idiosyncrasies into their features. So that now, they are all individual. It was an interesting interpretation on time and identity. Mr Grayley and I spoke for a further hour until the family finished their meal (I did not eat, you know I feel about eating in public) and then they bade me farewell. We shook hands and then they left, no doubt I will never see them again but I know that old hag's cataract will stay with me, just like that painting!

After my pleasant conversation with the Grayleys, I drank two more beers and then left my place at the table. I walked around the great drinking hall three times before a maid took my arm and sat me down at another table. Only one man sat at there. The maid sat me down on the bench opposite him and brought us two beers. The man in question was slumped over, his head in his hands, in front of him lay strewn papers and notations. He appeared to be sleeping. I leaned over the table a little and looked down at the papers. Madness, utter madness. I had no idea what they were – strange words and diagrams, bizarre equations and chemical compounds. As I scanned the papers, I saw intricate anatomical drawings of joints and ligaments...even a strange design for what looked like an oil derrick constructed of bone. However, one sketch in particular took my curiosity – it depicted a giant woman, perhaps a mile high, towering over a city, one arm reaching behind her, the other arm waving a great sword above her head. The scale of the statue and the power in her movement was the stuff of nightmares. I reached over to turn the page around, so that I could correctly orientate it and better understand its meaning.

As soon as my fingers touched the page, the sleeping man's arm shot out and grabbed my wrist. I was able to pull my hand free and I sat back down in shock. The man sat bolt upright, eyes wide and a look of slight bewilderment upon his face, as if he had just awoken from a strong dream and into a strange place. His eyes darted around the room briefly before they fell upon me. I smiled at him as I could not believe it. A familiar face. It was Brekker, our old family physician who diagnosed my epilepsy! He grabbed his pocket watch and checked the time.

I went to say hello but before the words came out, he had scooped up his papers, taken his beer and dashed off. I got up to follow him, pushing through the crowds and hoping that no maid would link my arm this time. Brekker wore his crooked hat; I believe the same ridiculous top hat he used to wear when he visited our home. As I tried to follow him, I felt a rising desperation inside me. Strange to describe mother, I just felt as if I had to see him – I had to catch with him and say "hello, do you remember me?" This desire made me push and pull at everybody around, but it seemed that I could not get any closer to the man – now just the peak of his top hat visible amongst the drinkers (who seemed madder to me, their leering and cheering enhanced by my desperation).

Finally I reached the end of the hall; I pushed the last man aside and stopped in my tracks. I was standing in a giant exhibition hall – but this one housed no artefacts of antiquity. I was standing on the threshold of the future, one foot in the past, one in the future. I stood amazed in that doorway and temporarily lost sight of Brekker. All around me great machines and contraptions – all working in chaotic automation. Great cogs turning, pistons pushing up and down – jets of steam, webs of electricity. Each of the machines, made by different inventors and companies lined the walls. A web of electricity crossing over the heads of everyone, high above like a glowing blue spider's web in a thunderstorm. My mouth dropped open and slowly, as if it took a lifetime, I stepped over the threshold and into that room. The charge in that hall made the hairs on arms stand on end – palpable excitement, a buzz of futurists walking around, talking and sharing ideas. Each with top hats that were straight and new, but I was looking for the crooked hat of Brekker. I walked slowly, turning around and marvelling at all I saw – a machine that ravelled cloth faster and more quietly than I could believe. I saw conceptual models of flying machines and helium dirigibles, even catamaran tanker. I was fascinated by the models and I took a moment to stare down upon them, taking in all the exquisite details and feeling like a benign deity looking down with pride at my creations. After a minute or so, I moved along from the models and came to a series of strange glass columns, supported by brass fittings – each standing six feet tall. Inside the tubes bubbled and churned strange, luminous liquids – thicker than water. Purples, greens and pinks. I was mesmerised by the colour and could even feel strange warmth emanate from them. The heat bathed my face and I closed my eyes, standing just six inches in front of them. The sounds of the room faded as coloured orbs of light danced under my eyelids, forming strange and attractive shapes before me. I felt in a void, but a welcoming and encompassing void. I guess I liken it to being back in the womb. The sound all around me became muted, faraway – a throb and a pulse. I reached out; eyes still closed and touched one of the tubes. As soon as I did, a sharp sting cracked up my finger and jolted me out of my trance. I jumped back, shaking my hand in stinging pain bumping into a gentleman. I turned around to apologise, and who should it be? Of course, it was Brekker.

The man was standing on near tip toes, trying to peer over the hats of the others. I apologised but he did not acknowledge me and so I stood next to him and tried to see what he was looking at. There was a commotion someway ahead. An excited chatter began to spread around the room as more people halted their private conversations and turned to look ahead. Brekker began to push forward, clutching his papers. I followed, excusing my way through the eager crowd. I caught snatches of excited talk as I pressed forward. "He's here," "the great one" and "a true genius" floated through the air.

As I moved forward, the crowd began to close in on me. Progress became harder, the air become more stifled. People all around me pressing in. My chest grew tight in a way that was a sickening warning sign of what was approaching. The top hats were spinning bars in front of my vision. I felt my jaw begin to clamp shut, my knuckles seizing. Ahead a bright white light. The top-hat bars began to spin in front of my eyes. My mouth went dry, the bright light burning, chest tighter, the bars and light providing an unbearable contrast. My jaw opened suddenly and clamped back down on my tongue. All went to black.

Brekker's Journal

I saw him, I saw the future. Pushed through the crowd, got to the front and stood in the glow of his mighty creation. There he sat, in the centre of a great glass dome – nonchalant, in command. Nikola Tesla, the great and magnificent. He stood up from his chair and signalled to an assistant on the outside of the globe. The assistant, a woman in a purple dress with a huge bustle (couldn't see her face, covered in veil) stood by a terminal, tubes and cables hooked up to the underside of the globe which was propped up eight-foot by a wooden stand. At the signal, she pulled two levers attached to the terminal and immediately the ground began to tremble. The hairs on my arms stood up, a hum emanating from the terminal. The woman turned and looked up at the globe. All eyes followed and Tesla stood forward and raised his arms, smiling down upon us. Then, from his chair, tendrils of purple and blue plasma – snaking out slowly, seductively towards the edge of the glass. First just five, then ten, then twenty. The hum in the room intensified as the plasma arms caressed the inside of the globe. I chanced a look at the people around me; they seemed fearful, stepping backward and holding their hats. Shuffling and looking around. Only I remained resolute. I looked then to the assistant and saw her raise her veil. Perfect grey eyes. She winked at me before replacing the veil and turning back to the terminal. She pushed the levers up and Tesla closed his eyes, turning his outstretched palms to the heavens. The tendrils combined and the globe was filled with bright white light. Before he was engulfed in the awesome spectacle, I saw his silhouette start to elevate and then the light enveloped him. I shielded my eyes as the woman powered down the globe. The light faded, the hum fell away and everybody took their hands away from their eyes. Tesla was no longer in the globe, but standing in front of it with that same, cool, nonchalant look about him. He turned away from the crowd just as they began to rapturously applaud him. I called out his name and waved my papers in the air, but I was drowned out by the masses that all surged forward to meet him. I was about to press forward also when I felt a hand on my shoulder, pulling me back and spinning me around. I was about to pull free when I saw Lucy in front of me – but her look was not that of elation at what she had seen, but concern. I was about to speak when she pulled me through the crowd in the opposite direction. We reached a small huddle of men, leaning over a man on the floor, his fingers bent at the distal and intermediate phalanges – as if gripping onto a ledge. Foam at his mouth, teeth clamped shut. Nobody was helping him – one man held some callipers and was measuring his cranium, another was pulling back his eyelids and shining a phosphorous stick into his eyes while another began groping around the poor man's chest – pressing on his chest plate, feeling his ribs. I wanted so much to ignore the situation and go to Tesla, but I could not. I could not stand to see this young man I vaguely recognised put through such humiliation. I pushed every one aside to give him some room. Some protested, but those protestations were short lived. They saw rage in my eyes. I bent down to the young man and put his right arm and a right angle to his body, palm upwards. Then I took his left across his body and put the back of his hand under against his check, holding it there so that his convulsions could not cause him injury. I then instructed Lucy to lift his right knee and bend it. This caused him to roll onto his side. Lucy stepped back and I held the arm. After a few seconds the convulsions stopped and the young man fell asleep.

The crowd stepped back, clapping politely. I let go of the young man's hand and looked up at Lucy. She smiled in relief.

How wonderful to see her face again, despite the circumstances.

How I have missed my friend.

Brekker's Journal

We met him. The 'great' Tesla.

We had taken the young man to the infirmary where he drifted in and out of consciousness. I took inventory of their medicines and took it upon myself to request his transferral to my mansion. Lucy agreed with me and we spoke in quiet tones about possible cures we could concoct for him. Though it was wonderful to be talking business with my friend and former assistant, I did not make mention of any of the breakthroughs I have made since she resigned from her post. While we spoke, I could not help but notice that Lucy kept glancing over to the patient. There was a look of concern in her eyes, but there was also something else, glistening behind her eyes.

We fixed the young man to a gurney and were about to take him to my carriage when we were stopped at the doorway by Tesla's assistant. She stepped around the frame and stood there, that veil over her eyes. We almost rammed her with the gurney. She lifted her veil and looked down at the young man. She is beautiful – sharp cheeks, strange eyes, and perfect skin. She regarded our patient quizzically, as if she had never seen a young man before. Then she fixed us with a stare.

"He has come," she said in a beguiling accent that I could not place, before stepping back behind the doorway. Then, ever the showman, from the other side of doorway stepped Nikola Tesla himself, his hat in his hands, his eye brow raised.

He looked at us both and then down to the patient.

"May I?" he said in a soft voice.

I stepped back from the gurney. Lucy remained and I saw her hand reach to our patient and cup his head, her fingers mixing with his hair.

Tesla smiled at Lucy and though that smile reassured me, I could tell it did nothing for Lucy. Tesla leant in low to the young man and listened to his breathing.

"Grand mal seizure," I said.

"I concur," replied Tesla.

"From your demonstration," added Lucy.

Tesla stood up, still holding his hat in his hands. "Forgive me, ma'am, forgive me doctor. My experiments are a little…progressive and the energy they generate can play merry havoc with certain brain patterns. I should put signs on the doors."

Lucy threw a sarcastic smile at Tesla. He turned to me and then he said.

"Good doctor, you were at the presentation and if I recall, as the light enveloped me, you were the only one looking."

"I was," I replied.

"And?"

"It is an impressive light emitting globe," I said. Then the 'great' man broke out into a condescending laugh.

"No my friend, it was no mere light emitting globe. It was the birth of a star…of sorts."

I handed him my notes and he took the papers with a wry smile.

"This is what I am working on," I said, rather meekly.

He looked over my notes and arched an eyebrow.

"What is this?" he said.

"Investigations into dreams and the place in between."

"Between?" he replied with a scoff. "No, my good doctor, it is not what's between that is the future, it is what is beyond."

And at that he tossed my notes onto the chest of the sleeping patient and left the room. I could taste the bile in the back of the throat. I could not look to Lucy. All I could do was grip the bar of the gurney and grit my teeth. And then, in his deep sleep, the young man lifted his arm and gently placed his hand upon the notes on his chest, his fingers brushing against the statue of my sword-wielding mother.

And so the 'great' Tesla shuns me – but seeing this young master in his dream reach out in this reality and touch upon my dream gives fuel to my ambitions.

Brekker's Journal

He rests, in my mansion. Still asleep. Lucy and I have concocted a potion that we believe may cure his epilepsy. I have added a few additional ingredients and have placed a journal by his side. I believe that I can cure him, and I simultaneously push him towards the other side and have him subconsciously record the dream, just as I did. As I know it is safe, I have doubled the dosage. Have not told Lucy. When we agreed, she requested to stay by his bedside while I mixed the medicine (which was fortuitous as I was then able to add my tonics unseen).

She is by his bedside now, holding his hand and rubbing his forehead.

The journal is by his side.

Cure injected. We wait.

———•◦•———

The dark void is over, light has come and I am on a cliff. A woman who is my mother, but does not look like her is standing on the edge. I am behind her and, behind me is my home. It is a white mansion with great pillars and a long porch. I do not recognise it, but I feel that it is mine. I feel that it is home. The same way that I know, in my soul, that the woman ahead is my mother. But she is young, perhaps twenty. She wears a flowing white dress, a string of green ivy embroidered on her hem. I can smell lavender. As soon as I do, four lavender bushes spring up around me. I run my hand through them, and I call to my mother. She turns to me and waves. With her other hand, she brushes her windswept hair from her face. She waves but she does not smile. I try to step over the lavender bushes, but I cannot. I cannot seem to lift my legs high enough and so I remain. The woman turns back to the cliff and looks out at the grey sky. A storm from the see is coming and I can see a small object approaching. At first a black dot then it becomes a strange flying machine that I cannot name. Spinning blades atop a glass bubble. My mother waves and so do I, but the grey sky seems to envelop it. Fog, fog all around me. I try to call out because I know that I am dreaming. As the dread of the fog takes my vision away, I know implicitly that I am dreaming.

As soon as I say this to myself, I understand that the woman was neither my mother, nor the mansion my home. I am dreaming and I want to wake up.

I scream this and as I do, I fall down to the ground, palms onto the grass. I press up, attempting to pull myself from the dream. I used to do this as a child, back home when I had nightmares. I press up, concentrating on the gesture and repeating "I want to wake up."

The fog turns everything to black and then I awake.

I sit bolt upright. I am truly home, in my bed. Everything is familiar. I recall the touch of the blanket – the fur on its trim; I recall the green lamp on my bedside. Calmness of pure serenity washes over me and I lie back down onto the soft pillow. I turn to the side to see a woman lying next me, her hair over her face. I gently stroke it to the side and I am confronted not by a woman, but a strange mannequin – the skin is canvas. She turns her head to face me, a living painting.

It is the Tsarina Angeline and her eyes are cataracts.

I am still dreaming, I gasp as if coming up from near drowning.

Brekker's Journal

He awoke and tried to jolt out of his nightmare. But he could not move. His muscles pulled taut from the exertion of his seizure. He lay back down, breathing hard and staring at the ceiling. His jolt knocked the journal from his hand and he fell back asleep. I had no time to replace it so that he could record what he saw and so we left the room and let him sleep. I have left the book upon his chest in case he awakes and decides to write.

Unsent letter from Gavrilo to his mother

Dear mother,

Please don't worry but today, I had an episode. As you know, I have not had one in seven years. I was at the Fayre and watching a demonstration by some magician I think (don't recall his name) and the light and movement was too much. It happened but somebody has taken care of me. I have awoken in a nice, pleasant room. Airy and clean but not in a hospital. Sheets are crisp. There is a dresser by the wall with pictures upon it, but I cannot see the faces. My head hurts a little and my vision is blurred. I have noticed a small mark on my arm – from a syringe no doubt.

Well, I am here and in a moment I shall go and find out who was so kind as to look after me. I thought I should write to you and say about my episode. I don't really have too many people in the academy to tell this too and I know, even if it means a little worry on your part that you would rather know than be in the dark. And, like I say, I am fine.

When I am well enough, I will return to the Fayre and maybe take whoever has aided me there for a drink.

I shall write again soon. Please reply as soon as you can.

With all my love,

Gavrilo

Gavrilo's notes

Whoever has taken me in was kind enough to leave my journal and a pencil with me. I feel strong enough to stand and I have dressed myself. I must have been out for a while, because my suit and shirt has been cleaned and pressed. They were folded neatly over the chair by the bedside. As I wander through the house, I shall take notes. Seems strange to do so, but I feel somewhat compelled. Leaving room.

Standing in grand mezzanine hallway. Wooden bannister highly polished. Winding stairs leading down to the to the entrance hall below. Carpet has pleasing green paisley pattern. Hallway lined with rooms. Decided to descend the staircase.

Entrance hall is grand indeed. A row of white doors underneath the mezzanine. Floor, wooden. Sends pleasingly hollow echo when I tap my heel on the floor. Ahead, in the centre of the wall beneath the mezzanine stand two open glass windows leading to another corridor.

Walked through glass windows and proceeded along corridor. Nobody around. No occupants, no staff. A ghost house.

Walked to the end of corridor, have stopped by the far doorway. Can feel a breeze floating through the doorway. Stepping through now.

Standing in a lovely sitting room. Plush chairs, globe bar, small table by the chairs. Breeze coming from open glass doors that leads out onto the lawn. The grass is lush and verdant. I can see through the doors the Heavy Hills behind which my house lies.

Going to step out onto the lawn.

Brekker's Journal

Night time – I am in my quarters, looking out at the lawn. Slight musculature pain, Slight ache in joints. A long, strange day.

Lucy and I sat in the gazebo, taking an afternoon brandy when Master Gavrilo walked out onto the lawn, notebook in hand. He stopped in the doors and looked around, casting his eyes off to the Heavy Hills and taking notes. Curious fellow. Then, his attention turned to us and he stopped writing.

I introduced myself, Lucy, our friendship and briefly outlined some of our work. He introduced himself and reminded me of his family lineage. A good family. I immediately recalled diagnosing him many years ago and I remember his dear mother and father. It had been many years since I had moved away and taken my practice with me (with the onset of symptoms) – locking myself mainly in the mansion with Agatha to work. And, as such, I was truly sad to hear of the tragic death of Master Gavrilo's sister Bella, aged just fifteen.

The three of us then walked through the grounds, talking endlessly. I am surprised to find so much wonder in a boy that lacks much intellect. It's endearing. He wants to understand, he wants to reach for the answers and ideals, but they are beyond his reach. However, he makes up for this lack of intellect with remarkable charm and many times he made us both laugh. He is warm and friendly and when he said that, as a child he was the saddest boy in the world, Lucy near fell about herself. I agreed with him, recalling how as a young boy all he would do was pick at things. On his own, by a doorframe or wall where paint was chipped. Picking at the flakes and looking at the grain. He looked to the ground when I said this and I could see him absently rub his left forearm. I conclude that when paint lost interest, he began to create scabs upon his arm with nails, knives and broken glass so that he could pick at the scabs.

We walked until sunset and then I retired to take my notes and mull over the day's activity in private. Tesla, what wasted talent, what arrogance. And here, delivered to me is a boy whom I believe could be a great investigator of dreams. I falsely told him that it was not safe for him to return home and that he should stay the night. My motives are that, in the morning, I shall broach some dangerous theory with him and see how he accepts it. He could prove to be a good test subject.

At present, Lucy and Gavrilo are still talking under the gazebo.

Brekker's Journal

Master Gavrilo is a good fellow indeed. He has taken me back to the Fayre and installed me in a tavern. I fetched some drinks and returned to find him scribbling a letter to his mother. He folded it away, unfinished when I returned with our drinks. Lucy was not with us, and immediately he used the opportunity to brazenly probe me about my relationship with her. I told him. Saw no reason to lie or give half-truths. He seemed jubilant to hear of her talents and depth of character. I turned the lamp onto him and asked similar questions. He was reticent at first to answer candidly about himself and it soon became apparent that the boy is somewhat introverted and ill at ease with such topics. I probed further and asked about the Academy and his studies. He became even more withdrawn and eventually revealed that he finds the work extremely difficult and that he does not have any friends to help explain things. He then, with eyes of a hungry, pleading dog, he asked me if I would help him revise. I said "no."

Crestfallen, he asked why.

"Because they are teaching you the wrong things," I replied.

Then I took a leap in the dark and laid out some theories for him. About the other side, about the in between. I even divulged a little of the city I travel to in my dreams.

He smiled as I mentioned this. I enquired about that smile, about its meaning.

"It seems to me," he said, "that the further forward we go, the deeper into ourselves we travel."

I broke out into uproarious laughter, perhaps the first time I have laughed in years.

I could not have said it better and so, we drank. Master Gavrilo is a good fellow to have around and I have a feeling that his inherent introspection and wide-eyed wonder, mixed with Lucy's intellect and dedication will help me greatly. What a team we'll make, what places we'll go to.

A good fellow, indeed.

My beloved Mother,

A short letter but an important one. Perhaps the most important any son can write to his mother about.

I have met someone, her name is Lucy and by the Grace of God, we are in love.

What else can one say to one's mother?

Your adoring son,

Gavrilo

Dear Vasili.

It has been so long since we spoke. Apologies for the drop in correspondence. But I thought you should know that our son is in love. A girl named Lucy whom I am yet to meet but sounds divine. I hope one day we could all meet. I hope Kamila is doing well. Congratulations on the birth of your fourth child together.

Very happy for you,

Regards,

Elizabeth

Brekker's Journal

Well there is no saving them now. It is clear that Lucy and Gavrilo are in love. I am happy for them, of course as they are dear friends. But I lament the passing of Lucy's talents and potential as she puts them aside to concentrate solely on her lover. Indeed, it would not surprise me if soon she will forsake all imagination and install herself in a home somewhere behind the Heavy Hills and produce nothing but children and homemade jam. For shame! But what can I do? Gavrilo too, though he keeps his inquisitive mind and nature, has changed somewhat of late. He has not been to class in weeks and has instead taken to working shifts in the outlying factories. He tells me it is to save for an apartment for them both. Do not know if they have discussed this together, or if he assumes this is what is best. I predict that within one month, he will have abandoned academia for good and taken to factory work. This makes me sad. Also, to note, the boy seems more introverted and comes across sometimes as sullen. We went drinking in Holstenwall two days ago. We sat at the bar and I began to try and explain some of my established theories and some of my burgeoning ideas. We drank and he nodded as I spoke, but he could not take his gaze from the bar – as if he were studying the grain in the countertop. His eyes fixed, his mind faraway. It was quite frustrating as most times, he is as I have said, inquisitive and eager…but sometimes, just sometimes, he seems so lost inside himself. It is frustrating because I am trying to sound out some grand theories and he isn't listening. He isn't there. Gavrilo sometimes, simply is not there.

However, I cannot let this sadness cloud my own visions. Indeed, I use it to power my machines, my drive. Of late my dreams have become more virile, more potent. It can be suggested that they are not dreams in the sense that they are my subconscious working through my anxieties and presenting them back to me, but more akin to visions. Presentations of fact. It started with anxious dreams of suffocating. Being subsumed by hardening concrete until I could not move. Normal nightmares. But soon, I began to step out of this nightmare, and view the events with a passionless gaze. Clinical. I looked upon myself and saw myself sinking into the concrete sarcophagus. Then, as I began to relive these dreams, I found that I could not only walk around the sarcophagus and view my 'demise' from whichever angle I chose, I could also turn away and walk through the vista of my dream. Every night now, whether dreaming under sleep, or under uranium tonic applications, I visit the same place. A vast, sprawling city of concrete. It is based in a flat plain that stretches on to the very edge of my subconscious. The buildings are of utilitarian architecture. Strong, foreboding forms. Huge tower blocks built to house a great work force. However, there are other municipal buildings – a hospital, a park with a Ferris wheel and even a school. It seems to me, that this place in my mind is the future of factory work. The workforce do not go to the factory and then leave, they live and breathe within the factory walls. They work the machines, they never tire. Magical. The power created from this place. However, the city is deserted. Not a soul saves me as I wander through it

This is the recurring vision I have. Sometimes, all I need to do is close my eyes to return there briefly. It has taken over my all things – it is my place, my destination. If I can find a way to that city and bring a workforce with me then I know that I can pull everything else with me and create my unified theory.

I need to go further into my dream to figure out how to do this, and to go further into my dream I need more power. As such, I have placed an order for a Tesla Coil. It makes me smile to know that the 'great' Tesla's grand machine will merely be the battery to mine.

It arrives in a few days. Lucy and Gavrilo will not be here. She has taken him away to her retreat up in the Austrian mountains. High, away and overlooking crystal lakes. I am sure they will be happy there.

While they are there, frittering away their time, I shall be pulling apart my dream to find myself a map to its location.

Dear Brekker,

Please find enclosed an initial concept sketch for your automated body brace. Your armour. Your living sarcophagus. You should have full mobility, great strength and longevity that will supersede your natural timeframe.

I will proceed with mark I version.

Regards,

J. Epstein.

#F 723

TheNeverPages

Brekker's Journal

Interesting day. Hard to put into words. Better if I list order of events.

1. Tesla Coil arrived this morning. Delivered by four workmen and Tesla's assistant who oversaw the installation of coil in laboratory.

2. Workmen paid for duty. They left. Assistant stayed behind to offer free demonstration of coil's operation. Thought it pointless. Operation obvious. Woman had ulterior motive. Plain to see.

3. Assistant revealed to be Tesla's fiancée. Her name is Evelyn.

4. Coil set up and test fired. Powerful machine. Satisfactory result. Thanked Evelyn and showed her to door. She stopped before leaving. Asked for drink.

5. Had plenty of brandy. Kept topping up my glass herself.

6. Knew she was here to steal secrets. Obvious. Already anticipated so papers left out for her to take. Papers of already failed experiments and erroneous theories. She didn't know.

7. Tesla sent fiancée over to distract and steal. Took the bait.

8. Despite slight ache in knees and elbows, made love in laboratory. Her passion comical. To ask her to come here and to do that, and for her to agree? Tesla and Evelyn disgust me. Still, played their game.

501

9. Evelyn left. After, I noted that of the 8 pieces of fool's gold I left for her, she had stolen 6.

Despite my disdain for Tesla and his methods, one cannot deny the power of his machine. After Evelyn left, I retreated to the laboratory and began to customise the coil. During demonstration, flailing limbs of electricity spiked around ceiling of laboratory. Have adjusted coils and attached thin rods designed to guide the lightning down, focusing on a single point in the floor. Mixed a compound, similar to liquid I ingest to venture into my dreamscape. Powdered form heaped on floor. Theory is to harness Tesla's power onto the compound and create a small gateway. Ingested compound sends subject inwards. If compound is activated by similar electrical charge that exists in us all, but is exposed outside, perhaps a gateway to that city of my dreamscape can be achieved. Perhaps one can step through and be corporeal. A literal doorway into one's own mind. How will time be perceived if one is standing in the threshold of one's own mind? What sorts of strain upon psychology will this produce? An ouroboros of mental flux, ever turning into oneself? Simple introduction of my compound to Tesla's machine and perhaps I may cross over?

Of course, this begs question – what if there is no way back? How to report? What findings? Will journal self-write as before? Need test subject.

Will sacrifice glory of being pioneer into what I have named TheNeverRealm for the benefit of objective observation.

Need test subject.

Hope Tesla sends back Evelyn to steal more fool's gold. I will use her body to sate carnal needs then subject her to my experiments.

Dear Mother,

I have decided to do the honest and right thing by Lucy and I fully intent to ask her hand in marriage, but before I do that I need to secure a future and to do that, I must work. In short, I have decided to put away the foolish, childhood dreams of academia and artistry and I intend to take up honest work in the factories. I shall work on the floor and, with my typing and draughtsman skills, I hope to progress up to the offices and become a clerk of some renown. This information my sadden you, what with our talk previous of me becoming a poet or a painter, but I think that if I am to honour Lucy then this is the only way. She cannot expect to have a future of uncertainty while her husband spends his time writing and painting and hoping that somebody will one day deem them worthy of a rouble. Nobody can live like that. No, I must put aside all these childish ideas and commit myself to the life of an adult – work, career, progress, a home, a wife, children and contentment.

Anyway, I must go now – I can see the queue for the factory forming already and if I am to be considered, I need to be within the first two hundred and fifty.

Hope this letter finds you well and not to downhearted about the decision I have made. If it is any consolation, forging ahead and doing all I can do to make Lucy happy is somewhat romantic, is it not?

Hope that is some consolation at least.

Best wishes

Gavrilo

PS – we will, of course, invite you to come visit Holstenwall soon. Once I am settled in a new apartment and have some money aside for a boarding lodge for you, we will send a train ticket for you. Lucy is keen to meet you.

Brekker's Journal

Strange addition to dream. Walked through concrete city as usual. As ever, no sign of life. No workforce. Walked through Municipal Park, passed Ferris wheel. Intended to map out the eastern blocks of town. Crossed through Wide Avenue as always. Turned corner and halted. Incredible column of earth towered in front of me. Higher than I can see. Could see edges of tower blocks protruding from the vast, brown column. Seemed as though this mass of earth has been brought into my dream, placed on top of city. Like child with circular building block, forcing it into square hole. Walked the circumference. Column of earth at least 600ft in diameter.

Monstrous and beguiling addition to dream.

Told Gavrilo over drinks about column of earth appearing in my city of unknown location. He grunted as he drank, only half listening. Even told him of my encounter with Tesla's assistant Evelyn.

Soon as I mentioned her name, he looked at me, eyes wide with fear.

"Angeline?" he whispered.

I corrected him on the name. He turned back to his drink and muttered something about recurring nightmares and the Tsarina Angeline of the Theresienwiese. Sometimes, he is so far away from this reality, that I cannot be sure if he is not sleepwalking with open eyes. Perhaps he is elsewhere – perhaps he is dreaming in another reality and we are all characters in his dream.

I might posit this notion to him the next time we go drinking, see if it sinks in. Doubtful, he'd probably mutter on about the Tsarina.

Brekker's Journal

Terrible accident. Lucy thrown from horse. Injuries catastrophic. Heart too broken to work today. Master Gavrilo too, though he visits Lucy, he returns to his shift in the factory. Brave, or callous?

Brekker's Journal

Received a graphein this morning. Was busy calibrating the depth machine ready for the final firing this evening.

Graphein reads: "Meet me on Charles Bridge. Come alone. 10pm. Important news. Evelyn."

Machine is configured and ready. I go to meet Evelyn, upon return I shall fire machine.

Brekker's Journal

Cannot write of what I have done. Too dangerous. Authorities are massing in the city. Watchmen all around. Timeframe increased. Must power machine for final drive as soon as I can.

Brekker's Journal

Abject failure. Fear of capture drove me to madness. Hastily prepared Tesla Coil for final firing. Incorrect calibration. Firing almost decimated mansion. Created 600ft wide sinkhole in garden. Cannot see bottom. Have not rope long enough to descend. No plumb line can reach bottom of abyss I have created.

Was too hasty. Worked too frantically. Fear of capture. Fear of imprisonment before work can be completed. As a result – Tesla Coil damaged beyond repair. Now faced with dilemma. To repair will take a month. Tesla is in Vienna and so construction and delivery of new coil, two months.

Need alternative power source. Need something to power my God Machine and open gateway to TheNeverRealm.

Need miracle.

Holsterhwall Herald

No XLV   Price 3d.   1st October 18

TESLA FIANCEE DEAD!

PREGNANT FIANCEE OF RENOWNED FUTURIST DROWNED IN VOLGA

Body of Evelyn Kübler-Ross found washed up on bank of Volga. Ms Kübler-Ross, due to marry Tesla in August was found to be in early stages of pregnancy. Blunt force trauma to victim's right eye give local Watchmen reason to suspect foul play. Mr Tesla, currently at Vienna State Exposition has been informed. Ms Evelyn Kübler-Ross has no immediate family.

Brekker's Journal

Lucy came to me. Walking so awkward for her, back hunched, shoulders useless. Simply said "make me better. Make me beautiful so Gavrilo will love me again."

Said I would. Have installed Lucy in laboratory, informed Gavrilo that I will cure her.

She will be my power source. Work begins in earnest. Threshold will be crossed soon.

Lucy is my miracle.

Dear Vasili,

Hope this letter finds you and Kamila well. I thought you should know that due to a tragedy in our son's life, he is returning to the family home. He shall continue to work in the factories but it is best for all concerned that he be near his mother in this most terrible time.

Forgive me for not divulging the nature of this tragedy, but I hope that it inspires you to write back and enquire of your son.

Regards,

Elizabeth.

Unfinished love letter from Gavrilo to Lucy

What to say that has not already been said? How can I say the things I want to say so that when you read this note your heart will say; "Gavrilo wrote this."

You may suspect that the handwriting has been forged, or that the note a fake in other ways...but the words, the worlds that the words herein create, how to construct a way to make you see that they are not but the burning truth. From in me they come and nobody in the world has ever laid them out in this way. They may have thought and turned over the quandary of making love eternal seem original...but the feeling, the words, the order are what vexes me so much. I cannot sleep and I cannot eat, I can only rail against this problem and drink. And oh Lucy! When I drink, the difference to me! What I become – loud, brash and angry to all around, but inside! But inside everything parts, the seas calm and the stars appear as garlands stretching over a great dance hall inside which you and I and I and you...that is why I drink... but how to write it down so you can pick up this not and say "yes, yes indeed, my Gavrilo wrote this and no other."

I will strive and continue on my quest and find some grand gesture. Something that nobody else has done or written – gone not only to a place that nobody has ever gone to, but gone through it and come out of the other side – for you, all for you and nobody else. You might shy away, you may baulk at my confession, that is a risk but I cannot stay my hand and nor do I want to. I cannot temper my heart when it comes to the divide between us and how I will traverse it.

Yes, your Gavrilo wrote this because you have given him a looking glass to hold up to his insides, to hold up to his heart and see things he never has done before. You have shown the destination, but not the way.

You, Lucy, are the eternal destiny, the eternal destination and I will come always to you. Always to you. Always.

And you will say "yes, my Gavrilo wrote this and no other. Yes he did this, and none other did."

It will feel like you are in love.

Dear Mr & Mrs Koromov and family.

I regret to inform you that at ten-to-ten this morning, 5th November, our son Gavrilo took his own life. I found him in the bathroom. He had found your old folding razor and taken it to his own throat.

There was no letter.

The funeral will be held at the municipal chapel in Couldwell at midday on the 11th November.

You may wish to attend. Family welcome.

E.W

Heavy Hills Tribune

VOL. IV.—No. 204

11TH NOVEMBER 18

City of Holstenwall Gone!

ENTIRE CITY INSTANTLY SUBSUMED BY SUPER-MASSIVE SINKHOLE.

TheNeverPages

Also by the Same Author

'Hat's off to Brandenburg'

London, 1815

The Roxy Playhouse is in trouble. The Roxy Playhouse Irregulars, those libertine artists and dreamers, are up to their necks in debt.

"Pay up in one month or its curtains for you all"

Dark times lead to drastic schemes and so the Irregulars decide to reinvent themselves as 'performance thieves', infiltrate High Society and 'Robin Hood' their way through it. However, getting embroiled in a dark and deadly plot to destroy the Monarchy was never part of their script. The Roxy Irregulars will have to stage the performance of their lives if they want to save the day and make it home in time for last orders.

OUT NOW IN PAPERBACK AND EBOOK

www.theneverpress.com

Maria & The Devil

The Devil, Montana's most feared outlaw has left his secret lover, Maria, alone in their secluded house deep in the wilds. If she had known that she was pregnant, the Devil might have stayed. That was almost nine months ago and Maria is still awaiting her lover's return and the arrival of her child. But while Maria waits for the Devil, a vengeful band of gunslingers are hunting him. Led by the relentless Rickman Chill, the gang have ventured deep into the dark wilds of Montana and they will stop at nothing to bring the Devil to Justice. Vengeance is a dangerous game, but as the Devil said to Maria before he left her: "there is nothing more dangerous than lovers"

Maria & The Devil is a supernatural thriller about motherhood, vengeance, solitude and self-preservation.

Lightning Source UK Ltd.
Milton Keynes UK
UKOW04f2338110316

270074UK00004B/199/P